Time To Go

Lisa
HARTLEY
TIME
TO
GO

CANELO

First published in the United Kingdom in 2019 by Canelo

This edition published in the United Kingdom in 2019 by

Canelo Digital Publishing Limited
57 Shepherds Lane
Beaconsfield, Bucks HP9 2DU
United Kingdom

A CIP catalogue record for this book is available from the British Library.

Print ISBN 978 1 78863 388 8
Ebook ISBN 978 1 78863 101 3

Look for more great books at www.canelo.co

Printed and bound in Great Britain by Clays Ltd, Elcograf S.p.A.

For Mum.

9 December

As Lot 9 arrived on the stage, the auctioneer stepped back from his podium and dabbed at his brow with a yellow silk handkerchief. His face was red, his suit stretched to capacity. He was supposed to have retired, but the promise of a significant regular cash boost to his pension had lured him back into the game. Once a month, he put on his best clothes, shined his shoes and lied to his wife.

Nothing new there. He lied as easily as he breathed these days. He had to. They had him trapped between knowing too much and disappearing too easily. They also knew he was desperate for money, which helped them keep him in his place. Standing here under the lights, sweating, shuffling, hating and loving it all in equal measure. Eyes glazed, feasting, trying to hide the tremor in his voice as he described the lots being paraded in front of them.

If he was honest, he knew there was no need. The punters all knew what they were here to bid on, had made their choices from the wares on offer days before. Depending on the lot, they might even have been offered an opportunity – try before you buy. His talents, the lyrical descriptions and the way he knew how to ignite the bidding into a battle of will and wits – wasted. He was wasted here.

If he closed his mind to the facts, the old excitement still fizzed, though. Allow the audience to gawp at each lot, then haul their attention back to himself. It wasn't easy, but he had a job to do, after all. He didn't have all night. An envelope of used twenties and a grubbier soul each time he left the building. Payment, and payback.

He could live with it. He had no choice.

Stuffing the handkerchief back into his trouser pocket, he licked his lips, ran a hand over his moustache and smiled.

'Shall we start the bidding at eight thousand pounds?'

—

In an office above the auction room, a man sat watching proceedings on a monitor. The room was in darkness, the glow of the screen the only source of light. He was invisible to those in the room below, and none of the people placing bids knew his name. The auction's location was a closely guarded secret, vital information that would allow the bidders access only revealed at the last moment. It was better that way, for everyone. If you knew nothing, you couldn't grass. It was a lesson he had learnt early, at his father's side. His dad had gradually grown to trust him, a little more each year, but the old man had still kept some secrets close. He didn't know for sure, but he had probably taken some to his grave.

There was a tap on the office door and he stood, strode over to open it. The man who stood there looked apprehensive.

The click of a lighter, the flare of a flame. He took the offered cigar with a nod of thanks as it was lit for him.

'Auctioneer looks nervous,' the other man said, waving a hand towards the stage.

He sat back down, squinting at the screen. 'Looks the same as always to me.'

'We can trust him, though.'

It wasn't a question. 'We know where he lives, where his daughter and grandkids live.' He lifted his shoulders. 'Same thing.'

A pause. He waited, putting the cigar between his teeth so that both hands were free. Just in case. He nodded towards a chair.

'You've men here?' the other man said as he sat down.

'Men?'

A quick jerk of the head. 'You know. In case something goes wrong. Someone gets… rough.'

He laughed. 'Rough? They wouldn't dare. Bid, pay, get out. They know how it works before they come in.'

'And if they don't?'

'Don't what?'

'Pay.'

He took his time replying, blowing smoke into the air and leaning back in his chair to cross his legs. 'Don't know. It's never happened.'

'It hasn't happened *yet*.' Definite emphasis on the final word. Shifting in the chair, one knee bouncing. The other man was nervous – he knew the signs. He sat up straight, his hand moving swiftly to his pocket.

'If you're having second thoughts—'

'I'm not,' the other man said quickly. 'It's just… the Albanians.'

'What about them?'

'They're…' He shook his head. 'I don't like working with them. Cut-throat bastards.' He glanced at the monitor, the auctioneer still speaking, pointing, nodding. Lot 9 displayed under a spotlight like a prize.

'They're businessmen, like us, buying and selling.' He nodded at the scene in front of them. 'You'd better watch your mouth; they're on the front row. Like I said, if you're having second thoughts…'

He set the cigar in the ashtray at his elbow and reached to turn on the desk lamp with his left hand, the right unlocking a drawer and removing a gun. It lay on his palm, squat and ugly. Threatening. He didn't raise it, didn't even look at it. Just held it. The other man gulped, swallowed, knowing he was looking at a weapon that had already killed. 'I'm not, I swear,' he said.

'Then why mention it? Why ask?'

'It's just… I've a lot of money invested in this scheme.'

'Scheme?' He chuckled. 'You make it sound as though we're robbing schoolkids of their lunch money. Scheme. Fucking scheme. A scheme is a gamble – might come off, might explode in your face. This isn't a scheme, it's a business, and it works.'

'You know what I mean. I'm risking everything.'

He thrust his chin forward, getting in the other man's face. 'Because you owe me. I didn't have to work with you, you know.'

Raised hands, wide eyes. 'I've never said—'

'You've caused trouble.'

The other man swallowed. 'Not intentionally.'

He turned the gun over in his hand, watching the light glint on the barrel and then skitter away. 'You can back out if you want to,' he said.

'Back out?' Eyes wider still. 'No, I—'

'But think of everything you'll be throwing away. The money, the respect. The opportunities.' He slipped the gun back into the drawer and locked it. 'I'll say it again – the money.'

'Yeah, all right. I get it. I'll shut up.'

'Make sure you do. I need to concentrate.'

He clicked the lamp off again as Lot 9 sold for eighteen thousand pounds.

Smiling, he did a couple of calculations. He'd reckoned they'd made over a hundred and fifty grand already, and the night was still young.

His phone rang and he tutted as he glanced at the screen.

'What?' He listened, puffing on the cigar. 'What are you talking about?' Another pause. 'All right, the more the merrier. Stay where you are. I'll be down soon.'

'What's wrong?' The other man was worried.

He turned to him, smiling. 'Nothing. Just a few special guests.'

'Guests? What are you talking about?'

'You'll see.'

If this were a film, she would hear footsteps behind her. They would grow closer; she would hurry, soon break into a run. Eventually she would stumble, turn her ankle, and he'd be on her. As it was, at first, there was no more than a vaguely unsettling awareness.

The lecture theatre had been too warm, the muggy atmosphere and droning tones of the guest speaker having a soporific effect. Lucy stumbled out into the street, tired and hungry, not relishing the forty-minute walk home in the freezing December darkness. She carried a tote bag of books, her laptop in a shoulder bag designed to look like it was carrying nothing more valuable than a shitload of lecture notes. Couldn't be too careful, not in London. Not according to her mother, who had her own wild ideas of danger, mostly conjured up in her own mind.

She started walking. The people she passed looked as weary as she felt, hurrying along to the station, to the bus stop, desperate to get home, get warm. Eat, sleep, wake tomorrow and do it all over again.

She was passing Warren Street Underground station when she became aware of the first nudge of unease. She couldn't have said what had alerted her, but she felt a tiny rush as her heartbeat quickened, her senses sharpened, her eyes beginning to search for danger. Her phone was in her jeans pocket and instinctively she felt for it. Still there. There were people around, a group in front of her waiting to cross the road. She increased her pace but the lights changed, and by the time she reached the crossing they were well ahead again. She waited, wanting to look behind her, to see if there was someone there. It was a ridiculous thought; of course there was. This was London – when were you ever alone? But this was different. She could feel eyes on her back.

Pretending to check the traffic, she glanced around. There were people behind her now, looking at their phones, their watches. They were all watching the lights, urging them to change so they could cross, resenting having to wait even for a couple of minutes.

That was when she saw him.

Standing by the entrance to the station, wearing dark trousers and a black coat with the hood up. Arms folded, feet apart, face invisible. Couldn't have looked dodgier if he'd tried.

She turned back. Maybe she was paranoid, seeing and feeling threats when there were none, but it wasn't the first time she'd felt as though she was being watched. Recently, it had happened several times.

She hurried across the road with everyone else, picking up her pace. Determined not to be rattled but feeling it nevertheless, she kept moving.

Another crossing. Again she had to wait. She turned again, looked back. He was there, head down, now no more than twenty metres away. The coat was baggy, all his clothes plain and unidentifiable. Lucy licked her lips, her mouth dry.

She'd already been warned.

1

'You're wasting your time. I'm telling you nothing, I'm not agreeing a deal with you. Take these off,' James Mulligan raised his cuffed hands, 'and let me go back to my cell.'

Across the table, Detective Chief Inspector Tim Achebe raised his eyebrows. 'You realise that if we do that, you'll be locked up for the rest of your life?'

Mulligan glared. 'Yeah, yeah. Better than being dead, isn't it?'

There was silence until Jen Somerville, Achebe's sergeant, sitting beside her boss, said carelessly, 'Is it?'

'Marginally.' Mulligan pouted. 'Things can happen to a person that are worse than death, you know.'

They did. Achebe said nothing, just watched him. In his grubby grey sweatshirt and jogging bottoms, his auburn hair unwashed, James Mulligan was a less than impressive sight. He had been arrested six weeks earlier when a botched drug deal had resulted in three men, including Mulligan himself, being shot. One had died, but Mulligan's bullet had gone clean through his thigh. He'd lost some blood but had never been in serious danger. That had come later, once he'd been released from hospital and into the prison system. Now, three beatings and an attempted riot later, they were trying to get him to talk again, and failing.

He looked from Somerville to Achebe. 'Is one of you going to speak? I've said all I'm going to, so get your fingers out of your arses and take me back to Belmarsh.'

Somerville tutted. 'Is that any way to talk to people who are trying to help you?'

'Didn't your mother teach you manners?' Achebe folded his arms.

Mulligan smirked. 'You know, she never said a lot to me at all.' He spoke in a high-pitched screech: 'Get your thieving hands out of my purse. I don't know who your father is, so stop fucking asking.' Reverting to his normal voice, he raised his eyebrows. 'You know, the usual.'

Somerville sketched a yawn. 'Yeah, poor you. No wonder you ended up a criminal when you had such a terrible child-hood.'

Mulligan tried to point at her. 'You can be a wee bitch when you put your mind to it, can't you?'

She beamed. 'You're learning.'

He scowled. 'But you're not. We're done. It won't work. Take me home.'

'Home?' Achebe's nostrils flared. 'An eight-by-six cell with a stinking toilet in the corner and the most psychotic cellmate you can think of in the other bunk? What do you reckon, James?'

Mulligan said nothing, making a point of ignoring him.

'How's your sister?' Somerville asked suddenly.

Mulligan's eyes narrowed. 'My…?'

'Sister, you remember. Girl who grew up in the same house as you.' She sat back in her chair and gazed at the ceiling. 'Lucy?'

Mulligan leant towards her. 'Is this some kind of—'

'Postgraduate student at the University of Westminster, isn't she?' Somerville inclined her head, checking with Achebe, who nodded, playing along as they had agreed earlier.

'I believe so. Studying cyber crime and forensics,' he said. 'Already holds a degree in computer network security.'

'Wow.' Somerville looked suitably impressed. 'Clever girl.'

'Very clever girl,' said Achebe. They both beamed at Mulligan like proud parents.

'She's twenty-fucking-four,' he spat. 'Hardly a girl.'

'Don't tell me you respect her?' Achebe smiled. 'I thought women were pieces of meat to you?'

Mulligan glared at him but stayed quiet.

'Still,' Somerville tipped her head to the side, 'a subject like that could come in handy.'

'We always need geeks,' Achebe nodded. It was true.

Mulligan's expression darkened. 'She wouldn't work for you lot. Never. Not if you begged her.'

'What's wrong, James? Scared we'll poach her? Wouldn't look good for you, would it? Your smart-arse little sister, working for the Met?' Achebe grinned at him. 'Don't tell me you haven't already asked her to do some work for you. Hacking, fiddling around with CCTV cameras? Sneaking into other people's bank accounts?'

Mulligan's eyes blazed, but when he spoke, he was calm. 'Leave her out of this. She's never been involved in any of my business activities.'

Somerville laughed. 'Is that what we're calling them? Business activities?'

'Whatever you say, they've made me more money already than you'll earn in your entire life.' Mulligan folded his arms.

'Congratulations. You must be proud of yourself. Now you can enjoy spending it.' Somerville widened her eyes in an exaggerated double-take, gazing around at the grimy walls and the barred window. 'Oh no, wait.'

Mulligan tried to applaud, the handcuffs making it impossible. 'Well done, love. Oscar-winning, that was.'

'Your sister's doing well for herself,' said Achebe. His tone had changed, serious now. Tired of playing games.

'Don't you think other people will have noticed that?' Somerville asked, backing him up.

'What do you mean?' Mulligan's eyes flicked between them. 'What are you bastards up to now?'

'We're concerned about Lucy.' Achebe leant forward, resting his forearms on the table between them. 'We want to keep her safe.'

Mulligan glared at him. 'Really? Good of you. Safe from what?'

'The two men who worked for you, the brothers? Albanian, not a brain cell between them?'

'Yeah, I remember them.' Mulligan allowed himself a smile. 'Been spilling their guts, have they?'

'You know they have,' said Somerville. 'Couldn't wait to tell us everything they knew in return for some time off their sentences.'

'Really.' A sneer. 'Won't have taken long. No loyalty, some people. No balls.'

'They say you were cooking your own crack, James. That true?'

His cheeks flushed. 'None of your business.'

'Come on, we know you were. We've been in all your properties, remember, including your cookshop. Your fingerprints all over the pans, DNA everywhere. Have to say, in a way, we were disappointed. We thought we'd brought in a major dealer when we arrested you. Then we discover you're a one-man band.' Achebe's expression was intentionally sorrowful. 'Not exactly Walter White, are you?'

Mulligan managed a grin. 'Even he had to start somewhere.'

'But we still think you can help us.' Achebe gave the other man a hard look. 'We need to put away the people you were working with. Otherwise we can't promise your sister will be safe.'

'I've already told you, no chance.' Mulligan leant back in his chair, focusing on the door. He raised his voice. 'Is anyone out there? I want to go back to my cell.'

No reply. Achebe folded his arms, waiting. Mulligan lifted his chin, pressing his lips together, making a show of staying silent. Achebe didn't care. Let him make them wait. He'd agree in the end, the DCI was certain. When he knew, when he was aware of what was really going on.

Once they'd told him his sister had already received death threats.

–

In the observation suite, two people were watching the detectives wrestle with James Mulligan.

'We're getting nowhere fast.' Assistant Commissioner Elizabeth Beckett began to push back her chair. 'I don't have time for this, Ian.'

Commander Ian Penrith smoothed his shirt over his belly, disturbing a few biscuit crumbs, which fell to the carpet. 'With respect—'

Beckett was on her feet now, sliding her chair under the desk, her fingers digging into the fabric. 'I don't know why you bother saying that. Respect doesn't come into it. It only means you're about to say exactly what you want to, whether I find it offensive or not.'

'With respect, I didn't ask you to be here.'

Beckett chose to ignore him. 'We were expecting James Mulligan to know most of the drug dealers, people traffickers and other criminals in London. Now it seems he's little more than an amateur, a waste of our time and resources. Resources that, as I'm sure I don't need to remind you, are growing sparser by the day.'

Penrith waved a hand. 'Yes, I read the memo. Budget cuts. Old news by now, surely?'

'Memo?' She made it sound as though he'd mentioned using an abacus to do his expenses, or something equally old-fashioned.

'Email, whatever.' He didn't look at her. 'Mulligan had a gun. He must have got it from somewhere.'

She scowled. 'Well I doubt he made it himself. Anyway, the victims weren't shot with Mulligan's gun.'

His turn to ignore her. 'As you've said, we also know he was involved in people trafficking. It's not just about the drugs.'

'Mulligan's not going to talk. Listen to him. Whatever he knows, he'll be killed if he shares it.'

'Or his sister will.'

Beckett threw up her hands. 'It's not going to work, Ian. I'll admit, it was worth a try, but we need to let Achebe handle the murders. We have other priorities, and yours is rebuilding the team.'

Penrith blew out his cheeks. 'Which I've been trying to do. Every other officer seems to want to work for us.'

'And how many of them have you considered actually speaking to yourself?'

Now he met her eyes. 'None.'

'Ian—'

'I know.' He shifted in his seat, the chair creaking. 'I know we need more bodies.' He smiled at the word. 'But they have to be the right ones.'

'This isn't a game. We've lost three undercover officers: one dead, one who's been medically retired and one—'

'Who resigned during a tantrum.'

Beckett's smile was cold. 'For the second time. She's made a habit of walking away. Now we're down to two men, and Ewan Davies has no experience. You have to admit, it's not ideal.'

'I haven't said it is. That doesn't mean I'm going to recruit just anyone who shows an interest.'

Beckett exhaled through her nose. 'She won't come back, you know.'

'Would you have her, if she agreed?'

'No.' The reply was immediate, as though Beckett had been expecting the question. She probably had. No doubt she had had questions to answer about the resignation of Detective Sergeant Caelan Small. Their prized asset, the jewel in their crown – gone. They'd already had to tempt her back once before, and Penrith wasn't convinced they'd be able to do so again. He didn't even know where she was. He'd wandered past her apartment building in Rotherhithe, had a word with the porter, but had discovered nothing. The man hadn't even admitted to knowing her. She had a habit of earning loyalty.

'What did you say to her?' Penrith hadn't asked before, but Caelan Small had told Beckett she was resigning during a conversation at the bedside of Nicky Sturgess, Caelan's former lover and colleague, who had recently been injured in the course of duty. Sturgess had also left the force, accepting the offer of an extremely early and well-pensioned retirement. Perhaps Caelan was with Nicky, but he doubted it. From what Penrith had heard, Nicky now needed a full-time carer, and he struggled to imagine Caelan nursing anyone. The pair had a complicated, troubled history, their relationship destroyed by a decision Caelan had seen as the ultimate betrayal on Nicky's part, when Nicky's death had been faked to protect her during an investigation. Caelan, believing she had seen her lover murdered, had been shattered. When Nicky had eventually reappeared hoping to rekindle the relationship, Caelan, stunned and furious, had walked away.

Beckett didn't answer Penrith's question, a faint blush staining her cheeks. Penrith noted this with interest. Elizabeth Beckett's emotions were usually imperceptible.

'Ma'am?'

She met his eyes. 'Does it matter? Caelan's gone and we need to move on.'

'I'd just like to know—'

'All right. She said she wanted to take some leave. I told her she wouldn't be able to stay away from the job for long. She called my bluff.' Beckett blinked at the memory. Penrith knew she wasn't regretting her behaviour or feeling guilty. She hadn't risen to the rank of assistant commissioner by accident. He imagined the scene: Nicky lying unconscious in the hospital bed, Caelan angry and emotional, Beckett unrepentant.

'And told you she was leaving permanently,' he said.

Beckett nodded. 'I also told her we were thinking about making Mulligan an offer.'

'And?'

'She wasn't interested.'

Penrith pinched his lower lip. 'Give me a week.'

He could hear the desperation in his own voice, knew Beckett would too.

'To do what?' She inclined her head. 'I've already said I don't want Caelan back here.'

'She's the best undercover officer we have.'

'She was the best undercover officer we *had*, I agree, but she also played by her own rules. I can't condone that.'

'You don't have to. I'm the head of covert policing now. If the shit hits the fan, it'll stick to me. Your name won't be mentioned; you can walk away without a scratch. Or a stain.' Penrith gave her a sideways glance, wondering if she would take the bait.

Beckett looked down her nose. 'Nice try.'

He laughed. 'Come on. Let me speak to her at least.'

'What will you tell her? That we can't manage without her?' She curled her lip, and Penrith smiled to himself. Beckett was pissed off because she knew it was true. Caelan had always been their star, and without her they were struggling.

'Flattery won't work. I'll tell her about the victims.'

'That's Tim Achebe's case.'

'And Lucy.'

Beckett considered it. 'A damsel in distress? She'll see through you.'

'Maybe.' Penrith bared his teeth. 'But she still won't be able to say no.'

2

Caelan had driven to Barmouth for the afternoon. Early December probably wasn't the best time to visit a seaside town in north-west Wales, but after days being trapped indoors by the weather, she had felt like escaping now the rain had finally stopped. Walking under the endless pale blue sky, the sea by her side, the beautiful Mawddach estuary behind her and the wind chilling her cheeks, was perfect. The village where she was staying was quiet, with a petrol station, two pubs and a grocery shop. People had been polite enough, even friendly, but the old urge to keep her head down was always there. Blending in, quickly becoming part of the furniture, had been vital to her safety for so long, it was now second nature.

It would take time to get used to being free.

She turned back towards the town centre, bought a tray of chips with a generous serving of mushy peas spooned over them, and found a bench across the road to perch and eat. Dressed in clothing of her choice, no need to report back to anyone about where she was or what she was doing. Spending her time reading, watching films, playing video games. Relaxing. Using her own name, smiling at people she met.

Telling the truth, living openly.

She had pretended to be someone else for so long, she had almost forgotten how being herself felt. Almost. But the solitude and the clean Welsh air were helping, the contrast with the bustle of London striking. If she didn't think about the job she had walked away from, or about Nicky, she was happy.

She dug into the chips, relishing the bite of the salt and the tang of vinegar. She was content, at least. She had decisions to make, and the time to think them through. She had a home to go back to in London when she was ready. She was healthy, she was young. She could start again.

As she ate, an elderly couple tottered by, arm in arm, the man carrying a bag of shopping in his free hand, the woman clutching an umbrella that she held over them both. Caelan nodded as they passed her, ignoring the sudden tightening of her throat. She crumpled up the polystyrene tray and dropped it into the bin beside the bench.

Clouds were beginning to skim across the sky.

–

Back at the house, she reversed onto the driveway, leaving the car ready as always for a quick getaway. She smiled to herself as she unlocked the front door. Old habits definitely died hard.

In the hallway she paused, listening. Usually she would step out of her shoes, but today she kept them on. With her phone in her hand, she crept down the hallway. The kitchen door stood open. Hadn't she closed it? She thought so but couldn't remember for sure. She stopped and waited.

Nothing.

She shoved the door open and marched inside.

The man sitting at the kitchen table, cup of coffee in one hand, chocolate digestive in the other, grinned at her.

'You took your time.'

She stared at him, anger rising. 'How did you get in here?'

Ian Penrith held up a bunch of keys, and Caelan shook her head. She leant against the door frame, ready to tell him where to go.

'Your friend Mr Davies needs to be more careful,' he told her, biting into the biscuit.

'You mean you stole them?'

Penrith lifted his shoulders. 'The keys were in his jacket pocket, which he'd left in my office. When I picked it up, they fell out. That's not stealing.'

'Couldn't you just have knocked?'

A smirk. 'Where's the fun in that? Anyway, you would have ignored me.'

'How did you know which was the right key?'

'I didn't. I brought the whole bunch with me and hoped one would fit. He's living with his sister at the moment, isn't he? He'll have to hope she's at home when he leaves work tonight, otherwise he's in for a chilly evening under the stars.'

Typical. Caelan refused to be persuaded to smile back at him. 'Still doesn't explain how you knew I was staying here. Did Ewan tell you?'

It was Ewan Davies's house. A former soldier and then police protection officer, he had transferred onto their team permanently just before Caelan had walked out. She liked Ewan, had trusted him as soon as they met. They'd worked together briefly, and the friendship between them had grown stronger. When he'd realised she needed a place to run to, he had offered her this house. He'd bought it when he was still in the army and rented it out, but was currently between tenants. On the border of Wales and England, it had seemed far enough away for Caelan to feel she was truly leaving her previous life behind. Now, suddenly, that life had barged back in, in the large and ungainly form of Commander Ian Penrith.

'No, Ewan didn't say a word,' Penrith said. He tapped the side of his nose. 'I worked it out for myself. Used to be a detective, you know.'

'Where did you park your car? I didn't see it.'

'In the pub car park, where I hoped you'd miss it.' His eyebrows danced. 'Thought I'd do my bit for local business and sample a half of bitter while I was in there.'

'Very clever. What do you want, Ian?' But Caelan already knew.

He smiled again. Somehow it never looked right on him. Penrith had a face made for scowling. 'Well, we're back here again,' he said. 'You resign, we run after you to beg you to come back into the fold. It's becoming a habit.'

'You're going to beg?' She moved further into the room though she didn't sit down. 'This should be interesting.'

He finished his coffee, thumped the mug onto the table. Reaching for the packet of biscuits again, he shoved a whole one into his mouth. 'Is Detective Sturgess here?'

Caelan stared at him, the question stinging as though he had slapped her. 'Nicky? No. Why would you think she would be?'

Penrith chewed, swallowed. 'Then where—'

'With her parents, at their house in Derbyshire.' Caelan spoke without emotion. 'Didn't you know?'

He shook his head. 'No reason why we should. She's definitely not coming back, so it's none of our business. I thought you and she might have patched up your differences.'

'She's made it clear she never wants to see me again. End of story.'

Penrith stared, and for a moment she thought he was going to sympathise. Instead, he took two more biscuits. 'More fool her then.'

In spite of it all, Caelan laughed. 'She blames me for what happened to her.'

'And you blame Assistant Commissioner Beckett.' It wasn't a question; he knew the answer.

'Did Beckett send you here?'

His mouth full, Penrith shook his head again, biscuit crumbs flying. 'No,' he managed to mumble. 'This is my show now.'

'Your show?' Caelan gave in, pulled out a chair and sat opposite him. 'It makes no difference. I'm not coming back.'

'Let me tell you what's going on before you throw me out.'

She snorted. 'I can guess. James Mulligan.'

'In a way.' Penrith slipped a hand into his jacket, removing a brown envelope from the inside pocket. He opened it, unfolded the contents and shoved them across the table towards Caelan.

'Whatever it is, I don't want to see.' Folding her arms, she turned her face away like a child.

'I'll explain, then,' he said. 'It's a post-mortem report.'

She snorted. 'Most people bring a bottle of wine when they visit.'

Penrith waited, but Caelan was determined not to blink first.

After a few seconds, he said, 'The victim was a young woman. We're not certain of her age, but her wisdom teeth hadn't come through. Based on that and other factors, the pathologist estimates she was between fifteen and twenty-one. We don't know who she is, or where she came from.'

Under the table, Caelan clenched her fists. He knew exactly how to draw her in. 'Description?'

'Dark hair, brown eyes. Thin almost to the point of emaciation. Evidence of drug use.'

She closed her eyes, seeing a face from the past, the face of someone she had failed. When she turned back towards Penrith, he pushed the papers towards her with a fingertip. She didn't pick them up.

'Tell me,' she said.

He took a breath as though to steady himself. 'She'd been beaten, raped, and not for the first time. She had injuries that proved she'd endured sexual abuse over a long period of time, and from a young age.'

Bile rose in Caelan's throat and she swallowed it down. Penrith's voice was a monotone, his face a mask. This was their job at its most sickening, crimes that tore them apart, filling them with a burning fury. She knew Penrith well enough to be aware of his ways of working, and was sure he wouldn't be using this as a way of persuading her to think about a return. Beckett would manipulate the situation to suit herself without thinking twice, but not Penrith. Not this.

'How was she killed?' she asked, aware of the tremor in her voice.

'She was shot in the back of the head.'

'An execution,' Caelan said softly. 'Where was she found?'

'Dumped in a bin on an industrial estate. She'd been restrained, burnt with cigarettes, and…' Penrith stopped, shook his head. 'You get the idea.'

'And you haven't identified her? Someone so young?'

Where were her parents, her teachers? Social services? But Caelan knew as well as any police officer that many young people were alone in the world, by choice or through the neglect and apathy of their families. Or to protect themselves from those same families.

'We don't know,' Penrith said. 'She's not been reported missing, as far as we can see. She's not the first.'

'What do you mean?'

He removed another envelope from the same pocket. He took out three photographs and studied them, then laid them on the table. Three faces. Three bodies. Three pairs of blank, unseeing eyes fixed on hers. 'Taking during their post-mortems,' he said unnecessarily. He pointed to one of the photographs. 'This girl was found first. Evidence of violent sex, restraint, beatings. Shot in the head and dumped.' He tapped the next one. 'This boy – the same story, and he was shot with the same gun.' Now his finger landed on the third face. 'This is the latest victim – I've already mentioned her injuries.' He nodded towards the envelope Caelan still hadn't touched. 'And you have her post-mortem report in front of you.'

'You think they were sex workers.' It was a statement, not a question. All the clues were there. Caelan stared at the three young, lifeless faces, a chill spreading through her stomach. 'Have either of the first two victims been identified?'

Penrith shook his head. 'No. We know the three are linked, though.'

'How?' Caelan couldn't take her eyes off the photographs. These were children, their bodies brutalised, used and thrown away. She was numb with horror, and with despair.

'They were all killed with the same gun, though their bodies were dumped in different areas.' Penrith paused, taking a moment. 'The bodies were washed, though whoever killed them didn't comb their hair.'

'What do you mean?'

Reaching into his pocket again, Penrith brought out a clear evidence bag. Inside was a tiny bright pink feather. 'The pathologist found this in the hair of the male victim. The girls didn't have feathers, but there was pink fluff in their hair that came from the same source.'

Caelan took the bag and studied the feather. The colour was vivid, garish. 'They were all in the same place at some point,' she said. 'Held somewhere maybe.'

Penrith nodded. 'And then maybe they did something wrong and were punished. Raped, beaten, murdered.'

She handed the evidence bag back to him. 'Absolute bastards.'

'It gets worse.'

'Worse?' She almost laughed. 'How could anything be worse than this?'

'In a million ways, you know that. It was the wrong word to use. I meant more complicated.'

He took out another photograph. 'Last one, I promise.'

This time Caelan looked down at the beaming face of a young woman. Hair the colour of treacle, wide green eyes. She blinked.

'Who is she?'

'Her name's Lucy. She's received death threats and... well, other threats. Threats of a personal and... vicious nature.' Penrith widened his eyes, inviting her to join the dots.

'You mean threats of sexual violence.'

'Correct.'

Caelan saw the flash of disgust in his expression, but his tone remained matter-of-fact. She swallowed. 'What does this have to do with...' She nodded at the other photographs, the post-mortem report.

'A photograph of the third victim's body, taken after she had been thrown into the bin with the other rubbish, was sent by text to Lucy. Untraceable.' Scowling, Penrith pointed at the photograph. 'And Lucy is James Mulligan's kid sister.'

He stopped, again appearing to be waiting for her to make the connection. She looked up at him, imagining she could feel the eyes of the woman in the photograph on her. She thought about it, not liking the possibilities coming into her mind. It was tenuous, but feasible.

'Are you saying someone's using the threats to the sister to send Mulligan a message?'

'It's possible. We have three victims we can't trace. They were obviously involved in sex work, possibly trafficked. We know Mulligan had his fingers in that particularly horrific pie.'

Sickened, Caelan considered what he was suggesting. 'Does Mulligan recognise any of the victims?'

'He says not. To be fair, he could barely look at the photographs.' Penrith screwed up his face. 'Not so easy to deny what you've done when you're brought face to face with the people whose lives you were involved in destroying.'

'Then the people Mulligan worked with are telling him to keep his mouth shut? Why would they? Why would they think he would grass?'

He sat back, folding his arms across his considerable belly. 'For the reason we're offering: to take some time off his sentence – a deal. Someone is obviously worried he might open his mouth – the same people who murdered, or ordered the deaths of, these three young people. What else could it be? Lucy Mulligan's doing well at university; there's never been any question of her being involved in anything dodgy like her brother. She has no enemies.'

'As far as you know.'

'She's had a brick thrown through her window, messages sent by text and email. She's even been followed, and now she's been sent a photograph of a dead girl? She's adamant she has no

22

idea what's going on, and Tim Achebe believes she's telling the truth.'

'But—'

'Achebe knows we're considering making Mulligan an offer,' Penrith went on. 'We want to use him to get close to the people he was working with. Lucy went to the local police about the threats, understandably worried and frightened. When she received the text with a photograph of an obviously dead girl, Achebe got to hear of it.'

'You're worried about the operation you've dreamed up involving Mulligan.' Caelan didn't bother to try to disguise the scorn in her voice, but Penrith was undeterred.

'And I'm worried about Lucy. If she's already under threat, and her brother's not even back on the streets yet… We know James Mulligan had contact with people traffickers. You can imagine what a laugh they'd think it would be to force his sister to work in one of their brothels.'

Caelan could visualise the horror only too well. 'She'd be dead within months.'

Penrith stared at her. 'You mean weeks, if not days.'

Silence.

'Has Mulligan said anything? Does he know who might be involved?' Caelan asked eventually.

A snort. 'He won't talk, not a word. He's terrified, and who can blame him? I think there's only one way to approach this. We're going to let him go and see where he leads us.'

Caelan couldn't believe it. 'What? I saw him shoot a man dead. You've evidence of his involvement in everything from selling crack to kidnap, torture and murder, and you're allowing him to walk free?'

Penrith grabbed more biscuits. 'Whatever he's done, Mulligan's classed as small fry. We want to offer him a compromise. We'll protect his sister if he helps us put away some of the real villains he knows.'

'Wouldn't him working with us put her in more danger? Why would he even consider it?'

'Because he's a selfish bastard who's terrified of prison.'

'Still.'

Penrith shrugged. 'It's a risk, but a risk to her, not to Mulligan. We're dangling a fairly huge carrot.'

Caelan shook her head. 'You're going to forget what he's done?'

He wagged a finger. 'I didn't say that. He'll still do his time, don't worry.'

'Beckett mentioned this before. I told her then I wouldn't be involved. Mulligan knows me, he's seen my face.'

'He offered you a job.'

'When he thought I had a kilo of coke to sell, yeah. Before he knew I was police. Once he found out who I really was, he told his men to kill me.' The memory was all too vivid. The gun pointed at her face, the blank eyes of the man holding it, and Caelan's own lack of fear. She had almost willed him to pull the trigger.

Penrith gave another snort. 'But they didn't. Mulligan respects you, I heard him tell you so himself.'

'What are you proposing?'

'Mulligan goes back to his old job – being a scumbag. You step in as his right-hand woman, learn the ropes. Maybe you're a cousin, a new girlfriend. We haven't worked out the details.'

'You don't think it'll look obvious? Mulligan suddenly reappears just when his sister's being threatened? Every dealer in London will have heard about him being arrested.'

Penrith was shaking his head. 'I don't think so. The word on the street is that Mulligan got away when his men were nicked. He ended up in hospital and was interviewed by the police but never charged.'

'Strange how rumours get around, isn't it?' Caelan knew Penrith would have told his numerous informants and contacts to start the whispers. 'I still don't buy it. Why would Mulligan have a new assistant all of a sudden?'

'Stands to reason. The two men he used for protection and as general thugs are in jail and will be for years. He can't do everything alone.' Penrith lumbered to his feet and went to the sink to fill the kettle.

'Mulligan and his men weren't the only people arrested that day,' Caelan reminded him. 'How are you going to keep Waits—'

Penrith flicked the kettle on to boil and held up a hand. 'Already dealt with. If Waits wants to see his baby, he'll play along.'

'Really? You think that'll work? The baby isn't due for months.'

'He's already agreed. He was easily persuaded, especially when we made additional promises. You know how much leeway we have when we need it. Better food, softer toilet paper...' He grinned. 'All of which can be rescinded when the job's done. Seriously, though, he's desperate to see the child. If we can make that happen – and we can – he'll do anything we want, including keeping his mouth shut.'

Caelan leant back, thinking it over. Penrith crossed to a cupboard, removed two mugs and found a box of tea bags.

'Make yourself at home, why don't you?' she said.

'Were you offering to make the drinks?' He waited. 'Thought not.' He poured water into the cups and sloshed the tea bags around with a spoon. 'What do you reckon?'

'I don't like it. It's too risky, and Mulligan especially can't be trusted.'

Penrith set a mug in front of her and sat back down. 'We're not doing it for him.' He gestured at the post-mortem report. 'We don't even know this girl's name.' Leaning across the table, he tapped a thick finger on the photograph of Lucy Mulligan. 'And this young woman has done nothing wrong, apart from being born into the same family as her worthless brother. We need to help them. Both of them.'

Caelan eyed him. 'I didn't believe you'd stoop low enough to use innocent people to get what you wanted. Seems I was wrong.'

He smiled. 'You think? Not only is Lucy Mulligan innocent, she's someone we can't afford to lose.'

'What do you mean?'

'She's a computer expert, and I mean the best of the best. A wizard. She has all sorts of top-secret government types sniffing around her, waiting for her to graduate so they can snap her up. We need to protect her. If we do, it'll make all of our careers. If we don't…'

'We'll be hung out to dry.' Caelan was beginning to see why Penrith had travelled here to speak to her himself.

'It won't bother you, of course, since you've abandoned your career yet again anyway. But some of us still have a mortgage to pay and are depending on having a pension when we retire.' Penrith sipped his tea, watching her over the brim of his cup. 'Think about it, Caelan. Think about these kids, dumped like so much rubbish. Remember those girls in the brothel you found. We're talking about people traffickers, the ones at the top of the chain. It's a chance to put them away for the rest of their lives.' He stopped, then said, 'Remember—'

'Don't.' It was a command, and for once, Penrith listened. Neither of them spoke, Penrith drinking his tea and Caelan staring at nothing, torn by what he had told her. She wanted to walk away and never look back, but what she had heard was like a siren call. She had no choice.

Penrith knew her as well as she had thought she knew him, and now she realised he wasn't above pressing every button he could think of.

'What does Mulligan say?' she asked eventually.

Penrith kept sipping. 'No.'

'What?'

'Mulligan said he wouldn't do it.'

'Then why—'

'We told him about the threats his sister had received, what they specified in graphic detail would happen to her if he talked, showed him the photographs of the three victims. He didn't much care, at least acted as though he didn't, so we told him he'd serve three years in an open prison if he spilled his guts. That changed his mind.'

Caelan was sickened. 'Only three years? Probably not even that.'

'It's a bluff, of course. Once we've got what we need, he'll never see the light of day, but he doesn't need to know that.' Penrith glanced at his phone. 'I have to get back to London.' He made her meet his eyes. 'What do you say? I'm not asking you to rejoin the force. You'll be a… contractor. You'll report to me, and only me. No need for you to liaise with Assistant Commissioner Beckett at all. No need for you to even see her.'

'Beckett's agreed to this?'

He shrugged. 'She's looking the other way.'

'Great. Then if it blows up in our faces, she walks away without a scratch?'

'As always.'

'And if we make arrests, she gets the glory?'

'If you want applause, Caelan, you're in the wrong line of work. You know that. Beckett plays the game; we do the dirty work. Always.' He stood. 'Well?'

She closed her eyes, hating herself. 'All right, I'm in.'

To Penrith's credit, he didn't gloat, didn't even react. 'Good. I'll give you tonight to close up this place. Come to my office tomorrow morning and we'll get you on your way.' He dumped his mug in the sink, picked up his phone and the bunch of keys. Holding them up, he grinned at her. 'Looks like Ewan might get these back tonight after all.' He left her sitting at the table, her head in her hands.

Once she'd heard the front door close, Caelan opened her eyes.

Penrith had left the photographs and post-mortem report on the table. She turned away from them, knowing he had done so deliberately. She had been manipulated, and now she acknowledged she had allowed it to happen.

Elizabeth Beckett had been right. Undercover work was like a drug, and once you had tasted it, felt the rush, there was nothing else like it. This time, though, it would be different. She wouldn't allow them to take complete control, not again.

She didn't trust them. She had grown used to thinking of Penrith as an ally, but now she wondered whether she had been fooled.

Lucy Mulligan smiled up at her as she took her mobile out of her pocket and scrolled to the number she wanted.

'Caelan?' Nicky's voice was weak, groggy. Caelan swallowed. 'How are you?' she managed to ask.

'I asked you not to call.' Nicky spoke quietly, but there was no mistaking the steel.

'I just wanted to let you know, I'm going away for a while.'

Nicky would understand what she really meant, Caelan knew. It was all part of the game. The doublespeak, the deception. There was silence, and Caelan moved the phone away from her ear, checking the screen to make sure the signal hadn't been lost. At last Nicky spoke again, her voice gentle.

'The job will kill you one day, you know. I mean it, Caelan. You saw what happened to me. Don't let them do the same to you.'

Caelan's mouth felt parched. 'I won't.'

'But you're still letting them rule your life?'

'No, I...' She allowed her voice to fade. What was there to say?

Nicky clicked her tongue. 'You can't stay away, can you? Even though it's destroying you and everything that should be important to you.'

Caelan's laugh was bitter. 'I don't think it was me who did that, do you?' She closed her eyes, regretting the words as soon as she had said them.

Nicky's tone changed, cold and clinical once more. 'Goodbye, Caelan. Please don't call me again, not ever. I'll be changing my number.' She was gone before Caelan could reply.

Mechanically Caelan pushed the handset into her jeans pocket and went upstairs to pack.

3

The evening had drawn in quickly, the house cold enough that she could see her husband's breath as he snored on the sofa. Lynn put down her book and slowly, painfully, struggled to her feet and made her way to the thermostat in the hall to turn the heating on. The arthritis in her hip seemed to be worsening by the day. She didn't need a walking stick yet, but she knew it wouldn't be long. Not a happy thought.

She limped into the kitchen, filled the kettle and set it to boil. She took two mugs from one cupboard, two hot-water bottles from another and then reached to the highest shelf for the locked metal cash box that held their medication. One tablet for her in the evening, several more for Pete.

She made the tea and carried the cups through to the living room separately, so she could use both hands to hold them steady, then did the same with two glasses of water. As she put the glasses down and sat beside her husband, he stirred and opened his eyes, smiling at her.

'I was going to make the tea,' he said. 'How long have I been asleep?'

'Not long,' she lied. He sat up and reached for the mugs on the coffee table, handing Lynn hers first. He saw the plastic medication boxes she'd brought through, seven days' supply of drugs for each of them already counted out into separate compartments.

'Tablet time again?' He grimaced. 'We'll soon be rattling.'

Lynn sipped her tea. 'Andrew sent me a text earlier,' she said. 'He wants to know if we'd like to go to watch Sophie's Christmas play with them.'

Pete nodded. 'Do you remember the year Andrew played Joseph in the nativity and knocked Mary off the stage?'

Lynn nodded. 'Accidentally.'

Pete grinned. 'Still. Her mum wasn't happy.'

'Well, you know what some parents are like. Their child has to be the star of the show.'

'No chance of that with ours.' Pete took a mouthful of tea. 'Both too shy.'

'You're talking about primary school, Peter. It's a long time ago.'

He looked at the pills lined up on the table. 'Don't I know it.'

'That girl, the one that played Mary, she always had her finger up her nose. I can't remember her name.' Lynn paused, looked at her husband. 'Is that someone at the door?'

'I didn't hear anything.'

She shuffled forward on the seat. 'I'll go and check. It'll be Andrew, it's his five-a-side night. He might not have his key.'

Pete put out a gentle hand to stop her, mindful of her sore hip. 'Stay there, I'll go. No point in you getting up again.'

He pushed his feet into his slippers, put his cup down on the table and made for the door.

The hallway was in darkness, but he could see a shadow on the step outside as he switched on the light. He frowned, wondering who was there. Andrew would have just knocked on the door until one of them opened it, or rung to say he was outside. He usually let them know if he was going to call in on his way home from football anyway. Pete wasn't a nervous man, but he slid the security chain on all the same as he fumbled with his keys and peered around the door. Instantly his expression changed as he recognised the person who stood there. Beaming, he wrenched off the chain and threw open the door.

'Hello, Dad,' Caelan said as she flung her arms around her father.

—

Five minutes later, she was sitting on the settee between her parents with a piece of home-made Victoria sponge and a coffee. Already she felt more relaxed. This was home: the house she'd grown up in, the people who loved her.

Her mum was grinning at her. 'This is a lovely surprise,' she said. 'You should have let us know you were coming.'

'And you'd have baked a cake?' Caelan smiled, her parents laughing at the weak joke, as she'd known they would.

'You're a long way from London,' her dad said. The house was south of Manchester, in an area called Withington.

'I need to be back there tomorrow morning, though,' Caelan said, knowing she was going to disappoint them. 'I'll have to leave before five, but I wanted to see you. I'm going away for a bit and I won't be able to call.'

Caelan had never told her parents exactly what her job entailed, but she knew they had probably figured it out. Most police officers didn't work nine to five, but they didn't disappear for months on end without a word either.

'You can't stay?' Her mum pouted. 'But we haven't seen you for ages.'

'I know. I'm sorry.' Caelan bit into the cake to avoid having to say more.

'It's Sophie's Christmas play tomorrow – if you stay, you could come to watch it with us.'

Caelan chewed, swallowed. 'I'd love to, but...' Sophie was at school already? In Caelan's mind, her niece was still a baby. She got to her feet, still holding her plate, and went over to examine the framed photographs that stood on the fireplace. Her parents on their wedding day, one of herself in a party dress with pigtails and a shy smile. Andrew stood beside her, a huge grin displaying his missing his top teeth. She picked up another photograph, this one of her brother and his family – Andrew holding Sophie's hand while his wife Jen cradled their other daughter, only a few hours old.

'Eleanor's walking now,' Caelan's mum said, coming to stand beside her.

Caelan stared at the baby in the photograph. 'Already?'

'She's ten months old, Caelan,' her mum said gently. 'It's not unusual.'

She put the photograph down. 'Sorry,' she said again.

'The girls would love to see you,' her mum said. 'You could stay here for a few days. You know your bedroom's always ready for you.'

'You know how busy she is, love,' Pete said quickly. 'More criminals in London than there are tourists.'

Caelan knew her mother was right. She didn't see them enough, couldn't even phone as much as she wanted to. Her job always got in the way. Now, though… Now that the Met didn't own her, she would change her ways. Her parents had always been older than those of most people her age, and it was beginning to show. Her mum had been thirty-five when Caelan was born, her dad eight years older, meaning they were now mid sixties and early seventies. When she'd spotted the medication on the coffee table, she'd had a shock. Now she nodded at the pills.

'What are all these for? Looks like you're going to open a pharmacy.'

Her dad laughed. 'The doctor insists we take them. Load of rubbish if you ask me.'

Caelan looked at her mum, who shook her head. 'Your dad's in denial, but his blood pressure and cholesterol are too high.'

Pete leant over Caelan and gave his wife's thigh a playful push. 'When you bake most days and then force me to eat it, what do you expect?'

Caelan sat back and sipped her coffee, allowing the warmth and comfort of home to soothe her. She would sleep in her childhood bedroom, knowing she was safe, and that she could forget every shitty thing that was part of her work and her life in London.

For the next seven hours, at least.

4

The bed was warm, the sheet beneath him soft and clean. Ryan Glennister opened his eyes, hours earlier than he usually did, and listened to the deep snores of the man lying beside him. Slowly, cautiously he pulled the duvet away from his body and rolled out of bed. Gathering his clothes, he stepped into the bathroom, washing his face and dressing as quickly and quietly as he could.

Back in the bedroom, he went to the man's jacket, hanging over the back of the room's single chair. He slipped his hand into the pockets, found a well-stuffed wallet and a mobile phone. He decided to leave the phone, but the banknotes he bundled together. With another glance at the man in the bed, he crept towards the door.

'Nice knowing you,' he said softly, smiling to himself. He stepped into the corridor and trotted downstairs to the hotel's reception area, remembering to keep his head down. He doubted the man would report the theft to the police. How would he explain who Ryan was or why he'd been in his room? The traces of white powder on the polished desktop would be difficult to explain away, too. No, he wouldn't go to the police. They never did.

Outside, Ryan hitched his rucksack onto his shoulder, the thick roll of money safe inside his pocket. Where to? He should eat, but first there was a certain other need he had to satisfy, and he knew just the place. Not so long ago, he'd been owned by his dealer, James Mulligan, forced to do the dirty work in return for his addiction being fed. Not anymore. He giggled to himself, revelling in what he'd done. Now he had the power. He was free to make a living any way he wanted – and turning over rich, stupid bastards like the man still snoring his brains out was one of them, though not the most profitable. He imagined Mulligan locked in a cell, ranting to himself, spitting fury but unable to act. He chuckled again, tapped the money in his pocket.

Perfect.

But his skin was beginning to itch, sweat gathering in the small of his back. His stomach felt cavernous, aching and tight at the same time. He needed food, plus his own favourite sustenance.

Ryan began to walk.

5

In the grey morning light, Enfield police station looked as uninspiring as ever. Caelan climbed slowly out of Penrith's car, Penrith himself hurrying around the vehicle to hover nearby, as though expecting her to change her mind and try to make a run for it. Remembering her conversation with Nicky, she was tempted. She saw Penrith wince as she slammed the door harder than was really necessary. Her parents had insisted on getting up early with her, making sure she had a decent breakfast, filling a flask with coffee. Driving away from the house, both of them in their dressing gowns, waving her off from the doorstep, hadn't been easy. Now she squinted up at the building and realised she wanted to go straight back up the motorway.

'Why here?' she demanded. 'I thought Mulligan was in Belmarsh?'

'He was, but he promised to behave himself, so here we are.' Penrith began to stride across the car park. Caelan hesitated, wondering what the hell she was doing.

Inside, she could see DCI Tim Achebe waiting. His expression was grim, but when he spotted her, he managed a rueful smile.

'Good to see you again, Caelan.' He held out his hand and she shook it.

'And to see you, but not to be back here.' She folded her arms. 'Where is he?'

Achebe inclined his head. 'In the cells. We're not taking any chances.'

He signalled that they should follow him. 'They'll take him into an interview room so you can talk to him.'

'I'm not sure about this, Tim,' Caelan said. 'You've spoken to Mulligan. What do you think?'

Achebe blew out his cheeks. 'Honestly? That we're crazy to be even considering working with him.'

'Thanks for the input, Chief Inspector.' Penrith spoke calmly, but Caelan saw him clench his jaw.

'Caelan asked.' Achebe pushed open a set of double doors and stood back to allow them through. 'I'm not going to lie to her. Mulligan's stone cold. I don't think he'd have a problem with his sister being hurt if it meant he was okay.'

'They'd get to him too,' Penrith said. 'He won't be safe inside, you know that. No one is.'

They reached the area where the cells were located. It was quieter and smelt better than many of the similar blocks Caelan had visited or been locked up in during her career. Then again, it was early. There was plenty of time for the place to be strewn with vomit and worse.

'He's in there.' Achebe pointed with his thumb.

Caelan peered through the observation hatch in the cell door. James Mulligan lay curled on the blue foam mattress of his bunk, his face turned to the wall. The man who'd given the order for her to be shot dead was almost unrecognisable. The smart clothes and sharp haircut were gone. Mulligan looked exhausted, pale and defeated.

Perfect.

'I'll talk to him in the cell,' Caelan said quietly. Achebe looked at her.

'You're sure?' He smiled, guessing what she was thinking, also keeping his voice down. 'The interview rooms aren't exactly welcoming either, you know.'

'They're still not a cell.' Caelan wanted Mulligan to remember his accommodation at Belmarsh. She'd never been inside the prison, but she knew his cell would have been cramped, airless and probably filthy. 'Who was his cellmate?' Maybe it was something else she could use to persuade him to agree to Penrith's plans. It was predictable, but it might work.

'The most recent was a geezer called Darrell Cornish.' Achebe came to stand beside her, peering through the hatch. He stepped back. 'Darrell has a bit of a temper – beat some bloke in a pub half to death because he bumped into Mrs Cornish on his way back from the fruit machine.'

'Nice.'

'Made a change from Darrell hitting her, anyway.'

'Sounds like she'll get a nice long break from him now, though?'

Achebe grinned. 'Yeah, about six years.'

Caelan waited for the door to be unlocked, then stepped inside, pushing it closed behind her. Even though she had shut the door herself and could knock and walk out any time she wanted, knowing she was now locked inside still made the flesh on the back of her neck creep. How anyone could survive a lengthy jail sentence, she had no idea. She had never been asked to go undercover inside a prison, though colleagues had. She hoped she never would be.

Except you don't work for them anymore, she told herself. She stood silently, waiting.

'What do you want, Achebe?' Mulligan said. 'I've told you, I'm not playing your games.' He didn't get up, didn't even turn his head. Caelan slipped her hands into her trouser pockets and relaxed her shoulders.

'Good to see you again, James,' she said.

He froze for a second but covered it well, unfurling his body and sitting on the edge of the bunk. His hands dangled between his knees and he linked his fingers as he looked up at her with a mocking grin.

'You. Hello, princess. My man definitely missed, then?'

Caelan smiled back. 'You know he did.' He hadn't even fired the shot.

Mulligan turned his mouth down at the corners. Sad face. 'I never could get the staff.'

'I feel sorry for you.'

'I'm sure, but don't bother yourself too much. I'm banged up while you can go on your merry way, cosying up to people, lying to their faces.' His expression hardened. 'I don't know how you sleep at night.'

'Pretty well.' She was lying, but he didn't need to know that. 'Compared to some, I've not done much to worry about. I've never trafficked people, for example.'

He smirked. 'Aye, very good. You know, I bet there are a lot of criminals who'd love to know who you really are. Where you live.' He licked his lips. 'What you look like in the shower.'

She laughed at him. 'Is that the best you can do? I'm not the one who's going to be worrying about having a shower, James.'

'Yeah, yeah, big men coming for me when my trousers are down. What a fucking cliché. Is that the worst threat you've got?' He sneered. 'They wouldn't dare.'

'Because what, they're scared of you? From what I've heard, you've already been beaten up more times than you've had lukewarm shitty dinners.'

Mulligan winked. 'Don't believe everything you hear.'

'Is that bruising under your eye, or make-up? Either way, purple's not your colour.' She looked him up and down, curled her lip. 'Looking good, by the way.'

He made a gun from his fingers and pointed it at her. 'If only Andri had been quicker.'

She smiled, enjoying the exchange. 'You'd just be looking at more jail time than you already are. But then you wouldn't be worried, would you? Not when prison is such a breeze.'

'It won't work, you know.' Mulligan ran his hand through his hair, leaving it standing up in greasy spikes. 'I'm not doing it.'

Caelan folded her arms. 'As you've already said, several times.'

He shook his head. 'Just trying to give you fair warning. If you've come in here to try to persuade me to do what they're asking, you may as well leave now.'

She leant against the wall, watching him through half-closed eyes. 'You offered me a job. Told me I had guts. Said you admired me.'

'I didn't know who you were then. What you are.' He spat on the floor. 'One of *them*.'

'You said you'd co-operate. Three quick years in an open prison, instead of…' She looked around pointedly. 'Instead of twenty-five banged up in the worst shitholes in the country.'

He turned away, pulled up his legs and lay down, facing the wall again. 'You don't get it, do you?'

'Get what?'

'You can threaten me with whatever you like, but you have to do everything by the book. Keep records. You think there aren't coppers in the force who'd sell information like that? If I'm part of what your bosses are planning, and I'm found out, I'll be killed very, very slowly. They'll break every bone I have, and that'll just be for starters. They'll strip my skin, burn me, cut me. The people I'm talking about are the real deal. They'll do anything to anyone.'

'And you were working with them. You provided young women for them to play with, and now suddenly you're shit scared? Know a thing or two about torture yourself, don't you, James?' Caelan's tone hadn't changed, but it was a struggle to rein her temper in.

'I didn't…' Mulligan swallowed, shook his head. 'That was business. This is—'

'Yeah, feels different when it's your own worthless hide we're talking about, doesn't it?' She took a step towards him, just one. He raised his head, sneering at her.

'You've no idea what you're talking about, who you're suggesting dealing with. Believe me, it isn't worth it. If they ever even suspected you were police…'

She gave an exaggerated roll of her eyes. 'I get it. It'd be bad.'

'Bad. You think?' He closed his eyes, making a pillow for his head from his hands.

'Whatever images you have in your head, visualise your sister in my place, because that's what they're threatening.'

'Only if I talk. If I don't, they'll leave her alone.'

'Come on, James, you know it doesn't work like that. As soon as they realise what she can do, they'll grab her, make her do whatever they want. With her skills, she's a criminal's dream.'

Slowly he pushed himself into a sitting position. His expression was difficult to interpret – cunning, sly, but she could see fear there too.

'Say I was to agree, say I paraded you around London as my new bit of fluff—'

'I'm flattered.'

'Don't be. I'll give you a list of my conditions, and you can go and tell them my terms, then we'll talk again. Fair?'

'Not really, but let's pretend you have some power at least.'

He laughed. 'You know I do.'

'You don't. We could do this without you. I fooled you, didn't I? Had you scurrying around wanting to buy from me? I could do the same to all your dodgy mates as well.' Caelan spoke with a bravado she didn't feel.

Mulligan scowled. 'Not for long. If I'd checked you out before the meeting, I'd have seen through you straight away.'

'I'm sure. Tell me what you want, Mulligan.'

'I don't want to serve another day in prison. Not now, not ever. Lifelong immunity, whatever I do.'

She raised an eyebrow, shook her head. 'Well, you can forget that one. What else?'

'It's not much to ask.'

'Not much? I saw you kill someone. You think that'll be ignored?'

'Why not? He was a wee shitebag. Who's going to miss him?'

'What else?'

'I call the shots. You do what I tell you to do. My world, my contacts, my rules.'

'Again, forget it. Anything else?'

He met her eyes. 'You sleep in my bed.' He licked his lips. 'I won't touch you. Promise.'

Caelan pretended to consider it. 'I could manage that, as long as you slept elsewhere. Mars, maybe.'

'Funny. You sleep with me. Going to look weird otherwise, isn't it?'

'Weird? Who to? Do you have an audience in your bedroom?'

He tried to bat his eyelashes at her. 'It could be arranged.'

'I'm leaving in ten seconds. If there's anything else, make it quick.'

'That what you say to all your boyfriends?'

'Eight seconds.'

'My sister goes into one of your safe houses and stays there.'

Caelan tipped her head to the side. 'You do care, after all. How sweet.'

His eyes narrowed. 'I don't want her to be used. Not by you, and not by the fuckers pulling your strings. And not by...' He pressed his lips together.

'Careful, James. You nearly mentioned a name.' She rested her hand on the cell door. 'Then you'll do it?'

He hunched his shoulders. 'Tell them what I want, especially the immunity. Then we'll talk.'

Caelan looked into his eyes, then nodded and turned away.

In the corridor outside, Penrith, Achebe and Somerville were waiting.

'Well?' Penrith couldn't stand still. Caelan shrugged.

'He'll think about it.'

6

Ninety minutes later, Caelan got off the Underground at Westminster and walked down Victoria Embankment. She wore her thickest winter coat, but a bitter wind cut through it, chilling her body and numbing her face. She glanced at the London Eye, rotating slowly on the opposite bank of the Thames, wondering how many tourists were braving the freezing London streets. She was already wishing she was back in Ewan's house in Wales as Big Ben chimed eleven o'clock.

Penrith had driven back to his office from Enfield, but Caelan had wanted some time alone to think about her conversation with Mulligan, and made the return journey using public transport. Achebe and Penrith hadn't been happy when she told them Mulligan's conditions, but that was their problem, not hers. If she went undercover, side by side with Mulligan, she wouldn't be doing it for them. Pleasing her bosses wasn't what drove her, as Penrith should know by now.

As she approached Penrith's office, she saw a familiar figure waiting in the corridor outside. Ewan Davies stood straight-backed as though he was still on the parade ground, and Caelan couldn't help smiling.

'Did you get your keys back?'

He grinned. 'Cheeky sod, isn't he? Yeah, he brought them to me last night. Woke everyone in the house including the baby when he hammered on the door, but he brought them.'

'I couldn't believe it when I walked in and found him sitting at the kitchen table.'

'Couldn't you?'

She laughed. 'All right, yeah. It was typical Ian.'

'He's waiting for you.' Ewan jerked a thumb towards the office door.

'And probably listening to every word we're saying.'

The door opened, and on cue, Penrith appeared. 'Sullying my reputation again, Caelan?' he said.

'No need. You did it yourself years ago.'

Penrith crooked a finger. 'Come in, both of you, and I'll tell you everything you need to know.'

She followed him into his office, dropped into a chair. 'Really? Makes a change.'

Squeezing around his desk, Penrith shook his head. 'I've told you, this is my show. I don't work like Elizabeth Beckett. She believes that the less you lot know the better, because if you aren't aware of the full story, you can't give any of it away if your cover's blown and everything goes up shit creek. I don't agree.' He picked up the phone on his desk. 'Coffee? Might even be able to rustle up some biscuits.'

'Thank you.' Caelan crossed her legs. Penrith requested the drinks and waited until Ewan had settled in the chair beside Caelan's before he spoke again.

'You know we're not going to be able to give Mulligan everything he wants, of course.'

'You wanted me to talk to him, which I did.' Caelan spread her hands. 'Do we need him?'

'You know we do. He's our way in,' Penrith said.

'You mean it'll be easier if he's around. I don't trust him.'

'None of us trust him, but he'll have to do as he's told.'

'Still. He'd expose me without a second thought if it helped him, or if he was in danger. He's already proved he can kill without regret.'

Penrith was nodding. 'That's the point.'

'What do you mean?'

'He's dealt in things most people don't even want to think about, like human trafficking. He can help us.'

'Until someone else moves into the area.'

This was why she had walked away with no intention of looking back. The endless seething mass of filth that polluted every part of London and beyond. The drug dealers, pimps and gangs, the shootings and stabbings. The relentless tide of misery and waste. People getting rich by any dishonest means they could imagine. And she and her colleagues stumbling around trying to stem the flow.

It was hopeless.

Penrith stared at her. 'Cheerful this morning, aren't you?'

There was a knock on the door and he heaved himself to his feet. He pushed past Caelan and Ewan and pulled the door open.

'Thank you.' He tutted. 'Digestives? Is that all we can stretch to?'

There was a mumbled reply and Penrith reappeared. Closing the door with a shove of his backside, he shuffled back to his desk and set the tray down on it. He poured them each a mug from an insulated coffee pot and held them out. Caelan took hers but didn't drink, and Penrith seemed to read the defeat on her face.

'Mulligan must have contacts,' he said. 'We need to know who they are, and they won't be small fry.'

'Hasn't he given you any names?' Ewan asked. Penrith stared at him, as though surprised to find he could speak.

'No, and he's not likely to until we guarantee he'll receive what he's asked for.' Penrith took three biscuits and piled them together, biting into them all at once.

'Is it worth it?' Should have stayed away, Caelan thought. Should have gone to Nicky, told Penrith where to stick it and started again.

Should have stayed away.

Penrith bared his teeth. 'I don't know. Is anything we do worth it?'

She stared at him, wondering if he could read her mind after all. 'I'm the wrong person to ask, Ian.'

He spread his hands on the desk. 'Bottom line, it's a fishing expedition. We want to find the person who killed our unidentified victim, and we don't want to upset anyone important who's watching Lucy Mulligan. You follow her delightful brother James around and see what happens. Keep your head down, your nose clean and all those other clichés.'

'It's a waste of time.'

His expression darkened. 'You've been in brothels before. Tell that to the girls who are drugged and starved, forced to have sex with as many men as their bodies can cope with, and then twenty more. If you hadn't gone in, they'd still be there. Ask them if they think what we do is worth it. Ask them if they want us to pursue the men who bought them and kept them as slaves.'

She glared at him. 'You're as bad as Beckett.'

'Maybe, and I know you better than she does.' He narrowed his eyes at her. 'The only reason you're here is because we've a chance of putting more of these bastards away. The desire for justice can be a strength or a weakness. In you, it's both. It always has been.'

She stared at him. 'Come on, Ian. That's a line from a soap opera, it has to be.'

He shook his head. 'Possibly, but I'm right. You want to rescue everyone, and sometimes you can't. That's what keeps you coming back for more, the ones you lost. *We* lost. Every operation is an attempt to save them all over again.'

She didn't look at him. 'You've made your point.'

Penrith said nothing.

Caelan took a breath. 'What's your plan?' She would do what they wanted, for a time. A short time.

'Mulligan has a house in Greenford. We're going to release him and he'll go there, pick up where he left off.'

'Greenford is near Northolt, and you know I can't go back there.' People knew who she was in that area of London. Who she really was. She had been unguarded, reckless, poking around in a case she should have stayed away from. It didn't matter that in the end she had been proved right.

'You mean the Rainey family?' Penrith snorted. 'Stay away from their house and their church and I don't think they'll trouble you.'

'The kids are old enough to be out, maybe in pubs or clubs. I could bump into them anywhere.'

'Rubbish. They'll never remember you.'

Caelan didn't agree. 'Fine. Send me in when you know there's a risk, when you know I could be compromised.'

Penrith ignored her. 'Ewan will be Mulligan's new muscle; you'll be his latest girlfriend.'

'No. I'll be his cousin, an old school friend, anything but that.'

He flapped a hand. 'It won't work. You need to be someone he's met before, and that means Kay Summers. Take a good variety of clothes, and the usual precautions. You know the drill.' He removed a thick brown envelope from his desk drawer and pushed it towards her. Caelan knew what it would contain.

'I'm not being Kay Summers again,' she told him. 'Too many people have heard that name.'

'You'll have to be. Kay is the one Mulligan was supposed to buy a kilo of coke from. She's the one with the fictional drug-dealing boyfriend, the criminal record. She's the one who was in the building with Mulligan when he was shot, and she was arrested with him and his men. You're Kay.'

Caelan gave the envelope a shove. It skittered past Penrith's meaty forearms and fell from the edge of the desk, disappearing onto the carpet beneath. He stared at her.

'Any need?'

'Every need,' she said. 'You're not listening. I need a new identity, someone I've never used before.'

'No. It'll take too long to set up.'

'Bollocks. Come on, Ian, I know how this works. You have identities ready, waiting for someone to come along and need them. Find me one that works.'

He pressed his lips together. 'You're putting me in a difficult position.'

'Really? Then the tables have turned for once.'

'You're supposed to use your own name, or one similar. Kay was all we had that works for you.'

Caelan folded her arms. 'I'm sure I'll manage.'

Penrith exhaled, closed his eyes for a second. 'All right. I'll need a couple of hours.' He pushed a second envelope towards Ewan, who reached for it, his face apprehensive. 'You're Owen Davison,' Penrith told him. 'Ex-army, convictions for GBH and assault. Born in some tongue-twister place in Wales on the same date as your own birthday. Passport, driving licence, cash, bank and credit cards, phone and charger, all inside the envelope.' He pushed himself to his feet. 'Now get out of here and let me rustle up a new legend for her ladyship.'

Caelan stood. 'We'll go and grab a coffee.'

'Grab whatever you like. Have lunch, enjoy yourselves. Use my credit card if you like.' Penrith hooked his suit jacket from the back of his chair and struggled into it, not bothering to attempt to fasten the buttons over his belly.

Ewan took the envelope, tucked it inside his coat. Penrith saw the expression on his face and paused. 'You can still say no.'

Caelan waited, her eyes on the ground, not wanting to hear that Ewan had changed his mind. If she was going to pull this off, she needed him with her. From their first meeting she had known she could trust him, and in this job, being able to rely on your colleagues could save your life.

'No, I want to do it.' Ewan patted his pocket, as though to reassure himself that his new profile would keep him safe. Caelan knew better. No fake identity could, not really.

–

'What have you been doing since we last worked together?' Caelan asked Ewan as they walked.

'Training. All the stuff I should have learnt before you forced me to start working with you.' He flashed her a grin, letting her know he was joking.

'Before you got shot, you mean.' He might be teasing her, but Caelan couldn't forgive herself. Ewan could have died because she had been arrogant and headstrong. Recognising her behaviour for what it was didn't make it any easier to stomach.

He grimaced. 'That too.'

They passed Whitehall Gardens, glimpses of the ravaged flower beds and drab grass visible through the bare trees. Caelan shivered, huddling deeper inside her coat.

As they turned onto Northumberland Avenue Ewan said, 'And I've been staying out of Penrith's way.'

'What was the problem?'

Ewan snorted. 'He's been a miserable bastard. Even more so than usual, I'm told.'

'Miserable? Why?'

He glanced at her. 'I'm guessing you disappearing had something to do with it.'

She wasn't going to comment. 'Who did you train with? Richard Adamson?'

'Yeah. Followed him across London, had him following me. Tried to lose him, failed miserably. He jumped me in an alleyway, had a knife to my throat before I realised he was there.' He smiled at the memory. 'Won't be making that mistake again.'

'Letting him catch you?'

'Letting him come back and tell Penrith about it.'

She smiled. 'What else? No need for firearms training.'

He glanced at her. 'Except… Well, you know.'

It wasn't a question, and Caelan guessed what he meant. When they had been shot at during their first assignment together, Ewan had gone to pieces. An experienced soldier, he had been discharged from the army after an incident in Afghanistan. Caelan couldn't imagine the horror, but she knew

Ewan was someone she wanted on her side, regardless of his past and its impact on his future.

'Penrith knows about it now too,' Ewan said. 'Guess who told him?'

Caelan shook her head. There was only one other person who had seen Ewan freeze as he heard the gunshots. 'Nasenby.'

'The very chap.' Ewan affected an upper-class accent. Michael Nasenby, Caelan's former boss, had lost his job and been imprisoned in the most unforgivable circumstances. He wasn't someone she wanted to waste time thinking about.

'What did Penrith say about it?' she asked.

'I don't think he cares.'

'Good. Hopefully you'll never be shot at again.'

A smile. 'If I am, I'll hide behind you.'

–

Penrith was back behind his desk, three white paper bags and a fresh mug of coffee waiting for his attention. 'Feeling suitably refreshed?' he asked.

Caelan pulled a bag towards her to look inside, but Penrith slapped her hand away.

'Almond croissant. Not for children.'

She scowled at him. 'Are we ready?'

Penrith raised his eyebrows. 'If you mean have I had half of London rushing around to do your bidding, yes.'

Another envelope appeared. Caelan took it, pulled out a passport. 'You've even had time to kick it around on the floor so it looks battered. I'm impressed.'

'Does the name meet with your approval?' Penrith said.

'Victoria Smith.' Caelan looked up at him. 'Was that the best you could come up with?'

'Smith is the surname of some of James Mulligan's real cousins.'

'And half of the population of Britain.' Caelan flicked through the pages of the passport. 'At least she wasn't born in Glasgow, like Mulligan. I'm not sure I'd manage the accent.'

'Everything you need is there.' Penrith nodded at the envelope 'Satisfied?'

Caelan examined the driving licence, saw her own face staring back at her. 'This is an old photograph. You don't want me to change my hair?'

'No.' Penrith looked her over. 'You're fine as you are.' He passed her a slip of paper and held up a bunch of keys. He grinned at Ewan. 'Not yours this time. Here's the address in Greenford. You need to go there as soon as possible. Mulligan will be arriving at six tonight.'

'And you don't want him disappearing before we get there.'

'Wouldn't be a great start, would it? I'll phone you later.' Penrith sat back, folded his arms. 'Remember what I said. Just stick close to him. I'll action our movements based on what you tell me.'

Caelan picked up the envelope, keys and piece of paper. 'No weapon?'

Penrith sniffed. 'Not yet.'

'And if I'm offered one?'

'Up to you. Come on, Caelan, you know how this works. Use your judgement.' He leant forward, studying her face. 'Not lost your nerve, have you?'

Caelan felt Ewan flinch beside her. 'You know better. I'll talk to you later.' She looked at Ewan, smiled. 'Come on then. Time to go.'

The address Penrith had provided led them to a residential street, properties built in pairs, most of the small front gardens converted to hard standing for cars. A few houses were well looked after; more were run-down or heading that way. Mulligan's house had been rendered, then painted white. It had two bay windows at the front and a smart black front door. Caelan raised an eyebrow. She'd been expecting a dump, but this place looked anything but.

Ewan parked on the paving at the front of the house and they climbed out, retrieved their bags. Caelan had the keys ready, wanting to look as though she knew what she was doing, giving the impression she belonged here. The house next door had no cars parked outside and was in darkness. Hopefully the residents were still out at work.

They were in a hallway, the stairs to the left and a door to the right. Caelan opened it. The living room beyond was in darkness, and when she flicked on the light, she saw it was comfortably furnished with two large sofas, a huge TV and a couple of games consoles. She beckoned Ewan inside and turned off the light again.

'Penrith said Mulligan owns several houses. He won't be able to hold on to them, will he?' Ewan asked.

'Not if he bought them with the money he made from dealing and whatever else, which seems likely. They'll be working out how much of his assets were the proceeds of crime and he'll probably be looking at a hefty repayment.'

Ewan smiled. 'Hard to feel sympathetic.'

She snorted. 'Don't waste any time on him.'

The living room led to a dining area, and there was another door to the kitchen, which was modern, kitted out with shiny appliances and gleaming cupboards. Caelan filled the kettle from a complicated tap while Ewan wandered around examining everything.

'He's spent thousands on the gear in here, I reckon,' he said.

Caelan leant against the nearest work surface. 'He looks after himself.' She opened a wall cupboard, searching for mugs. 'Could you find the milk please? Someone should have been in and cleaned the place up, filled the fridge with fresh stuff.'

Ewan checked cupboards until he located the fridge, and handed the milk over. He opened a drawer, held up a sheaf of takeaway menus with a smile. 'How about some food?'

She considered it. 'We should probably wait for Mulligan.'

Ewan pouted. 'Why?'

'Because the people around here will be used to him. The takeaway owners will probably know him. A couple of strangers ordering food to be delivered to his house might look weird, especially if they know he was arrested.'

'But we don't even know if this was Mulligan's home.'

Caelan spread her arms. 'Look around. I doubt he rented the place out. Would you, if you could live here? It's an ordinary house on the outside, but in here, where it matters, everything's top of the range, or near enough.'

'Fair point. All right, let's wait.'

They took their drinks into the living room. Ewan moved to turn on the light again, but Caelan held up a hand. 'Why don't we leave them?'

He smiled. 'You want to surprise Mulligan, don't you? You want him to think we're not here.'

'Except the car's outside.'

'I could move it.' Ewan put down his cup.

'No, you'll never find a space.' She flicked the light switch. 'Let Mulligan worry about where he's going to park.'

'He'll have a car?'

Caelan scowled. 'Got to make it look authentic.'

Outside, the street was busy as people returned home from work, those without their own parking area shuffling their cars into anything resembling a space. Caelan checked the time.

'He'll be here soon. Shall we have a look at the bedrooms?'

Ewan grinned at her. 'You're sharing with Mulligan, aren't you?'

'Not unless he drugs me.' Caelan blinked, remembering Nicky. Ewan said nothing, waiting, but Caelan kept talking. 'I think we should say that you and I are together.'

He stared. 'You mean we pretend to be a couple again?'

She smiled at him. 'Yeah. Is it such an awful thought?'

Ewan was blushing. 'No, but...'

'I know it's not what Penrith suggested, but I'd feel happier. That way, we can watch out for each other, stay close without raising suspicion. It'll be safer, especially with the people we're hoping to meet. I'll still say I'm Mulligan's cousin.'

'Makes sense, but I don't think Mulligan will like it.'

Caelan led the way upstairs. 'You know what? I don't care.'

The first bedroom was at the front of the house, large and luxurious. Caelan pulled a face at herself in the huge mirrored wardrobe. The king-size bed was ready to sleep in.

'Look at the state of it,' she said. Ewan pursed his lips.

'Black silk sheets not your thing?'

'Are they anyone's? Except Mulligan's, obviously.'

She turned away. The next room was smaller, containing only a double bed with plain white covers, and a chest of drawers.

'Why don't you have this one?' Ewan asked. She lifted her shoulders.

'Are you sure? You haven't seen what the other one's like yet. It might be Mulligan's sex dungeon.'

He smiled. 'Nah, I checked. Single bed, wardrobe. It'll do.'

As they came down the stairs, headlights lit up the hallway. Caelan slid her hands into her jeans pockets and took a deep, calming breath. Time to put on the mask.

'Ready?' she said.

Ewan cleared his throat. 'Think so.'

They went to the living room window. There were three cars. One approached the house slowly; another stopped at the kerb, while the third held back and waited.

'The first is our lead vehicle,' Caelan said. 'The driver will have stayed just in front of Mulligan all the way, escorting him. The one in the middle, the one that's stopped, will be Mulligan himself.'

'And the car behind is making sure he doesn't try to escape. They've made sure he gets here as planned without it being obvious he's under escort. Clever.' Ewan nodded.

'Sometimes we get it right,' Caelan said. She turned away, tension tightening her throat, not wanting Ewan to witness her bringing herself under control. This would be his first real undercover operation; he would be nervous enough without sensing her anxiety – and she knew he would if she didn't disguise it. She was the experienced officer and had to take the lead. She also knew she couldn't risk Mulligan realising she was nervous. She didn't trust him and knew he would use anything he could to his own advantage. He had nothing to lose.

Her heart rate increased as they waited for him to appear, the familiar hum of adrenalin and apprehension beginning to crackle through her veins. There was always some anxiety; it was part of what made the job so addictive. No turning back now.

They heard a key in the lock, the door being flung open. Mulligan stomped into the room and glared at them.

'You couldn't have waited outside? Cheeky bastards, making yourselves at home.'

'Good evening, James,' said Caelan.

His smile was mocking. 'Cousin Victoria. Lovely to see you.'

Caelan stepped closer, getting in his face. 'Let me make something clear. You behave yourself, as agreed. You do nothing to draw attention to yourself, or to either of us. You know what happens if you do.'

Mulligan turned away, threw himself down on the sofa. 'You tell tales, and I go back inside. Not going to happen.'

'As long as we understand each other.' She folded her arms.

He glared at her. 'We do. I'll do as I'm told, as long as you stick to the deal.'

Caelan shrugged. 'I'm here, aren't I?'

'Aye, for now.' Mulligan spotted the takeaway menus Ewan had left on the windowsill. His face brightened. 'What's for dinner?'

8

They ate at the dining room table, Mulligan scooping out rice and tearing into naans, not looking up from his plate.

'First decent food I've had in weeks,' he said through a mouthful of curry. 'The stuff you get in prison isn't fit for pigs.'

'Anyone would think you were there to be punished,' Caelan said.

'Punished?' Mulligan swallowed. 'Aye, good one. You'd have us breaking rocks, would you? Hard labour?'

She snapped off a piece of poppadum. 'It's none of my business.'

'Doesn't stop you getting us locked up, though, does it?'

Caelan said nothing, kept eating. Mulligan shook his head, checked his watch.

'Right, I'm away for a shower.' He grinned. 'You two better get yourselves ready. It's going to be a late one.'

Caelan looked at him. 'Where are we going?'

He pushed back his chair, not bothering to clear away his plate or the detritus around it. 'Club called Stand.'

'Stand?' Caelan looked at Ewan, who shook his head. 'What kind of name's that?'

'It's a new place in Shoreditch. Exclusive. Wouldn't have expected either of you to have heard of it.' Mulligan rubbed his eyes. 'Not that I'm in the mood for clubbing, and my leg still aches like a bastard, but I've got to show my face, haven't I? Let people know I'm back?'

'That's the idea,' Caelan said. 'You've been to this place before? Met people who'll be of interest to us there?' She wanted to be sure Mulligan wasn't just fancying a night out.

He nodded. 'It's the kind of venue where you can be introduced to useful people, you get me? Worth your while, I promise.' A grin. 'And you can have a dance and get pissed at the same time. Can't argue with that, can you?'

'We can't drink, and neither can you,' Caelan said. Mulligan scowled at her.

'All right, Mammy. I can have a couple of beers, they said. Got to make it look realistic, haven't I? They'll think I've taken holy orders if I'm in there all night drinking lemonade.'

'If you make it alcohol-free beer, then yeah.'

Mulligan's frown deepened. 'Joking, aren't you?'

'Tell people you're still on medication, antibiotics or something. You were shot, remember?'

'Vaguely.' He rubbed his thigh, leering at her. 'Want to see my scar?'

She ignored him. 'What kind of place is it?'

'How do you mean?'

'You said exclusive. Is there a dress code? We don't want to be stopped at the door while you're allowed inside.'

Mulligan smirked. 'Don't you? Spoilsport.' He turned away, headed for the hallway. 'It's casual.' Sticking his head back inside the room, he pointed at Ewan. 'That doesn't mean patched jeans and a Wales rugby shirt, pal. Smart casual. Make an effort.'

Ewan flushed but said nothing, moving to help Caelan as she began to pile the takeaway cartons together. Mulligan stepped closer and watched, hands on hips.

'Know your place, don't you?' he said.

'What, the kitchen?' She spoke mildly, knowing he was trying every trick in the book to wind her up. Mulligan laughed.

'You reckon I'm that pathetic, that I think women should stay in the kitchen? Be seen but not heard? No. I meant you're supposed to be working for me, doing as you're told. Good to see you getting some practice in.'

Caelan rinsed the plastic containers ready for recycling and dumped everything in the bin. 'Who can we expect to meet at this club?'

'Few hundred people.'

'You know what I mean.'

'I've told you, people who might be useful. Wait and see.'

She went to the sink to wash her hands, knowing that pressing him would be pointless. Better to go and see whether he was telling the truth. They had nothing to lose. 'Forget it.'

Mulligan smiled. 'You've got an hour.'

–

The doorman watched them approach, his face blank. Mulligan strolled towards him, hands in pockets. Behind a cordon, a line of shivering people huddled, waiting to see if they would be deemed worthy of entry. Caelan could already hear the music.

Mulligan nodded at the doorman. 'Good to see you, Rico. Busy tonight.'

Rico didn't smile. 'Didn't expect you to show up. Heard you'd been arrested, thought you were inside.'

'Inside? Nah. Questioned and released.' Mulligan licked his lips. 'In the end they realised they had nothing on me.'

Assuming a puzzled expression, Rico rubbed his chin. 'They questioned you for six weeks? Shit. Is that even legal?'

Mulligan forced a laugh. 'Aye, good one, pal. I've been in hospital – took a bullet.'

'I heard.' Rico's hands went to his hips and he took a step towards Mulligan. 'Missed your head, though, didn't they?'

'Luckily.'

Rico made a sound to indicate he didn't agree, and Mulligan nodded towards the door of the club. 'Just let us in, will you? Too cold out here for me.'

Looking down at his own padded black jacket, jeans and heavy boots, Rico shrugged. 'Feel sorry for you. Join the line.'

Mulligan gaped at him. 'But… Listen, pal, I've been in here every week, almost every night, for months. My bar bill is probably paying your wages.'

'And? Like I said, if you want to come in, you need to wait over there.' Rico folded his arms, already looking over Mulligan's shoulder. Caelan stepped back, touched Mulligan's arm.

'Come on, James. Let's do as the man says.'

The look Mulligan shot her was pure venom. 'Vic—'

Rico grinned. 'Why don't you do as you're told, *James*?' He made the name sound like an insult.

'Didn't you say this place is the best night in London? Let's just wait.' Caelan made herself sound enthusiastic. Mulligan clenched his jaw but allowed her to lead him to the back of the queue. They watched as a trio of young women approached Rico and were waved straight inside.

'Should have worn a shorter skirt,' Mulligan said to Caelan.

'With your legs?' She smirked at him, saw the couple in front of them glance at each other, laughing. Mulligan shoved his hands into his trouser pockets, stamping his feet, hunching his shoulders. 'Fucking Rico. All about the power. He could have let me in, he usually does. Oh fuck.' He started, half turning away. Caelan tried to see what had spooked him without looking obvious.

A group of people had surrounded Rico, talking, laughing, bumping fists. There were three women and three men, though one hung back, his eyes fixed on the screen of his phone. Caelan stood still, lowering her voice as the rest of the queue shuffled forward.

'Do you know them?'

'Shut up.' Mulligan's voice was quiet, tight. He glanced at the man with the phone, closing his eyes for a second.

'Tell me who he is, or I'll go and ask him myself,' Caelan told him.

'Don't. I owe him money, all right?'

She glanced at the man again. He didn't look familiar, but there was no reason he should. 'How much?'

'Ten.' Mulligan kept his face turned away.

'Thousand?'

'No, fucking magic beans.'

'They're going inside,' said Ewan. Mulligan turned his head, eyes narrowed.

'Good. Now you know what he looks like, you can help me avoid him.'

'And you can tell us who he is,' Caelan said.

'All right. He's called Stefan Harris.'

Caelan made a mental note of the name. 'And why do you owe him ten grand?'

'We did a deal. I bought some merchandise, paid half up front, sold it on. Let's say I forgot to pay the rest. Then...' He spread his hands. 'Then I got shot and you know the rest.'

'What did you buy from him?'

He stared at her. 'I told you. Merchandise.'

'Drugs.'

'No comment.'

Meaning yes. 'Can't you just give him his money?'

Mulligan bared his teeth. 'Are you kidding? I don't have any money. It's all been confiscated by your bastard colleagues.'

'Keep your voice down,' Caelan told him as they moved forward.

'Stop asking stupid questions then.'

Caelan let the comment go, nodding towards the doors as they reached the head of the queue. 'You still want to go in?'

'Yeah, come on. Fuck him.' Mulligan raised his chin, straightened his jacket. He marched towards Rico, who stepped back, grinning.

'Have a good night,' he said as he waved them past. Caelan saw Mulligan's shoulders tense, but he kept walking. Seeing Stefan Harris, whoever he was, had obviously rattled him. She hid a smile as he looked around him warily. There was no sign of Harris or his friends, and he seemed to relax.

Caelan paid their entry fees, and they headed towards the thumping music. The club was cavernous, the main dance floor already full. Spotlights arced and soared, illuminating bare brickwork, steel walkways and huddles of people. The place was packed. Mulligan headed for the nearest bar, pushing towards the front of the crowd around it. Caelan leant close to Ewan.

'We need to stay with him,' she said. 'I don't trust him. He's going to try to lose us, and if he does, he'll say it was because it's so busy in here. Don't let him out of your sight. Go into the toilets after him if you have to.'

Ewan nodded, and they followed Mulligan to the bar. He had a young woman at his side, his arm around her shoulders, and was already drinking from a bottle of lager. He lifted it in a toast as they reached him.

'Sláinte,' he said. 'This is Beth. She's a friend of mine.'

Beth gave an awkward smile. 'We've only just met.'

'Don't be shy. I bought you a drink, didn't I?' Mulligan leered at her.

'He's got a wife and three kids at home,' Caelan said.

Shaking her head, Beth disentangled herself, disappearing into the crowd. Mulligan rounded on Caelan.

'What did you say that for?'

She moved close to him, grabbing his arm and holding it tight, her mouth almost touching his ear. 'You're not here to socialise, and I told you not to drink. This isn't a game.'

Mulligan turned his head, close enough to kiss her. Caelan forced herself to remain where she was, not allowing him to make her feel uncomfortable. She could smell beer on his breath, the curry he'd eaten.

'And if I stand here whispering to you, pointing people out, that isn't going to look suspicious?' he said. 'I have to behave normally – talk to my friends, have a beer, maybe a dance. Otherwise this isn't going to work. Someone will notice, and then we'll all be in trouble.'

63

She released his arm, seeing the sense in what he said. People had to believe Mulligan was free, and not under suspicion. 'Fine,' she said. 'We do it your way, for now.'

He moved away, smiled at her as though they were friends. 'Are you having a drink?'

'We've discussed this.'

Mulligan's eyebrows danced as he downed the rest of his beer and smacked his lips. 'Right. Three alcohol-free lagers coming up.'

He moved back to the bar, waving a twenty-pound note. Ewan stepped closer to Caelan.

'He's got a point,' he said.

'I know.'

'This isn't the kind of place I expected.'

Caelan smiled. 'Too classy?'

'Well, yeah.' He glanced around. 'I know it's stupid, but I thought it'd be... well, dodgy. People starting fights, making deals. Gangsters in suits, an atmosphere. Like a film.' They watched a group of laughing women go by, dressed to impress, followed by three men wearing designer shirts and smart trousers. Everyone was well groomed, happy, looked prosperous.

'We need to be careful,' Caelan said. 'Mulligan could be trying to pull a fast one, pretending that coming here is worth our while when all he wants to do is get shit-faced.'

'Got it. That bloke we saw as we were coming in, though – Stefan Harris? Mulligan seemed terrified of him.'

'If I owed someone ten grand, I'd want to avoid them too. Maybe I need to find Harris, see what he's doing here.' Caelan knew she would need to speak to Ian Penrith about Harris as well as grilling Mulligan about their business dealings, but now wasn't the time to start digging.

Ewan frowned. 'Mulligan said he wants to stay away from him.'

'I'm not asking him to come with me.'

They saw Mulligan heading their way, three beers held close to his chest as he pushed through the crowd.

'Here we go. Get those down your neck.' He thrust the bottles towards them, drank deeply from his own. He pulled a face. 'Well, it's cold at least.'

Caelan moved away, trying to find a quieter corner where they could talk. Mulligan followed, pouting like a child, casting a longing glance at the dance floor.

'Do you know who owns this place?' she asked. Mulligan shook his head.

'You're talking to the wrong person. You saw how Rico treated me – I'm a nobody.'

'Then why are we here?'

His eyes were searching the crowd. 'I told you, it's the place to be.'

'If you're a criminal?'

He smiled. 'If you're anyone.'

Caelan drank some beer. 'Tell me about Harris.'

'Nothing to tell.' Mulligan wouldn't look at her.

'You remember what you agreed? Why you're not spending tonight—'

He interrupted her. 'I remember.'

'All right. Then can you introduce me to him?'

'Bad idea. He won't be happy to see me, especially when he hears I can't pay him. You think he's going to be in the mood to chat to you?'

'I want to speak to him.'

A splutter. 'Then you're dafter than I thought. He's got a reputation around women.'

'The ones he arrived with seemed happy enough.'

'You think?' Mulligan curled his lip. 'See the blonde, her name's Abbie? He broke her nose last year.'

'And she's still with him?'

'She's one of many. Believe me, he's not a man you want to get any closer to than you already have.'

'I don't have a choice. You know that.' Caelan leant closer again. 'Tell me. Is he someone I should be looking at?'

Mulligan hesitated. 'Your call.'

'What does he do?'

'His family own a pizza shop, a chippy and a taxi firm.' Mulligan widened his eyes. 'So, you know, he fries food and drives people around.'

Businesses where lots of cash payments could be expected. Fronts for laundering drug money? Based on what Mulligan had said, it seemed possible. 'I'll ask again. What did you buy from Harris?'

Mulligan shifted. 'White.' His lips barely moved.

Cocaine. Not a surprise. 'When?'

'Does it matter?'

'Is he still selling?'

'I don't know. Ask him.'

She smiled at him. 'I might. What would he do if I told him I'm here with you?'

Mulligan blew out his cheeks. 'Tonight? Here? Nothing. This isn't the sort of place you'd start trouble. You come here to be seen, noticed. To announce yourself. Look around you. I could spit in any direction and hit two footballers and a reality TV star.'

She'd have to take his word for it. 'If you know you're safe here, why are you still staying out of Harris's way?'

'Come on, you know how it works. You saw the two lads with him? Look like pit bulls in polo shirts? Maybe tonight, when I'm tucked up in bed, they'd pay me a visit and remind me of the debt I owe their boss. They might leave it even longer, to really put the willies up me.' He took a gulp of beer. 'As it were. But sometime soon, they'd turn up, rip my arms off and shove them up my arse. And that'd be for starters.'

'Then why did you bring us here, if you knew you might see Harris?'

Mulligan scowled. 'Because I'm trying to hold up my end of the bargain. I knew if you were seen in this place, where it's safe, people would recognise you when we go to some of the… livelier places I know.'

'We could have walked away, come back tomorrow.' Caelan knew they were here to do a job, but putting Mulligan at risk wasn't part of the deal. For now, they needed him.

'He's going to find out I'm back anyway,' Mulligan said. 'At least here, the doormen should keep a lid on things.'

'Does Harris know where you live?'

Mulligan forced a smile. 'Not as far as I know. Still alive, aren't I? But I'm sure he could find out.'

Caelan turned to Ewan, handing him her beer. 'Cheers. I'm going to have a wander around.'

He nodded, his face professionally blank, though Caelan guessed he wasn't happy about being left alone with Mulligan.

'Off to powder your nose?' Mulligan asked her.

Caelan smiled. 'Not in the way you usually mean, no.'

She left them, planning to complete a circle of the club, intending to scope out the exits as well as track down Harris and his friends.

Pushing through the crowd, she headed for the toilets, giving the impression she had a reason for leaving Ewan and Mulligan in their corner. Several people caught her eye, but she ignored them, not wanting to encourage anyone to try to talk to her.

The queue for the women's loos was already out of the door. Caelan hesitated, then kept moving, as though she'd decided she could wait. She was circling around the main dance floor when she spotted Stefan Harris, standing alone as the rest of his group headed off to dance. She studied him, wondering how to make her move. He was a shade under six feet tall, muscular, shaven-headed. No doubt his appearance was intended to make him seem intimidating, and Caelan had to admit, it was effective. Abbie, the one Mulligan had said Harris had attacked, kept throwing him anxious glances from the dance floor, as though by leaving his side she was doing something she'd pay for later. Harris was looking at his phone again, sipping from a bottle of beer. Caelan moved closer, not looking at him, making a show of studying the crowd.

'Looking for someone?' He was grinning at her, his eyes travelling over her body. Caelan stopped, smiled back.

'Yeah, my boyfriend. He must have gone to the bar.'

Harris stepped closer. 'Why don't me and you have a chat while you wait for him?'

Caelan pretended to hesitate. 'Well, I...'

Abbie had stopped dancing and was watching them, frowning.

'Come on,' Harris said, beckoning to Caelan. 'Never seen you in here before.'

'No, it's my first time.'

He winked. 'Bet you say that to all the boys.'

She managed a laugh while promising herself that if Harris touched her, she'd break his arm. 'I need to get back to my boyfriend.'

'What's your name?' Harris leant closer.

'Victoria.' She didn't miss a beat.

'I'm Stefan. Good to meet you.' He held out his hand.

Caelan nodded, keeping her own hands by her sides. 'Like I said, I'm with someone and he—'

'Come on, sweetheart, we're just talking. More fool this fella of yours for leaving you alone.' Harris looked over Caelan's shoulder with a sneer, and she knew he was making sure Abbie was watching. 'How about a dance?'

'No thanks.'

His expression darkened, and he took another pace towards her. 'What's your problem?'

'I don't have a problem, I have a partner.'

'A partner.' Harris snorted. 'Right. What does he do?'

'What?'

His hands were on his hips, chest puffed out. 'I'm a businessman, made a profit of over a hundred grand last year. This boyfriend of yours can compete with that, can he?'

Caelan gave him a level stare, knowing that if he was into the kind of business she suspected, he'd have made much more than that. 'No, he can't,' she said. 'But I can.'

He chortled. 'You? Yeah, course you can, sweetheart.'

'Straight up. I've made some decent money up in Scotland; now I'm down here looking for… opportunities.'

'And what line of business are you in?'

Caelan smiled. 'Buying, selling. Importing sometimes, depending on the deal.'

Harris rubbed his chin. 'Food, furniture, what?'

'Like I said, it depends on the deal.' She turned. 'See you around.'

This time he didn't move to stop her walking away. Caelan didn't look back, knowing she'd planted a seed. She'd said nothing to suggest she was into anything dodgy, but Harris could make what he would of what she'd said. Sooner or later he'd probably hear she was linked to James Mulligan, and would draw his own conclusions.

Mulligan was scowling when she found them again. Caelan smiled at Ewan, who rolled his eyes in Mulligan's direction.

'Harris seems nice,' she said.

'You're going to get me killed, you know that?' Mulligan told her.

'Why? I never mentioned your name.'

'You didn't need to. He'll find out soon enough, and then—'

'Hello, stranger!'

A young woman bounced up beside them and slung an arm around Mulligan's neck, beaming at him, at them all. Mulligan's expression altered immediately, and he grinned as though seeing her was the best thing to happen to him in months.

'Hello, darling, I wondered if you'd be around.' He kissed her cheek.

'Aren't you inside?' She laughed at herself. 'Obviously not.'

'Nah, they had nothing on me.' Mulligan's eyes were on Caelan as he spoke. 'Had to let me go. No charges.'

'Good. I was worried about you.' She pulled a face at him. Mulligan winked. 'No need, princess. No need.'

'Aren't you going to introduce me to your friends?' She treated them to another smile, blue eyes wide, teeth gleaming. She wore a tight black dress and was holding a garish cocktail.

Mulligan waved a careless hand towards Caelan and Ewan. 'Victoria and Owen. Vic's a cousin of mine. And this is,' he broke into the Dolly Parton song, 'Jolene, Jolene, Jolene—'

She punched his ribs, none too gently. 'Shut up, Mulligan.' She held out a hand to Caelan and said, 'Jolene Townsend. My mum was a big fan.' The grin reappeared. 'Of Dolly, not of you.'

Caelan smiled back. 'Who isn't?'

Jolene took Ewan's hand. 'Hello, you.'

On cue, Ewan blushed. Mulligan muscled back in, snaking an arm around her waist.

'Who are you here with, Jo?' he asked.

She took a gulp from her glass. 'Reuben, but then he heard his brother was around, so he left.'

Mulligan clicked his tongue. 'They fallen out again?'

She raised her eyes to the ceiling. 'You know how they are.' Draining her drink, she raised the empty glass. 'Good to meet you two. And you,' she poked Mulligan's arm as she pulled away from him, 'stay out of trouble.'

He gave a mock salute as she danced away.

'Reuben?' Caelan said.

'Reuben Nash.' Mulligan concentrated on his beer.

'Who is he?'

'Someone I know.'

Caelan saw his reluctance to talk about Nash. 'And you've done business with him?'

Mulligan glanced around. 'Can we discuss this later? It's not really the place.'

'What about Nash's brother? The one your friend Jolene mentioned?'

'Nathan? You don't need to be worried about him.'

'I'm not,' Caelan said. 'What's the problem between him and his brother?'

Mulligan looked mutinous. 'Why do you care?'

'He's someone you know. That makes him of potential interest to us.'

'Reuben Nash owns a club – dump of a place compared to this one. Nathan helps out there. I try to stay out of his way. He's a psycho.'

Ewan said, 'You know the bloke you wanted to avoid? Harris? He's heading this way.'

'Oh shit.' Mulligan looked stricken as he set his beer down on the nearest table. 'Has he seen me?'

'He hadn't, but one of his friends is pointing you out,' Caelan said, scanning the crowd. 'Or maybe they're talking about me.'

'Why would they be? I told you speaking to him was a bad idea. Why didn't you listen, you stupid—'

Stefan Harris swaggered towards them, shouldering his way past Ewan. 'Fancy seeing you here,' he said, looking down at Mulligan, arms folded across his chest.

Mulligan attempted a laugh but sounded more like he was choking. 'Stefan. This is a surprise,' he said.

'I'm sure it is.' Harris looked over his shoulder at his two huge friends. They grinned back, their expressions making it clear they were eager for the command to rip Mulligan apart.

He turned to Caelan, disgust clear on his face. '*This* is your boyfriend? This lying, thieving piece of Scottish shit? Fuck me, love, you must be desperate.'

Caelan stepped closer to Ewan, snuggling against his side. He slid an arm around her waist as he met Harris's eyes.

'She's with me,' Ewan said. His tone was perfect for the role he was playing – possessive with a hint of steel, warning Harris off. In the real world, Caelan would never have been in a relationship with someone who thought they owned her, but from the little she'd seen of Harris, she thought Ewan's caveman act well judged. She kissed his cheek and met Harris's eyes, a

71

challenge in her gaze. Ignoring her, Harris looked Ewan up and down, nodding as though he had passed some kind of test.

'You're a lucky man. Might want to rethink your choice of friends, though,' he said, sneering in Mulligan's direction.

'Vic's my cousin,' Mulligan said. He sounded calm, confident, though Caelan could see his face had paled as the strobing lights swept over them.

Harris snorted. 'Unlucky, sweetheart. Definitely a bad apple on the family tree, this one.'

'They all are on his side of the family.' Caelan gave Mulligan her sweetest smile. He didn't react.

'Wait a second.' Harris narrowed his eyes, and Caelan's stomach lurched. No matter how long you'd been in the job, certain phrases set alarm bells jangling. 'Wait a second' was one, 'Don't I know you from somewhere?' another. Harris kept talking. 'If you're cousins, how come you,' he pointed at Caelan, 'don't have a Scottish accent, but you,' he nodded at Mulligan, 'sound like fucking Braveheart?'

Caelan spoke immediately, not looking at Mulligan or giving him a chance to say a word. She knew who she was supposed to be, and even a thug like Harris might notice if she hesitated. 'My dad was in the army, and we moved around a lot.' She smiled at Harris. 'I wasn't even born in Scotland.'

Harris sniffed. 'Lucky escape. Haggis for every meal, and those fucking awful bagpipes.' He grinned at Mulligan. 'It's a shithole, isn't it, James?'

Mulligan said, 'Aye,' through gritted teeth.

Abbie, Harris's girlfriend, appeared, hovering behind him as though afraid to interrupt. Harris turned his head to snarl at her. 'What?'

She tried a smile. 'I'm going to the bar, would you—'

'Do you really need to fucking ask? You know what I drink.'

He turned back as she scurried away. Caelan told herself to stay quiet as Harris grinned at Ewan.

'Got to keep them on their toes, haven't you?' he said. Behind him, his friends guffawed, nudging each other like schoolkids. Ewan laughed too, nodding, his arm tightening around Caelan's waist. She played along, making sure her body stayed relaxed as fury coiled in her belly. She felt an irrational burst of anger towards Ewan, wanting to push his arm away and storm off, even though she knew he was playing a part. She watched Abbie hurrying over to the bar, red-faced and humiliated. She wondered where the other women were, the ones Harris had arrived with. Abbie had been dancing with them, but they'd disappeared.

Harris pushed his hands into his trouser pockets, bouncing on the balls of his feet. His eyes roamed the room, and when he looked back at them, he seemed to struggle to focus. Caelan wondered if he was drunk, or if he'd been sampling his own wares.

'Still, it's a bonus, her being your cousin,' he said, jerking his head towards Mulligan.

Mulligan frowned. 'A bonus?'

'Hasn't she told you what an amazing businesswoman she is?' Harris looked gleeful. 'Maybe you should ask her to lend you a few quid, James. The way I remember it, you owe me ten grand.'

Mulligan looked stricken. 'Listen, Stefan—'

Harris stepped forward, his two huge friends behind him. He shoved a finger in Mulligan's chest and leant closer. 'Ten grand, plus interest. We'll call it a round fifteen. You've got two days.' He took hold of the front of the other man's shirt and twisted it in his fist, forcing Mulligan to stand on his tiptoes. 'Forty-eight hours, James. Or we come and take it from you ourselves.'

Caelan heard Mulligan swallow from three paces away.

'And if I don't have it?' he said. Harris gave a lazy smile as he released his grip.

'We'd have to reach a compromise.' He turned back to Caelan, his eyes exploring, lingering, as intrusive as if he was touching her. She felt Ewan stiffen beside her, but he didn't speak. 'Like I said, why don't you talk to your cousin here? I'm told she knows ways to make a few quid.'

Caelan stared back at him, defiant. She might have a role to play, but her character wouldn't be cowed so easily, not if she really was working with a man like Mulligan. You'd need guts, arrogance.

'He'll have the money,' she told Harris. She heard Mulligan take a shuddering breath, as though he'd been punched. Harris smiled.

'Good. I'd hate to have to spoil a pretty face.' He pointed at her. 'Let's see if you're as good a businesswoman as you claim to be.'

Her turn to smile. 'I am, I promise you that.'

All at once, Harris's face was a few inches away. 'Good. Because if he can't pay, you'll have to. You're family, aren't you? Blood's thicker than water, and all that? You told me yourself you'd turned a decent profit. Fifteen grand, sweetheart.' He held her eyes for a moment longer, then turned and walked away, his friends scrambling to follow.

'See you in two days,' Caelan called after them. Harris raised a hand in acknowledgement, not looking back.

Mulligan waited for them to be out of sight before he exploded. 'Are you fucking mental? "See you in two days"?'

'What was I supposed to say?' Caelan moved away from Ewan, giving him a quick smile. He didn't meet her eyes, his mouth twisting, and she wondered why. Was he embarrassed by the way he'd been forced to behave, by what Harris had said? Or was he worried by how Caelan had responded?

Mulligan was dragging his hands through his hair, panicked. 'I don't know. Anything. Anything but what you actually said. I could have talked to him, persuaded him to give us more time—'

'Us?' Caelan rounded on him. 'Us? This is your debt, not ours.'

Mulligan shook his head. 'Not according to Harris. What's mine is yours, Cousin Victoria. Harris doesn't care whose bones he breaks, as long as he gets his money. I hope you've got a stash of used notes tucked away somewhere, because fuck knows I haven't.' He glared at her. 'And what did Harris mean when he said you were an amazing businesswoman, that you've turned a profit? What bollocks have you been telling him?'

'Keep your voice down.' She scanned the room, but no one seemed to be taking any notice of his histrionics.

'Keep my voice down?' Mulligan spoke in a squeak, his tone ingratiating. '"Of course he'll have your money. Yes, Mr Harris. No, Mr Harris. Why don't you bend me over the bar right now, Mr Harris?"'

Caelan's hand shot out, seizing his arm. The tips of her index and middle fingers found the spot she was looking for as her thumb nestled into place on the other side of Mulligan's wrist. She increased the pressure and twisted. The movement was discreet, almost imperceptible, but it caused enough pain to make Mulligan's eyes bulge. Caelan knew she was taking a risk – if anyone noticed, they might wonder what was going on. She was supposed to be Mulligan's assistant, not his boss, certainly not someone who would manhandle him to make a point.

But he deserved it.

He gasped. 'What are you doing, you crazy bitch?'

Caelan spoke pleasantly. 'Shut your mouth, Mulligan. We're here to have a good time, remember? To meet people?' She let him go and he stumbled away.

'Yeah, well strangely enough, I'm not enjoying myself,' he said.

'Poor you. Tell me about Reuben Nash.'

'Listen, why don't we call it a night?' Mulligan said. 'We can go home, make some cocoa, have a chat. I'll tell you anything you want. Scout's honour.'

Caelan glanced at Ewan. 'Had enough?'

He smiled. 'Before we got here.'

'You're a miserable bastard, you know that?' Mulligan said.

Ewan drained his beer. 'It's been said.'

They retrieved their coats, headed outside. The queue waiting to enter the place was even longer than before. Caelan reckoned there must have been about a hundred people in the line. Rico was still there, joined by another man, both of them laughing as they saw Mulligan.

'What's wrong, is the music too loud for you?' Rico called.

Mulligan kept walking, didn't reply.

As they approached the end of the queue, Caelan saw a man say something to the woman he was with and move towards them. He looked to be in his early twenties, hair expertly styled, clothes clearly expensive. Mulligan saw him and grinned, held out his fist to be bumped.

'Leyton, pal, how have you been?'

'Good. I heard you'd been banged up?'

Mulligan scoffed at him. 'Heard wrong, didn't you? Hospital, that's all.'

'Your hair, man.' Leyton shook his head, his expression sorrowful. 'What've you done to your hair?'

'See Leyton?' Mulligan said to Caelan and Ewan. 'Best barber in London. Ask anyone.'

Leyton laughed. 'Not just *anyone*. Some people are beyond help.' He cast a critical eye over Ewan, whose hairstyle could be described as casual at best. Ewan stared back, and Caelan was pleased to see he was unembarrassed. He might not be the most experienced, but she was glad he was with her. She knew she could rely on him to back her up whatever the situation, and in their job, that could be the difference between life and death.

'Like I said, I've been in hospital,' Mulligan was saying. 'Getting a haircut doesn't seem so important when you collapse in a pool of blood and wake up in intensive care.'

Caelan wanted to remind him that she'd lost more blood the last time she donated than he'd done when he'd been shot, and that the nearest he'd come to intensive care was being pushed past the entrance on his way to the X-ray department.

Leyton looked suitably impressed, eyes wide, mouth slightly open. Caelan could see the woman he'd been standing with frowning at him as the queue began to move. She interrupted Mulligan's boasting. 'They're letting people inside.'

Leyton turned to gawp at her. 'What?'

Caelan jerked a thumb, and his eyes widened.

'Shit. See you around, Mulligan.' He trotted towards his girlfriend, calling over his shoulder: 'And come into the shop, yeah? We'll get that barnet sorted.'

They kept walking, Caelan scanning their surroundings, Ewan walking a couple of feet behind them. After a few minutes, Mulligan glanced at Caelan's face, saw her expression.

'What?' he asked.

There was no one nearby, no one listening. 'Intensive care?' She nudged him. 'You've a good imagination, I'll give you that.'

Mulligan laughed. 'Aye, all right. But I've been away six weeks. People are going to ask questions if I tell them the truth – that they took one look at my leg, stuck a plaster on and sent me on my way with a sticker and a lollipop.'

Caelan had to concede it was a fair point. 'Just don't…'

'Don't what?'

She looked at him. 'Say too much. Stick to something like the truth. It's safer. *You'll* be safer.'

Mulligan huffed. 'Safe? Good one. You saw Harris and his mates. You told him we'd have fifteen grand for him within forty-eight hours. If you're planning on us staying safe, you should have kept your mouth shut.'

–

Back at the house, Mulligan threw himself onto the nearest sofa and closed his eyes, kicking off his shoes. Ewan went through to the kitchen to make coffee while Caelan paced the room.

Mulligan opened an eye. 'Can't you sit down? You're making me nervous.'

Caelan stopped and stood in front of him, hands on hips. 'I want to ask you about—'

'No.' He said it wearily, his chin on his chest. 'Not tonight.'

She frowned down at him. 'You said—'

'I know what I said. Now I'm saying I'm knackered, and we can play twenty questions tomorrow. All right?'

It wasn't, but Caelan knew there was no point pushing him. If this was going to work, she had to keep him onside. 'Fine.' She sat on the other end of the sofa, drew her feet up underneath her. Mulligan watched, his eyes half closed. Caelan remembered the face of his sister in the photograph Penrith had left with her at Ewan's house. Those same green eyes.

'What do you think of the house?' Mulligan spoke softly, and Caelan almost missed the question.

'It's nice,' she said automatically.

He gave a soft laugh. 'Nice? Aye, I suppose it is. I own it outright, you know. No mortgage, none of that crap. All mine. Can you say that?'

She looked at him. 'What?'

'You're what, late twenties? Wee bit older? And you'll be paying off your mortgage until you die, or it'll seem like it. Or giving rent to some greedy bastard who never fixes anything and could kick you out any time if they felt like it. Won't you?'

Caelan thought about the flat in Rotherhithe, how she had come to live there. 'Not exactly.'

'Yeah?' Mulligan shifted position, turned to face her. 'Look at your job.'

'What about it?'

'The day we met, you were close to death, and I'm guessing it wasn't the first time. So I'll ask you – is it worth it?'

Caelan rubbed her eyes. It had been a long day. 'It's what I do.' She wasn't going to tell him about the loneliness, the isolation, the soul searching.

A smirk. 'And you're a real hero. Let's say you *had* died that day. What do you think would have happened?'

'I don't understand.'

'Don't, or won't?' He sat up straighter, warming to his theme. 'I'll tell you what would have happened – nothing. The world would have kept turning, wouldn't even have noticed, certainly wouldn't have given a shit. A quiet funeral, no big do with full honours for you, because let's be honest, no one knows who you are. You're faceless.'

Caelan said nothing, her head beginning to ache. He was right, but she wasn't going to give him the satisfaction of telling him so.

'Do you have a family?' he asked. 'Husband?'

She stared at him then, couldn't help it. Mulligan leered, realisation dawning. 'Wife?'

'Shut up.'

He wriggled in his seat. 'Wait until Jolene hears. She swings every which way, that one. She'll be round here—'

Caelan narrowed her eyes. 'Don't you dare.'

'Aye, right, she thinks you're loved up with Action Man in there.' Mulligan jerked his head towards the kitchen, where Ewan could be heard clattering around. A smile. 'I'm not much good at this undercover thing, am I?'

'We're undercover, not you. You just have to be the same hateful little shit you've always been.'

He pulled a face, held a hand over his heart. 'I'm wounded. That hurts, it really does.'

'More than your leg did, I'm sure.' Caelan glanced towards the kitchen.

'Does he even know how to make coffee?' Mulligan raised his voice. 'Oi, we're gasping out here.' He met Caelan's eyes. 'As I was saying, look around you. When we walked into that club tonight, people knew who I was. You'll never know what that feels like.'

'Thankfully.'

'Come on now. Have you never been tempted?'

'To do what?'

He grinned. 'To sample life on the other side. Never taken a bribe, a backhander? Never seized a load of drugs and skimmed some off to see what all the fuss is about?'

Her face was solemn. 'Never,' she said truthfully. Mulligan slapped his thighs with both hands.

'Never, Mother Teresa? Then I feel sorry for you. I might be grabbing the shitty end of the stick right now, but I'll tell you what, I've no regrets. I've done everything I ever wanted, enjoyed every minute. You only have one life, sweetheart. Maybe you should try enjoying it. Let yourself go a little, you know?'

'And the best way to do that is to be like you? Ruining lives so you can live like a king?' Caelan was aware how prissy she sounded, but she enjoyed winding him up.

'Ruining lives? Whose lives are we talking about?' Mulligan spread his hands. 'Come on, tell me.'

'Anyone who ever bought drugs from you, for a start.'

He smiled at her. 'You believe that, do you?'

'Fairly obvious, I'd have thought.'

'Shall I tell you something?' He drew himself up, looking as though he were preparing to make a speech.

'Do I have a choice?'

'Well, you could walk out of here now, and I'll do the same. How about it? Nah? Right. Then you listen. The people who bought from me, they were looking for a bit of happiness.'

'Happiness. You're serious? Happiness?'

'That's what I said. Anything to take them out of their shitty lives for an hour, half an hour, even a few minutes. Even a second, because you know what? It's better than reality. Even using a drug you know is killing you is better than looking around and realising what your life is. They couldn't do it, couldn't cope with the reality.' Mulligan licked his lips, kept talking. 'Some had probably been abused, some might have had mental health issues, learning difficulties, whatever. Never given any advice or help, just been pushed aside and forgotten about. And eventually they were offered a little something to make the misery disappear for a while. Why wouldn't you take it? In that situation, who could refuse? Could you?'

'Any day of the week,' Ewan said as he appeared carrying three mugs. He handed one to Caelan, held one out to Mulligan, who scowled at him as Ewan crossed to the other sofa and sat down.

'You spit in mine?' Mulligan demanded.

Ewan grinned. 'Never know, will you?'

Mulligan grunted, peered into the cup. 'All I'm saying is, some people will always find ways to destroy themselves. They choose different ways to do it, that's all. Drugs, drink, too much food, too little food, gambling. Taking risks. It's how they think, how they're made. Self-hatred, self-sabotage, call it what you like. It might take years, it might be over in minutes. But they'll find a way. They punish themselves, do things they know will destroy them in the end. A long, slow suicide, because it's what they think they deserve. I see it all the time.' He blew on his coffee, watching Caelan's face. He nodded at her, then smiled. 'Anyway. Shall we see what's on the TV?'

Camden, 11.24 p.m.

Lucy needed some paracetamol from her cupboard downstairs in the kitchen. It was late, she was tired, and though she didn't like to admit it, she was scared. Her room had always felt like a sanctuary, until recently at least. Now she felt watched, threatened. She wanted to lock her door and get into bed, but she knew she would have to wait. The headache had been there all day, but now it was worse, pounding and pulsating. She needed painkillers. Swearing quietly, she made her way downstairs.

The house was silent, everyone either out or in their room. She paused as she reached the front door. The kitchen was in darkness, the hallway silent and still.

Then, movement. A man stepped out from behind the kitchen door. He was dressed in black, a cap pulled low over his face. Horrified, Lucy gaped at him, a scream rising in her throat. She swallowed it as he raised a finger to his lips. Staring, she stood frozen. He had something in his hand. Was it a gun? He saw her eyes move to it, and grabbed her arm, his grip surprisingly gentle.

'It's a taser,' he whispered. 'I won't use it, not unless I have to. You understand?'

She nodded, knowing she wouldn't be able to speak if she tried.

'Let's go.' He pulled on her arm. As the front door opened, another man standing outside, she turned her head, looking back at the empty kitchen, the silent house.

No witnesses.

9

Caelan was trying to put Mulligan's words out of her mind as she got into bed. She shouldn't have listened, should have told him to shut up. A drug dealer, suspected people trafficker, trying to justify his actions now he'd been caught. He could dress it up any way he wanted, but he had sold misery packaged in pills or powder. And if he had been involved in trafficking… She closed her eyes. She was here in his house, lying in a bed bought with the profits of his shitty dealings.

And she'd allowed him into her head.

She wouldn't let it happen again.

She'd wanted to talk to Ewan, to ask if he was okay, but Mulligan had given them no opportunity to do so. Maybe now, with the three of them tucked up in their separate bedrooms, she could cross the landing to have a quiet word.

Pushing back the duvet, she swung her feet to the floor. As usual when she was working, she wore a T-shirt and jogging bottoms to sleep in, her trainers and a rucksack containing clean clothes, her phone and all her ID and bank cards ready at the side of the bed in case a quick getaway was needed.

She hadn't quite closed the bedroom door, and slowly, soundlessly, she pulled it open and stepped onto the darkened landing. She stopped and listened, hearing a murmur of voices. Was it coming from Mulligan's room? He must have switched the TV on when he'd got into bed.

She was about to tap on Ewan's door when she remembered. There was no TV in Mulligan's bedroom.

She marched across to his door and barged inside without knocking.

His bed was empty.

She turned, not allowing herself to panic. She'd locked the doors herself, and the keys were in her pocket. The windows were locked too – she'd checked. Mulligan must still be in the house, and he couldn't have let anyone else in. Could he? She paused on the landing, listening. His voice was low and she couldn't make out what he was saying. She couldn't hear anyone responding.

She jogged down the stairs, switching on lights as she went, not bothering to hide the fact that she was awake and looking for him. Again she told herself to stay calm, but it wasn't easy. Mulligan had been out of prison less than eight hours. He'd known he was going to be released, down to the hour; been aware he would be coming back to this house. She and Ewan had been through the place when they'd arrived, but she admitted they hadn't been as thorough as they might have been. She'd known Penrith would have sent people in to get it ready for them, but that could have been days ago. Someone could have been hiding here since then, ready for Mulligan's return, either to hurt him or help him. Unlikely, but possible.

Also, Mulligan knew she and Ewan were police. He could have traded that information for his own safety, or his sister's. Caelan had made plenty of enemies over the years, and London wasn't that big a city. She stopped and listened once more, but she knew there was little point in being cautious now. She heard a soft thud, and tensed, tilting her head as though it would help her hearing. Had Mulligan closed a door? A window? Had someone just left the house? She told herself it was impossible, but she knew that wasn't true. The house had been standing empty for weeks. Duplicate keys for the windows or doors could have been acquired, either on Mulligan's orders or without his knowledge. Panic gripped her chest, and she forced herself to breathe normally. Whatever was going on, she had to deal with it professionally. It was too late to wish again that she'd never agreed to get involved.

Mulligan was silent. Had he been attacked, abducted? Caelan moved forward. The living room was in darkness, but a light was on in the kitchen beyond. She kept moving. No movement, not a sound.

A tap was turned on in the kitchen, the clunk of the pipes and sudden gush of water making her jump. She swore under her breath, knowing she was on edge, being ridiculous, and kept moving.

She stood in the kitchen doorway, hands loose by her sides. Mulligan, wearing a navy bathrobe, his feet bare, was by the sink, drinking a glass of water. He nodded at her.

'You're awake. Come to join me in a nightcap?' he said, raising the glass as though proposing a toast. He looked calm, unruffled. No hint of guilt or concern.

Cautiously she moved into the room, maintaining a distance. 'Who were you talking to?'

He took another sip of water. 'No one. I don't have a phone, remember? The landline's been disconnected, and they confiscated my mobile when I was first arrested. I told them I'd need it back to make this charade a wee bit more realistic, but they didn't agree.'

Caelan leant against the worktop, alert and still listening. 'And you took matters into your own hands?'

Mulligan opened the dishwasher, placed his glass inside. 'I've been supervised since I left the prison, first at Enfield, now here. Where the hell would I have found a phone?'

'We both know the answer. You brought it with you from the prison. It's not difficult to get hold of them inside.'

Mulligan inclined his head. 'Been believing what you read in the tabloids? Shame on you. Anyway, I was searched before I left Belmarsh, and again when I left Enfield.' He pulled a face. 'Intimately searched. You know how it is – they delve into all your nooks and crannies.'

'And?'

'You know, it's shocking that you have so little faith in your colleagues. Don't you think that if I'd had something hidden away I shouldn't have, they'd have found it?'

'Depends if you'd bribed them, doesn't it?'

He looked suitably shocked. 'As if. If I *had* given one of Her Majesty's prison officers a few quid to rummage the other way when they had their finger up my arse, why would I give myself away on my first night of freedom by having a conversation loud enough for my two babysitters to hear?'

Caelan paused. It was a question she'd asked herself on the way down the stairs. Mulligan wasn't stupid – he might have known he'd be overheard. He could have sent a text silently, and neither she nor Ewan would have been any the wiser. What was his game? Had he wanted to lure her down here? She eyed him – the confident stance: feet apart, arms folded, the hint of a smile on his face. She couldn't trust him.

'I'll ask again,' she said. 'Who were you talking to?'

'Myself. A little habit I picked up in prison. Twenty-three hours a day in your own company tends to have that effect.'

'You were never in a single cell.'

'Wasn't I?' He smiled. He was casual, unconcerned.

Caelan glanced at the window. Was someone out there? Half of the window was locked, the other side divided into a fixed pane and a smaller section that could be opened but not locked. He could have opened it to have a conversation, or for a contact on the outside to pass something through.

Or he could just be winding her up.

'Empty your pockets,' she said. He laughed at her.

'No way.'

'Do it, Mulligan.'

'Are you going to make me? I'm wearing a dressing gown and nothing else, princess. Not much room to hide anything in here. You're welcome to check, of course.' He spread his arms as though offering a hug. 'Feel free.'

She felt more inclined to kick him in the balls. 'Fine.' She stepped towards him, noting with satisfaction the panic on his face. 'But I'll warn you now, my hands are cold.'

Mulligan stepped back, bumped into the sink unit behind him. 'You can't. You have to be the same sex to search someone.'

'You gave me verbal permission. Or I could call Ewan down. Your choice.' Caelan moved closer, and Mulligan held up his hands.

'All right, you win. Fucking hell, you love a power trip, don't you?'

She glared at him, breathing easier now she knew there was no one else in the room. 'No more than you do. Where have you stashed it?'

He dug into his dressing gown pocket, held out his hand. On his palm was a tiny mobile phone.

'Take it. I'll warn you, though, I've lost count of how many arses it's been inside.'

Caelan wrinkled her nose, keeping her hands by her sides. 'How about a compromise? If it had been down to me, I'd have given you your own phone back. I agree it would support your story – that you were questioned and released without charge. I'll have a word, try to get it back for you if you hand that one over. The whole idea is you carry on doing what you were doing before.'

'Not much of a dealer without a mobile, am I?'

'Not really.'

He squinted at her. 'And what do I have to do in return?'

Now she smiled. 'You only use it when I'm with you. If we're separated for any reason, the phone stays with me. You tell me who calls and what they want, and sometimes, you let me speak to them.'

'Won't work. The people who ring me don't want to chat.'

'You think I do? Final offer. I'm supposed to be learning the ropes. You need to let me talk to them.'

He scowled. 'All right, fine. But don't blame me if—'

Behind Mulligan, the window shattered, the sound as sudden and shocking in the silence of the night as a gunshot. Instinctively Caelan flung herself at him, the two of them crashing to the ground in a tumble of arms and legs. She pinned him against the cupboards, keeping her head down as a brick skidded across the floor and came to rest near the door. She counted to twenty before disentangling herself, a glance at Mulligan's terrified face telling her he had no idea what was going on.

'Stay there, and don't touch anything,' she told him as she pulled keys from her pocket and stumbled towards the back door. Ewan appeared in the door from the living room, his eyes widening as he took in the shattered glass and the brick.

'What the hell's going on?'

Caelan saw he was already wearing his shoes and pointed outside with her thumb. 'Can you see if anyone's out there? I won't be a second.'

He met her eyes, nodded and ran out of the door. Caelan hesitated, torn between protecting Mulligan and rushing outside herself. Whoever had thrown the brick must still be close by, though she didn't think Mulligan was in immediate danger. This was a warning. Decision made, she picked her way through the shards of glass glinting against the tiled floor and raced up the stairs. Her bedroom light was off, and she didn't switch it on. A quick glance out of the window revealed nothing but darkness in the small garden below. She couldn't see Ewan, or anyone else. As she pushed her feet into her trainers and bent to tie them, her heart seemed to thump in the back of her throat.

Who had thrown the brick? Was it linked to the mystery phone conversation Mulligan had been having? Or to Stefan Harris? If Harris had ordered someone to come and lob a brick through the window, he had moved quickly. From what Mulligan had said, though, it didn't seem like Harris's style. The fact that the brick had been thrown as Mulligan was standing there seemed to suggest someone had been watching the house, though she supposed it could have been coincidence. Or perhaps the idea had been to lure Mulligan outside and... what?

She hurtled back downstairs and into the kitchen. Mulligan was still on the floor, still huddled against the cupboard doors. He was wide-eyed, pale, but as Caelan stood over him, he managed a smirk.

'Knew I should have paid the window cleaner's bill before I went inside,' he said.

She couldn't help laughing, despite the situation. 'Did you see anyone out there?'

He shook his head. 'I didn't look, had my back to the window the whole time I've been in here.'

'Don't move.' She glanced at the back door. 'Has Owen been back?'

Mulligan frowned. 'Owen?'

She glared at him. 'That's what I said.'

He blinked, remembering. 'No.'

'You okay?'

'Fine.' He waved a hand towards the back door. 'Just... find out what's happening?' He tucked his dressing gown around his legs with a shudder. 'And, you know. Watch yourself.'

Caelan snorted as she went outside, not believing for a moment that he was actually concerned about her. She had her phone in her pocket but was reluctant to use it as a torch. It was difficult to move covertly when you were lit up like a Christmas tree.

Standing still, she listened, giving her eyes a few seconds to adjust to the darkness. There was no movement, no sound except the vague hum of traffic, despite the late hour.

She began to move as shapes revealed themselves in the gloom. Bins, a bicycle, a table and four chairs. She stopped again. Nothing.

The surface beneath her feet changed as she moved towards the rear of the garden: decking, then grass. It was long, wet, her trainers soaked in seconds, though the lawn could only have been ten feet square. She could be obliterating any footprints made by whoever had thrown the brick, but she wasn't concerned. This wouldn't be a job for their forensics people. Mulligan wasn't someone who would call the police, no matter what happened to him, and it was vital he keep to his usual patterns of behaviour. They would need to alert Penrith, but she knew he wouldn't want any fuss either.

In the farthest corner of the garden, a gate was set into the fence. It stood open. Caelan approached with caution, treading lightly. She stepped through into a narrow alley that ran the length of the road, separating the back gardens on Mulligan's row from those of the houses in the next street. It was dimly lit by three street lamps: one at either end of the alley, and one halfway along. Plenty of shadows, numerous places to hide. Caelan still couldn't see or hear Ewan, or anyone else, and knew their chances of catching up with whoever had thrown the brick were slim. They could have nipped over the fence of any of the nearby gardens and made their escape well before Ewan had got outside. At least she hadn't found him in a pool of blood.

Yet.

As she stood deciding which way to run, she saw movement at the end of the alley. Ewan. He held up a hand, began to jog towards her. She met him halfway.

'Anything?' she asked in an undertone. They needed to be cautious, because they didn't know who might be hiding nearby and listening, but she wasn't worried they'd given themselves away by rushing outside to see what had happened – the people they were pretending to be would surely have done the same.

'No.' Ewan's hands went to his hips. 'I've seen nothing, didn't hear anyone running away.' He turned, spread his arms. 'They could be anywhere. I did hear a car start up nearby, but it might have been coincidence.'

Caelan looked up and down the alley, knowing they were wasting their time. 'Let's go back inside.'

She led the way, another thought arriving in her head as she retraced her steps. What if the idea had been to lure her and Ewan out of the house, leaving Mulligan unprotected? He would be the target after all, not them. Anyone who knew how people like him operated would expect him to have some protection. Ewan fitted the bill perfectly, which was why Penrith had decided he should pose as Mulligan's new muscle man. Fuck. She began to run, Ewan hurrying to catch her up.

'What is it?' he said as they sprinted back towards Mulligan's garden.

Caelan didn't reply, focusing only on getting back to the house as quickly as possible, her mind still hurtling through motivations for the attack. Mulligan knew all about their operation. What if he had told his contacts on the outside who they really were? Could the attack on the property be intended as a warning to them? She didn't doubt he would betray them in a second to save himself from a beating, or worse. He might not care about his sister, but he would always make sure to protect himself. Caelan didn't know him well, but she didn't need to. He had made his desire for self-preservation unashamedly clear.

Or the phone call had been him calling for help, for rescue. In the second after the brick had hurtled through the window, he had looked so stunned and frightened she hadn't believed he had been expecting it, but how could she know for sure? He'd admitted to having the phone in his possession whilst in prison. He might have asked a friend to come and lob the brick through the window, then be waiting nearby with a car to spirit him away. Could that explain the engine Ewan had heard?

Mulligan could already be five miles away, on his way to a motorway or airport.

She pounded through the gate and back into the garden, all thoughts of discretion gone. If Penrith could have seen her, he'd have gone ballistic – she wasn't following protocol. Charging around in the dark like a blindfolded elephant went against normal procedure, but out in the field, events often overtook even the most detailed planning. Part of her brief was always to think on her feet, responding to shifting situations instantaneously, but she also had a responsibility to protect members of the public. In this case, that meant Mulligan, however distasteful the thought.

The back door stood open, as she'd left it. As she crossed the lawn, she cursed herself. She should have locked the door behind her, preventing him from escaping and stopping anyone else getting inside, either to help Mulligan or to hurt him. Stupid. She was behaving like an amateur.

Cautious again now, she sidled up to the back door and peered inside, not allowing herself to dwell on the possibility that he might have done a runner. She had no desire to have to break that news to Penrith. Though surely if he had arranged an escape, he would have scheduled it for the middle of the night. It would make more sense to wait until he could be sure she and Ewan were asleep. She also guessed he would have been wearing something more substantial than a bathrobe. It wasn't the ideal outfit to do much more than sit around the house in.

'James?' she said softly.

No reply.

She stepped into the silent kitchen, Ewan close behind. Immediately she became aware of two things.

Mulligan wasn't there, and there was blood on the floor.

It wasn't a huge amount, more a smear, and she told herself not to panic.

'James?' she called. 'Where are you?' Louder now.

'Through here.' His voice came from the living room. He sounded subdued, but at least he was there and able to speak. Caelan headed towards him, again avoiding the glass on the kitchen floor.

Mulligan was standing in the middle of the room, lights blazing, curtains drawn. There was no one else there, and Caelan, who had imagined him being held at knife- or gunpoint, relaxed a little. He had his back to them, and she approached, touched his arm.

'Are you hurt?' she asked, her tone business-like.

He turned. He looked unharmed, but she saw he was holding a piece of paper. 'I heard the letter box clang just as you left the house,' he told her. 'Cut my foot on the glass on the kitchen floor as I came rushing in here.' Caelan glanced down, saw blood staining the toes of his right foot, smudges on the carpet where he'd moved towards the front door.

'I told you to stay where you were,' she said.

Mulligan scoffed. 'Yeah, well I was a sitting duck in there, wasn't I? Anyway,' he held out the sheet of paper, 'this is what they put through the door. I think the brick through the window was just to make sure I was awake and found it.'

Caelan took the sheet, noting the tremble in Mulligan's hand. Beneath the bravado, he was frightened. It was an A4 page that had been folded in half and then quarters. There was an image, a scanned photograph, printed on it. Two children – a boy and a girl. The boy, several years older, held the handlebars of a bike, while the girl had a football under one arm. Both were beaming at the camera, the girl missing several teeth. Caelan's stomach dropped.

'Is this…?' She didn't really need to ask. The resemblance between them as children was more obvious than in the adult versions.

'Me and my sister Lucy.' Mulligan swallowed audibly. 'That photograph… She has the original in a frame, on the wall of her bedroom in the house she shares. She sent me a text when she first moved in and told me about it. She always tried to stay in touch, but I thought it best to keep my distance.' He managed a smile. 'Seems I was right.'

Caelan knew she had to speak to Penrith. She held out the keys to Ewan. 'Can you lock up, maybe put the kettle on, please?'

He nodded, took the keys. Mulligan watched as he left the room.

'What are we going to do?' he asked.

'*I'm* going to speak to my boss. You're doing nothing.'

He thrust his hands into the pockets of the bathrobe. 'Bollocks to that. I've still got friends out here, you know, friends who can make things happen. Let me make some calls.'

She eyed him. 'You don't have a phone, remember?'

'You didn't take it.' He held up a fist, showing her the phone still in his hand. 'How about we forget you saw it?'

'How about you go back to prison tonight?'

He took a step towards her, jaw clenched. Caelan didn't react, didn't even move, just kept scrolling on her phone. Mulligan stopped in front of her, leant in.

'You think you can stop me?'

She glanced up, took a step back and drove her foot into the side of his knee. It wasn't the most vicious kick she could have delivered, but it had the desired effect. Mulligan let out a howl and his leg crumpled, the phone tumbling from his grip as he staggered. He dropped to the floor, scrabbling to retrieve it. Caelan's foot shot out, pinning his hand to the ground.

'Don't fuck me around, James,' she said, her voice cold. He stared up at her, his expression difficult to read. There was fury there, and frustration. It was understandable. No doubt he was hating every minute of being Penrith's puppet. Caelan increased the pressure on his hand, all the time knowing she had to get him back onside. Weeks before, when he'd realised she'd fooled him, when he'd been told the woman he thought was going to sell him cocaine was in fact an undercover police officer, he had accepted the fact with a grin and a shrug. Even when he'd given the order to his men to kill her, he'd been matter-of-fact, almost apologetic. Like it was all part of a game he had won, and she would have to accept defeat.

'Believe it or not, we're on the same side,' she told him now.

Veins stood out in his neck as he fought to keep the pain he must be feeling from showing in his expression. 'Like fuck we are.'

She kept her weight on his fingers. 'I don't care about you, it's true, but I don't want your sister caught up in the fallout from whatever shit you've pulled in the past.'

'Makes two of us, but don't think for a second that means we're friends.' He tried to wrench his hand away, and she allowed him to. He scrambled to his feet, dressing gown flapping, breathing hard. He pointed at her.

'Get your boss on the phone. I want him here.'

'Why?'

'Because I've changed my mind. I'm not working with you bastards for another minute. And I want to make an official complaint about you.'

Caelan feigned boredom. 'Really.'

Ewan came into the room with three mugs in his hands. Mulligan watched him through narrowed eyes.

'I don't want any fucking tea.'

'It's coffee,' Ewan told him. Mulligan's face reddened further.

'You think you're so clever, the pair of you. I want to speak to your boss, now.'

Caelan leant against the wall, held out her phone. 'It's ringing.'

Mulligan snatched it, held it to his ear. 'This is James Mulligan. Who am I speaking to?' He listened, face thunderous. 'Yes, she's here… Because I told her to ring you. I'm sick of being told what to do, like a fucking schoolkid. And I want to make a complaint about this crazy bitch. She's tried to break my fingers and shatter my kneecap already. You may as well let the real criminals at me.'

Ewan shot Caelan a glance, his eyebrows raised. She lifted her shoulders.

'I want to know where my sister is, to see with my own eyes that she's safe. I don't believe a word you fuckers say any more.' A pause as he listened. 'Fine. I'll be ready.' He thrust the phone towards Caelan. 'He wants to talk to you.'

She braced herself. 'Hello?'

'Been having fun?' Surprisingly, Penrith's tone was mild.

'Something like that.'

'Why are you doing what Mulligan tells you to?' Penrith cleared his throat. 'Though I'm sure you have your reasons.'

Caelan kept her eyes on Mulligan. 'There was an incident this evening.'

His voice sharpened. 'What do you mean?'

'You might want to send someone over to Lucy's house.'

'Why? You think there's an immediate threat?'

'Possibly.' Quickly she told him about the brick, the photograph.

She heard him muttering, issuing instructions. 'Right. Get Mulligan in the car, bring him back to Enfield. You can give me all the details when you get here.' He blew his nose, loudly and at length. 'This isn't what we expected, especially on the first night.'

'Join the club,' Caelan said.

When he didn't speak, she waited, expecting an explosion of fury. She heard him sniffing. 'See you soon,' was all he said.

Caelan moved the phone away from her ear, glanced at the screen. Penrith had gone. She looked at Mulligan, who was waiting, hands clenched into fists at his sides.

'We've got an appointment,' she said. 'You'd better get dressed.'

10

Police stations at night always took Caelan back to her days in uniform. The still, gloomy corridors, the noise and bustle of the custody suite. The bellowing, the threats.

The misery.

The drive from Greenford had taken about an hour, Mulligan swearing and muttering in the back seat, Ewan sitting beside him, watching his histrionics like an anxious, exhausted parent.

Caelan swung into the car park, spotting Penrith's car immediately, Achebe's too. She reversed into a space, turned off the engine, called Penrith.

'We're here,' she told him. 'How do you want to do this?'

He didn't hesitate. 'Stay where you are. We'll come to you.'

Leaning back, she closed her eyes. She'd been ready for bed, but it didn't look as though they were going to be able to rest any time soon.

Mulligan bounced in his seat. 'What are we waiting for?'

'An escort,' Caelan told him.

'What?' He turned his head, watching as Penrith and Achebe appeared and walked towards them. 'Why?'

'Because no one trusts you. Haven't you figured that out yet?' Caelan took off her seat belt and opened her window. Penrith stood back, hands in pockets, while Achebe leant in.

'Evening, all.' He held out a pair of handcuffs. 'Going to have to ask you to slip into something more uncomfortable, James.'

Mulligan glowered at him. 'You're not serious?'

Achebe straightened. 'I've now been at work for almost eighteen hours. Do I look like a man who's in the mood for having a laugh?'

Penrith gestured towards the building. 'Shall we?' he said.

Inside, the place was quiet. When they reached the custody suite, even the cells were silent. Achebe inclined his head.

'No guests tonight? Everyone around here behaving themselves, for a change?'

The custody sergeant looked up from his desk. 'Seems they are. Give it an hour. It won't last.'

'Never does.' Achebe kept walking. 'We'll be in Interview Four.'

The sergeant waved a hand. 'Enjoy.'

—

The room was bleak and cold. Mulligan sat at the table, Penrith opposite him, while Caelan, Ewan and Achebe remained standing. Mulligan cast his eyes around the room.

'This is cosy, isn't it?' He looked up at the video camera mounted high in the corner. 'Is that recording?'

No one replied. Mulligan was putting on a convincing show of nonchalance, but Caelan could see he was rattled. Being in the police station again, the slamming doors, the handcuffs, was getting to him. He licked his lips, his right leg jiggling under the table.

Penrith leant back in his chair, rubbing his eyes. 'Mr Mulligan, I'm afraid we have bad news.'

Mulligan stared at him. 'What do you mean?'

Caelan wanted to ask the same question, but she kept quiet.

'We sent officers to your sister Lucy's home in Camden. They arrived forty minutes ago, but I'm afraid she wasn't there.' Penrith looked at the ceiling, clearly feeling uncomfortable, or pretending to. Mulligan shot Caelan a glare before focusing again on Penrith. She tried to catch Achebe's eye, but he was staring resolutely at the far wall. She frowned. Was Penrith winding Mulligan up? She hoped so, because if not and Lucy really had vanished, they were all in the shit, Lucy most of all.

'Well, she's a student,' Mulligan said. 'She's probably out getting pissed or shagging in a single bed somewhere.'

'Let's hope so.' Penrith didn't sound convinced.

'What are you talking about?' Mulligan demanded. 'Where is she?'

Holding up a hand, Penrith looked sorrowful. 'We did offer Miss Mulligan more… secure accommodation, but she declined, against our advice.'

Caelan expected Mulligan to start ranting, but instead he watched Penrith through half-closed eyes, his voice soft, dangerous. 'I'll ask you again. Where is she?'

Ignoring the question, Penrith pulled a handkerchief from his pocket and wiped his face. 'When we spoke to her house-mates, they told us Lucy had met a new boyfriend and hadn't been spending much time at home. We found her handbag, Oyster card and phone on her desk.'

Mulligan swallowed. 'Meaning?'

'Meaning,' Penrith said, 'wherever she is, she didn't take several items most people these days wouldn't ever consider leaving behind.'

Caelan couldn't read him, had no way of knowing whether he was being truthful or not. It was easy to underestimate Penrith, with his biscuit crumbs and his badly fitting clothes. How much of it was a front and how much was genuine, Caelan had never been able to say for certain, but she did know that he would never have had a sniff at his current rank if he hadn't been able to outwit chancers like Mulligan without even trying.

Mulligan tipped his head to the side, imitated Penrith's voice. 'Indicating, without evidence to the contrary, that it's safe to assume she didn't leave the premises of her own free will?' His own accent resurfaced. 'That this prick in fact wheedled his way into her life so he could grab her once her guard was down?'

Penrith nodded. 'I think we have to consider the possibility.'

Mulligan was halfway across the table, his cuffed hands reaching for Penrith's throat, before Achebe reached him, grabbing his shoulders and hauling him back into his chair.

'Behave yourself, or you'll stay in the cells until you can,' Achebe told him. Mulligan sat back, panting, his face red. Penrith hadn't moved, watching Mulligan with disdain.

'Start talking,' he ordered. His voice and manner had transformed. Gone was the genial, slightly bumbling middle-aged police officer; in his place sat the Commander Ian Penrith Caelan knew and grudgingly respected.

Mulligan was sullen. 'Not happening.'

'Not even to save your sister?' Penrith folded his arms. 'We've no idea where to start looking for her. London's a big place, James.'

'How do I know she's actually missing?' Mulligan set his cuffed hands on the table. 'How do I know you're telling me the truth?'

Penrith sighed. 'Tim?'

Achebe nodded, left the room. Caelan didn't move, though she wanted to follow Achebe and demand to know what was going on.

No one spoke, Mulligan seething on his side of the table, Penrith happy to sit and fiddle with his phone for a while.

Achebe returned after a few minutes, a clear evidence bag in his hand. He held it up so they could all see what was inside. A wooden photograph frame, the picture inside obscured by a web of broken glass. Caelan exchanged a glance with Ewan. Broken glass was becoming something of a theme tonight.

'Let me see that,' Mulligan said. Achebe moved closer, held it out to him. Mulligan peered at the frame, and his shoulders slumped.

'Is it—' Caelan started to ask him.

'Of course it is,' Mulligan snapped. Penrith turned in his chair, blinking up at Caelan.

'This is the original of the image that was posted through James's door tonight,' she said. 'Didn't you say someone had thrown a brick through Lucy's window too?'

Penrith nodded. 'Luckily she was in a lecture at the time.'

Mulligan sat up straight, eyes wide. 'What the fuck?'

'When did it happen?' Caelan asked.

'Last week,' said Penrith.

'Then they've known for a while where she lives, have probably been watching to work out when the room would be empty.' Caelan was guessing, but she was following Penrith's lead.

'Why would they give a shit?' said Mulligan.

'Because they wanted to warn you, not hurt her. Not yet.' Caelan took a few steps so she stood near Penrith, but slightly behind him, meaning Mulligan had to keep moving his head to focus on whoever was speaking. 'You obviously didn't listen.'

'How could I?' Mulligan tried to run a hand through his hair but was restricted by the handcuffs. 'I didn't know about it. She didn't tell me.'

'You've been dealing with some nasty people, James. It can't be a huge surprise if some of them want you to keep your mouth closed now that we've caught you and they're still out there enjoying their freedom.' Penrith gave him a smile that was anything but friendly.

'You don't know who I've been dealing with,' Mulligan told him.

'But we're hearing a few names.' Caelan folded her arms. 'Stefan Harris, Reuben Nash, his brother Nathan?' She waited a beat. 'Jolene Townsend?'

As she'd expected, Mulligan bridled, trying to point a finger at her. 'She's nothing to do with this.'

She smiled at him. 'But the others are?'

He ignored her.

'You arranged the murder of Jackson Hobbs, one of the city's most established drug dealers,' Caelan went on. 'Surely you expected repercussions?'

'I wasn't involved in Hobbs's death. No one can say otherwise.' Mulligan sat back, cuffed hands in his lap.

'Ryan Glennister could,' said Caelan.

'Ryan? You reckon?' Mulligan chuckled. 'You'd have to find him first. And then get him to remember what day it is.'

Penrith turned back to Mulligan. 'As I said, your sister wasn't in her room when our officers arrived tonight. The door was locked, but we managed to get inside.' He held out his phone, and Mulligan peered at the screen. 'As you can see, the place was a mess. No one in the house heard anything, but there was clearly a struggle.'

Mulligan's mouth twisted. 'Aye, Lucy would have fought,' he said. 'She never was one for being pushed around.'

'Tell me who you were working with. If you want us to find your sister, you need to help us,' Penrith told him.

'What about Stefan Harris?' Caelan said. Penrith glanced at her, as though irritated she had spoken again. Mulligan shook his head.

'I owe Harris money, but he wouldn't take it out on Lucy. He'd get his men to give me a battering, no more.' He jabbed a thumb in Caelan's direction, looking at Penrith. 'Hasn't told you she's promised to pay him the fifteen grand he's owed yet either, has she?'

Penrith didn't blink. 'Is it relevant to your sister's disappearance?'

'Don't know, do we?'

'Then it doesn't matter.'

Mulligan's knee was still bouncing. 'Will do when Harris comes looking for it.'

'I'm sure we'll cope,' Penrith said. He drummed his fingers on the table. 'If you owe Stefan Harris money, you must have bought something from him.'

'White,' Mulligan said. Penrith nodded.

'And what did you sell him?'

'Nothing.' Mulligan didn't flinch, kept his eyes on Penrith's face.

Penrith inclined his head. 'You didn't? Not even a few people?'

'Not even once.' Mulligan's cockiness was back, and Caelan wondered why. They knew Mulligan had trafficked people – the two men who had worked for him had said so – but perhaps he was telling the truth about his dealings with Harris. When she remembered all the crimes they believed him guilty of, she asked herself again why she had agreed to work so closely beside him. He represented everything she despised.

'You're supposed to be helping us find out who's trafficking people into the area.' She wanted to grab him by the throat and squeeze. 'Not being much help so far, are you?'

'Come on, James, we know what you were selling. People who believed they were coming here to start a new life. Didn't quite work out like that, did it?' Penrith said.

'Again, I know what you've heard. But those two fuckers who worked for me, they were the ones who found the girls and did the talking. They told them what an amazing life they were coming to. I don't…' Mulligan gulped. 'You think I enjoyed it? I'm not a monster. I saw it as giving them an opportunity.'

Caelan couldn't help it. 'An opportunity? A fucking opportunity? Are you kidding me?'

Mulligan held up his cuffed hands. 'All right, bad choice of words. It's a terrible business, I know.'

'Business?' Caelan couldn't look at him.

'You want me to tell you the truth?' Mulligan swallowed again. 'I'm fucking haunted by it. There were only a couple of shipments…' Again he raised his hands. 'Sorry. But that's what they called them. I played the big man, aye, of course I did. Didn't want to lose face, but once I was involved, I realised I hated it. There was one girl, they brought her over to my house.' He nodded at Caelan. 'The one we're staying in.'

'I'll sleep better now, thank you.' She felt ill.

'Hear me out. She was young, terrified, but already used to having sex with whoever she was ordered to. She went upstairs, undressed. Got into my bed, lay there waiting for me, passive as you like.' He chewed on his bottom lip. 'She looked... I didn't... I couldn't. She lives in Glasgow now. I found her a job with one of my cousins – my *real* cousins. She's training to be a chef.' He didn't look at them, his face crimson.

'Who brought her?' Penrith asked.

Mulligan's head snapped up. 'What?'

'You said "they" brought her to your house. Who did?'

'Fuck's sake. Does it matter?'

'It does, because this is why we're here. I'm sorry if we haven't been clear. You're giving us cooperation and information in exchange for a lighter prison sentence. We've established that, haven't we?' Penrith sniffed.

'I don't know who brought her, all right? The doorbell rang, and there she was. Mine for the night, because I'd done whoever owned her a favour.'

'What favour?' Penrith wanted to know.

'We'd agreed a deal. I was going to be one of their suppliers, give them a discount. They needed a fair bit of gear to keep the women sweet.' Mulligan looked at Caelan to see if she was going to react. He was disappointed.

'Then you know who it was,' was all she said. He made a noise of impatience.

'No, I don't. No names, no strings. I was given an address, some empty house. A squat. I knocked on the front door, and a hand reached out, gave me a packet of cash. Took the gear, and I was away home. We didn't say a word to each other. Next thing I know, I get a text telling me there's a present on the way. Mine to do what I wanted with, then sell on. Bit of a bonus from her owner, I suppose.'

'Her owner?' It was the first time Tim Achebe had spoken since he'd come back into the room, and his disgust was clear.

Mulligan turned to look at him. 'That's what I said.'

'Wasn't this "owner" a little pissed off when she disappeared off to an actual new life in Glasgow?' Achebe folded his arms.

Mulligan shook his head. 'Not when I paid the going rate. I replied to the text saying I'd had such a good time, I wanted to keep her. I was given a price, took the cash to the same squat.'

'How much?'

Mulligan glanced at Achebe as he asked the question. 'Twenty grand.'

'The price of a life. Fuck.' Achebe turned away, and Mulligan stared at the floor. Caelan wondered if his shame was real. She doubted it.

'And who did own her?' Penrith asked. Mulligan exhaled.

'Like I said, these people don't shake your hand and introduce themselves. No real names are used, not even nicknames.'

'You expect us to believe you've no idea who you were working with, or for? Forgive me if I don't,' said Penrith.

'It's the truth. It's like a… a secret society. You know? You indicate you're willing to trade in…' Mulligan rubbed a hand across his mouth, 'well, in people. And customers make themselves known.'

'Word got around? There must have been a middleman, someone who knew both of you.' Penrith said.

'Don't know. Don't think so. Friend of a friend of a friend, maybe. You can't find out who told who, no way.'

Penrith shrugged. 'We'll try, if it's all the same to you. I'll need the address of that squat, for starters.'

Mulligan's lips twitched. 'Gladly.'

They all knew it would be a dead end.

Caelan said, 'How did these mystery people contact you? Did they phone, come to your house?'

'I had a burner phone, changed the number every few days. No doubt everyone else did too. I don't know how the numbers were passed around, but they always were. Like I said, there are people pulling the strings, but I don't know who they are. It was mainly calls, yeah. Short ones – the requirements, a location for the drop-off.' He paused. 'The price.'

She studied him. 'You sure you weren't selling second-hand cars?'

'What?'

'Requirements, drop-offs? We're talking about people here.' She took a breath, told herself to stay calm. Mulligan would love knowing he had got to her. Sure enough, he leered across the table.

'Getting emotionally involved, Victoria? Not allowed in your job, is it?'

'We need names, Mulligan.' Penrith tried to bring them back to the point. 'I'll remind you, one of these customers of yours could have your sister.'

'Told you, I've none to give you.' Mulligan tapped his foot against the table leg. 'Would if I could, but the whole point was, no one knew the identity of anyone else. Then if one of us got nicked, we wouldn't be able to give them up to you lot.'

'Then you've nothing to bargain with.' Penrith began to rise from his seat. 'We're wasting our time. You can go back to prison, for good this time.'

'What made her different?' Caelan asked softly. Penrith hesitated, sat back down. Mulligan looked at her.

'What?' he said.

'This girl you were lent for the night.' She hated speaking so casually, but she wanted Mulligan to tell her the truth. 'Why didn't you have sex with her? I'm assuming you hadn't been troubled by your conscience before? There must have been other girls.'

He tried a smile. 'Would you believe me if I said no? Not like that.'

'No, I wouldn't.' She paused, thinking about it. 'Did she look like your sister?'

She watched his face and knew she was right when he blinked rapidly.

'Not exactly, but there was a resemblance,' he said. 'And I… Well. It made me think. I put her on the train up to Glasgow Central the next morning.'

'Not back to her home?'

He winked at her. 'She didn't want to go. Anyway, I didn't want her telling tales.'

Caelan bit back a torrent of abuse. He wasn't worth it.

'And now your sister could be in the same situation,' Penrith said. 'Like I keep saying, time for you to start talking.'

Mulligan tried to rub his face. 'Aye, all right. The people who brought the girls over from Albania – I never knew their names, never met them. My boys – the fuckers who've stitched me up and told you everything they know – they're Albanian too. You've no doubt noticed.' A hint of his usual grin. 'They knew where to find the girls, and who could get them here. I didn't ask questions.'

'Not what your two former employees have told us,' Penrith said.

'Told you I did it all myself, did they? Aye, right, because I speak fluent Albanian. You better talk to them again, though it won't do you any good. The people at the top of this game are careful. They don't meet face to face; they use go-betweens to exchange money, and then the go-betweens turn up dead. They're like shadows. It's not a pleasant business.' Mulligan shook his head, as though disappointed. As though he'd never been involved.

'You led us to believe you could be useful to us. Now I'm not so sure.' Penrith glanced at his phone, checking the time. 'Your sister's probably in a brothel somewhere by now, preparing for her first client.'

Mulligan studied him, unmoved. 'That's all you've got, isn't it? That's your ace, and you're going to play it over and over again.'

Penrith gave him a cheerful smile. 'That, and the fact that we can have you put away for the rest of your life. You can bleat on all you like about how you saved an Albanian innocent, but the fact is, we're giving you a chance you don't deserve.'

'Tell me something,' Mulligan said, his voice quiet, thoughtful. 'Why would my sister be snatched now?'

'What do you mean?' Penrith shifted in his chair.

'I'm just back on the streets after a stay in hospital, and questioning. If I was going to spill my guts to you, wouldn't I have done it while I was in custody? While I was trying to save my arse?'

Penrith leant closer. 'Maybe you did. Maybe that's why you were released.' He gave another grim smile. 'Maybe people are already wondering what you told us while we had you under lock and key.'

Mulligan leapt forward again, clawing for Penrith. 'You fucker, what have you been telling people? If my sister's been snatched because of you lot, if she's hurt—'

'It'll be your fault.' Penrith reached into his pocket, pulled out and held up a mobile. 'Yours, I think?' He left it on the table in front of Mulligan as he pushed back his chair, stood this time. 'Use it wisely. I know Caelan will be keeping an eye on you. I want you to introduce her and Ewan to Reuben and Nathan Nash, and any other lowlifes you can think of. Reuben Nash owns a nightclub, doesn't he?'

Mulligan stared. 'If you can call it that. It's a shithole. How do you know about it?'

Penrith chuckled. 'We have intel people, you know. Anyway, you're not the only one who makes secret phone calls. Caelan called me earlier, reported in on your evening at Stand. Sounded like fun. We know who you spoke to once you got home, by the way. Quite touching, really.'

'Fuck off.'

'You tried to call your sister, but only got her voicemail. Not surprising at that time of night, but it makes me wonder why you did it.'

'Do I need a reason? I'd just got out of prison. I wanted to say hello.'

Amazed, Caelan realised Mulligan was blushing. He could talk about his crimes with barely a blink, but catch him showing concern for his sister and he was embarrassed. Again she was reminded that she had to remember who he was, what he'd done.

'Did you want to warn Lucy?' Penrith rocked back on his heels. 'Perhaps someone had used her as a threat before? Were you worried?'

Mulligan snorted. 'What do you think? Yeah, I was worried. She's a young woman, and she's clever, but she's vulnerable because she doesn't know… well, about my life. My lifestyle. I wanted to tell her to watch her back.'

Caelan stepped towards him, suddenly suspicious. 'Did you tell her you were working with us, with the police?'

'I—'

'*Did* you?'

He shook his head. 'Course I didn't. I stuck to the story. Released without charge. You think I'm crazy? May as well have shot her in the head myself. Working with the police is even worse than grassing someone up to them.' He licked his lips again. 'Anyway, can't you listen to the message, hear what I said? I don't remember the exact words, but there was nothing about you lot.'

Slowly Caelan moved away. For once, she believed him. He wouldn't do anything to put himself at risk.

Penrith was halfway through the door. 'We'll speak again over the next few days. I'll expect you to have introduced my officers to everyone in your address book by then. Last chance to give us information we can use, Mulligan, or at least point us in the right direction. If you don't, the deal's off. We'll start sniffing around your friends, see if we can find your sister. Goodnight, all.'

The door banged behind him and Mulligan gazed at Caelan and Achebe, head on one side. 'Goodnight? Is he taking the piss?'

'Probably,' Achebe told him.

11

8 December

Heading for a narrow gap between a kebab shop and an estate agent's, Mulligan led them down the kind of dingy alley usually reserved for emptying your bladder or dropping your trousers for some other reason. There were a few people about, several already staggering as they approached the queue waiting by the club's entrance. Two bouncers, one male, one female, were on the door, smiling and chatting as they waved people inside. A group of middle-aged women cackled and nudged each other as three younger blokes joined the queue behind them, the men exchanging awkward grins as they shuffled their feet, embarrassed. Caelan saw one of the women wink at Ewan as they approached the back of the line, and tucked her arm through his possessively.

'You were right,' she told Mulligan.

'Had to happen sooner or later. How do you mean?'

'This place really is a shithole.'

He pretended to wince. 'Wait until you get inside.'

Caelan watched a couple wearing jeans and trainers move past the bouncers, who didn't give them a second glance. 'They're not even checking people's bags.'

'Not that kind of place,' Mulligan said.

She could believe it. 'Asking for trouble.'

They moved a few steps forward. Mulligan's hands were in his pockets, head up. Back in the game.

'People come here to relax, maybe do some business,' he said. 'No one wants to be searched on their way in.'

'And the management won't want to do it anyway. Not in their interests.' Caelan lowered her voice as another group stumbled up behind them. 'No doubt you can sell anything in here as long as you hand over a cut of the profits.'

'No comment.' Mulligan grinned as he gave a jaunty wave to someone near the front of the queue. 'And don't let Reuben hear you say that, or anyone else.'

Caelan smiled back. 'I'll be subtle.'

'Aye, I'm sure.' He made a sound of disgust.

The club's entrance was anonymous, black doors with a small silver sign above them. Caelan squinted up at it.

'Reuben's? That's imaginative.'

The male bouncer caught her eye as they passed. 'Have a good evening,' he said. She nodded, trying to look as though she couldn't wait to get inside, but suppressed a sigh as they made their way down a gloomy corridor towards the music. This was going to be a long night. Nightclubs weren't her favourite places, especially when she was working. There were dark corners where someone might hide or lie in wait, and keeping track of one person was next to impossible. The music made it difficult to talk, and people under the influence of alcohol or drugs weren't always rational. All in all, she would rather Mulligan had taken them anywhere else than two different nightclubs on consecutive nights, but it was out of her control.

Ewan glanced down at her, his smile questioning, and Caelan gave him a tiny nod. At least on this job she wasn't alone, as she had been so many times before.

The smell of sweat and cheap aftershave was as over-whelming as the crush of bodies around the bar. There were a few spotlights making lazy circles on the black-painted ceiling, the music loud but nowhere near as crisp as it had been in the Stand the night before. Drugs were changing hands, shots being downed. People were here to enjoy their evening, and who could blame them? In some ways Caelan wished she could march over to the bar, order a double vodka and join them.

Their shoes already sticking to the floor, Mulligan led them to a table in a dark corner. The table was battered, the chairs covered in dark red fabric dotted with stains and spills.

'Good vantage point, you see?' he said as he flung himself down. He had perked up since the meeting with Penrith, especially after a few hours' sleep and another takeaway. 'I'm getting good at this.'

Caelan took the chair beside Mulligan's and leant towards him.

'Who have you seen so far?'

He pursed his lips. 'Big guy over there? Blue shirt, black jeans?'

She glanced over discreetly. 'The miserable-looking one?'

'Aye, that's him. Nathan Nash, Reuben's brother. Always looks like he's at his mam's funeral.' Mulligan looked at Ewan as he pulled out a chair. 'You away to the bar, big man?'

Ewan frowned. 'Why not.'

Watching him walk away, Mulligan smirked. 'Don't think your boyfriend's happy. You could be a bit more affectionate, you know? I think he's pining.'

Caelan ignored that. 'What does Nathan Nash do?'

'Helps his brother here.'

'Nothing else?'

'Like what? Charity work?'

'Something legit.'

Mulligan wagged a finger. 'I haven't said they're into anything dodgy. They run this place, maybe turn a blind eye to a bit of dealing or thieving.'

'Then why are we here?'

'I told you. Stand is the club to be seen in; Reuben's is the place to do business. Look around you. Most people are your average punters, here for the cheap booze. But you've also got those who aren't just here to enjoy themselves.'

Caelan waited for five young women to pass their table. 'Tell me who I should be watching.'

Mulligan laughed. 'Watching? I've already seen you have a good look at a few people – the blonde in the red dress who just went by for one.'

Caelan refused to smile. 'Is Reuben Nash around?'

His eyes flicked over the crowd. 'Not yet. He'll be in his office upstairs; he'll come down later on. He likes to get a feel for how the evening's going, or so he says.'

'What about Stefan Harris?'

Mulligan's nostrils flared. 'What about him?'

'Will he be here?'

'I'm not his secretary. Look, Reuben Nash hates Harris. Don't ask me why, because I don't know. Harris comes here sometimes because he knows it'll be worth his while. He and Nash are polite, but in that strained way, you know?' Mulligan raised his eyebrows. 'As though it wouldn't take much for them to start punching each other.'

'Like you and me.'

Mulligan laughed, but his eyes were cold. 'Aye, you're not kidding.'

There was a silence. Caelan watched Mulligan fiddle with the buttons on his shirt, run a hand through his hair. He was doing his best to appear calm, confident, but she realised he was anything but. He hadn't mentioned his sister, and Penrith hadn't been in touch, so they had no idea what was happening. It seemed unlikely, given the mess in her bedroom and the items she had left behind, that Lucy had gone voluntarily, but Caelan knew better than most that things weren't always what they seemed. She sat back, hoping she looked relaxed, as though she was enjoying herself.

No chance.

She remembered the faces of the three young people in the photographs Penrith had shown her. She had to focus on them as well as Lucy. Someone knew who they were, why they'd died. Had they seen too much? Asked questions? Protested at being used like pieces of meat? She knew she had to trust Achebe and Somerville to do their jobs, but finding justice for the three unidentified faces was her responsibility too. She needed to talk to Penrith, to ask whether she could have some background details on any of the people she had met through Mulligan so far. In her job, it wasn't always deemed a good idea to be given a lot of information about a suspect or person of interest. If you had background knowledge, it could lead to you mentioning something or someone the person in question hadn't told you about. She'd known covers blown by an officer mentioning a place or person they shouldn't have been aware of. It didn't happen often, should never happen at all, but she and her fellow officers were human, and where there were humans, there were mistakes.

Ewan appeared, clutching three beer bottles, trailed by Jolene Townsend, the woman Mulligan had introduced them to the night before. Mulligan leapt out of his chair and bounded towards her as Ewan set the beers on the table.

'You're slumming it tonight, Mulligan,' Jolene said, watching him over the rim of her glass.

'On your own?' he asked.

She smiled. 'For now. Non-alcoholic lager?' She gestured towards his beer bottle. 'Gone over to the dark side, have you?'

Mulligan's face froze for a second, but he quickly recovered. 'Still on the painkillers. Got to avoid the drink for the time being. You know how it is.' He pulled out a chair for her, guided her into it. He jerked his head towards Caelan and Ewan. 'Owen's driving, Vic's here to work.'

Jolene met Caelan's eyes, one eyebrow raised. 'Work?'

'I'm showing her the ropes.' Mulligan spoke lightly, but Caelan knew what the words were costing him. Here was the subterfuge, and with it the admission that he might need help. He was being forced to acknowledge that he'd been rattled by his run-in with the police and was worried about the future of his business if they should start sniffing around again.

'I don't understand.' Jolene was talking to Mulligan but still looking at Caelan, her expression guarded. Caelan hesitated,

114

waiting to see what Mulligan would say. He leant towards Jolene, speaking quietly.

'Vic knows my game inside out, and she's family. You remember Andri and Erdi?'

'Your thick-as-pig-shit assistants?' Jolene scoffed. 'Hard to forget them. Banged up, aren't they?'

'Exactly. And a man can't run a business empire like mine on his own.' Mulligan stretched his legs out in front of him and drank some beer. 'When Vic heard what had happened, that my boys were out of the picture, she volunteered her services.'

Again Jolene's eyes were on Caelan, the hint of a sneer in her expression. Caelan wondered why.

'And what about him?' Jolene jerked her head towards Ewan.

'Owen?' Mulligan said. 'He's the muscle, and unlike my Albanians, he can think for himself. Win-win.'

Caelan had to admit, Mulligan sounded convincing. Ewan's face was set as he drank his beer, his eyes constantly scanning the crowd, playing his part to perfection. Jolene's gaze flicked from Mulligan to Ewan and back again.

'So you're back in the game?' she said.

Mulligan raised his bottle. 'Never left it, princess. Let people know, though, won't you? Don't want everyone thinking I've gone into retirement.'

'No worries.' Jolene stood. 'You got anything to sell?'

Mulligan spread his hands. 'Not yet, but the night's young.'

With a glance at Caelan and Ewan, Jolene lowered her voice. 'Why don't you speak to Stefan?'

'Bit of an issue there, unfortunately.' Mulligan cleared his throat. 'Fifteen thousand issues, actually.'

'You owe him money?' Jolene shook her head. 'You stupid bastard.'

'I know, I know.' Mulligan rubbed his face with both hands. 'I need a deal, one that's going to make me enough to pay Harris off and give myself and these two a decent pay packet. Have you heard of anything I might be interested in?'

Jolene was already moving away. 'No. You know me, I like the quiet life. See you.'

As she disappeared into the shadows, Mulligan scowled. 'Fuck.'

'What's the problem?' Caelan said. 'She'll go and tell everyone she knows that James Mulligan is desperate to make some money.'

'What, and you think they'll be queuing up to sell to me?' Mulligan finished his beer and slammed the bottle onto the table. 'Not going to happen. I got caught, remember? Anyone I used to trade with won't want to be associated with me now, not when I've had the police at my door.'

'Then we're wasting our time. Make up your mind, Mulligan. Either you can get us close to the major players around here or you can't.'

'Didn't know I'd be treated like a fucking leper, did I?' Mulligan took a couple of deep breaths. 'You saw how Jolene was just now. She doesn't want to know me, and neither will anyone else. Good thing you promised to pay Stefan Harris back yourself, because fuck knows how I'd be able to do it.'

'Jolene didn't have to come and speak to you if she didn't want to,' Ewan said. 'She was talking to some other bloke at the bar, but when she saw me, she asked if you were here and then followed me over.'

Mulligan frowned. 'What other bloke?'

Ewan lifted his shoulders. 'Six foot, dark hair, skinny. Wearing a suit. The bar staff got a shift on when they saw him, so I'm guessing he either manages the place or owns it.'

'Right the second time.' Mulligan's grin looked forced. 'Reuben Nash. What's he doing out of his office already?'

'Maybe he heard you were here,' Caelan said. 'Is he a friend of yours?'

Mulligan's lips tightened. 'Not exactly.'

She exhaled. 'How much do you owe *him*?'

'Nothing.'

Caelan watched his face. 'What then? What's Nash involved in, other than this place?'

'You'd have to ask him.'

'No rumours?'

'He's a nasty bastard who owns a dodgy nightclub. That's all I know.'

'Nasty?'

Mulligan nodded. 'Though not as nasty as his brother.' He sat up straight. 'And right on cue...'

Caelan looked up to see the man Ewan had described striding towards them. He stopped in front of Mulligan, rocking back on his heels.

'Heard you were back, James. How's the leg?'

Mulligan stood, held out his hand. Nash glanced at it but kept his own hands by his sides. Mulligan blushed but kept smiling. 'Good to see you, Reuben.'

'Who are these two?' Nash demanded, his eyes skimming Ewan then Caelan. She flashed him a smile.

'You mean Jolene didn't tell you?' she said. Nash showed his teeth, more of a grimace than a smile.

'She said Mulligan had found some little helpers. I was expecting two brick shithouses, to replace the idiots he had before.'

Caelan felt Mulligan tense beside her, and knew he was worried what her response would be.

'He decided he wanted people with a brain between them this time,' she said. 'People he can trust.'

Nash curled his lip. 'You can't be that clever, working with him. He's a fucking disaster.'

Caelan gave a slow smile, allowing her gaze to linger on Nash's face. 'Good job I know exactly what I'm doing then, isn't it?'

'She's my cousin, Victoria. She had a successful operation running up in Edinburgh,' Mulligan put in. He was frowning. Nash's pop at his business prowess had clearly hit home.

'Yeah, I heard.' Nash rubbed his jaw. 'Why's she in London, if she was doing so well up there?'

'Split up with my ex, met Owen,' Caelan nodded at Ewan, 'and decided it was time for a change of scenery.' Sometimes you had to think quickly and deviate from the cover story, but she would rather not have had to. Now she'd have to get Penrith to create a convincing former partner for Victoria Smith, one who was known for dealing drugs. Something else for him to moan about.

'Sure you didn't come to rescue your cousin here?' Nash said.

'Work with, not rescue,' Caelan told him.

Nash said nothing, scrutinising her face, and Caelan didn't give in to the temptation to elaborate further. Giving details meant she would have more to remember about the person she was supposed to be. Mulligan, shifting in his seat beside her, started to speak, but Nash talked over him.

'We should have a coffee, Victoria, talk about how we might be able to help each other.'

Ewan leant forward, his expression belligerent. 'Hang on, mate. She's with me.'

Caelan reached out, laying a hand on his arm as though to calm him. 'I think Mr Nash is talking about a business meeting, not a date.' She met Nash's eyes. 'Aren't you?'

He stepped back, inclining his head in Ewan's direction as though offering a challenge. 'Of course.' Lifting a hand, he walked away. Mulligan watched him go, then turned to Caelan.

'Reuben Nash with a twinkle in his eye. Never thought I'd see the day.'

Caelan suppressed a shudder. 'Might be a good idea for me to meet him, though. You sure this is his only business?'

'Far as I know.'

'What does he think I'd want to discuss with him then?'

'He probably wants to give you permission to peddle drugs in here. And he wants to get into your knickers.'

'Arrogant bastard. Like a woman couldn't say no him.' Ewan drained his beer as Mulligan laughed.

'You do remember she's not really your girlfriend, don't you? You get that?'

Ewan wasn't going to bite. 'It was the way he asked, like no woman would dream of turning him down, even if they already had a boyfriend.'

'Like I said, it might be in our interests for me to meet him, see what he wants to talk about,' Caelan said.

'I've already told you. Drugs.' Mulligan spread his hands. 'This place runs on them.' He raised his eyebrows. 'Watch.'

Caelan followed his gaze, saw the other Nash brother, Nathan, go over to a young man who wore a padded jacket and a pair of pristine trainers. They were one of the most expensive designs on the market, as Caelan knew from the shopping trips she had made when preparing for new assignments. Several of the women she had pretended to be would have killed for those shoes. A badge saying *Drug Dealer* couldn't have made him more obvious. Nathan grabbed the man's shoulder, stooping to speak into his ear. With a nod, the dealer turned away, heading for the shadowy booths at the back of the club.

'Supply and demand, or whatever they call it.' Mulligan said. 'Demand's high in a place like this, and Reuben Nash only lets certain people trade here, so anyone wanting to buy has to fork out top dollar.'

'Unless they bring it in with them,' Caelan pointed out. 'The security on the door is hardly going to stop them.'

'You reckon?' Mulligan shook his head. 'It'd be like taking your own food into a cafe and then expecting to be allowed to sit at one of their tables while you ate it. Not polite, and not allowed.'

'How would Reuben Nash know where people bought their drugs? It's not as though they have a label on them.'

'He wouldn't, not for sure, but the threat of Nathan interrogating you about it is enough to put most people off.'

They watched Nathan Nash lean against the wall, arms folded, blank-faced.

'Look at him, eyeing everyone like Big fucking Brother,' said Mulligan. 'Barrel of laughs, isn't he?'

'Why do people come here then?' Caelan asked. 'The music's nothing special, they can get their drugs cheaper elsewhere...'

'And their drinks,' Ewan put in.

'...so why bother?'

Mulligan gave a slow smile. 'Because, like I said, you can meet new contacts here, make a deal. Buy pretty much anything.'

'Like a gun?' Caelan said.

Mulligan frowned. 'Why? Don't tell me you want one?'

'No. But you did.'

He smiled, understanding. 'The one I shot Adam Waits with? Andri got it for me. I never asked where from.'

'How convenient.'

'What you don't know, you can't get put away for.' Pushing back his chair, Mulligan got to his feet and bellowed, 'Leyton!'

A head turned in the crowd, a hand was raised.

'Leyton Grey – you met him last night?' Mulligan said as he sat back down. 'Doesn't look like he's coming over. He's with a different girl tonight – little shit's like a dog on heat.'

'What's his story?' Caelan asked.

Mulligan pulled a confused face. 'Story? I told you, he's a barber. Cuts the hair of footballers, TV stars, you name it.'

'And yours.'

He pretended to preen. 'Aye, and mine.'

'If he's just a barber, why did you introduce us to him?'

'I'm not following.'

'What does he do on the side?'

Mulligan looked shocked. 'Nothing. Why would he? His shop's a gold mine. If you remember, *he* came to speak to *me* last night. I didn't even see him. He's my barber, and a pal. That's it.'

'Hmm.' Caelan wasn't convinced. She didn't believe Mulligan would be friends with anyone if there wasn't something in it for him. 'I want to talk to Jolene Townsend again, and Nathan Nash.'

'Not tonight.'

'Why?'

'Too obvious. Anyway, talking to Nathan is like trying to have a conversation with a wall. He's not exactly chatty.'

'We'll see. Anyone else?'

Mulligan leant back in his chair. 'See the laddie over there, grey hair, baggy jeans, looks like someone's grandad?' He held up a finger. '*Is* someone's grandad.'

Caelan looked. 'Yeah?'

'Pimp. Runs a load of girls out of a house in Perivale.'

She blinked. 'What's his name?'

But Mulligan shook his head. 'Woman dancing over there with her back to us? Bleached hair, terrible frock? Loan shark. Employs her two sons to beat the shit out of people who don't pay.'

'Tell me—'

'Wait, there's plenty more. Young fella in the black T-shirt, double sleeve tattoos?' Mulligan paused. 'Go on, guess.'

Caelan set her jaw. 'Unless you're going to give me some names, I'm not playing.'

'Go on.' He bounced in his seat. 'Pretty-boy looks, Gucci loafers?'

She looked at the man, scrolling on his phone. 'No idea.'

'Con artist. He cosies up to lonely middle-aged women – and men – and they buy him anything he wants, take him on holiday, you name it. Then when he's bled them dry or he's had enough, he changes his mobile number and fucks off into the sunset.' Mulligan looked gleeful.

'You sound as though you approve,' Caelan said.

'I admire his…' He paused, searching for the right word. 'His guile. His initiative. Anyone who can fool people like that—'

'Yeah, very impressive.' Caelan got to her feet.

'You should go into that line yourself,' Mulligan told her. 'Jolene's an expert—' He caught himself and closed his mouth. Caelan smiled.

'Interesting. Maybe I'll have a chat to her about it. Where did you say Reuben Nash's office was?'

He stared at her. 'I didn't, and I wouldn't advise you to go looking for it.'

'He offered me a coffee, didn't he?'

Ewan was frowning, but again he didn't protest.

Caelan walked away, conscious of their eyes on her back.

9.37 p.m.

Lucy Mulligan lay in darkness. Her head thumped, her elbow throbbing where she'd smacked it on the door of the van they'd bundled her into. She had no idea where she was, or what would happen next. Rolling onto her side, she reached for one of the bottles of water she'd found in the room and drank. She felt sick, worry and fear combining, meaning her stomach was causing her as much discomfort as her head.

Restless, she put down the bottle and stood, pacing over to the door. It was locked – she'd checked several times. She had no idea who might be out there, who could be waiting for her, and she knew that trying to leave this place was impossible. She was alone here, unable to contact her friends, or her brother.

Turning from the door, she clenched her fists. James. James and his schemes. She had promised herself – and her mother when she'd been well enough to take an interest – that she would never set foot in her brother's world. Now, though, it seemed she had been dragged into it against her will.

A door slammed, and she heard voices in the room next door. Male voices. She froze, pressing her back against the wall. Who were they?

And more importantly, why were they here?

12

As she had done the previous evening, Caelan made a slow circuit of the nightclub. It wasn't as busy as Stand had been, and it was easier to move around. There was only one bar, and a dance floor with a metal staircase, blue paint flaking from it, leading to an upper floor half the size of the one beneath. She trotted up the stairs, reasoning that Reuben Nash's office was most likely to be up there, out of the way. She paused at the top, looking down on the DJ sitting in an enclosed glass booth at one corner of the dance floor. Nathan Nash stood beside it, arms still crossed, looking like he'd rather be somewhere else. Caelan knew the feeling. She turned, narrowly avoiding being barged to the ground by a staggering young woman. She hiccuped an apology as Caelan moved past her.

There were several scruffy red leather sofas placed at intervals along the walls, as well as chairs and tables, mostly occupied. Caelan saw Mulligan's friend Jolene on a sofa in the corner, her legs draped across the lap of the man she was with. As Caelan passed, Jolene locked eyes with her, a challenge in her gaze. Remembering what Mulligan had almost said about her, Caelan kept walking. Maybe the man was the latest in a long line of victims she had conned, maybe he wasn't. It was not Caelan's concern.

There was a door set into the furthest wall, marked *Private*. Caelan smiled to herself and tried the handle.

Locked.

Instantly she moved away, turning so her back was against the wall, scanning her surroundings to see if anyone had spotted her.

No one seemed to have even glanced in her direction, but she moved away, deciding to go back down to Ewan and Mulligan.

Then Nathan Nash appeared at the top of the stairs.

He strode towards her, his face thunderous. She stood her ground, hoping he was heading for someone else.

No such luck. He stood in front of her, hands on hips, preventing her from moving away from the wall. His shoulders and chest were heavily muscled, his hands huge. Caelan had been well trained in the art of defending herself, both fairly and outside the rules, but Nash looked as though he would take some beating. He stared down at her, enjoying the fact that he was so much bigger, no doubt expecting her to be intimidated.

No chance. Caelan knew she couldn't give an inch.

'Can I help you?' she said.

He gave a slow, sardonic, unsettling smile. 'I was going to ask you the same question.'

'Well, one of us should answer, otherwise we'll be here all night.'

His eyes narrowed. 'I own this place, and you've just been trying the door of my office. You want to explain why?'

'I was looking for your brother.'

That surprised him. 'You know who I am?'

'I'm here with James Mulligan. He pointed you out.'

Nash chuckled. 'Bet he did.'

She wasn't going to ask him what he meant. 'I thought Reuben owned the place,' she said. 'Doesn't that make this *his* office?'

'We're partners, not that it's any of your business.'

'Equal partners?'

His fists clenched. 'Straight down the middle.'

Raw nerve, Caelan thought. 'I've met your brother already, and he thinks we might be able to help each other.'

'Yeah?' He looked unimpressed. 'How?'

'You better check with him. He didn't tell me.'

Nash tipped his head to the side. 'Who are you?'

'Like I said, I'm here with James Mulligan. He's my cousin, and I'm here to help with his business while he recovers from his operation.'

That amused him. 'Operation? When he got shot in the arse, you mean?'

Caelan put her nose in the air. 'I think you'll find it was his thigh.'

A silence. Nash leant closer. 'Shame the bullet didn't hit him between the eyes.'

She looked up at him, hoping she appeared calculating. 'You're not the first to say it.'

Nash's lips twitched. 'Not his biggest fan either?'

'I walked away from a successful business up in Scotland to come down here and help James out. He told me he was doing well, that I could make a fortune, but he owes money and it seems he's nowhere near as successful as he told me. I'm wondering if I've made a mistake.'

Nash lifted his shoulders then let them fall. 'Why are you telling me?'

'Because your brother told me James is a disaster. I'm wondering if it might be worth my while making some contacts of my own.' Caelan waited. She was playing a dangerous game, and if Mulligan could hear her, he would be furious. The problem was, no one seemed to be taking him seriously. If she was going to find anything out worth knowing, she might have to bypass Mulligan, or get rid of him altogether. Send him back to Belmarsh and forget about him. Do the job on her own.

Nash appeared to be considering her words. 'We don't know you,' he said finally.

'Maybe that's why your brother suggested we have coffee, a chat.'

'I doubt he meant tonight.'

Caelan tried a smile. 'No time like the present.'

His face closed. 'We're working. The place is heaving, same as every night.'

'I can see that. How many people do you employ?'

He hesitated, and she guessed he was torn between telling her to mind her own business and boasting about how well he and his brother were doing.

'Officially, around fifteen,' he said.

'Right. And unofficially?'

His face darkened. 'What is this, twenty questions? Why do you want to know?'

She held up her hands. 'Hey, calm down. I'm just making conversation.'

'Yeah, well it feels more like you're fishing for information.'

'Maybe I am.' She folded her arms. 'I want to know if having a meeting with your brother is going to be worth my while.'

Nash's eyes bulged, and for a second Caelan thought she had gone too far. She'd belittled Nathan Nash himself, his brother Reuben and their business in one sentence. She waited, watching as Nash visibly brought himself under control. When he spoke again, his voice was low, his aggression reined in, but only just.

'You're a cheeky bitch, you know that? If I were you, I'd turn around and walk away now. You think you can march into our club, our city, and start dictating what's going to happen? If we want to do business with you, we'll let you know. It's not up to you to pick and choose.'

Caelan uncrossed her arms, put a hand on her hip. 'You think? Here comes the man who makes the decisions.'

Nash spun around to see his brother approaching. Reuben flashed Caelan a grin.

'Can I get you a drink?' he said.

Nathan started spluttering. 'You know what I caught her doing?' he demanded.

Reuben shrugged. 'Dancing? Enjoying herself?'

'Trying to get into the office.'

'I tried the door, yeah,' Caelan said. 'It says "Private", and I thought there must be a corridor, more than one room. If the

127

door leads straight into your office, then I apologise. Of course, I'd never walk in without your permission.'

'Gave it a go, though, didn't you?' Nathan snarled.

'She's already said she tried the door, Nath.' Reuben tried to slip an arm around his brother's shoulder, but Nathan pushed him away. 'Why don't you let me handle this?'

'Handle it? Fucking handle it? You've never heard of her before tonight, never met her, and you want to talk business? She's related to James Mulligan. That should be all you need to know.'

Reuben scowled, moving close to his brother. 'I think you're overstepping the mark here, don't you?'

'Fuck off.'

'Why don't you go and collect some glasses or something?'

'You're a prick,' Nathan snarled at him.

Reuben smiled. 'Takes one to know one. Now get the fuck out of my sight.'

It looked like Nathan might argue, but in the end, throwing Caelan another furious glance, he marched away. Reuben looked at her, seemingly amused, then pulled a key from his pocket and held it up. 'Shall we?'

–

'I've owned the place for three years,' he told her once they were sitting down with cups of coffee. The office was windowless, about sixteen feet square, with a desk and chair at one end and a couple of sofas, a low table and a complicated coffee machine on a wooden cabinet at the other. The walls were painted a light grey, with black and white canvases of city skylines and landmarks hanging at intervals along them – the Eiffel Tower, the Empire State Building, Tower Bridge. There was a second door leading off the room, and Caelan wondered what was through it. A cash office, perhaps? There must be a safe somewhere. A place like this would no doubt only accept cash payments. She made a point of not studying the door, which was timber-clad and ordinary-looking, though she was willing to bet it had a steel core and frame as well as a six-point locking system at least. No doubt Ewan and Mulligan were wondering where she was, Ewan at least probably worrying, but the chance to talk to Nash privately was too good to pass up.

'It was a dump when I first bought it,' Reuben Nash was saying. He sipped his coffee, watching her over the rim of the cup. 'You're probably thinking I haven't improved it much.'

'Your brother gave me the impression you and he were business partners,' Caelan said. 'Is that not the case?'

Nash chuckled. 'Well, we are in a sense. Nathan spent years in the army. When he left, he didn't know what to do with himself. He had some savings, so I offered him a role in my business, let him invest a bit of money so he didn't feel like a charity case. But equal partners?' He took another mouthful of coffee and shook his head. 'No.'

'What's his role?'

'His role? You're taking quite an interest in my brother. Isn't your boyfriend downstairs?'

Caelan smiled. 'I'm trying to get an understanding of how things work around here, that's all. And I'm pretty sure your brother hates me.'

'He's cautious, maybe even paranoid. He doesn't like change or taking risks.'

'And I represent both?'

'Not in my view.'

Nash's tone hadn't changed, but his expression had. There was a veiled threat in his words and in his eyes, like a fox approaching a chicken coop. The chickens might feel safe behind the wire, but the fox knew it was an illusion, that it could break in and destroy them any time he wanted. Caelan realised she couldn't afford to underestimate this man. Stefan Harris had been brash, upfront, boasting about how he made his living. Reuben Nash was reserved, courteous and no doubt much more dangerous.

'I suppose being in the army would teach you to be cautious,' she said. She tasted the coffee. 'This is delicious.'

'It should be, it's stupidly expensive.' Nash gave a slow smile, and again Caelan felt a flicker of unease. 'Most people only get the supermarket own-brand stuff, but I'm willing to make an exception tonight.' He set his mug on the table between them and leant back, crossing his legs. 'Now, can we talk about you?'

Ignoring the tiny voice in her head telling her to run, Caelan said, 'Of course.'

'Cards on the table,' Nash said. 'I know Mulligan's a drug dealer, so I'm guessing that's your business too?'

'It's a safe assumption.' She was going to be cautious, because in this situation, Victoria Smith would be. Also, she guessed Nash would be expecting it.

'Anything else?' he asked.

'How do you mean?'

He exhaled sharply. 'Come on. There are lots of different ways of making money.'

'True. Why don't you tell me how you make yours?' She waved a hand. 'Other than this place, I mean.'

'I'm a businessman. That's all you need to know.'

'You said we could help each other.'

'The way I see it, you're new to London, wanting in on what happens around here. I can help, introduce you to people, put in a good word, but I'll need something in return.'

Caelan's stomach clenched, but there was no sign of fear in her voice. 'Oh really? What?'

He smirked. 'I haven't decided yet.'

She put down her cup and got to her feet. 'Well, get back to me when you've had a think about it. I'm a busy woman.'

In two steps he was beside her, using his height as his brother had to try to intimidate her. He didn't touch her, because he didn't need to. Caelan stood her ground, staring into his face.

'What can you offer me?' His expression made the insinuation clear.

'I need to make some money, and quickly.'

He inclined his head. 'Can I ask why?'

'His name's Stefan Harris.'

She saw the rage in Nash's expression before he controlled himself and shut it away.

'Let me guess. Mulligan,' was all he said.

Caelan nodded. 'And since James can't pay, Harris is expecting me to.'

Nash moved away, hands in his trouser pockets. 'But you don't have the money.'

'Or the inclination to bail James out.'

'Guess you're fucked, then.' Nash didn't sound overly concerned.

'Unless…'

'Unless?'

She raised her eyebrows. 'Someone gives me a chance to make some cash.'

He went to the door, held it open. 'Nice talking to you, Victoria. Give my regards to Stefan Harris.'

Caelan walked past him, chin up, not looking back. Let Nash think he'd scored a victory. She would find out what his game really was, and then she would destroy him.

13

Downstairs, Ewan was looking fretful, Mulligan furious. As Caelan slid back into the chair beside his, he turned on her.

'Well that was the longest piss in the history of the world.' He was jittery, eyes flitting around the room, his knee bouncing again.

She reached for the fresh bottle of beer on the table in front of her. 'What's happened?'

'Stefan Harris is here,' Ewan told her.

'He asked where you were,' Mulligan said. 'And we didn't know what to say. Harris doesn't like not getting an answer.'

'Poor thing.' She glanced around. 'Where is he?'

As she spoke, the crowd around the bar shifted and parted, and she saw Harris. He wore a white T-shirt and jeans and was looking at his drink as though there was something unpleasant floating in it. The same two men were with him, each with a pint in his hand. Harris said something and both started laughing.

'Fucking sycophants,' Mulligan said.

Harris spotted them and raised his glass in a mock toast. Mulligan groaned.

'He's coming over.'

'So?' Caelan sat back.

'We don't have his money.'

'He gave us forty-eight hours, remember?'

Mulligan squirmed. 'You think he plays fair?'

Caelan sighed. 'Fine. I'll talk to him.'

'Vic—' Ewan began to say. Caelan smiled at him.

'It's fine. What can he do?'

'Tear you to fucking shreds,' Mulligan muttered.

Caelan was already on her feet, Harris smirking as she approached.

'Here she is, the woman who's going to bring me my fifteen grand. In less than…' he made a show of checking his watch, 'one day.'

His companions chortled, and Caelan nodded at them.

'Evening, all. Not brought your walking punchbag with you tonight, Stefan?'

Instantly his face changed. 'What?'

Caelan continued as though he hadn't spoken. 'Would you like the cash delivered to your home, or somewhere else?'

Harris shifted position, aware that people around them were listening. 'Wherever you like, sweetheart. As long as I get the money, who cares.' He leered at her. 'And dress yourself up a little, yeah? We could go out. I'll treat you to dinner.'

She smiled. 'If every other person in the world dies between now and then, and I've no other option, maybe.'

Furious, Harris opened his mouth to scream at her, then seemed to reconsider. He forced a smile, though his eyes burned. 'You're funny. I'm sure you'll still be laughing when you can't pay and my boys here come to take whatever they like as compensation.'

'You're terrifying, you know that? Not quite as terrifying as your boys, but scary all the same.' Caelan made to turn away, but Harris grabbed her arm, as she had intended. Before she could react, she felt him being dragged away from her. Two of the bouncers had him by the arms, holding him still as he struggled. His friends hovered nearby, confusion clear on their faces, unsure whether to wade in and help their boss or to stay out of it and hope for the best. Three more bouncers arrived, faces set. They stopped nearby and waited. Reuben Nash stood watching, arms folded, his face impassive.

'You're not welcome here, Stefan,' he said.

The music was still playing, but everyone in the place had fallen silent, moving closer to see what was happening.

Harris stopped struggling and sneered at Nash. 'What are you going to do, bar me? That'd be a mistake.'

The bouncers holding him yanked his arms back as he tried to break free, their eyes on Nash, waiting for instructions. Nash chuckled.

'I think that's my decision, don't you?'

'And mine.' Nathan Nash had pushed his way through the crowd and strode over to stand beside his brother.

Reuben didn't look at him. 'Let me deal with it.'

Harris gave a mocking laugh. 'You going to let him talk to you like that, Nathan? He treats you like a kid.'

Nathan's face was red, his shoulders tensing, but he said nothing. There was a crowd around them now, people jostling each other, muttering, a few laughs. Nathan turned to glare over his shoulder but kept his mouth closed, and Harris tried again.

'He's taking you for a mug, Nathan. How much does he pay you? Less than he does the barmaid he's shagging, I bet. Call yourself a partner? You're a fucking joke.'

Nathan pressed his lips together, and Caelan saw fury in his eyes. Snarling, he threw himself at Harris. A gasp went up from the crowd as his fist connected with the other man's jaw, the bouncers staggering, only just managing to keep Harris on his feet. The music had stopped now, and the main lights were coming on, while Reuben stood as though frozen.

Nathan went for Harris again, and Reuben came to life, yelling his brother's name, trying to grab his arm. Shaking him off, Nathan reached inside his jacket. Caelan recognised the glint of a blade before she registered the knife in Nathan's hand. Instinctively she shouted a warning. The bouncers had allowed Harris to slump to the floor and were moving away as quickly as they could. Caelan didn't blame them. People were scrambling clear of the scene, the bar staff huddled together in a corner, the DJ making a run for it.

Nathan's eyes were wild, his teeth bared. He grabbed the front of Harris's T-shirt, jammed the blade under his chin.

'You never did know when to keep your mouth shut, did you, Stefan?' He spoke calmly, as though he and Harris were chatting over a pint. Harris's eyes were wide, his face glistening under the lights. Caelan saw him swallow, the blade pressing against his Adam's apple.

'Let's calm down, shall we?' he managed to say. His jaw was swelling, bruising from the punch he'd received already visible.

'Funny how you can be polite now there's a knife at your throat.' Casually Nathan moved the blade, giggling as Harris squirmed. Caelan wondered whether he'd been sampling some of the wares on offer in the club.

'Come on, I was joking,' Harris choked out. 'Your brother's the one you want to be having words with.' He lifted his hands as though in surrender. 'Let me go, mate, and we'll say no more about it.'

'You've no respect, Harris, not for me, not for my brother. You'd be nothing if we hadn't helped you out.'

Caelan could see from Harris's face that he didn't agree, but he was trying to nod. 'Like I said, put the knife away. Let's have a drink.'

'A drink?' Nathan shook his head. He removed the knife, let go of Harris's T-shirt and stepped back, blinking as though he'd just woken up. Harris got to his feet, taking his time, trying hard to look as though nothing had happened.

Reuben turned to his brother. 'Finished?'

'Fucking right he has,' Harris said. He nodded to his men and, shamefaced, they moved towards him. Harris met Reuben's eyes, hawked, and spat on the floor. 'Not welcome here? I wouldn't piss on the place if it was on fire.'

He walked away, his men scurrying after him.

The place was close to empty, just a few people still gawping. Beside Caelan, Mulligan shifted.

'Let's get out of here,' he whispered. 'The police will be here next.'

Reuben turned away from his brother without a word and marched towards the stairs. Mulligan raised his voice.

'Might want to make yourself scarce, Nathan,' he said, cupping a hand around his ear. 'Reckon I can hear sirens.'

Nathan started. 'Shit,' he said. 'Shit.' He gazed around as though lost, making no move to leave. Mulligan walked over, gave him a gentle push.

'Go on, clear off. You're found with a knife, you'll be doing time. You'd better hope no one filmed what just happened.'

Nathan's eyes strayed up to the next floor. 'But I need to talk to—'

'You need to leave. Don't worry about Reuben. I'll talk to him.' Still Nathan lingered. 'I mean it, pal.' Mulligan jerked his head towards the exit. 'Get lost. You want to go inside again?'

Nathan shook his head, finally seeming to register what Mulligan was saying. He took off at a run, pushing past the last remaining punters, skittering over the dance floor, disappearing from view. Mulligan turned back to Caelan and Ewan.

'Daft bastard,' he said. He yawned, rolled his shoulders. 'Bedtime, I think.'

'What about Reuben?' Caelan said.

Mulligan glanced in the direction of the upstairs office. 'None of my business. They're always arguing about something; they'll sort it between them. Come on, I'm fancying a kebab.'

'Do you think anyone's really called the police?' Ewan asked as they made their way towards the door.

Mulligan sniffed. 'Not if they know what's good for them. Or they've no idea what sort of place this is. Most people would just forget they were here tonight.'

'The people you know might,' said Ewan.

Mulligan pulled a face. 'That hurts, it really does.'

As they reached the bar, the staff filed out from behind it and stood in a huddle. There were four of them, two male, two female, early twenties at the most. One of the men had cropped hair and a thick beard, the other sported carefully cultivated stubble and glasses with thick lenses. The women had both pulled their hair back into ponytails for work, one dark, one strawberry blonde. They looked uncomfortable.

'Has Reuben… Is he still here?' one of the men said. He glanced at his colleagues. 'It's just…'

'We haven't been paid,' the woman nearest Caelan told them. 'It's not closing time, but everyone's cleared out, so we don't know whether to leave or tidy up, or…' She shrugged. 'And yeah. We need our money.'

Mulligan nudged her. 'Don't expect many tips tonight, princess.'

She narrowed her eyes at him. 'Here's one for you. Don't call people that, you patronising prick.'

He laughed, delighted. 'Aye, fair enough.'

'So, is he still here?' the man demanded.

'Upstairs,' Caelan told them.

'You go, Megan,' the blonde woman said. 'He likes you.'

Megan screwed up her face. 'Doesn't mean I like him.'

'Still. He'll listen to you.'

With a glance towards Nash's office, Megan shook her head. 'I'm not going up there. He'll be in a terrible mood.'

'Doesn't it bother you?' Mulligan asked.

She looked down her nose at him. 'What do you mean?'

'Working in a place where there's just been a knife fight?'

'It was hardly a fight,' the man with the glasses said. 'Just Nathan losing it for a second. It happens.'

'I can think of safer ways to earn minimum wage,' Mulligan told them.

The four members of staff smirked at each other.

'Minimum wage. Right,' the bearded man said.

Mulligan looked at him. 'You mean Reuben's a little more generous? Pays you to keep your mouths shut, does he?'

More smirking.

'No comment,' said Megan.

Caelan exchanged a glance with Ewan.

'We're going home,' she told Mulligan. 'Are you staying?'

'Home? You mean the house you're staying in, which actually belongs to me?' Mulligan looked at the bartenders, waiting for a reaction. None came. 'I might as well. Looks like there'll be no more action in here tonight.'

Megan stepped forward.

'Do you know Reuben?' she asked, her eyes on Caelan.

Caelan remembered what Harris had said about Reuben's relationship with one of the bar staff. She scanned Megan's face, but saw no sign of anger or jealousy. 'I only met him tonight,' she said. 'Why?'

'I saw you talking to him and Nathan when I was collecting glasses. Just thought you might be able to go and have a word if you were mates, see what he wants us to do.'

'Sorry.'

Ewan nodded towards the stairs. 'You can ask him yourself.'

There was an immediate rush to be back behind the bar when their boss arrived. The blonde woman opened the glass-washer and began to load it, while the two men collected empties and handed them to her. Megan disappeared through a door at the back of the bar, reappearing with a crate of bottles. She began to restock one of the fridges.

'Are you scared of him, or trying to impress him?' Mulligan asked in an undertone. Megan scowled.

'Fuck off.'

Reuben looked relaxed, Caelan noted. He had removed his tie, untucked his shirt.

'How's it going, guys?' he called as he strolled up to the bar. The bearded man nodded.

'Yeah, fine.'

Reuben stood with his hands in his trouser pockets, watching them work. 'Listen, do a basic clear-down and then go home, yeah? I'll pay you until the end of your shift, but you don't need to stay.' He smiled. 'I think we've all had enough tonight.'

'We were just going ourselves, Reuben.' Mulligan smoothed his hair. 'See you around, pal.'

'Where did Nathan go?' Nash glanced around. 'Not after Harris, I hope?'

'Nah, I told him to make himself scarce,' Mulligan said. 'Thought the law might show up.'

Nash scowled. 'Let them come. We've nothing to hide.'

'Not now the building's empty, anyway.' Caelan flashed him a smile, and Nash frowned at her.

'Like I said, let them come.' He pulled his phone out of his pocket and stabbed at the screen. Holding it to his ear, he began to pace. 'Nathan? Call me back when you get this. Immediately, you understand? We need to talk.' He ended the call. 'Where the fuck is he?'

He sounded more irritated than concerned. Mulligan checked his watch.

'He's been gone ten minutes. Could be a few miles away by now.'

Nash's face darkened. 'Why did you tell him to go? He needed to stay and calm down, not run away.'

'You wanted him to wait around until the police got here? They'd send him down, you know that, with a knife involved.'

'Police? They wouldn't bother.' Nash spoke with confidence, and Caelan wondered why. It wasn't as though there were no witnesses to what had happened – there had been a couple of hundred people inside the club at least. Surely one of them would talk if questioned? They couldn't all have been up to something dodgy.

'No one will have seen anything, and Harris would hate police involvement as much as we would,' Nash was saying. 'Nathan knocked him on his arse. He won't want people to know that.'

'Loads of people saw Nathan go at him with the knife,' Caelan said. 'It only takes one of them to open their mouth.'

'They won't.' Nash's voice was cold, the threat clear. He meant no one would dare.

'You don't think it'll be all over Facebook and Twitter by now?'

Nash rounded on her. 'Harris had it coming. It was a fight, nothing that doesn't happen in most clubs any night of the week. No, Nathan shouldn't have pulled the knife, but Harris shouldn't have provoked him. He knows what Nathan's like.'

'And what is he like?' Caelan knew she was on dangerous ground, risking pushing Nash away for good, but she decided the woman she was pretending to be would want to know as much about the Nash brothers as she could if she was going to work with them.

'As you've seen tonight, he's got a temper. He won't let anyone disrespect our family and he won't be pushed around.' Nash's smile was cold, and Caelan could feel Mulligan shifting beside her.

'Except by you?' she couldn't help saying. Nash surprised her by laughing.

'Yeah, except by me. Like I told you upstairs he works for me, whatever he says.'

Mulligan cleared his throat. 'Vic, if we're going to find a taxi…'

Nash gave another chuckle. 'I see you can't wait to get out of here, Mulligan. What's wrong, had enough of the coppers lately? I told you, they won't come here.'

'Can you blame me?' Mulligan smiled weakly.

Heading for the door, Nash beckoned to them. 'Let's get you off the premises then.'

With a glance at each other, Caelan, Ewan and Mulligan trailed after him. Nash stood in front of the exit.

'Could I have your phone number, Victoria?' He glanced at Ewan. 'Purely for business purposes, of course.'

Caelan gave Ewan a look of her own. He stared at his feet, scowling, not wanting to say no, but obviously not happy either. Caelan pulled out the phone she'd been issued with.

'Give me yours and I'll send you a text,' she told Nash. 'Then you'll have mine.' She didn't want him to realise she didn't know the number. He dictated his own and moved away from the door.

'If you see Nathan out there sulking, send him in, will you?' he said as he turned away.

'Arsehole,' Mulligan muttered as he followed Caelan out, Ewan bringing up the rear again.

As she stepped into the alleyway, Caelan froze. Mulligan crashed into her back, Ewan stumbling into him. Mulligan swore.

'What the hell are you—'

'Shut up and stand still,' Caelan told him. Mulligan peered around her.

'Oh fuck,' he said softly.

Nathan Nash was dead.

He lay on his back, his eyes staring up at the sky, but the blood around his head told its own story. Caelan's stomach back-flipped and she closed her eyes for a second. This was a disaster. Had their presence here triggered it? She didn't see how, especially after Nathan's run-in with Harris, but it had to be considered. Was the perpetrator waiting outside? She glanced over her shoulder at Mulligan, trying to calm her thoughts and figure out the best course of action. She needed to keep him safe, but they also needed to remember who they were supposed to be. She couldn't be seen to be protecting him.

Ewan stared at the body, his face working. 'We need to call the police.'

'No, we don't,' Mulligan told him. 'We need to get out of here.'

Ewan grabbed his arms and held him. 'You're going nowhere.'

Mulligan squirmed. 'Don't tell me you've got a knife as well, big man?'

Caelan moved back towards the club. 'Someone needs to tell Reuben.' And Penrith, she thought.

'Shouldn't we phone the police first?' Ewan said again.

Caelan lowered her voice. 'I want to see Reuben's reaction,' she whispered.

Ewan's face was stern. 'I understand, but—'

'Okay, you know who to ring. You'll be kept on the phone otherwise. I'll go in and tell Reuben. Don't move, Mulligan,' she told him.

'Couldn't if I wanted to.' He tried to wrench away, but Ewan held firm.

'Give me three minutes, then come inside,' Caelan told Ewan. He nodded.

She took a breath and pushed back through the door. Inside, the bar staff were still busy. Reuben was sitting on a stool with a bottle of beer in his hand, scrolling on his phone. He turned as she walked towards him and smiled at her.

'Couldn't stay away?' Then, seeing her expression, he said, 'What?'

He was already on his feet when she reached him. The bar staff were watching while pretending to still be working. Reuben rounded on them. 'Get out, now, all of you. Go home. Finish this tomorrow.'

'They need to stay here for the time being,' Caelan said quickly. 'I need to speak to you privately.'

He tipped his head to the side, watching her. 'They need to stay? Why? What's going on?'

'Just… You need to know something.'

Nash shrugged. 'All right.' He looked at his staff. 'You lot, wait in the cellar for now.'

He watched them raise their eyebrows at each other, grab jackets and bags. 'Now!' he bellowed. They fled through the door at the back of the bar. Nash stepped closer to Caelan. 'Tell me.'

She met his eyes. 'It's your brother.'

He grabbed her wrist. 'Nathan? Where is he? Is he hurt?'·

Caelan shook him off. 'I'm so sorry, Reuben. We've just found his body. He's dead.'

He stared at her, his eyes wild. 'Dead? What are you talking about? He can't be. You're wrong, you must be.'

Ewan and Mulligan appeared, and Caelan shot Ewan a glance, hoping he would understand. He nodded, remained by the door, grabbed Mulligan's shoulder to prevent him moving. Mulligan looked at Nash and didn't protest.

'I'm sorry,' Caelan repeated. 'Your brother's dead, Reuben.'

'But…' Nash gave his head a violent shake. 'I don't believe you.' He turned towards the door. 'I want to see him.' Caelan tried to grab him, but he broke away from her, charging towards the door. Ewan intercepted him, held him tight, Mulligan seizing his other side as Nash fought and kicked.

'Let me go, you bastards,' he screamed.

Caelan raised her voice. 'We need to call the police, Reuben.'

He stopped struggling, raised his head, his eyes burning, his cheeks white. 'No. No police.'

'We've no choice. This isn't something you can deal with yourself.'

The look he gave her was a mixture of fury and resolve. 'Watch me,' he said. 'I know where Stefan Harris lives. I can finish this tonight.' He made another attempt to wrench himself free, screaming threats and abuse when Ewan and Mulligan held on.

Caelan took out her phone. 'I understand why you don't want them here, poking around your business, but we have to call them. Nathan's dead, and you need them to find the person who killed him.'

'I know who fucking killed him,' Nash spat. 'Let me go and I'll show you.'

'You don't know Harris was involved,' Caelan told him.

'Are you kidding me?' He gave a high-pitched laugh. 'Of course Harris did it. He hates us, even more so after Nathan kicked his arse tonight.' He made another attempt to tear himself free. 'Let me fucking go!'

'Have you anything on the premises you wouldn't want the police to find?' Caelan said. He didn't reply, and she raised her voice. 'Reuben. Listen to me. Is this place clean?'

'Clean as a fucking whistle,' he snarled. 'You think I'm stupid?'

'Then I'm making the call. The longer we leave it, the worse it's going to look. You'll be the first person they suspect anyway.'

Nash laughed again. 'Me? He was my brother. Why would I—' His voice broke. 'Let me see him.'

'You need to let the police deal with it,' Caelan said. 'You've no choice, Reuben.'

'Why are you so keen to call those bastards in?' he demanded. 'I thought you were a businesswoman. Why would you want them sniffing around?'

She sighed, making sure he heard her. 'I don't. None of us do, but we're talking about murder here, Reuben. This isn't petty theft or someone dealing on your patch. Your brother's dead.'

'So you say. How do I know you're not lying?'

Caelan didn't bother to answer him, and Nash let out a sound of frustration.

'Why won't you let me go out there? I need to see him for myself.'

'You can't go out there, Reuben. The police will need—'

'Fuck what the police need,' Nash screamed. He raised his foot, stamped on Mulligan's toes, then flung out a fist, catching Ewan between the legs. Both men crumpled, and Nash broke free, sprinting for the door again. Furious, Caelan ran after him, but he was already outside when she reached him, cradling his brother's body in his arms.

3.32 a.m.

The door opened without warning. Instantly Lucy was awake, scrambling away until her back hit the wall. A man stood there, filling the doorway. Instinctively she wrapped her arms around her body, making herself as small as possible as he stepped into the room and closed the door. Her heart hammered, her breathing fast and uncontrolled. Who the hell was he? Why was he here in the middle of the night? She could think of only one reason, and realised that lying down made her more vulnerable. As he turned to lock the door, moving quickly, she pushed herself to her feet.

'Who are you?' She heard hysteria in her voice and ran a hand across her mouth. 'Leave me alone.'

He didn't reply as he turned on the light. Lucy's hands covered her eyes, temporarily blinded after the hours she'd spent in darkness. She forced them down, blinking, ready to fight, but he hadn't moved. He was watching her, looking amused.

'Why are you here? What do you want?' Wildly she looked around for a weapon.

He smiled as he moved towards her.

14

'You know that between you, you completely buggered up the crime scene?' Ian Penrith said. He was wedged behind the desk in his office, Caelan and Ewan standing in front of him. They had been transported to Acton police station along with Mulligan, Reuben Nash and the four members of staff. Caelan and Ewan had then secretly been brought to see Penrith after giving statements at Acton as Victoria Smith and Owen Davison. He'd allowed them to shower and change into the clean clothes his operatives always kept in lockers near his office.

He picked up a paper bag from his desk and removed a croissant, taking a huge bite. 'You may as well sit down,' he said without looking at them. 'You've some explaining to do.'

Caelan sat, pulling out the chair beside her for Ewan. 'Come on, Ian. We didn't expect to trip over Nathan Nash when we left the club.'

'Even so. Once you'd realised he was lying there, one of you should have stayed outside to preserve the scene.' He pushed more croissant into his mouth.

'Difficult to do that without compromising our cover,' Caelan said. 'Most civilians would run from a dead body, not stand guard over it.'

'You could have improvised.'

He wasn't going to let them off the hook easily, Caelan saw. He was being unfair, but he wouldn't care.

'I wanted to tell Reuben Nash his brother was dead. I wanted to see his reaction,' she said.

Penrith grunted. 'As you've told me. But you knew other officers were on their way. And once you'd gone back in, Reuben should never have been able to get to the body.'

Caelan saw Ewan shuffle in his seat, blushing. 'That was my fault, sir,' he said.

Swallowing the last of his croissant, Penrith screwed up the paper bag and lobbed it towards the door, where it bounced on the rim of the bin and then nestled inside. 'I heard. Hit in the balls, I'm told.' He shook his head sorrowfully. 'Not good enough.'

Ewan's head dropped. Caelan said, 'Nash was hysterical, struggling and kicking. I doubt three men could have held him.'

'I'm not going to argue with you. You already know that the victim's brother crying over the body, holding it and having to be forced away could compromise the investigation. Forensics aren't happy.'

'It couldn't be helped.' Caelan wasn't going to apologise for something that had been out of her control. 'What do we know so far? When's the post-mortem?'

'You don't need to know. Come on, Caelan, this is basic stuff. You can't know any more than is reported in the news.'

'I'm guessing he died from the blow to his head?'

Penrith held up a warning finger. 'Nothing's been confirmed.'

'I can keep my mouth shut, Ian.'

He gave her a level stare. 'You're not going to be given the opportunity to do anything else, not yet anyway. And what about the fifteen thousand pounds?'

'What about it?'

'You think we've room in the budget to pay off drug debts?'

All at once, Caelan was exhausted. It was now 10.30 in the morning, and she and Ewan had been awake for over twenty-seven hours. 'What was I supposed to say? I'll have to talk to Harris, try to reason with him. I said we couldn't trust Mulligan. I think this whole operation is a waste of time and resources.

He's introduced us to a few people, but they all seem to regard him as a joke. I think he made himself sound more important than he actually is.'

Penrith looked thoughtful. 'You don't think he knows anything?'

'Not as much as we thought. Not as much as he pretended to.'

'You're saying he lied about how much he could help us so he'd receive a lesser sentence.'

'Is it such a surprise? He told you he never knew the names of the people who organised the people trafficking, said we needed to speak to his two assistants again.'

'Which we've done,' Penrith said.

'And?'

'They say the same as Mulligan – all done anonymously, burner phones, go-betweens, et cetera. They don't have any names to give us.'

'Convenient for them.'

'I think if they could have helped us, they would have. They think Mulligan's looking at life for murder. They've no loyalty to him now he's not paying them, and they know they're also looking at lengthy prison sentences.'

Caelan could believe it. Mulligan's men, Andri and Erdi, had been his employees, not his confidants or friends. They were mercenaries, paid to do the dirty work. She knew Penrith was right – if they'd been able to trade information to help themselves, they'd have done so in a second.

'Okay, so getting information from the brothers is a dead end. What about Ryan Glennister?'

Penrith picked at his lower lip. 'Who?'

'Come on, Ian, you know who I mean. He worked for Mulligan, one of his little helpers.'

'Isn't he in prison?'

'Why are you asking me questions you already know the answers to? Glennister was allowed to walk away. We got him into a rehab programme.'

'Did we?'

Caelan held back from throwing herself across the desk and throttling him. 'He might be able to help. I could try to track him down.'

'No.'

'Why not?'

Penrith shrugged bulky shoulders. 'From what Mulligan said, Glennister didn't know which way was up. Mulligan didn't confide in him, he used him. It's a dead end.'

She stared at him, not believing what she was hearing. 'You're taking Mulligan's word for it? Of course he'd say Ryan knew nothing, because he doesn't want us talking to him. We know Mulligan kept him sweet with crack, feeding it to him like you'd give treats to a dog. When I saw Ryan, he was barely conscious. If that happened regularly – and I've no doubt it did – Mulligan won't know how much he knows, and it'll be worrying him.'

Penrith seemed to be thinking it over. 'Glennister walked out of the rehab clinic without completing the programme.'

'Shit.' She was disappointed. She'd felt sorry for Ryan Glennister, made to dance like a puppet by Mulligan, who'd exploited the other man's addiction shamelessly. But then he'd been given a chance to start again, and it looked as though he'd turned his back on it.

'Feeling less sympathy for him now?' Penrith said, with a knowing look.

'No. Why was he allowed to leave the clinic?'

'They don't hold people prisoner. If someone wants to go, how can they stop them?'

She closed her eyes for a moment, seeing Glennister's vacant face. She had hauled him to safety during the incident where Mulligan had been shot. Mulligan himself had fired at two men, one of whom had died at the scene. Caelan was certain he would have killed Glennister too if he'd had the chance. 'Ryan should have been sectioned,' she said.

'That decision wasn't ours to make. When he was assessed, it was decided the rehab clinic was the best place for him. You know all this.'

'I still think he might be able to help us.'

'He was interviewed at the time, more than once. He didn't tell us anything. He's terrified of Mulligan.'

'As far as he knows, Mulligan's in prison.'

Penrith pressed his lips together. 'As I said, he left the clinic and he had no fixed address. He could be anywhere by now. Looking for him would be futile.'

Caelan didn't agree. 'How do you know he didn't finish the programme?'

Was Penrith blushing? She couldn't believe it.

'I... kept an eye on him.' He coughed, cleared his throat. 'When I heard we were considering sending you out with Mulligan, I mean.'

She laughed. 'For an undercover expert, you're a terrible liar. Don't tell me you were concerned about him?'

Penrith scowled. 'You and I were both concerned, but he made his own decision. Like I said, we'll never find him.'

'Can I at least try?'

He held up his hands, and she took the gesture as acquiescence, though she'd no idea where to start looking. No point worrying about that now. She decided it was time to change the subject.

'You told Mulligan he had one chance to give us information we could use, and he hasn't done it,' she said. 'He's introduced us to a barber, a con artist, two drug dealers and an ex-soldier who's now been murdered.' Caelan blew out her cheeks. 'Not a resounding success so far.'

'He must know more than he's told us,' Ewan said. Penrith and Caelan both looked at him. 'If he doesn't, why would someone bother to threaten his sister?'

Caelan nodded, returning her attention to Penrith. 'Have you found her?'

'No. We don't know where to look. The threats she received by text and email are untraceable. No one saw her leave her house; there are no useful CCTV cameras in the area. There's also no sign of any communication between her and this mysterious new boyfriend we were told about. We're still going through all the contacts on her phone in case she had his details stored under a different name, but so far everyone checks out.'

'That seems strange. Or suspicious,' she said. 'How else did they communicate, if not by phone?'

Penrith raised his eyebrows. 'Maybe they spoke face to face. I hear some people can still manage it.'

'He could be married,' Ewan suggested. 'Or her lecturer maybe – a relationship they need to keep quiet for some reason.'

'It's possible, but why would she tell her housemates about it if she needed it to be a secret?' Penrith said.

'Because they kept asking where she'd been and she wanted to give them a reason they'd believe?' Caelan replied.

'Meaning you think she was doing something else?' Penrith frowned. 'You're not going to come up with another of your wild theories, are you?'

'You mean the wild theories that have been proved right more often than not?' She grinned at him, and he gave her a tiny smile.

'They're the ones.'

'She's an intelligent woman, who I assume knows how to access all kinds of information. If I were in her position—'

'She's not you, Caelan,' Penrith said quickly.

'If I were in her position, I'd want to know what was going on. Why I was being threatened, who was behind the threats. Where the danger was coming from.'

'You would because of your job, your training. Most people would get into bed and pull the duvet over their head until it was safe.'

'Something else is going on here. We need to find out what it is.' She folded her arms.

'I *know*. We'll keep digging,' Penrith told her.

'What about her bank account? Debit and credit cards?'

'No recent activity.'

Caelan blinked. It wasn't looking good. 'Social media?'

Penrith spread his hands. 'So far, we've drawn another blank. She doesn't seem to have any accounts, at least none we've found.'

'A computer expert who doesn't use social media? Probably wise,' Caelan said.

'I didn't say she doesn't use them, I said we haven't found them.'

'Do you think the new boyfriend exists?'

'Who knows? But why would she lie about it?'

'Have the housemates been questioned again?' she asked.

He was nodding. 'They don't know any more than they've already told us.'

'Did they meet the boyfriend, or did Lucy just tell them about him?'

'They said he'd never been to the house. We're doing everything we can to find out more about him – speaking to students on her course, her parents... Nothing. It's early days though.'

She pursed her lips. 'Maybe I should talk to the housemates myself. I'm supposed to be a cousin of Lucy's, after all. I could go there, play the concerned relative.' She knew there wouldn't be much acting involved. The thought of anyone being held prisoner by the kind of people they were assuming were involved was unbearable.

'No,' said Penrith. 'You're not the only person on the force, Caelan. You need to trust that some of the rest of us also know what we're doing.'

'What harm could it do? The people Mulligan knows don't seem to conduct much business during the day. We wasted yesterday sitting around watching him play video games.'

'Badly,' added Ewan.

'Regardless, your brief is to integrate yourself with Mulligan's contacts, not his sister's student friends,' Penrith said.

Caelan tipped her head to one side. 'All right, Ian, where have you stashed her?'

Penrith's expression didn't alter. 'I've no idea where she is. I wish I had.'

He didn't move, didn't fidget. Watching his face, she had no idea if he was telling her the truth or not. 'Then like I said, we need to find her. Shouldn't that be more of a priority than going after Mulligan's cronies?'

'We're doing both. And now we also have a murder to investigate.' Penrith closed his eyes for a second as though weary, then seemed to perk up. 'Guess who's SIO?'

Caelan considered it. 'No idea.'

'Detective Chief Superintendent Adele Brady.' He gave a grim smile. 'Assisted by Tim Achebe and team, of course.'

Caelan had encountered Brady before. At first they hadn't known whether they could trust each other, though they had got the job done. Even so, she knew she would need to be on her toes. 'Brady's okay.'

'There's a ringing endorsement.' Penrith checked his watch. 'What are your plans for the rest of the day?'

'Depends what you're going to do with Mulligan.'

'I think I'll have another chat with him.'

Caelan cleared her throat. 'I was thinking…'

Penrith gave her a sharp glance. 'Well?'

'Do we need him anymore? Like I said, he's introduced us to small-time criminals, and even they think he's pathetic. Stefan Harris and Reuben Nash seem to be the biggest players, but they're drug dealers, not people traffickers.'

'You've decided that after two days?' Penrith pulled a face. 'They're not going to broadcast the fact that they're bringing people here and forcing them into slavery, are they? Not to someone they've known for a few hours.'

'No, but—'

He frowned at her. 'I think you're already impatient because you don't want to do this. You haven't believed in the operation from the start.'

Her laugh was scornful. 'You blackmailed me into—'

'Blackmailed?' Penrith let out a guffaw, and she glared at him.

'You used the threats made to Lucy, whether they were genuine or not, to persuade me to do this job, just like you tried to use them to change Mulligan's mind.'

Penrith leant forward. 'And your point?'

'I've already made it. We need to find her, because if we don't do it quickly, she won't be alive when we finally do.'

Now he looked pained. 'Don't you think I'm aware of that?'

'Then let me go and talk to the housemates, the friends, anyone. Mulligan can come with us; Ewan will keep an eye on him.'

Penrith snorted. 'Yes, that's obviously his area of expertise.'

Ewan blushed again, and Caelan scowled at Penrith.

'And if Mulligan is seen to be poking around, searching for his sister, it might bring the person who snatched her out of the woodwork,' she said.

'Or they might kill her.'

'They've no reason to. The threats were about him grassing to the police, and as far as they know, he's said nothing. Trying to find her himself is different.'

'Maybe.' Penrith clicked his tongue against his teeth a few times, thinking it over. 'Let me speak to Adele Brady.'

'Why? This has nothing to do with the murder of Nathan Nash.'

'As far as we know. Anyway, she's going to need you to talk to the people Mulligan's introduced you to so far, the ones who knew Nash. Maybe they'll be more open with you than they would with us.'

Caelan had to admit it made sense. 'What about the three people who were murdered? Is there any progress?'

'Not as far as I know, but that's not your concern.'

'Not my concern? After you used their deaths to persuade me to do this?'

He held up a finger, infuriating her. He made her feel as though she was always trying to catch him up, like a child struggling to keep pace with a parent.

'That wasn't my intention,' he said. 'Your role is to stick close to Mulligan.'

'I'm a bodyguard now?'

'No need for that. Mulligan would be dead by now if someone wanted him to be. The attack on his house would have been the perfect opportunity.'

Especially as I went charging outside and left him in the house, Caelan thought. She was glad Penrith was unaware of the full details of what had happened, knowing there had been mistakes on her part. Maybe he was right, and she wasn't as invested as she had been in past operations, despite the three murders and Lucy Mulligan's disappearance. The thought sickened her, guilt and anger at herself pushing their way to the surface. She was a hypocrite. All right, she would never sell information to criminals, but she knew her actions could have put Mulligan at risk.

All the more reason for her to push for more involvement, but she knew she'd have to tread carefully. Penrith was no fool.

'Can't I speak to Brady myself? Find out what she wants me to ask Harris and the others?'

Penrith narrowed his eyes. 'You're asking for orders? What are you up to?'

Nowhere near careful enough, then. 'Nothing,' she said.

'Which in my experience always means something, especially with you. You don't need to be told what to ask, Caelan. It's a murder investigation. You ask them the same questions you'd ask if you weren't undercover, but in a subtle way that won't get you killed.' He gave her a hard stare. 'As you already know.'

She met his eyes, didn't look away. 'I just want to help.'

'Your priority is speaking to Mulligan's friends. Nathan Nash's murder is a complication, but it might actually help us. We need to have a good look at his life, his friends and enemies, his past and his business activities.'

'You'll want me to talk to his brother, then,' Caelan said, not relishing the prospect. She remembered Reuben Nash falling to his knees beside Nathan's body, desperately searching for a pulse, and his guttural howl of grief when he was unable to find one. Penrith was right: he should never have been allowed near the scene. Caelan knew he would be a suspect, top of the list. If he had killed his brother, any traces he might have left while doing so could now be explained away by a defence lawyer because he had come into contact with the body after death.

'But we didn't see Reuben leave his office,' Ewan said. 'He would have had to walk past us to get outside, unless there's an exit we don't know about.' He glanced at Caelan. 'Would he even have had enough time to get outside, attack Nathan and then come back in?'

It was a point she had been going to raise herself, but as Ewan had been speaking, she had realised something else. 'Did you see him go upstairs?' she asked.

Ewan looked confused. 'Sorry?'

'Reuben. Once Harris left, he went storming off towards the stairs. I assumed he'd gone up to his office, but I was watching Nathan, listening to Mulligan telling him to make a run for it. I didn't actually see Reuben go upstairs.'

Ewan's eyes were wide. 'Now you mention it, me neither.'

'He could have gone through one of the fire doors, met his brother outside and killed him.' Caelan frowned, thinking it through. Penrith stayed quiet, though she knew he would be absorbing everything they said.

'We need to check with Mulligan. He might have seen where Reuben went,' she said.

'I doubt it,' said Ewan. 'He was too busy telling Nathan what to do. Anyway, Reuben must have been in his office. We saw him come down from the floor above.'

'I only saw him at the bottom of the stairs,' Caelan said. 'Did you see him walking down them?'

Ewan shook his head. 'When I looked over, he was there.' He paused. 'You don't think he went up there at all? He would've been taking a hell of a risk.'

'Looking at the body, I think Nathan fell and hit his head. Whether he was pushed or punched is another matter.' Reuben could have shoved his brother, not meaning to really hurt him. It was possible.

'But how would he have known Nathan was going to leave the club? He only went because Mulligan told him to. He looked like he was in a daze, like he was shocked by what he'd done,' Ewan said. 'Isn't it more likely Stefan Harris was waiting for him outside?'

'Probably,' Caelan said. 'But Nathan hadn't taken much of a beating before he died, as far as I could see.'

'Which is why we wait for the post-mortem.' Penrith glanced at her. 'It's taking place this afternoon.'

'Thank you,' she said.

He held up his hands. 'I accept you might have a point about speaking to Lucy's housemates. Go to the house, see if any of them are around. Remember you're her cousin, without access to any of the information you'd have as a police officer. I don't want Mulligan anywhere near them. He can stay at Acton until I decide what to do with him. I'll let you know.'

'And you'll speak to Brady?'

He scribbled on a piece of paper and pushed it across the desk. On it was scrawled an address in Camden. He made a 'go away' gesture with his hands. 'If I can. She's no doubt fairly busy, with the murder case and all. Probably won't be happy about being bothered.'

'I want to help.'

He didn't reply, just folded his arms.

Caelan picked up the address and pushed back her chair, Ewan doing the same. 'You want us to report back here?'

'If I could trouble you.' Penrith was already stabbing at the screen of his phone, but Caelan hadn't finished. She had irritated him already, why not go for broke? She had concerns, and he was her supervisor, or had been. Who else could she go to?

'The timing of all this, though…' She thought back to what Mulligan had said when she'd first spoken to him in the cell at Enfield: that there were officers who would sell what they knew.

Penrith's head snapped up, his eyes narrowing. He had accused Caelan of following her own wild theories before. 'What?'

'Mulligan's released from hospital and custody without charge, as he keeps telling everyone. His sister, who's already been threatened, disappears.' She shrugged. 'It's as though someone *did* know Mulligan had wangled himself a deal.'

'What are you suggesting?' Penrith spoke quietly, but there was no mistaking the steel. No officer liked a suggestion of corruption.

'Nothing.' She paused, as though thinking aloud. 'But sometimes information is shared that shouldn't be, whether by accident or not. You know that.'

'You think there's a leak? That whoever's threatening Mulligan and his sister is paying someone on the force for information?' He had both hands on the desk, palms down, as though he was going to vault over it.

Did she? Caelan found it as hard to accept as Penrith apparently did. 'I don't… No. I don't think so. But you have to admit, the timing's worrying. It's happened before.'

'That was different.' Penrith blew out a long breath. 'You can't make these accusations without evidence. I shouldn't need to tell you that.'

'It's not an accusation. It's a suggestion.'

'Do you have a suspect in mind?' He leant forward. 'The commissioner, perhaps? Adele Brady? Tim Achebe? Me?'

Caelan got up. 'I wanted to discuss this with you, but it seems you're not willing to listen. Forget it.'

Penrith waited for her to reach the door before he said, 'Caelan.'

Furious, she turned.

'I'll keep it in mind.'

15

There was a cafe on the corner of the road where Lucy Mulligan lived. Knowing that Ewan must be as exhausted as she was, Caelan suggested they make a quick stop for food.

'We can see the house from here,' she said quietly. 'We'll observe for a while.'

Ewan grinned as they headed towards it. 'We would still have stopped to observe if there hadn't been a coffee shop nearby?'

She laughed. 'This is London, of course there was going to be a coffee shop. Why don't you grab a table?'

He held open the door and she touched his cheek as she passed. They'd walked hand in hand since leaving the Tube, knowing that any of the people around them could be Lucy's housemates. Behaving like colleagues on the way to the house and then a couple once they arrived wasn't a good plan. Ewan smiled at her, and she remembered Mulligan teasing him about realising Caelan wasn't really his girlfriend. She felt a flicker of unease, hoping it had been nothing more than Mulligan trying to provoke a reaction. Anything else could affect the working relationship, the friendship she and Ewan were building, and she didn't want that. It wasn't easy to pretend to be closer than you were, or to give the impression of being colleagues and nothing more, as she and Nicky had learnt to. The lines sometimes blurred, for one person or the other. Occasionally both.

'Coffee and a bacon butty?' she said, making sure she spoke naturally.

'Read my mind.' Ewan shot her another smile and made for a table by the window, where they'd be able to see Lucy's house. The cafe was deserted, which suited their purposes.

Caelan turned to the counter, saw the woman behind it watching Ewan. She hid a smile as the woman blushed, realising she'd been caught staring at someone else's boyfriend. Caelan allowed a little frostiness into her tone as she asked for their breakfasts, as though unimpressed by what she'd seen. Still red-faced, the woman hurried towards the kitchen, muttering that someone would bring their order over.

Ewan was gazing out of the window, oblivious. As Caelan sat down, she murmured, 'You've got a fan over there.'

He looked across at the counter, then back at Caelan. 'What do you mean?'

She grinned at him. 'Never mind. Has anyone left the house?'

'No, but everyone living there's a student, so I'm guessing they're either in lectures or still in bed.'

'Lucky them.'

'And we could be wasting our time.'

'But we couldn't call ahead and check they were at home. Mulligan might have Lucy's address, but not the phone numbers of everyone who lives there.'

'Yeah, I know.' He brightened. 'Still, at least we're not stuck babysitting Mulligan again.'

'For a while, at least.'

'You really think trying to find out what he knows is point-less?'

Caelan lifted her shoulders. 'Do you? I think he's doing everything he can to stay out of prison. We know he lied about the scale of his business, and he didn't mention the money he owed. He's concerned about his sister, but not as much as he is about protecting himself.'

Ewan nodded. 'And he still won't give us any names.'

'None worth having, anyway.'

'Do you think he's too frightened to tell us what he really knows?'

Caelan thought back to Mulligan curled on the bed in the cell at Enfield police station, describing the torture he knew would be inflicted on him if the people he had been working with discovered he had betrayed them. Remembering his descriptions gave her an idea, and she was angry with herself for not thinking of it before. She resolved to mention it to Penrith when they were back in his office.

'Nathan Nash, though...' Ewan rubbed his chin. 'Surely Reuben wouldn't be stupid enough to kill him on their own doorstep, even if it was an accident? And Stefan Harris would be stupid to attack Nathan so soon after what happened in the club.'

'The Nash brothers are probably involved in all kinds of things we don't know about yet. There could be hundreds of suspects.'

Ewan screwed up his face. 'Do you think Penrith will talk to Detective Chief Superintendent Brady?'

Caelan saw a burly man in a chef's jacket and blue and white checked trousers emerge from the kitchen carrying a tray. He went to the coffee machine and poured two cups, scowling towards the kitchen as he grabbed a small milk jug from the cold cabinet. Caelan smiled to herself. Seemed Ewan's admirer wasn't brave enough to face them.

'I think he'll speak to her. Whether Brady will want us anywhere near her case is another matter.'

Ewan glanced at her. 'Us?'

She nudged him. 'We're a team, aren't we?'

He spotted the chef approaching and picked up the tomato ketchup. 'Definitely.'

–

The house where Lucy Mulligan lived was three storeys of red brick. It was well maintained, the black gate newly painted, blue ceramic planters filled with heathers standing guard at either side of the matching black front door. Ewan stepped back as Caelan knocked, looking up at the floors above.

'Not like any student house I've seen before,' he muttered.

Caelan had to agree. In the cafe, she'd had a look online at rooms being offered for rent in the area and guessed Lucy Mulligan would have to be forking out between seven and nine hundred pounds a month to live here, more if her room was en suite.

'How's she affording this place?' Ewan wondered. 'She's a postgraduate student, so she'll have been studying for years.'

'Student loans, I assume.'

'She'll be paying them back forever.'

'Isn't everyone?' Caelan knocked again, then put her ear to the door. Nothing. She squatted, poked her fingers into the letter box so she could hold it open and peer inside. She heard Ewan shuffling his feet and knew he was uncomfortable with what she was doing.

'Anything?' he asked.

She straightened. All she'd been able to see was a few pairs of shoes and a stretch of wooden flooring that needed washing. 'No.'

Hands on hips, she turned and surveyed the street, then stepped away from the house and looked at the upstairs windows.

'Curtains are closed up there,' she pointed out. 'I bet someone's at home but still asleep.'

'Or they just didn't open their curtains when they went out this morning. Or they're ignoring us.'

She nodded, acknowledging the point. 'This is stupid. Bloody Penrith, we could be waiting around for hours. He could have given us a couple of names, or some clue about who lives here.'

'Wouldn't that be against protocol?' Ewan said the word self-consciously, as though afraid she would laugh at him.

'So's looking through letter boxes. Anyway, Penrith's not above breaking the rules when he feels like it.' Caelan moved back towards the gate, hands in pockets, and glanced up the road, a plan forming. She grinned.

'How about using your charms, Ewan?'

–

There were more people in the cafe now, workers on early lunch breaks calling in for a sandwich or snack. Ewan waited behind two women wearing fleeces, work trousers and safety boots. They were chatting in a language he guessed was Polish, though he couldn't be sure. Despite travelling all over the world with the army, he could only speak English, some Welsh and a little half-remembered schoolboy French. The thought embarrassed him when he realised he could hear several different languages being spoken in this small cafe alone.

There were four people waiting in front of the women, plus another two behind Ewan. The place was full, and Ewan didn't see how he was going to be able to do what Caelan had asked.

Two suited men left the front of the queue, takeaway coffees in hand, and everyone shuffled forward. The woman who had taken Caelan's order was back behind the counter, joined now by a surly-looking teenage boy. He was on the till while she doled out the food, and they scrambled around each other to make drinks as needed. It looked a chaotic system, but it seemed to be working.

There was only one person in front of Ewan now, and he licked his lips, rehearsing in his head what he wanted to say. This was the part of the job he worried about, that made him nervous. It was all very well shadowing Caelan, staying a pace behind her and out of the action, but she had asked him to do this alone.

It was a fishing trip – they had no idea whether Lucy or her housemates had ever been in the cafe. Thinking back to his own days as a student, before he joined the army, he wouldn't have had the money to buy coffee on his way to college. Caelan had thought it worth a try, though, and there was a newsagent's shop further down the road she was going to check out too. In Ewan's opinion it was a long shot, but unless someone answered the door of Lucy's house, what else were they supposed to do? Now that Penrith had agreed to allow them to poke around, they had to make the most of the chance.

Ewan was in no hurry to go back to being Mulligan's child-minder. The bloke was stringing them along, he was sure of it. Caelan had told Penrith as much, and Ewan agreed with her. But a brick had been thrown through Mulligan's window, and his sister had apparently been snatched. Unless it was all part of an elaborate ruse Mulligan had dreamed up to delay his return to jail, there was someone else involved, someone skulking in the shadows. And now the murder of Nathan Nash had rattled Ewan more than he wanted to admit.

'Take your order?' The teenager on the till was staring at him, his hand poised over the order pad.

'Oh, a latte and a…' Ewan glanced up at the menu board, 'toasted teacake, please.'

'Eating in?'

He confirmed he was and handed over his money. Sitting back at the table where he'd waited for Caelan, he took out his phone, just any other customer. He had no real texts, no genuine emails, because this wasn't *his* phone. It belonged to Owen Davison, and everything on it was a lie. The phone numbers would ring but never connect, and the texts were sent by someone at headquarters. Ewan wanted to speak to his sister, to text Holly, a woman he'd been out with a few times recently. He'd explained he was going to be working away and she'd been miffed when he'd said he wouldn't be able to keep in touch. Like an idiot, he'd mentioned he was being partnered with a female officer, which had annoyed her all the more. He smiled to himself, knowing there was no chance of Caelan ever looking at him as anything other than a colleague. She didn't even seem to have friends.

He put the phone on the table, wondering if he had made the wrong decision when he joined the undercover unit. Already he was missing his family and friends, and his freedom. He was used to doing as he was told – you didn't last long in the army if you didn't – but constantly pretending to be someone else, thinking about every word and action, was taking its toll. Maybe this job wasn't for him.

He saw the woman from earlier heading his way with a tray and made eye contact. For now, Caelan was relying on him and he wasn't going to let her down.

'Still hungry?' the woman said as she set the mug and plate down in front of him.

He nodded, smiling at her. 'My girlfriend's gone to the newsagent's, so I thought I'd come back here.' He lifted his mug. 'Great coffee, and the service is pretty good too.' Shut up, Ewan, he thought, but she laughed.

'Don't let your other half hear you saying that.'

He gave an exaggerated eye roll. 'She's not happy. We've travelled across London to visit her cousin and she's not at home.'

The woman put a hand on her hip, leaning towards him. 'Selfish madam.'

'She lives down the road, though I'm guessing she doesn't come in here. She's a student, and you know how they're always pleading poverty. No money for cafes.'

He took a bite out of the teacake and waited.

'We do have a few students come in.' She pursed her lips. 'You hear them talking about uni as though no one's ever been before.' Her smile was sad. 'I wanted to be a nurse, but here I am.'

Ewan swallowed. 'I joined the army as soon as I could,' he said. 'Not my first choice, but when you need to earn some money...' He saw the teenager glaring from the counter as the queue grew even longer, and knew he had to hurry. 'Don't suppose you've seen her? Long auburn hair, green eyes?'

She was losing interest, conscious of the queue. 'There's a lot of student houses on this road, and we get hundreds of people in here, sweetheart. I'm sorry.'

'The students, do they come in for breakfast, or lunch?' He didn't even know why he was asking. She was backing away, frowning now.

'Breakfast, I think. Look, I need to get on.'

She hurried back to the counter, leaving Ewan red-faced and furious with himself. He felt like leaving but knew he would look even more suspicious if he did, so he took his time nibbling the teacake, sipping his coffee.

He definitely wasn't cut out for this.

Eventually he finished. He set the cup tidily on the plate and got to his feet. As he turned towards the door, he noticed a man sitting at a nearby table watching him. He was mid twenties, bearded, dressed casually in a hoody, jeans and a padded jacket. Ewan ignored him, kept moving towards the door.

Outside, drizzle was falling and he stopped to button his coat.

'Why were you asking about students?'

He turned, knowing who he would see. 'Sorry?'

The other man folded his arms. He was shorter than Ewan, and slim. No threat. 'You were asking questions about students,' he said. 'Seems a bit weird to me.'

Ewan stepped closer, remembering he was supposed to be a thug. 'Why do you care?'

'Because I'm looking out for my friends. And I'm two seconds away from calling the police.'

'Friends? You mean you're a student too?'

Blushing now, aware that he'd given himself away, the man pulled at his beard. 'What if I am?'

'Listen, mate, I'm not up to anything dodgy. We came here looking for my girlfriend's cousin. She's missing, you see.'

The other man blinked. 'That's not what you told the waitress.'

'You heard, then?' Ewan smiled. 'No, I didn't want to tell her any more than I had to.'

The man frowned, clearly wondering whether Ewan was telling the truth. 'Who is it you're looking for?'

'Why, is there more than one person missing from the area?' Ewan was trying to lighten the mood, but it didn't work. The other man just glared at him. 'All right, I'll be straight with you. We're looking for Lucy Mulligan.'

The man's head jerked up. 'Really? Then maybe we should talk.'

—

Caelan pushed open the door of the newsagent's. There was no one behind the counter, but a woman wearing a navy-blue tabard was stacking tins on the shelves in the next aisle. She turned around with an attempt at a smile, though her eyes were red-rimmed and she looked exhausted. Her face froze as she recognised her customer.

It was Mulligan's friend, Jolene Townsend.

Caelan stopped, hesitated. Jolene worked in a shop on the same street Mulligan's sister lived on? Why hadn't Mulligan mentioned it? Silently she answered her own question. Because he couldn't be trusted. To be fair, he hadn't known she and Ewan would be coming here, but still, it was a hell of a coincidence. Now she would need to think quickly. As far as she was aware, Mulligan was still at Acton police station, and if Jolene had heard what had happened, she might wonder why Caelan was already free to wander around London.

Jolene flicked her hair over her shoulder. 'What are you doing here? Did Mulligan send you?'

'Send me? No, why would he?'

'Thought he might be lying low after last night.' Jolene ran a hand over her eyes. There was something theatrical about the gesture, but Caelan suspected she was genuinely upset. 'Glad I wasn't there.'

'Why would James need to lie low? He wasn't involved.'

'No, but he needs to stay away from the police. They let him go, then he finds a dead body? Not ideal timing, is it?'

'Suppose not. When did you leave the club?'

Jolene narrowed her eyes as if she was going to ask why Caelan wanted to know. 'Soon after you saw me upstairs. I was with someone I... wanted to spend some time with.' She met Caelan's eyes. 'I'm told Nathan attacked Stefan Harris with a knife?'

'He punched him, then held the knife to his throat.'

'Shit. Do they think Stefan killed Nathan?'

'No idea,' Caelan said truthfully. 'Would you be surprised?'

'I'm surprised anyone would kill him right outside the club.'

'That doesn't answer my question.'

Another flick of the hair. 'Didn't realise I was under oath.'

Caelan held up her hands. 'Sorry. It was... Well, I've had better nights out.'

Jolene managed a grin. 'Welcome to Reuben's.' She pulled her phone out of her jeans pocket and glanced at the screen. 'What are you doing around here? Where's your boyfriend?'

'Gone to get us some coffee. I wanted to see where Lucy lives. I'm worried about her.'

Moving behind the counter, Jolene picked up a bottle of water and drank. 'Don't see what good looking at her house is going to do.'

'I was hoping to speak to her housemates, see what they can tell me.'

'Run off with her boyfriend, Mulligan told me.' Jolene sniffed. 'I don't understand what all the fuss is about. She'll be home when she's ready.'

Mulligan hadn't told Jolene about the threats Lucy had received then, or she was pretending he hadn't. He would have been instructed not to disclose anything relevant to his sister's disappearance, but that didn't mean he would have listened.

'Maybe,' was all Caelan said.

'Do you even know who her housemates are?'

'No,' Caelan had to admit. 'Do you?'

'Why would I?' Jolene's eyes flicked from right to left and Caelan moved closer to the counter, effectively penning her in. She was lying.

'They never come into the shop?' she pressed.

'Wouldn't know, would I? Since I don't know what they look like. Anyway, I only work three days. My uncle owns the place; he's here the rest of the week.' This time Jolene kept her eyes fixed on Caelan's. If she was a confidence trickster, as Mulligan had accidentally hinted, Caelan thought she'd be a successful one.

'James doesn't know either.'

'He tries to stay away from Lucy. They live in different worlds.'

'Does she know about his... business?'

Jolene drank more water. 'How should I know? I've never met her, and Mulligan doesn't talk about her much.'

The door opened again, and a man came in. He wore a baseball cap, kept his head down, the collar of his jacket turned up. Jolene glanced at him, then at Caelan.

'Look, are you going to buy anything? Because I'm busy.'

Caelan turned to look at the man, who was now shifting from foot to foot as he studied the display of crisps, his arms wrapped around his stomach. 'Think he's hungry,' she said.

A look of fury crossed Jolene's face, but she only said, 'Here's your boyfriend.'

Ewan appeared in the doorway. His mouth opened as he recognised Jolene, the look of confusion on his face almost comical.

'Hi, Owen,' Jolene said. She sneered at Caelan. 'Looks like he forgot your coffee.'

16

The student's name was Tom Haslam. Back at the house, he led them into the hallway Caelan had already seen through the letter box, and through into the kitchen. It was clean and tidy, the furnishing basic but functional. Caelan looked around.

'No huge piles of washing-up? Are you sure you're students?'

She was trying to put Haslam at ease, but when he didn't reply, she wondered if he'd felt patronised. Eventually he smiled. 'We're grown-up students. The place I lived as an undergraduate was a hovel compared to this. Tea?'

They both accepted and Haslam busied himself with kettle and cups. When his back was turned, Ewan sidled closer to Caelan, as though he was going to whisper a question. She guessed it was going to be about Jolene, but she had no answers to give. Gently she pushed him away.

'Not here,' she mouthed.

He held up his hands in apology, and she smiled at him as Haslam turned back, holding out mugs of strong tea.

The living room had the same feel as the kitchen – beige carpet, magnolia walls, IKEA furnishings. Haslam gestured towards the sofa and settled in one of the two armchairs, cradling his tea against his chest. He met Caelan's eyes.

'I'm told you're Lucy's cousin? I suppose I should have asked for some ID.' His hand went to his beard as he realised he had invited two strangers into his home.

'Maybe, but I'm not sure how I could prove I'm related.' Caelan smiled at him. 'I haven't brought my family tree.'

'I don't remember her mentioning you.' His expression wasn't hostile, but Caelan knew she'd have to work to get him to trust her. She decided to be as honest as possible.

'We've never actually met. I know her brother James, but not Lucy.'

Haslam stiffened. 'Why are you here then?'

'James wants to know where Lucy is, but he was injured recently. I said I'd come here instead, see what I could find out.' Caelan held his gaze. 'I'm worried.'

'Injured?' Haslam scoffed. 'Shot because he's a dodgy drug-dealing bastard, don't you mean? Does that mean you're a criminal too?'

Ewan shifted in his seat and Haslam gave him a wary glance.

'No, it means Lucy's family and I want to find her,' Caelan said.

'Yeah, well it's a little late for James to be concerned about her now.'

The bitterness in his voice surprised Caelan, and she hesitated. 'What do you mean?'

'Lucy told me about him one night. He'd sent her a text asking how she was, wanting to know if they could meet. She said she didn't want to see him, and I wondered why.' He snorted. 'Do you know Lucy's area of study?'

'Something about criminals and computers?' Caelan was deliberately vague, assuming a confused expression as if it was all too complicated for her.

Haslam nodded. 'Close enough. You can understand why she wanted to keep her distance.'

Caelan realised she would have to change her approach. Haslam was telling them nothing new.

'Were you around the day Lucy disappeared?' she asked.

Haslam's eyebrows went up.

'No. I missed her in the morning because I had to get to the library. Sometimes we have breakfast together...' He looked wistful. 'I got home around five, and she wasn't in. I thought nothing of it until a couple of police officers turned up at the front door.'

He spoke respectfully, Caelan noted; not saying 'coppers' or any of the other more offensive nicknames for the police.

'What did they say?' she asked.

'That they needed to speak to Lucy, and was she at home? I assumed something had happened, an accident involving a member of her family. When I went up to her room and knocked, there was no answer. Her door was ajar, not locked as it usually was when she was out. I called her name a few times, then looked inside.' He blinked as though remembering was painful for him. 'I saw straight away that something had happened. The room was a mess, and before you say it, not a student mess. It had been trashed.'

Caelan exchanged a glance with Ewan. 'Trashed? What do you mean?'

Haslam swallowed. 'Books thrown around, everything from the desk shoved onto the floor, the cushions from the bed chucked in a corner. A couple of photographs had been smashed, clothes and bedding everywhere. Lucy was tidy, she wouldn't have left it like that. I called down to the police officers and they came upstairs. They didn't go into the room but they had a look. One of them asked me to try calling Lucy. When I did, her phone rang inside her room. She hadn't taken it with her.'

'And then?'

He lifted his shoulders. 'Then they told me to go downstairs.'

And went into the room to retrieve the smashed photograph to show Penrith.

'Shit. This sounds... scary,' she said.

Haslam glared. 'You think so? Try having it happen in your home, to your friend.'

'Have you been in the room since? Can we go inside?'

'The police put some tape over the door. Someone came to do fingerprints or whatever a few hours later, but...' He shook his head. 'What I don't understand is why the police were here in the first place. They can't have known Lucy was missing – *we* didn't, and we live with her.'

How was she supposed to explain that one? 'Don't know. A tip-off, maybe?'

'From who? The people who took her?' He ran both hands over his cheeks. 'It's got to be because of her brother, something he's done. Pissed off the wrong people maybe.'

His words were too close to the truth for comfort.

'James doesn't seem to know anything about it,' Caelan told him. 'The police came to ask him when he last saw Lucy, and that was the first he'd heard.'

'Yeah, right. He wasn't going to say it's because of something he's mixed up in, was he?' Haslam made as though to stand. 'Where does he live? I'd like a word with him.'

Ewan looked him up and down. 'Shouldn't bother, mate, or you'll have me to answer to. Stay out of his way.'

'Why the fuck should I?' Haslam snapped. Ewan laughed, and Haslam subsided, red-faced, his expression furious.

'Was anyone else at home the day Lucy went missing?' Caelan asked.

Blinking, Haslam stared at her. 'No. All four of us were out all day. I don't know why Lucy was at home; she's usually at uni all day, even when she doesn't have lectures.'

Interesting, Caelan thought. 'She was committed to her studies then?'

Haslam's glance was scornful. 'She's doing an MSc. You have to be.'

'Didn't she ever relax, have some fun?'

'She…' Haslam paused, staring at the carpet. 'She told us she had a new boyfriend. She'd been spending a lot of time with him.'

And you hated it, Caelan realised. She sat forward, as though what Haslam was saying was new to her. 'What's his name? Do you have his number?'

'No. Lucy never brought him here. I know nothing about him.'

Except that he was where you want to be – close to Lucy. 'Is he a student too? Someone she met at uni?'

He slammed his empty cup down on the coffee table by his chair. 'I've already told you, I don't know.'

Caelan said nothing, waiting, hoping Haslam would fill the silence. He got to his feet.

'If you don't mind, I've an essay to write.'

The implication was clear, and Caelan doubted he could tell them much more in any case.

As they stood, they heard the front door open and close. Haslam tutted but didn't speak.

A young woman bounced into the room, a huge bag on her shoulder, blonde hair flying. 'Been making friends, Tom?' she said, her tone implying there was a first time for everything. Haslam turned away and stalked out of the room. The woman beamed.

'His manners don't improve.' She held out a hand. 'Liss Tucker. It's Felicity really, but,' she rolled her eyes, 'no thank you. Parents might as well have called me "had a pony and went to boarding school", don't you think?'

Caelan laughed, shaking her hand and introducing herself and Ewan. As Tucker seized Ewan's hand, she said, 'Don't mean to pry, but who are you? Can't be friends of Tom's, he doesn't have any, and we'll all die of old age before he thinks to introduce us.' She made an expectant face. 'So?'

Caelan introduced herself, then Ewan.

Tucker gaped at her. 'You're Lucy's cousin? I bet you're here to see where we've stashed her?'

'Something like that. The police have told her brother nothing and we're worried.'

'Understandable.' Tucker jerked her head towards the sofa they'd just vacated. 'Shall we sit?'

Caelan didn't move. 'You think you can help us?'

175

'Don't know yet. I'll try.' Tucker flung herself into the nearest armchair and crossed her legs. 'Now. Shame you spoke to Tom first. He's taken it personally.'

'Personally?'

'That Lucy's done a runner.' Tucker leant forward, lowered her voice. 'Jealous, you see. Furious.'

'I got the impression he might have… well, a crush. Feelings for her.' Caelan also spoke quietly as she retook her seat on the sofa.

'A crush?' Tucker snorted. 'An obsession, I'd call it. Always asking where she'd been, where she was going. If she made the mistake of telling him, he'd often turn up. Lucy was polite about it, but I know she found him creepy.' She grinned. 'The joys of house shares.'

'I assume he wasn't happy she had a new boyfriend?'

Tucker leant forward so far Caelan worried she might fall out of the chair. 'Shall I tell you a secret? I don't think she did. I think it was a ruse to put Tom off.'

'You're saying she lied about it? Really?' Considering they had found no trace on Lucy's phone of anything resembling romantic texts or messages, Tucker's words made sense. 'Did Lucy tell you that?'

Tucker shook her head. 'Not in so many words. But she didn't talk much about him, never brought him here. She was hardly at home, which made Tom cross, as you can imagine. When he asked where she was going, she said she'd met someone, they were going for a drink. Tom went purple, Lucy went out. I thought nothing of it, but when I asked her about it later, she wouldn't say a word.'

'Didn't you find that strange?'

'In a way, but it's really none of my business. Lucy and I live in the same house, we're friendly, polite, but we're not close. If she wanted me to keep my nose out, I respected that. I think even Tom became resigned to it.'

Caelan asked, 'When did she first tell you she'd met someone?'

Tucker thought about it. 'About three weeks ago? I can't remember exactly. Didn't she tell her brother about him?'

'No. They're... not close.' Caelan echoed Tucker's own words.

'Ah. Families.' Tucker gave a knowing nod. 'Bet she didn't mention the brick through her window, either.'

Again Caelan acted surprised. 'What? What do you mean?'

Tucker folded her hands in her lap. 'Now that was strange. My room's on the floor above, and one evening as I came down the stairs I saw Lucy leaving her room with a brick in her hands. I've seen many strange things during my time in shared houses, but never a pet brick.' She smiled, but Caelan could see she was concerned. Unlikely though it sounded, maybe Tucker hadn't considered a possible link between Lucy's disappearance and the brick through her window before. 'You don't think someone has taken her, do you? Against her will?'

'I don't know.'

Now Tucker looked stricken. 'I never imagined—'

'Not even when you heard Lucy's room had been trashed on the day she disappeared?' Caelan didn't mean to snap, but the young woman's jokey manner was beginning to grate.

Tucker stared. 'Trashed? What do you mean?'

Caelan realised Tom Haslam hadn't told her. He'd probably been advised by the police to keep his mouth shut. She repeated what Haslam had told them about the mess in Lucy's room.

'Did the police question you?' she asked.

Tucker nodded. 'Briefly. I couldn't tell them anything.'

'Did they ask about Lucy's boyfriend?'

'Yes, though as I've said, I had nothing to tell them, apart from a vague feeling she might have made him up.' Now Tucker looked ill.

'What did they say to that?'

'Nothing. They made notes, but...'

If Penrith was aware of this, he hadn't mentioned it. Caelan sat forward in her seat, forcing Tucker to meet her eyes. 'Is there anything else you can think of that might help us find her? As you can understand, we're extremely worried.'

'Of course, as am I now.' Tucker chewed on the inside of her cheek as she considered it. 'A man came to the house one day,' she said suddenly.

'A man? What man?' Caelan allowed some aggression into her voice. 'Who was he?'

Tucker shrank back. 'I don't know. I answered the door, and he asked if he could speak to Lucy.'

'Just "Lucy"? Or did he use her surname?' Caelan made it clear Victoria Smith was losing patience.

'No, I'm pretty certain he just said Lucy.' Tucker gave a few rapid blinks. 'As though her knew her, you know?'

'When was this?'

'A few weeks ago. Soon after she mentioned the new boyfriend. It wasn't him, though, I'm sure of it. He was…' She shook her head. 'No, he wasn't her boyfriend.'

'Then who was he? How can you be sure? Did he give a name?'

'No, and I didn't ask.' Tucker wrinkled her nose. 'He was filthy, smelt terrible. Not someone I would have assumed Lucy knew. She wasn't in, and he said he'd come back. I don't know if he ever did.'

Caelan thought she knew the identity of the visitor, though how he could be involved, she had no idea. She took out her phone and found James Mulligan's Facebook page, which was still active. Scrolling through his photographs, she found the one she wanted. The image showed Mulligan standing by a bar, toasting the camera with a glass of whisky. In the background another man lurked – scruffy, thin-faced. Caelan stood, shoved the phone under Tucker's nose.

'Is this the man who wanted to see Lucy?'

Tucker said, 'Just a second. Need my specs.'

She rummaged in her handbag, put on the glasses and peered at the screen. 'Yep.'

'You're sure?'

'Completely. I only spoke to him for a few seconds, but I felt I needed a shower afterwards. That's him, I'd swear it.'

'Did you mention this to the police?'

Tucker bowed her head. 'No. I'd forgotten about it.'

Caelan put the phone away.

Swear it? Tucker might have to.

17

Back on the street, Ewan made sure they were away from the house with no one near enough to overhear before he asked, 'Who was it?'

'Ryan Glennister.'

'The bloke who worked for Mulligan? The one he kept loyal by paying him in crack?'

'The one I just asked Penrith if we could track down, yeah.' There was no satisfaction in Caelan's voice, no sign she was pleased to have possibly been proved right, because she wasn't. Glennister's involvement raised more questions.

'Penrith didn't say no,' Ewan reminded her.

They stopped at the kerb, waiting to cross the road. The Underground station wasn't far, and Caelan was in a hurry to get back to headquarters.

'He didn't say yes either, which means if I pursue it, he's covered his own arse,' she said. 'He wouldn't have bothered before, when Beckett was in charge, but now he's leading the unit he seems to be playing the game.'

They scurried across the road, squeezing between a double-decker bus and a truck as the traffic came to a standstill.

'Why do you think Glennister went there?' Ewan asked as they reached the other side.

'I don't know, but I'm looking forward to asking Mulligan about it.' Caelan pulled her phone from her pocket and found the alias one of Penrith's numbers was under. He picked up immediately. 'Victoria.' He coughed. 'A pleasure.'

She noted his use of her cover name. 'Can you talk?'

A pause. Penrith was on the move. She heard a door close. 'Be sensible,' he said.

He meant, anyone could still be listening.

'Acton. Is he still there?' Caelan asked.

She could hear Penrith snuffling, but he didn't speak. There was some mumbling, then he said, 'For now. Is there a problem?'

'Possibly.'

Penrith grunted. 'What are you talking about?'

'The person we spoke about earlier, the one you told me I couldn't try to find? He was at our missing person's house recently.'

'You mean our addict friend?'

'That's the one.' Caelan shook her head at Penrith's choice of words.

'Bollocks,' he said.

'Exactly.' Caelan waited.

A sigh, long and heartfelt. 'All right, meet me at Acton. If I get the Tube, I'll be around forty minutes.'

Caelan considered the route they would need to take. 'Us too.'

'Can't wait.' Penrith was gone.

—

When they left the train at Acton Town station, Penrith was lurking outside, phone pressed to his ear, pacing up and down a short stretch of the pavement. He made no sign he had seen them and turned away as they passed.

'Keep walking?' Ewan said softly.

Caelan nodded, tucking her arm through his. 'It's not far.'

She could hear Penrith lumbering along behind them, still talking. She forced herself not to turn and look at him, but it wasn't easy. She wanted to slow their pace so she could overhear, but she knew he was too canny for that. Maybe he was organising a search for Ryan Glennister. She hadn't asked who was leading the investigation into Lucy's disappearance, but Penrith would want it done quietly, meaning he would be doing it himself, or leaving it in the hands of one of his own team. Since there were only three of them, and Caelan and Ewan were already operational, there was only one person left for the job.

'Richard fucking Adamson,' Caelan mumbled.

–

Mulligan was back behind a locked door, wearing prison-issue sweatshirt and jogging bottoms again. When Caelan peered inside, he was lying on the bunk in the same position as she had seen him in the cell at Enfield. The door was opened, and she stepped inside.

'Fancy seeing you here,' she said.

Mulligan turned his head. 'Where have you been?' He took in her jeans, T-shirt and coat. 'How come I have to wear prison pyjamas and you're all dressed up?'

Caelan smiled. 'These old things?'

'What do you want?' He sat up, crossing his legs, lounging against the cell wall as though he was back in his own living room. 'Who are you today, by the way?'

She took a quick pace towards him, surprised to see him flinch. 'Shut up and listen. Why would Ryan Glennister have been to your sister's house?'

His mouth opened, his eyes widening. 'What are you talking about?'

'It's a simple question.'

Now he was angry. 'The scrawny little fucker. If he's involved in her disappearance, I'll kill him.'

She ignored his bluster. 'Does he know Lucy? Have they met?'

Mulligan stood, running his hands through his hair. 'Not as far as I know. Why would I introduce Ryan to anyone? He's a liar and a thief, and he fucking reeks. Who told you he was there?'

'Doesn't matter. The point is, we know he was.'

'When?'

Caelan told him what little she knew. She and Penrith had agreed that he would need to be told the truth if they were going to find Glennister. Mulligan was agitated, striding around the tiny cell swearing to himself. Caelan moved back against the wall, arms folded, waiting for him to calm down.

'Why isn't he in prison, anyway?' Mulligan demanded. 'He steals – I've seen him with my own eyes.'

'Not to mention working for you – a drug dealer and people trafficker.'

Mulligan wagged a finger. 'You think I'd have involved Ryan in anything important? He's a crack addict. He'll do anything for drugs or money, and I mean anything. I wouldn't trust him to wipe his own arse.'

She nodded, acknowledging the point. 'Is it true he used to be a rent boy?'

'It's what I heard, but who knows? He worked for me sometimes, aye, but I didn't exactly ask for a CV or references.' Mulligan moved back to the bed, threw himself down. 'Wouldn't surprise me, though. Like I said, if it could earn him money for drugs, he'd do it.'

'Where can we find him?'

'Ryan? No idea. He never had a proper home, used to sleep wherever he fell.'

Caelan unfolded her arms, moved so she was standing over him. 'He was at your sister's house. If you didn't send him, who did?'

He looked up at her, jaw clenched. 'If you didn't send him? What are you implying?'

'Maybe you were trying to warn her, maybe you just wanted to see her. But maybe…' Caelan touched a finger to her lips, making a show of thinking it through, 'maybe you wanted to use her as bait, allow whoever's threatening you to take her. Giving her to them would have saved your skin, wouldn't it?'

As she had expected, Mulligan leapt from the bed and threw himself at her, fingers curled into claws as though he was going to rip out her throat. Caelan took a step to the side, watched him crash into the wall. As he spun around, she grabbed his arm and stuck out her leg, using the momentum of his body to twist him over her thigh and onto the floor. She kept hold of his wrist, forcing his arm up towards his shoulder blades, her knee in the small of his back. Mulligan cursed and struggled, but he couldn't throw her off. Unwittingly he had answered her question. Caelan eased the pressure on his wrist slightly, but not enough to allow him a chance to escape.

'I'm going to let go, but you need to listen to me. You didn't know Glennister had been there, did you?'

He snarled and bucked, flinging back his head, trying to smash it into Caelan's face. She was ready, moving well out of reach.

'James, stop. Listen to me. We're wasting time. I know you didn't send Glennister – your reaction just proved it. We need to find him.' She spoke softly, not knowing if he would respond. If not, he could stay here and they would look for Ryan Glennister without him.

Finally Mulligan lay still. 'How do you know it wasn't me? Not exactly known for telling the truth, am I?' He twisted his head, trying to look at her. Caelan released his arm and scrambled to her feet.

'No, but I can tell by now when you're lying to me.' She nodded towards the door. 'We all can. You had no idea Glennister was involved, you're not that good an actor.'

Dragging himself upright, Mulligan rubbed his arm. 'Aye, very clever. Do you have to be so aggressive about it?'

She smiled. 'That was defensive.'

Mulligan pouted. 'Felt aggressive to me. You don't know whether Ryan went to the house again, though, do you?

Once he'd heard Lucy wasn't in, he probably just ran back to whichever squat he'd come from.'

'He might not have needed to, if he was only asked to confirm whether Lucy lived there, whether she was at home.'

'But you said this was three weeks ago. What difference would it have made if they weren't going to grab her until now?'

Instead of answering his question, Caelan asked one of her own. 'I assume you were in Belmarsh three weeks ago?'

'Yeah, squeezed into what was built to be a single cell with another prisoner. He was going through heroin withdrawal, twitching and sweating, pacing like a bastard. Happy days.'

'Did you have the phone then?'

His look was sly. 'Why do you want to know?'

'Did anyone contact you? Threaten you? Give you any hint your sister would be hurt if you didn't keep your mouth closed?'

He was quiet for a moment. 'Who's out there listening?'

'No one.' Caelan was telling the truth. 'Penrith's busy.' He'd gone in search of coffee, content to allow her to report back on her conversation with Mulligan afterwards. Neither of them believed he would tell them anything new.

Mulligan frowned. 'Honestly?'

'Absolutely,' Caelan told him. 'If there's anything to say, I'll let Penrith know. You know how it works. Why?'

'I just...' For a second, Mulligan looked anguished, and again Caelan almost pitied him. 'Someone has my sister, and I don't know who,' he said. 'It could be your boss, could be someone I've done business with. Whoever it is, whichever way I turn, Lucy's in trouble.'

'Or you are,' Caelan couldn't help saying.

His mouth twisted. 'I know what you think of me, but she's my sister and she's done nothing wrong. You think I want her hurt?'

'Then give us some names,' Caelan said gently. 'Tell us who might have her.'

Mulligan's head dropped. 'I can't. I've told you, I don't have names to give you.'

'Tell me who contacted you when you were in prison.'

He looked at her. 'No one, honestly. I'd say if someone had. It would give you a clue, wouldn't it? The only person who had the number of the phone I bought would be the bloke I bought it from, and he could have sold the information on.'

'What's his name?'

Mulligan hesitated. 'Bramwell. Kev Bramwell. He's Belmarsh's Del Boy, could get you anything you liked. I reckon one of the… the prison officers must have been helping him. Before you ask, I don't know which.'

She moved over to the bed, sat down. Mulligan watched her, frowning. 'What are you doing?' he said. Caelan patted the bed beside her in invitation. He gave her a suspicious glance.

'There's no pillow, if you're thinking of smothering me,' he said as he sat. She smiled.

'You remember when I spoke to you in the cell at Enfield?' she asked. Mulligan nodded, his expression wary. 'And you described what would happen to you if it was discovered you were working with the police?'

'Did I?'

'In detail. You said they'd break every bone you have, strip your skin, burn and cut you, and I was wondering…' Now she stood, the movement quick and fluid. 'Were you so specific because you'd seen all that being done to someone else?'

Mulligan's mouth opened. 'No, I—'

'Or because you'd been told, or shown photographs?' Caelan moved towards the cell door. 'Maybe you should think again about whether you can help us.' This was what she had wanted to discuss with Penrith, the thought she'd had in the cafe earlier. She had suggested to Penrith that they should check, look for victims of assaults or murder victims with corresponding injuries. He had agreed, but Caelan knew it would take time, while the man who might be able to tell her more was standing in this tiny room with her.

186

Mulligan was on his feet, closing the gap between them. Caelan stood her ground, knowing she could take him down again if she needed to. There were officers further down the corridor outside – if she made enough noise, they'd hear her. Mulligan stopped in front of her, lifted a hand as though he was going to take hers, but held back. There was no violence there now. He looked lost, in need of reassurance.

'Can you help me? Help my sister?' His voice was low, urgent, as though by saying the words he was betraying himself and the life he had led.

'We're trying to,' she said.

He pressed his lips together. 'I think Penrith has Lucy and is using her as bait.'

'If that were true, wouldn't he have allowed her to stay at home? He could have had people watching her constantly, keeping her safe, but she'd have been able to go about her life as usual.'

'I don't know.' He held his palms to his cheeks. 'This is a fucking nightmare.'

'We'll find her, but you need to tell me what you know.'

She thought he was going to scream at her, but he took a shuddering breath, allowed his hands to fall to his sides. His eyes roamed the cell and he moved closer still, his voice no more than a whisper. 'You have to trust me. I'm doing my best to point you in the right direction, but I can't give you names. I swear I don't know who's at the top of the ladder, but someone must.'

Caelan put her mouth close to his ear. 'Then you need to trust me too. I'm the only one who can help you. Let's get out of here, and we can talk.'

Mulligan gave a quick nod and turned away as Caelan banged on the cell door with her fist and called for it to be unlocked.

18

'Mulligan's on his way back to the house in Greenford, Ewan too,' Penrith said. 'You've made a deal with the devil, then?'

'Well, with Mulligan. You aren't supposed to know about it.' Caelan leant against the wall of the empty office where she'd found Penrith waiting for her. 'He doesn't trust you. He thinks you know where his sister is.'

'And you're inclined to agree?' Penrith gave a grim smile. 'I don't know where she is. I've already told you, she refused a safe house. I could have kidnapped her myself and moved her into my flat, but it didn't seem appropriate.'

'Did she say why she didn't want to go?'

He waved a hand. 'Busy at uni, assignments to complete, world would stop turning if she didn't.'

'But you told me she was terrified.'

'Evidently not terrified enough.'

'You said someone followed her?'

'Yes, as she was going home from the university.' Penrith frowned. 'It's a forty-minute walk and she didn't know whether the tail was there when she left the building or if she picked him up on the way.'

'Him?' Caelan ran through the possibilities.

'She thought so.'

'Could she give a description?'

'Not really. Average height, wearing a thick coat so no idea on build, hood up, head down.'

'Then it could have been Ryan Glennister.'

'You're not going to look for him, Caelan. He knows who you are, who you really are, and he's a drug addict. He'd probably part with information for a pound.'

'Which is why we need to find him.'

Penrith pulled at his tie. '*We* will. *You* can't. I'll talk to Adele Brady about it.'

She decided to change the subject, knowing he wouldn't be moved, and told him about Kev Bramwell, the man in Belmarsh who could provide prisoners with whatever they wanted. Mulligan had said no one had used the phone to contact him with threats about Lucy, but Caelan was sceptical and knew it was worth having a quiet word with Bramwell all the same.

'Interesting,' Penrith said. 'We'll have to tread carefully, but it's worth following up. I'll have a word with Achebe.'

'What about one of these government departments you said are so eager to hire Lucy Mulligan? Could they have hidden her away somewhere if they're keeping tabs on her?'

Penrith pulled a handkerchief from his pocket and blew his nose. 'Doubtful. She's nothing to them at the moment – she couldn't give up information or passwords because she doesn't know anything.' He glanced at the contents of the handkerchief and pushed it back into his pocket. 'However keen they might be to employ her in the future, for now she's on her own.'

'Was there a computer or laptop in her room?'

'A desktop computer, yes. Someone had done a good job of smashing it to pieces, though. It's being examined, but they're not hopeful.'

'There wasn't a laptop? That seems strange for someone like her.' Caelan realised she should have thought of this before, asked Tom Haslam about it. She found it difficult to believe Lucy would only have one computer, and if she did have another and it was missing, questions would need to be asked about where it was.

Penrith seemed unconcerned. 'Well we didn't find one in her bedroom. We're trying to access the machines she used at the university too.'

'Did you speak to Brady?'

A quick nod. 'She's waiting outside.'

Caelan stared at him. 'I thought she was SIO? What's she doing here?'

'Maybe she missed you. It's been a while.' Penrith checked his watch. 'We'll talk later.'

She was halfway through the door when he called her back.

'Remember – I'm still your boss, contractor or not.'

She smiled. 'When do I send in my first invoice?'

Penrith's face was stony. 'When we make an arrest.'

—

Caelan trotted across the car park, heading for a small silver car she believed belonged to Brady, but as she drew level with a shiny black estate, the driver's window was wound down and Brady's face appeared. Caelan stopped.

'You've changed your car,' she said.

Brady pointed at her. 'Spot the detective. Get in.'

Caelan did as she was told. Brady glanced at her as she fastened her seat belt. 'Not supposed to say that, am I?' she said. 'Bit of a giveaway when you're undercover.'

'You think so? No one's around.'

Brady fiddled with the sat nav, started the engine. 'Know that for sure, do you? Where's your boyfriend?'

Leaning back, Caelan closed her eyes. She needed to sleep. 'I assume you mean Ewan?'

'Well, I know where Mulligan is. Two of my officers are escorting him home.' Caelan heard her tut. 'Waste of time and resources, but who am I to complain?'

'You're trying to find out who killed Nathan Nash. Your team brought Mulligan in for questioning, so it makes sense you'd also take him home.'

'Does it?'

Caelan forced her eyes open, studying Brady's profile. 'Why are you so pissed off?'

'What am I doing here, Caelan? You think I don't have a thousand things to get on with? Why is it I have to jump when your boss calls?'

'Because he's a commander and you're—'

'In charge of a murder investigation.' Brady shoved the indicator on with more force than was necessary. 'I need you to stay out of my way. It's going to be difficult enough tiptoeing around half the criminals in west London without a couple of pretend villains under my feet.'

'I've already met some of the people Nathan Nash knew. You can use me.'

'Can I?' Brady clicked her tongue. 'What if I don't want to?'

'Then don't.' Caelan rubbed her eyes, a headache beginning to build in her temples. 'But Ewan and I found the body.'

'And Mulligan was with you. I've been hearing about him.' Brady braked as traffic lights changed in front of them. 'Penrith says you're not convinced the operation around him is worthwhile, that you'd rather focus on finding his sister.'

'She's missing and innocent, he should be in prison. Who would you prioritise?'

'Not my decision, or my problem,' Brady said. She waited for a moment. 'Reuben Nash tells me you can give him an alibi. That true?'

'No. I couldn't swear he was in his office when he seemed to be. It's in my statement.'

'In Victoria Smith's statement, you mean.' Brady released the handbrake as the lights changed again. 'Don't make my life easy, do you?'

'Have you found anyone with a motive for killing Nathan?'

'I'm told Stefan Harris had an axe to grind. Not had the pleasure of meeting him myself.'

'He's the obvious suspect,' Caelan said.

'But the wrong one?'

'I don't know. Has Reuben Nash been allowed to go home?'

'By now, yes. He's the victim's closest relative. We have to respect that, even if…' Brady shrugged.

'Even if he's also a suspect.' Caelan waited a beat. 'I'll go and talk to him today.' Brady started to interrupt, but she held up a hand. 'Come on, Adele. Reuben Nash thinks he and I, or he and Victoria Smith, could work together. He knows Victoria's desperate to make some money. That's my way in.'

'His brother was murdered last night. You really think he'll be in the mood to talk business?'

Caelan remembered the way Reuben had spoken to his brother, as though Nathan was an irritating child. 'I'm sure he will. He'll want revenge, if nothing else.'

'Revenge?' Brady groaned. 'Just what this investigation needs.'

'Are you still searching the club?'

'Reuben's? Go to all the nice places, don't you?'

'I've been in worse,' Caelan said truthfully. 'Worked in worse, too. Is there any way Reuben Nash could have left his office, other than down the main stairs? No back rooms or staff-only stairs? Because if not, I don't see how he could have killed Nathan.'

'Nothing obvious so far, but we'll be poking around for a while yet.'

'What about CCTV?' Caelan's hopes weren't high, but it never hurt to ask.

'Well, there are plenty of cameras both inside and outside the building. Problem is, none of them actually work.'

Caelan had spotted a few but hadn't noticed anything unusual about them. 'You mean they're dummies?'

'No, they're real enough, they're just not switched on,' Brady said. 'It's almost as though things were going on there that Reuben Nash didn't want caught on camera. Strange, that.'

'What about Nathan's phone? Anyone ask him to meet them outside, anyone threaten him?'

Brady glanced at her. 'You realise I'm not supposed to be giving you information, don't you?'

'Well, you don't want me to try to provide any by questioning people, so what else are we going to talk about?'

'Okay, let's compromise.' Brady sounded as though it was the last thing she wanted to do. 'You have to keep talking to Reuben Nash, Stefan Harris and whoever else for your work for Penrith anyway. If you happen to hear any whispers about the murder, I don't suppose it'll do any harm if you pass them on to me.'

Caelan looked at her, but Brady's eyes were fixed on the road. It wasn't the definite agreement she had been hoping for – Brady clearly wanted to protect herself too. She could say she had never officially agreed to Caelan's involvement if she felt she needed to. 'Have you spoken to Harris yet?' she asked.

'He's given a brief statement, but we'll be talking to him again.'

'What does he say happened at the club?'

'You mean when Nathan Nash had him at knifepoint? He never mentioned it.'

'Because it would give him a motive for killing Nathan. No surprise there,' Caelan said.

'None. There was some impressive bruising to his jaw and a plaster on his throat, but no marks on his hands to suggest he'd punched anyone.'

'And that's relevant?'

Another sharp glance from Brady. 'Don't play games, Caelan. You know as well as I do what killed Nathan Nash – a bloody great bang on the head. You'd have guessed as soon as you saw the body: no knife or gunshot wound, no sign of strangulation. He fell back on the pavement, and smack. Maybe someone pushed or punched him – we think his jaw was broken, but it's not been confirmed yet. We know Nathan attacked Stefan Harris, but from what we've heard, Harris didn't retaliate.'

'He didn't, at least not then. He didn't have a chance.'

Brady tapped her fingers on the steering wheel. 'Didn't you say Nathan said something about him and his brother helping Harris get started?'

'Yeah, something like "you'd be nothing without us".'

'Interesting. We know Harris is a dealer. I wonder what else he gets up to.'

'Maybe I could find out.'

Brady ignored her. 'Whoever smacked Nathan didn't hang around. He might have survived if they'd called an ambulance and got him into surgery.'

'They might not have realised how seriously he was injured.' Caelan looked at Brady. 'I'll be interested to hear whether Nathan had taken anything. The way he was behaving, I wouldn't be surprised.'

'Maybe he was drunk?'

'He didn't seem to be. I didn't smell alcohol on his breath, and he stood pretty close when he caught me trying the door of their office.'

'Subtle,' Brady said. 'That wasn't in your statement.'

'Victoria Smith wouldn't have mentioned it, so neither did I. It meant she had a reason to be pissed off with Nathan too. Didn't Reuben Nash tell you about it? He came to rescue me, to put Nathan in his place.'

'What a gentleman. No, it wasn't in his statement either. Maybe he's taken a shine to you.'

'I hope so. I could use it to get closer to him.'

Brady laughed. 'Lucky you.'

Caelan said, 'You think Reuben did it, don't you?'

'At the moment, I don't think anything.' Brady moved from one lane of traffic to the next. 'I'm guessing we won't have many people who were enjoying themselves at the club last night volunteering to give statements. It seems that kind of place.'

'There might have been some upstanding citizens.'

'I won't hold my breath. We've put an appeal out, but I doubt there'll be many takers.'

They were nearing Mulligan's house in Greenford and Caelan knew she didn't have long. 'Adele, listen. People are going to be talking about Nathan Nash's death anyway. What harm can it do if I ask some questions? I'm not going to get in your way.'

Brady was silent, then said, 'Okay, but it goes through Penrith. I don't want you coming directly to me with anything. Don't contact Tim, Jen Somerville or anyone else.'

'Why would I? It's not as though I'm new to this.'

Brady didn't reply, slowing the car, and Caelan knew she was still reluctant to agree absolutely. 'You can walk from here, can't you?' she said, glancing at the sat nav before pulling in to the kerb. 'It should only be five minutes away. I don't want to get too close to the house. Don't want the two officers from my team recognising me – they might wonder why I'm giving Reuben Nash's new girlfriend a lift.'

Caelan froze, one foot on the pavement, the rest of her still inside the car. 'What?'

'That's what Nash is telling people anyway.' Brady gave her a big grin and a wave. 'Hope you're very happy together.'

As she sped away, Caelan began to walk, hands in her jacket pockets. Brady hadn't told her much, but what she had said was interesting. It was no surprise the security cameras in and around the club weren't working. Reuben Nash would have wanted them as a deterrent, possibly to satisfy the terms of his insurance policy, but no doubt they hadn't been switched on since the day they were installed.

Brady's team had already spoken to Stefan Harris, albeit briefly. Caelan decided she would pay him a visit too. She didn't have his money, but perhaps a compromise could be reached. Fifteen grand was a lot to pay off in favours, but since it seemed unlikely Penrith was going to authorise a payment to clear Mulligan's debt, she would have to work out a solution on her own.

She was hungry, tired, her head aching. She would need to rest before heading out again. Turning onto Mulligan's street, she saw Ewan get out of a taxi outside the house. He spotted her, lifted a hand.

'Quite a night,' he said as she reached him.

Caelan smiled. 'Never been questioned by the police before?'

'No. I was shitting it the whole time, knowing I had to answer... well, as someone else.'

She took his arm, steered him towards the house. 'You must have done okay. They seem to have believed you.'

The front door was ajar. Caelan stopped, frowning.

'Wait,' she said.

'What do we do?' Ewan whispered.

'Take it slowly.'

'Is Mulligan here?'

'He should be by now. Two police officers were bringing him home.'

Ewan gestured towards the house. 'Should we...?'

She nodded, moved forwards. The door hadn't been forced or the lock tampered with, as far as she could see. She pulled her sleeve over her hand and pushed the door wider, just enough to see inside.

James Mulligan lay face down on the hallway floor, blood pooling around his head.

19

'You need to stop stumbling over bodies,' Penrith said as Caelan and Ewan sat down. 'I'm getting tired of debriefing you about it. Here you are again, littering up my office, drinking my coffee.'

'I'd rather not make a habit of it,' Caelan said. Penrith was trying his best to appear blasé, but she could see he was rattled. He was twisting a pen in his fingers, his hands never still. 'How is he?'

'Critical but stable. You know how hospitals are, never a straight answer. They reckon whoever did it used a baseball bat. Enough to disable him, not quite enough to kill him.' Penrith looked at her as he leant back in his chair. 'Yet. It still might.'

She winced. 'Stefan Harris has to be a suspect.'

'Because of the money Mulligan owes him? But you'd already said you'd pay. Why would he attack Mulligan now?'

'To warn me to keep my promise?'

'Doubtful,' Penrith said. 'Isn't it more likely it's linked to the attack on his house and the disappearance of his sister? He can't inform on anyone from intensive care, can he? Anyway, they probably meant to kill him.'

'I don't know.' Caelan rubbed her eyes. 'It doesn't make sense.'

'Unless Mulligan's been lying to us. He might know more than he's ever let on. He was beaten up in Belmarsh, more than once. How do we know they weren't warnings to keep his mouth closed too?'

'But no one knew he was going to be released then, not even him,' Caelan pointed out.

'Wouldn't matter. He'd be as likely to grass in prison as on the outside – probably more likely, once he'd had a taste of life inside,' Penrith said.

'If what you're saying is right, it means someone knows he was in prison, not hospital. Meaning they could also guess that us suddenly appearing is a set-up.'

Penrith was sceptical. 'There's no reason why they should.'

'Come on, Ian. Mulligan was banged up for murder and a string of other offences, then suddenly he's free?'

'It happens.'

'No one was supposed to know he'd been inside.' Caelan remembered Mulligan's mobile phone, the one he'd had in Belmarsh. He'd said there had been no threats, no contact while he was in prison, but he might have lied. The phone was being examined to see who he had contacted apart from the call he'd tried to make to his sister the night he was released, but Caelan knew it would take time. Any texts and call logs had been deleted, and there were no contacts saved other than his sister's name and number.

'What if this ties into what I said before, about someone leaking information?' she said.

Penrith pressed his lips together. 'Very few people knew about the deal with Mulligan. Three of us are sitting in this room now.'

Caelan thought about it. Herself, Ewan, Penrith; Assistant Commissioner Beckett, Adele Brady, Tim Achebe and Jen Somerville.

Somerville...

Newly single, having to manage on her own wages? Maybe she'd been tempted. Caelan hated herself for the direction her thoughts were taking, but she had to consider it.

Then again, she could be guilty of paranoia and listening to a man desperate to keep himself out of prison.

'What if one of the other prisoners in Belmarsh recognised him?' Ewan said.

'And word got back to the people he was working for? It's a possibility.' Grateful for the suggestion, Caelan was thankful she hadn't voiced her thoughts about Somerville. She looked at Penrith. 'Worth following up?'

He was already nodding. 'I'll mention it to Tim Achebe.'

Caelan thought of something else. 'Mulligan was supposed to have two of Brady's team with him,' she said. 'Where were they when he was attacked?'

Penrith scowled. 'They dropped him off at the kerb, didn't bother to wait to see if he did a runner or got inside the house safely. Their arses are being kicked as we speak.'

'Someone must have been watching the house,' said Ewan. 'They probably followed him in as he unlocked the front door.'

Penrith folded his hands across his belly. 'It's possible.'

'Are Scenes of Crime at the house?' Caelan blinked, exhaustion threatening to overtake her. Discovering Mulligan lying there had shaken her more than she wanted to admit.

'Yes. After an ambulance turned up and carted Mulligan away, I didn't see any point in being discreet,' said Penrith.

'Shouldn't we be at the hospital? Should have followed the ambulance really. His real cousin would have done.' Caelan had made the emergency call as Victoria Smith, the panic in her voice genuine. What did the attack on Mulligan mean?

'No point worrying about that now,' Penrith said. 'Victoria's supposed to be only recently arrived from Scotland anyway, and she and Mulligan have never really been close. Mulligan's mother is in a secure unit near Edinburgh, so she won't be popping down to visit, and no one knows who his father is. There's no other close family apart from his sister, and we're all aware of the problem there.'

'I'll go and see him later,' Caelan said.

'Why?' Penrith looked unimpressed. 'You don't need to feel guilty, or concerned, or whatever it is that's bothering you. Mulligan has made his own choices in life.'

'Not this time, though. This time it was down to us.'

He glared at her. 'He knew the risks. He only agreed because he'd be getting something out of it. His conscience was clear despite everything he'd been involved in, and yours should be too.'

Caelan didn't argue, but also didn't agree. 'The officers who took Mulligan back to the house – were they in uniform? Driving a marked car?'

'I doubt it, since they were Adele Brady's team. Why do you ask?' Penrith narrowed his eyes, thinking about it. 'You're wondering if we've been rumbled? Whether someone was watching, realised Mulligan had been speaking to the police?'

'He was a witness to what happened at the club last night, and he was one of the people who found the body. It's understandable the police would need to talk to him,' Ewan pointed out.

'Maybe they didn't want to take the chance. Then again, if they wanted him out of the picture permanently, there are more reliable ways of doing it,' Caelan said.

'The hospital said his pockets were empty. No wallet, no phone. Either whoever attacked him wanted it to look like a mugging, or...' Penrith paused. 'Or they wanted to see who he'd been speaking to.'

'Shit.' Caelan considered what this might mean. 'Then they'll have contact numbers for us?'

'Under the names you've been using, yes.' Penrith drummed his fingers on his desk. 'It might not be a bad thing. Of course, I wouldn't have wanted Mulligan to be hurt,' he bared his teeth, 'but it might mean your phone number is now in the hands of the person or people we're trying to catch.'

'Reassuring.' Caelan spoke lightly, but she knew he was right. 'What do you want us to do?'

'Exactly what you were planning to do before Mulligan was taken out of the equation. Brady's agreed to you speaking to Reuben Nash, Stefan Harris and the rest.' Penrith's mobile began to ring. 'Stay in touch and try not to get smacked over the head. I can do without the paperwork.' He answered the call, and Caelan turned to Ewan.

'Seems we're dismissed.'

—

'I'm knackered,' Ewan said as they headed down the steps to the Underground.

'They'll have to get us hotel rooms for tonight,' said Caelan. 'Mulligan's house is a crime scene.'

They dodged around a crowd of tourists, all enthusing about the Houses of Parliament. Ewan hesitated, glancing around.

'Where are we heading? Ealing Broadway?'

'No, we're going back to Camden,' Caelan told him.

'You want to see Jolene Townsend again?' Ewan took Caelan's arm as they made their way through the crowds, and she glanced down at his hand, surprised. She had taken his hand, put her arm through his lots of times, but he had never initiated contact before. Hopefully it was a sign he was becoming more comfortable with them posing as a couple.

'I want to know what she's selling to some of the people who come into the shop,' Caelan told him. 'I don't know what the bloke we saw in there earlier was after, but I doubt he wanted to pay his newspaper bill.'

Ewan grinned. 'Maybe he wanted some pick and mix?'

'Is that what they're calling spice and crack these days?' Caelan gave a mock shake of her head. 'I can't keep up.'

They managed to board the next train and squeezed into a corner.

'Why do you want to see Jolene?' Ewan asked.

'She was shifty earlier when I asked her if she knew who Lucy's housemates were. I want to know why.'

'Maybe she sold… whatever she's selling to some of them.'

'Could be. Also, when we met her in Stand, she told Mulligan she'd been there with Reuben, but he'd gone home,' Caelan said. 'I'm hoping she can tell us more about him.'

'Maybe she can give us his address?'

'She probably could, but I think I'll call Reuben and invite myself over to the club instead. I don't want to go to his house, not yet.'

He glanced down at her. 'I wouldn't be going with you?'

She smiled. 'No, I'm planning on cheating on you. Sorry.'

Ewan laughed. 'I don't think even you would go that far for your job.'

Caelan didn't reply.

–

Jolene looked no happier to see Caelan than she had before, though she managed a smile for Ewan as they walked through the door. She was talking to an older man by the counter. He appeared agitated, pointing to the shelves as he spoke. He ignored Caelan and Ewan as he stalked away, heading for the back of the shop, running his hand over his balding head and then smoothing his moustache. Jolene moved to sit at the till, sipping from an energy drink.

'You're back,' she said. 'Did you find Lucy's housemates?'

Caelan ignored the question, not speaking until she was standing beside the other woman.

'Have you heard from Reuben?' she said. Jolene's eyes narrowed.

'What's it got to do with you?'

'I wondered how he was doing, that's all. He must be devastated.'

Jolene curled her lip. 'You think so, when his brother was killed last night? Amazing really.'

'So you've spoken to him?' Caelan glanced at Ewan. 'We swapped numbers last night, and I wondered if I should give him a call.'

Beside her, Ewan folded his arms. Jolene looked at him and laughed. 'Strictly business, of course,' she said.

'What else would it be?' Ewan gave Caelan a hard stare, and she reached out to touch his arm.

'Reuben just wants to discuss some opportunities,' she said.

Jolene flicked her hair. 'Yeah, opportunities for him to get into your knickers.'

Caelan lifted her chin. 'Is that what happened to you?'

'What are you talking about?'

'The other night, at Stand. You said you were there with Reuben.'

A mocking laugh. 'I was, for a while, then I left with someone else. Sometimes Reuben and I spend time together, sometimes we don't. Both of us do whatever, and whoever, we like. Doesn't that happen where you're from?'

Shooting Ewan a wary glance, Caelan said, 'Not to me.'

'Yeah?' Jolene sniffed. 'Figures.'

There was a pause, Caelan wondering whether to pretend to take offence, Ewan scowling, and Jolene sipping her drink without a care.

'Reuben will want something from you,' Jolene said. Her eyes roamed Caelan's body. 'Wonder what that could be.'

'I'll rip his fucking head off,' Ewan snarled.

Jolene scoffed at him. 'Course you will. Reuben's got more bouncers than Mulligan has inbred cousins. They'd batter you, chew you up and shit you out, but you keep telling yourself that.' Her eyes widened as she realised what she'd said. 'I didn't mean they... They'd never have hurt Nathan. I was—'

'Have you heard about James?' Caelan cut across her bluster.

'Mulligan?' Jolene's eyes strayed towards her phone. 'I've not spoken to him today.' She looked up, alert now. 'Where is he?'

'Intensive care,' Caelan said, deliberately blunt. Jolene's hand went to her chest.

'What? What do you mean?'

'Someone laid him out with a baseball bat earlier today.' The wobble in Caelan's voice wasn't entirely faked. 'He might not survive.'

Jolene snatched up her phone, stabbing at the screen. 'Why didn't you say before? Fuck.'

'Who are you texting?'

A scowl. 'None of your business. Mulligan has plenty of friends; they'll all want to know what's happened.' She paused, staring at Caelan. 'Why didn't you say when you came in? All that crap about me and Reuben. Nice to see you give a shit about your cousin.' She leant over the counter. 'Maybe that's it. Maybe you wanted Mulligan out of the way so you can take over his business yourself.'

Caelan snorted. 'Yeah, you're right. You figured it out.'

'Why don't we calm down, ladies?' Ewan said. They both turned to glare at him, and he retreated, hands in the air.

'Someone did this to my cousin, and I want to find out who. If anyone you know can help me with that, you need to tell me.' Caelan leant over the counter, grabbing a pen from beside the till and a newspaper from the display stand next to her. She scrawled her mobile number on the paper and threw it at Jolene, who gaped at her. 'You can tell your friends I'm looking for whoever's behind this. You see now why I want to speak to Reuben?'

'But why Mulligan? What's he got to do with…' Jolene closed her mouth as Caelan set her hands on the counter and leant forward, getting in the other woman's face.

'With?'

'I mean, he's been away for six weeks, and he's… well, he's a nobody.'

'As I'm finding out.' Caelan stepped back, hands on hips. 'He told me he did decent business down here, but from what I'm seeing, no one takes him seriously.'

Jolene managed a smile. 'He's trying to trade in a busy area. It'll take time.'

'Which he might not have now,' Caelan reminded her. 'Listen, Jolene, if you hear anything… The police are looking into what happened, but you know what those bastards are like. James isn't going to be a priority.'

Jolene's face closed. 'I don't know anything about it. I didn't even know he'd been hurt until you told me.'

'I know, I'm just saying—'

'I've got stock to put out.' Jolene got up, grabbed her phone and disappeared into the darkened area behind her, leaving the newspaper with Caelan's phone number on the counter. Caelan picked it up, scribbled *Ealing Hospital, intensive care unit* beside her phone number and threw it onto the chair Jolene had been sitting in.

'Let's go,' she told Ewan.

He followed her outside. 'Who do you think she's going to phone?'

'No idea. Reuben?' Caelan took out her own mobile. 'Let's see.' She found his number, made the call and listened. 'Voice-mail.'

'Could be a coincidence.'

'Or she and Reuben could be closer than she'd have us believe.'

20

Reuben called back as they got off the tube at Oxford Circus, but Caelan ignored him. Ewan looked up at the street names as they walked.

'How much do you think renting a shop around here would set you back?

'No idea. Fifty or sixty grand a year? Maybe more.'

He whistled. 'And people still make a living? We're in the wrong business.'

She smiled. 'Always.'

'Reckon that's the place.' Ewan nodded towards a small shopfront. In the window stood a single barber's chair, and Ewan grabbed Caelan's wrist as he saw the man sitting in it, his face lathered, ready for a shave.

'Bloody hell, he plays for Spurs,' he hissed.

'How can you tell under all the shaving cream?' Caelan looked up at the black-painted shop frontage. 'Place doesn't even have a sign.'

Ewan ran a hand over the top of his head. 'I don't need a haircut.'

'Don't have one then,' Caelan said. 'Have a shave, or a facial.'

'They do facials?' Ewan didn't sound keen.

'We can ask.' Caelan pushed open the door, beaming at Leyton Grey, who stood beside the footballer in the chair, cut-throat razor ready to go. 'Hi, Leyton,' she said. He stared at her, confused. 'We met at Stand,' she told him. 'Vic and Owen? We were with my cousin, James Mulligan?'

His face cleared. 'Oh, yeah. Have a seat.' He grinned at Ewan. 'We'll see what we can do.'

Twenty minutes later, Grey escorted the footballer to the door. As his client walked away, he turned back to Caelan and Ewan. 'Comes in here twice a week, regular as you like. He's a fussy bastard, but at eighty quid a throw, I'm not complaining.'

'Eighty quid for a shave?' Ewan sounded panicked, and Grey grinned at him.

'Don't worry, mate, I charge my customers on a sliding scale. Your man who's just left is on over a hundred grand a week according to the papers, so I reckon a few quid for a shave and a trim isn't going to bankrupt him. You, though – let's call it thirty and a couple of beers next time I see you.'

'Are you sure?'

'Mates' rates.' Grey waved him into the chair. 'Any time.'

Ewan thanked him, sat down. 'Just do whatever you think,' he said.

'Quick tidy-up. No worries.' Grey got to work, and Caelan met Ewan's eyes in the mirror. They were here on a fishing trip, wanting to see how many of Mulligan's mates knew about the attack on him, and who had told them. Mulligan had said Leyton Grey was nothing more than a barber, but she had been keen to see his shop for herself.

'Do you employ anyone else here?' she asked.

'Nah, it's just me. I work ten, twelve hours a day sometimes, but it doesn't bother me. I enjoy it. Come in on a Saturday, the place is rammed. I do okay.'

'James said you've a gold mine on your hands.'

Grey laughed. 'Yeah, he would, but it's not from any money he pays me. I give him a free cut because he's put so much business my way, told all his mates and contacts about me.'

'You must be doing well to afford a shop around here.'

Grey glanced at her, looking sheepish. 'Truth told, I only pay half the rent I should. My dad's mate owns the building – it's been in his family for years. The shop had been empty for a while, and he said he'd rather see it being used even if it meant cutting the rent. So here I am. Had a little place in Camden before this.'

'Camden? We've just been there.'

'Yeah?' Grey seemed to be only half listening, frowning at Ewan's hair. 'Few white ones coming through here, mate. You'll have to dye it soon.' He winked at Caelan in the mirror.

'We went to see Jolene Townsend,' Caelan told him.

'She still working in that shop? Used to go in there for my fags every morning.' He stepped back, tipped his head to the side, assessing his work. 'Looking better already.'

'You know her, then?'

'Everyone knows Jolene.' Grey's tone was matter-of-fact, nothing lascivious about it.

'James introduced us to her. We wanted to talk to his friends, see if they'd heard. See if they can help us.'

Grey turned, bemused. 'What do you mean, see if they've heard?'

'Someone attacked James with a baseball bat today.'

He stared. 'James? You mean Mulligan?'

'He's in intensive care.' She looked at the ground, then back at Grey. 'You hadn't heard.'

Wordlessly Grey shook his head. His mouth worked and he cleared his throat. 'You said you're his cousin? Have they let you see him?'

'We found him, but we haven't been to the hospital yet. I'm not his next of kin, so…'

He nodded his understanding. 'They wouldn't let you in anyway. Shit, it must be serious.'

'You can see why we're asking questions. I want to know who did this.'

'Aren't the police—'

'I don't trust them. What do you know about James?'

His eyes slid away. 'Like I said, we're mates.'

'You know what he does for a living?'

'I've an idea.'

'Well then. You'll understand why I don't think the police will be prioritising this. James probably wouldn't want them poking around too much anyway.'

Grey went back to Ewan's hair. 'I don't think I can help you. I'm a barber, not a… I mean, I've never done business with Mulligan.'

'But you cut the hair of some of the people who do?'

He wouldn't look at her. 'I don't want to get involved.'

Caelan folded her arms. 'Do you know Nathan Nash?'

'I know he's dead.'

'Reuben Nash? Stefan Harris?'

Grey's shoulders were up around his ears, as though he was expecting a blow to the head himself. 'I've told you, I don't want to be a part of this. I've a business to think about.'

'I'll take that as yes.'

'Take it as whatever you want.' He stepped away from Ewan. 'You're done.'

Ewan stood. 'Cheers.' He brought out his wallet, but Grey waved him away.

'On the house. Just leave me alone. Please.'

Caelan tried to meet his eyes, but Grey had turned his back again. He picked up a broom and began sweeping up Ewan's hair. There was a desk at the other end of the shop, and Caelan went over and picked up an appointment card and a pen.

'I'll leave my number.'

'Don't bother,' Grey said without lifting his head. Caelan wrote it anyway and left it beside the till with two twenty-pound notes.

—

As they headed back to the Underground station, Ewan said, 'Why are you giving everyone your phone number? If you didn't and then one of them rang you, we'd know they could only have got the number from Mulligan's phone, the one that whoever attacked him took.'

Caelan tucked her hands into her coat pockets as a cold breeze whipped around them. 'Because it would look strange if I didn't. I don't know, maybe I shouldn't have. Sometimes it's impossible to know what's the best option.' She remembered Reuben Nash's call and pulled out her phone. He answered on the second ring.

'Victoria. Good to speak to you.' He sounded hoarse, his voice catching in his throat.

'How are you?' Caelan asked. The man's brother had just been murdered, after all.

He sniffed. 'Trying to carry on as normal. Nathan wouldn't want me sitting around feeling sorry for myself.'

Caelan grimaced at this unconvincing show of brotherly love. 'Then maybe we could meet, have that chat?'

'I heard about Mulligan,' Reuben said. 'You're not wasting any time.'

'Meaning?' Caelan wanted to ask how he knew. She guessed Jolene had told him, probably in the text she had sent when Caelan and Ewan were still in the shop.

'Come on. You came down here to help Mulligan out, but I'm guessing you're hoping to step into his shoes permanently. Here's your chance.'

Caelan lowered her voice, hoping she sounded flirtatious. 'You're suggesting I'd exploit my cousin's misfortune for my own ends? That would be despicable.'

Ewan shook his head, but Reuben chuckled.

'It would indeed.'

'I'm actually trying to find out who attacked him.'

'So you can shake their hand?'

She snorted. 'Funny man. No, because I want answers.'

'Listen, why don't you meet me at the club later?' Nash said. 'I'd invite you to my house, but I don't usually bring business home.'

She sighed. 'I'd like to, but...'

'But?'

'It depends what Stefan Harris does to me. James owes him fifteen grand, and Stefan's decided I'll have to pay up instead.'

'I heard. Last night, just before my brother went for Harris with his knife.' His voice was little more than a whisper. 'I'll come with you to see Stefan. I need to have a chat with him anyway.'

Caelan kicked herself mentally. 'You sure that's wise?'

Nash's voice hardened. 'I think it's my decision, don't you?'

'No, not if you're planning on coming along with me. I don't want him to think I can't handle things alone.' She waited, guessing she might have just blown her chance to get closer to Nash.

After a pause, he laughed. 'You know, you remind me of my mother.'

'Really?' Caelan wasn't sure how to respond.

'Yeah. She wouldn't take any shit from me either. I'm glad she's not here to see one of her sons buried.' He was silent again, and Caelan waited. Eventually he said, 'Do you think Harris is behind the attack on Mulligan?'

She knew there was no point in lying to him. 'Maybe.'

'Wouldn't surprise me. He's a vicious bastard.'

'He didn't seem vicious when Nathan had a knife to his throat.' Again Caelan braced herself, and again Nash surprised her.

'Stefan's got a big mouth, and it often gets him into trouble. Once it does, he backs off and lets other people handle it, because he's shit at fighting and he hates getting hurt. Why do you think he goes around with two bodyguards?'

'I'd assumed it was a status thing – you know, look at me with my staff.'

'No, it's because he's a wimp and a coward.'

'I heard he beats up his girlfriend,' Caelan said.

'You know about that? No doubt Mulligan told you. He was the one who took her to the hospital, did he mention that?'

'James did?' Caelan couldn't keep the surprise from her voice, and Nash laughed.

'Proper good Samaritan. It happened outside my club. Harris and Abbie had argued, and he'd punched her and stormed off. She was shocked, crying and bleeding. Mulligan got her into a taxi and took her to A and E. I didn't know anything about it until the next day, or I'd have helped her myself. Nathan wanted to go and beat the shit out of Harris, but I persuaded him it wouldn't be a great idea.'

'Not good for business?'

'Not good for Abbie,' Nash said softly. 'Anyway, let me know when you've spoken to Stefan.'

'I thought you wanted to come along?'

'Changed my mind. If he did... if he killed Nathan, or he was there while one of his mates did it, I'll catch up with him sooner or later. I need to ask around first, get my facts straight. Have to say, though, he's at the top of my list.'

'Do you have his phone number and address?'

'Harris's, you mean? Yeah, don't you?'

'No, he never gave me it. There wasn't much time between him flirting with me, then demanding money, then promising me his men would take the fifteen grand in kind if he told them to.'

'Fucker,' said Nash.

'James also said you and Harris hate each other.'

Nash coughed. 'Stefan's never been my favourite person, even before all this kicked off. We've had a few misunderstandings, some business deals that have gone sour for one reason or another. He tends to hold a grudge.'

Caelan noted the fact that Reuben had said he'd attempted to work with Harris, because it meant there was more to his business than being a nightclub owner. Then again, with the amount of dealing she had seen happening in his club, it wasn't a surprise.

'Would you text me his number then, please?' she said.

Nash sighed. 'Okay, but you should be careful. Like I said, Stefan isn't the easiest man to deal with.'

'And you are?' Her voice was almost a purr, and Ewan stifled a laugh as she mimed vomiting. Nash gave a throaty chuckle.

'You'll have to find out for yourself. Speak soon.'

He ended the call and Caelan turned to Ewan. 'The worst part of this job isn't the danger or the terrible hours, it's flirting with people like Reuben Nash. I feel as though I need a shower, and we weren't even in the same room.'

'You were convincing, though. Reckon he thinks he's in,' Ewan said with a grin.

'Lucky me.'

Her phone beeped and a mobile number appeared on the screen. 'Oh, he's sent me a kiss along with Harris's number and the address of his cab company. How sweet.' Caelan saved the number to her phone and sent a quick text. 'I've told Harris we're on our way. I'm not going to call, but I want to make sure he's there when we arrive.'

Ewan screwed up his face. 'I'm pretty sure he'll want to see you.'

'Even if I don't have his money?' Caelan pulled a face of her own. She was playing it down, but her stomach turned over when she thought of facing Stefan Harris again. She remembered the predatory look in his eyes, the way he had spoken to his girlfriend, and the promise that his men would take back the money any way he wanted. If they were looking for people traffickers, Harris had to be the prime suspect. She needed to keep talking to Nash, but she knew she would have to be careful. Nash might appear friendly, almost chatty, but he had told her little of value so far. She needed to continue to build up his trust.

Her phone began to ring, and she checked the screen, expecting it to be Stefan Harris.

'Where are you?' Penrith said without bothering with a greeting.

'Oxford Circus. Why?'

She heard him click his tongue, then mutter to someone. 'You haven't been to the hospital?'

'The…' She realised he meant the one where Mulligan was being cared for. 'No, not yet. Why?'

'Don't bother. We're posting an officer to guard him, and you won't have clearance.'

'What's happened?'

'A minor incident,' Penrith said. 'A phone call was made to the hospital's main switchboard. The caller was subtle, but they were trying to find out which ward Mulligan is on. Who have you spoken to, and what have you said?'

She told him. 'Jolene Townsend knows which hospital Mulligan is in, but I didn't tell Leyton Grey. Was the caller a man or a woman?'

'We don't know. The call wasn't recorded, and the receptionist said it was a bad line, lots of crackling, the voice faint and muffled.'

'Like someone whispering through a scarf and a few sheets of paper?'

'Exactly like that, I'd guess.' Penrith crunched something. It was probably a couple of boiled sweets but sounded more like gravel. 'She reported it immediately, knowing Mulligan was the victim of an assault. It could be a friend who's concerned about him, of course, but we're not taking any chances.'

'Jolene must have told someone where he is,' Caelan said. 'The only other way of finding out is to phone every hospital in London.'

Penrith paused for a moment. 'You know, a more cynical man than me would say you gave Townsend the information to see what she would do with it.'

'No comment.' Caelan smiled to herself.

'Why did you go to see Grey?'

'Because he's a mate of Mulligan's and he appears to have loads of money. He seems to have genuinely built up a decent business, but I thought it was worth a visit.'

'Casting your net far and wide?'

'He admitted to cutting the hair of some of Mulligan's more dubious friends. Who knows what else he's done for them?'

Penrith heaved a breath. 'I'll leave it to your judgement, but don't waste time.'

'You're the one who's been talking about fishing trips and casting nets.'

'Keep me updated. And you'll be getting a call from our mutual friend.'

He was gone, leaving Caelan staring at her phone and wondering who he was talking about. Tim Achebe? Assistant Commissioner Beckett? She baulked at the thought.

Immediately the phone announced the arrival of a text, and she saw that Harris had replied.

The message said: *I'll be waiting.*

21

An hour later, Caelan and Ewan stood outside an estate agent's premises pretending to look at properties advertised in the window. The sky was grey, rain clouds gathering overhead as a strong breeze picked up litter and flung it at their shins. The address Reuben Nash had provided was a scruffy-looking place a few doors down, with several vehicles parked outside, all emblazoned with the company name in silver lettering. There were saloons, an estate and a minibus with blacked-out rear windows.

'Kwik Kabs. Wonder how many seconds it took him to think of that,' Ewan said. 'Doesn't look as though they're busy, either.'

'According to Mulligan, Harris's family also own a pizza place and a chip shop. Maybe they're all frying fish today.'

'Fish and chips. That's what we should have for tea tonight.' Ewan nudged her, and Caelan knew he was trying to lighten the mood. She was apprehensive, and she could feel his unease too.

'If Harris leaves us any teeth to eat with,' she said. 'Come on, let's get it over with.'

'Wait a second. How are we going to do this?' Ewan blushed. 'I mean, I don't want to mess anything up.'

She smiled. 'Harris is going to think he's in control, because we're on his turf and we owe him – apparently. To a point, we'll have to see how it plays out. I don't have the money, and there's no point pretending I can get it.'

Ewan scowled. 'Bloody Penrith.'

'He was never going to hand it over. Maybe two or three thousand, but fifteen?'

'Not him who has to face Harris, though, is it?'

She lifted her shoulders. 'I should never have said I'd repay it.'

'You didn't have a choice, not with Harris standing there, his men ready to kick the shit out of Mulligan.'

'Yeah, couldn't let that happen, could I?' She smiled. 'Are you ready?'

He nodded, and they turned to cross the road. As they waited for a break in the traffic, a black BMW sped towards them and screeched to a halt behind one of the Kwik Kabs vehicles. Harris climbed out with a jaunty wave, the bruising on his jaw visible even from across the street.

'Where are his guard dogs?' Ewan murmured.

'Probably inside, chewing on someone's remains.'

Harris waited on the pavement, leaning against the wall. As they reached him, he said, 'No huge suitcase of cash? Hope you've brought your chequebook, then.'

Caelan met his eyes. 'Can we talk?'

He gave an unpleasant smile. 'If you don't have the money, I think we need to.' He pushed away from the wall, waved them inside with mock politeness. 'After you.'

Inside, the place was even dingier than it looked from the outside. There was a square room with several white plastic garden chairs for people to wait for their cab, another door, and a hatch in the wall where they could see a woman at a desk barking orders into a phone.

'Meet my mum,' Harris said. 'Worked here every day since she was sixteen. Built the place up from nothing, didn't you, Mum?'

She waved a hand but didn't turn.

'Salt of the earth. Now,' he jerked a thumb towards the door at the back of the room, 'upstairs.'

Caelan started to move, and as Ewan made to follow, Harris's hand shot out and grabbed his forearm. 'Not you. You can stay down here, keep my old mum company.'

Ewan looked down at Harris's hand. 'Not going to happen.'

Harris smirked as one of his muscle men appeared behind Ewan, the other in the doorway that apparently led upstairs. 'Think you better do as you're told, sunshine, don't you?'

Caelan turned. 'I'll be okay, Owen. Let me talk to him.'

Ewan seethed and snarled, but in the end threw himself down in one of the plastic chairs.

'I'll look after her.' Harris leered. 'Promise.' He glanced at the man standing behind Ewan. 'Stay with him. Don't let him out of this room.'

The man nodded, planting his feet as though he expected Ewan to charge at him.

'Can they even speak?' Caelan asked.

Harris took her arm. 'They can say "yes, sir", and that's all I need.' He squeezed. 'All I need my women to say too.'

He marched her through the door, the other man following behind like a puppy. The stairs were on the right, and on the left was an open door, a toilet and grimy sink visible. For a moment Caelan toyed with pretending she needed to use them, but she quickly dismissed the idea. Harris would no doubt think it a good laugh to deny her the chance.

The last thing she wanted was to allow him to drag her upstairs, but if only one of his men was coming with them, she still fancied her chances if things got rough. He was bigger, heavier, definitely stronger, but she doubted he'd had the training she had. Ewan could always wade in too, unless Harris or the others were armed… She didn't allow her mind to consider the possibility, focusing instead on the details of her surroundings, wanting to learn everything she could about Harris's home territory. So far, it wasn't much. The place was bare, neglected. Functional. Even the stairs were uncarpeted.

Halfway up, she pretended to stumble, and Harris almost lost his footing. Yanking her upright, he snarled, 'Clumsy bitch.'

Caelan ignored him, kept walking. His grip on her arm had tightened and she knew he would leave bruises, but for a second, he'd panicked, and she'd had the upper hand.

At the top of the stairs was a landing with one door leading off it. Harris looked down at her.

'I'm going to let go of you so I can unlock the door. You'll be a good girl, won't you? I wouldn't advise running, because you won't get far. Johnny here would happily throw you down the stairs, wouldn't you, mate?'

Johnny laughed, rubbing his hands together like a pantomime villain. Caelan gave him a disdainful glance.

'Why would I run?' she said. She didn't say 'I'm not afraid of you', but they all knew she meant it.

Harris scowled and barged the door open. 'Get inside.' He gave Caelan a shove and she allowed herself to be pushed through. 'Wait out here, Johnny. Don't let anyone in,' Harris ordered.

Johnny might have replied, but anything he said was lost as Harris slammed the door and locked it. Caelan felt her heartbeat rocket, her body begin to hum. Adrenalin. The familiar sensation, somewhere between excitement and fear. Harris moved close, trapping her against the wall, then smiled and abruptly turned away, giving her a chance to look around the room for the first time.

It was clearly his office, kitted out slightly more impressively than downstairs, but not by much. There was one window, on the opposite wall to the door, which was now at Caelan's back. There was a desk with a computer, a leather office chair that Harris was settling into, and a dining chair on the other side of the desk. In the corner was a filing cabinet and a large plastic toolbox. Caelan eyed the toolbox. She knew the hideous uses ordinary tools could be put to in the right, or wrong, hands. Pliers, screwdrivers, nail guns… She told herself to focus. Harris was a loudmouth and a bully, but she would not allow him to hurt her. Then again, in a room this size, the only door locked, would she be able to fight him off? She shut the thought down, took a few steady breaths. Of course she would. Stay calm. Concentrate.

'Sit down,' Harris said. His demeanour had changed – he was now playing the reasonable businessman. She did as she was told, sitting up straight, only the balls of her feet making contact with the floor, appearing casual and relaxed but ready to spring out of the chair if necessary.

Only she knew that her heart was hammering against the back of her throat.

'You don't have the money,' Harris said.

'Nope.'

'Then we've got a problem.' He leant back in his chair, eyes half closed. 'You promised me you'd have it.'

'I said James would have it.'

Harris inclined his head. 'From what I've heard, your cousin's in no position to do anything but stare at a hospital ceiling for a while.'

'Who told you that?'

'Doesn't matter. And before you ask, it wasn't me who attacked him. If I wanted Mulligan put out of action, I'd make it permanent, but he's not worth the effort. You, though...' Now he leant forward. 'You I think I could get used to having around.'

She said nothing, staring back at him with what she hoped was a disdainful expression. It didn't seem to bother him.

'Let's talk about the money you owe me,' he said. 'It's not that I need it, more... Well, it's about respect, isn't it? Responsibility. I made the sale in good faith, and Mulligan screwed me over. It's time to settle the debt.'

'Yeah, well, like I say, I can't pay you.'

He leant back again, rubbing his jaw. 'And yet you told me you'd made decent money in Scotland. Were you lying about how successful you've been?'

'Why should I bail out my cousin?' She allowed some belligerence into her tone. 'Would you pay a debt for Reuben Nash?'

Harris scowled, furious, as she had expected. 'I'd step over Reuben Nash if I saw him dying on the street. Anyway, he's nothing to me. Mulligan's your family, and I'm getting my money. I don't care which one of you pays, but someone's going to.'

'What's the problem between you and Reuben?'

'Apart from the fact his brother's a psychotic bastard who's attacked me more than once?'

She watched him. 'His dead brother, you mean? The one who's been murdered?'

'Murdered? Come on. Way I heard it, Nathan hit his head. How's that murder?'

'Depends if he fell or was pushed, doesn't it? And after the incident with the knife, you're probably the first person the police will want to talk to.'

Now he laughed. 'You think? You saw Nathan, he was off his face. He probably just tripped over his own feet. The police have been round here already, and I told them the truth. I left the club, got straight in a taxi. I was going to go to A and E to see if that fucker had broken my jaw, but in the end I didn't bother. I went home, then to bed. Whatever happened to Nathan, it was nothing to do with me. My mum backed me up; she heard me come in.'

Caelan hid a smile. 'You live with your mum?'

He glared at her. 'No, she lives with me. Something wrong with that?'

'Not at all.' She nodded towards the door. 'What about your friends out there? Johnny and…?'

She waited for him to fill in the gap, but he said, 'They dropped me at home, and where they went after that is their business.'

'Back to the club to give Nathan Nash a kicking? To kill him?'

His nostrils flared. 'I've told you it was nothing to do with us, and even if I'd wanted to teach him a lesson, I wouldn't have done it outside his brother's club. I'm not that stupid.'

Caelan wondered about that, but didn't comment. 'Then who do you think did it?'

'No idea. Why do you care?'

'I want to know who tried to kill James, and it seems too big a coincidence for him and Nathan Nash to be attacked within hours of each other if there's no link.'

Harris gave a dismissive shrug. 'Forgive me if I don't give a shit. We're here to talk about my money.'

She risked a smile. 'Well, unless I've won the lottery in the past five minutes and haven't been told, I still don't have it.'

He didn't laugh. He pushed back his chair, got to his feet. Caelan didn't turn her head as he moved around the desk to stand behind her. She forced herself to stay still, her body thrumming with energy, ready to attack or defend herself.

It was a mistake.

His hands were on her shoulders, gentle as a lover. He caressed them, his mouth close to her cheek, cigarettes and coffee on his breath. Caelan burned with anger, revulsion, but she knew she couldn't react. This was a test, one she was determined to pass.

His fingers moved down her arms, encircling both biceps for a second before sliding back up to her shoulders.

Then, suddenly, they were around her throat.

She froze, her body urging her to fight, or run. Harris didn't speak, but he was breathing faster. He was enjoying this – the power, the control. Her options flashed through her mind – drive her fist into his groin, shove the chair back into his body, then grab it and batter him with it. Her seated position would make any attempt to throw him off difficult, though, and she was furious with herself for allowing him near her. She waited, sensing that he had hesitated.

'You're going to work for me until you've paid off your debt,' he whispered. The pressure on her throat increased, but only slightly.

'Doing what?' she managed to say.

More pressure. 'Whatever I want. Whatever I tell you.' He laughed softly, his lips brushing her ear. 'Whenever I want.'

Caelan fought the rising panic, the disgust and fury. He wasn't hurting her, not yet. This was posturing, a show of dominance. How far was he willing to go? She didn't know, didn't want to risk finding out. He had locked the door, put the key in his pocket, and to retrieve it she would have to get close to him. Even if she'd put him out of action, that would leave her vulnerable again. She knew she would struggle to exit the room unless he opened the door himself. On the other hand, that meant Johnny, the man outside, couldn't get in to help his boss out unless he also had a key, which Caelan doubted. She imagined Harris would want to keep them to himself. Everything he did was a display of power. She knew she could hurt him, kill him if she had to, unless he got in a lucky punch. She was well trained, but a punch in the face would put her flat on her back as quickly as it would anyone else. The secret was to strike first and not allow the other person back up.

Harris's right hand slid up her throat and he gripped her jaw and chin. Viciously he yanked her head around so that their cheeks were pressed together.

'You've been getting on well with Reuben Nash, haven't you?' His voice was low, husky, and Caelan knew the situation was exciting him. The thought revolted her, and she cursed herself for coming here at all.

'I've spoken to him,' she croaked.

'Am I hurting you?' Harris whispered. Caelan said nothing, and he wrenched her jaw and chin again, hard. She made a small sound of distress, and he nuzzled her neck. 'Well?'

'A little.'

His left hand increased the pressure on her throat. 'You know, in your position, I'd be telling the truth. You were in Nash's office, just the two of you, nice and cosy. I want to know what he said to you.'

She didn't reply, and he squeezed. She choked, coughing, and he laughed as he released his grip. Caelan swallowed. He hadn't hurt her as much as he thought, but she knew she had to give him what he wanted. With him standing behind her, she was too vulnerable. It wasn't as though Reuben had passed on state secrets.

'He asked what my business was, said maybe we could work together, that he'd introduce me to people,' she said. 'I told him I needed to do a deal soon, because Mulligan owed you money. When he heard your name, he backed off. Didn't seem to want to know any more.'

His left hand was back at her throat, the right still gripping her face, his thumb digging painfully into her jaw. 'What else?'

'Nothing, I swear. He asked for my number later on, but then we found Nathan's body and...' She allowed her voice to trail away.

'You're sure there's nothing else?' This time he grabbed a fistful of her hair, twisting it, pulling her head back so her chest rose. Caelan knew that if he touched her breasts she would have to react. She couldn't allow this to go too far. 'Did Reuben tell you how he makes his money?' Harris said against her ear.

Caelan spoke quickly, as though she was panicking. Harris didn't know how close he was to having his fingers snapped. 'He said all I needed to know was that he's a businessman. He asked whether I dealt, like James.'

'What did you say?'

'I told him it was a safe assumption.'

Abruptly Harris let her go. Caelan made a show of half falling out of her chair. She pretended she was struggling to sit upright, fighting the temptation to rub her jaw, to explore her aching throat with her fingertips. She decided she would not give him the satisfaction, and kept her hands clenched in her lap.

He stepped away and stood over her, grinning. 'Do we understand each other?'

She lifted her chin. 'I think I'm beginning to get the picture.'

He laughed. 'You're a mouthy bitch, you know that? Usually I don't like women who talk back to me. They only ever try it once.'

'I'll try to remember that.' She looked at him. 'But no promises.'

His eyes narrowed. 'Careful.'

She didn't reply.

'I want you to find out what Nash is up to,' he said. 'He allows people to deal in his club, but he's never let me near. I want to know why, who his major players are. I know faces, but not names. More importantly, I want to know how else he makes his money.'

'What do you mean?'

Harris waved an impatient hand. 'His place is a dump, yet Nash seems to be loaded. Where's the money coming from?'

'I don't know. Don't people pay him to trade in the club?'

'Who told you that?'

'James.'

'Mulligan?' He made a sound of disgust. 'How would he know? He asked Reuben if he wanted to buy some of the crack he was peddling. Reuben laughed in his face.'

'Why?'

'Because Mulligan's small-time. Not worth the bother, especially now.' He checked his phone. 'Talk to Reuben. Anything you find out, let me know. I want that bastard's business.'

'His business?'

'The club. I made an offer when he bought it, but the seller was someone I'd pissed off years ago and he told me where to go.'

Caelan frowned at him. 'Why would you want it? You've just said it can't make much of a profit.'

'I have plans for it. The rest is none of your business.' He held up a hand, threw the key on the floor behind her. 'Now get out.'

She stood up slowly. 'All you want me to do is talk to Reuben?'

His smile was predatory. 'For now. But remember, I know you're staying at Mulligan's house, and I can visit any time I like. If I was you, I'd do as I was told. And don't think about running back up to Scotland or anywhere else. I'll find you.'

Caelan picked up the key, unlocked the door. Ignoring the urge to hurl it at his face, she left it in the lock. As she opened the door, Harris said quietly, 'And remember, you owe me fifteen grand. It's going to take you years to pay that off, and I'll own you until you do.'

22

Downstairs, Harris's mother was still hunched over her desk.

'Lovely son you've got there,' Caelan muttered as she strode past. She was ignored.

Ewan stood when he saw her, his face anxious. His eyes went to her throat, and Caelan saw his expression darken. Johnny came clattering down the stairs and nodded to the other bodyguard, who stepped away. Caelan took Ewan's hand and squeezed.

'Come on,' she said. 'Time to go.'

Ewan flung a look of hatred at Harris's heavies, then up at the ceiling.

'What did that bastard—'

'Leave it, please,' Caelan said, beginning to drag him towards the door. The bodyguards were laughing, each giving a little wave as they stepped onto the street.

'Are you okay? What the hell happened up there?' Ewan demanded.

'Let's just get away from here,' Caelan told him. She had been shaken by her encounter with Harris, but now she knew she needed to put some distance between them. She was raging too much to think clearly, and in her job that could be fatal.

Ewan didn't argue, didn't ask for explanations, and she was grateful. They walked quickly, hand in hand again, though after what Harris had done, Caelan had to force herself not to recoil from the contact.

It was only when they were on the Tube, speeding away from Harris's patch, that she began to explain what had happened.

Ewan listened silently, still holding her hand, staring at the floor of the carriage with his jaw clenched. When she'd finished, he turned to her.

'He could have—'

'I know what he could have done,' she said quietly. 'He didn't. Anyway, I wouldn't have let him get that far.'

Ewan nodded. 'Sorry.' He blew out his cheeks. 'What now?'

'We talk to Reuben, as instructed – we were going to anyway. And we'll need to check in.'

He nodded again, knowing that she meant with Penrith. Caelan also wanted to speak to Adele Brady to ask if any progress had been made on the enquiry into Nathan Nash's death, but Brady had said not to approach her directly. 'You know, on second thoughts, Reuben said to meet him later, at the club,' she said. 'Why don't we see the boss, then go and get a few hours' sleep? Don't know about you, but I'm dead on my feet.'

'Good plan.' Ewan hid a yawn behind his free hand. 'You said something about hotel rooms?'

'Well, we can't go back to the house. There's a place in Southwark they sometimes use. One of the chain places – nothing fancy, but clean and comfortable.'

They sat quietly for a while, Caelan beginning to realise that Ewan holding her hand was now giving her comfort, rather than feeling like an imposition. She wasn't attracted to him, never could or would be, but he was a good friend and a safe, reassuring presence. She shifted slightly, and he glanced at her, misinterpreting the movement.

'Sorry, I thought we were still...' He sat up straighter, releasing her hand, but she shook her head and took it again. Looking up at him, she saw he had realised what she needed him to do, and they sat in companionable silence until the train arrived at Westminster.

–

228

'Why didn't you kick the shit out of him?' Penrith asked.

Caelan shrugged. 'Didn't think you'd approve.'

'Never stopped you before.'

'We're looking for people traffickers, and Harris seems a good place to start. He treats women with contempt, like property. He thinks it's his right to touch them when he chooses, to insult them and beat them.' She paused. 'Why *didn't* I kick the shit out of him?'

'Because you're a professional,' Penrith said. 'Harris isn't worth it, not unless it's necessary to subdue him.' He gave Caelan a hard stare, which she took to mean that he understood how close she had been to having to put Harris out of action, and that he wasn't impressed with the risks she'd taken.

'Earlier you mentioned a mutual friend,' she said. 'Did you mean Adele Brady?'

'I did. She was going to call to update you, but we didn't think it wise in the end. You're supposed to be undercover, after all.'

Caelan frowned. 'Update me about what?'

'Tim Achebe and Jen Somerville have quietly been asked to look into the attack on Mulligan.'

'But—'

Penrith held up a hand. 'They're already working on Nathan Nash's death. I know. The point is, they've been involved in trying to persuade Mulligan to work with us from the start. They know him, and some of his background. Maybe you should speak to them about both cases.'

Caelan closed her eyes for a second. 'We'll need some rest first.'

'Fine.' His expression said it wasn't, but even Penrith recognised exhaustion when he saw it. 'I'll ask Tim and Jen to come to you. There are rooms reserved for you.' He named the hotel and location.

'Not the usual place, then?' Caelan said.

'No. We've used it a little too often. Safety first and all that.' Penrith peered into the mug that sat close to his right hand.

'Bugger. Empty. I won't offer you coffee because you'll only hang around for longer.'

'You're all heart.'

'It's interesting that Harris has asked you to spy on Reuben Nash for him,' Penrith mused. 'Hopefully it'll help us out too.'

'If I can get Reuben to trust me, maybe.' Caelan leant her head against the back of the chair, a dull pain beginning to pulse in her temple. 'Have you heard any more about Mulligan?'

'No change. There's a guard outside his room now, as I told you. No more phone calls trying to find out where he is, as far as I know.'

'Harris already knew about the attack on him.'

Penrith considered it. 'Jolene Townsend?'

'Maybe.' Caelan thought back to the previous evening. 'When Mulligan mentioned that he needed to raise some cash, Jolene suggested he speak to Harris. She must know something about how he makes his money.'

'She told us Mulligan was a nobody when we spoke to her earlier,' Ewan pointed out. 'If that was true, why would she think Harris might have a deal for him?'

'Everyone keeps telling us that. She also said, "What's he got to do with—" as though something was going on that Mulligan wasn't a part of,' Caelan said.

'And what did she mean?' Penrith demanded.

'No idea,' Caelan admitted. 'I couldn't press her without looking suspicious.'

'What's suspicious about it? Your cousin's been attacked and left for dead. And you want to know what happened. Go back to her. She knows something.' Penrith pulled a face, frustrated. 'I'm beginning to think you were right and none of this is worth the effort. Let them all kill each other if that's what they want to do.'

'Except Lucy Mulligan is still missing,' said Ewan.

There was silence, then Penrith sighed.

'We should have been more forceful with Mulligan. He must know more than he's told us, and now we can't speak to him at all.'

'He told me he was doing his best to point us in the right direction, but swore he didn't know who was involved,' Caelan said.

'And that was when we should have beaten it out of him.' Penrith screwed up his face to show he was joking. 'As we can't do that, especially now that someone else has had a go at him, let's go over the possibilities. Mulligan made a point of taking you places where you'd meet Stefan Harris, Reuben and Nathan Nash and Jolene Townsend. What about Leyton Grey?'

Caelan shrugged. 'We saw him at Stand and at Reuben's. Mulligan made him out to be a simple barber, but it seems he knows some of Mulligan's friends. I think he stays on the list.'

'What else do we know?' Penrith opened a desk drawer, took out a pad of paper and a pen and began to scribble.

'Reuben Nash and Stefan Harris can't stand each other. Harris wanted to buy the club Reuben now owns but the bloke who sold it wouldn't accept his bid because he also hates Harris.' Caelan paused, collecting her thoughts. 'We should probably track down whoever sold it to Reuben.' She watched Penrith make another note. 'And Harris says the club can't be making much of a profit so he wants to know where Reuben's money is coming from.'

'Don't we all.' Penrith tapped his pen against his front teeth. 'Maybe Reuben Nash is the one Mulligan was trying to point you towards.'

'Could be. Anyway, I'm seeing Nash again later,' Caelan said.

Penrith glanced at Ewan. 'Don't you mean "we are"?'

'I'm not invited,' Ewan told him.

Penrith focused on Caelan instead. 'Is that wise?' he asked.

'If we want him to talk, I think it probably is. Believe me, I'm not looking forward to it.' Caelan touched her jaw with her fingertips. It was tender, aching.

'Let Nash see what Harris did to you,' Penrith advised.

'He can hardly miss it,' Ewan said, anger clear in his voice. Penrith looked at him but didn't comment.

'What about Jolene Townsend?' he said.

'She admits to having a casual relationship with Reuben. Mulligan hinted she's a con artist, but she also works in a newsagent's, owned by her uncle. She knows Harris is a major dealer but backed away when Mulligan said he owed Harris money.' Caelan shook her head. 'I don't know, maybe she's afraid of Harris. She knows everyone Mulligan has introduced us to, but he seems protective of her.'

'Protective of her, yet he also told you she's a confidence trickster. Interesting,' said Penrith.

'You think it was a hint?' Caelan gritted her teeth. 'Why did he have to be so bloody cryptic? And when I spoke to him this morning, just when he seemed to be about to trust me and possibly tell me more, he—' She gave Penrith a sharp look. He gazed back at her.

'He…?'

'He was smacked around the head with a baseball bat.'

Penrith gave a slow nod. 'And I was the only person who knew what he'd said to you. Did I sneak out and do it myself, or send someone else after him? I see your dilemma.'

'Oh shut up, Ian. I'm wondering whether Mulligan contacted anyone while he was being taken back to Greenford. The officers with him would have noticed a phone call, but he could have sent a text without them realising.'

'We don't have his mobile, and it'll take a while to find anything out without it,' Penrith reminded her.

'I know.' Caelan covered her mouth as she yawned. 'This is hopeless. Could you ask Jen and Tim to give us time to get some rest before they show up, please?'

'You have four hours.' Penrith checked his watch. 'Starting now.'

Caelan pushed back her chair. 'You're a shit, you know that?'

He grinned. 'It's been mentioned. I want to speak to you after you see Reuben Nash.'

Ignoring him, Caelan headed out into the corridor with Ewan at her heels. As they made their way back onto the street and towards the Underground station, Ewan said, 'Likes to keep us on our toes, doesn't he?'

'Dancing to his tune, you mean,' Caelan said.

'I don't have any other clean clothes, or a toothbrush or razor.'

She nudged him. 'Use your credit card. We have them for a reason, you know.'

His smile was uncertain. 'Are you sure?'

'Definitely. I need stuff too, but just the essentials. At the moment, sleep is my priority.'

'Mine too.'

All at once, Caelan wanted to be alone. 'Then I'll see you at the hotel. There are probably rooms reserved for Jen and Tim too, so they look like guests rather than visitors.' She checked the time on her phone. 'See you soon.'

She walked away without looking back.

–

Ninety minutes later, Caelan was in her hotel room. She ran a bath, making sure the water was as hot as she could stand it. Lying back in the bubbles, she felt herself relax for the first time since she'd been at her parents' house. While she'd been doing the hurried shop for clothes and toiletries, she'd bought a flannel, and now she soaked it in the scalding water and held it to her bruised face and then her throat. She closed her eyes, knowing she couldn't linger for long. Two and a half hours' sleep wasn't going to be nearly enough, but she had learnt early in her career to make the most of a chance to rest whenever the opportunity arose, however brief.

She shampooed her hair and soaped her body, wincing again as she washed her face and throat. Once dry, she went through into the main bedroom, made herself a coffee and climbed into bed. Being reminded of her injuries had given her an idea, but she wouldn't be able to act on it until she had spoken to Achebe and Somerville.

Settling back on the pillow, she scrolled through the news on her phone while she drank her coffee. Though exhausted, she knew she was going to find it difficult to sleep. Now that she was alone and there were no distractions, Lucy Mulligan's face appeared again in her mind. Where was she? What was she going through? With Mulligan himself lying helpless in hospital, Caelan felt even more of an obligation to find his sister.

She didn't want to look too closely at what her motivations might be, knowing that despite everything she knew Mulligan had done, all he stood for, she felt responsible for the attack on him. At the end of their last conversation, in the cell at Acton, he had shown glimpses of conscience, of vulnerability. Something had shifted between them, especially when he had begged Caelan for help and agreed they should trust each other. How much more might he have said had they had the opportunity to talk again? She knew Mulligan was wily, but at that moment, he had appeared sincere. He had volunteered the information about the man who had provided him with the phone in Belmarsh, and Caelan knew it was because he was becoming increasingly concerned about his sister, whatever he said and however hard he tried to convince them that he couldn't care less.

She turned off the lamp, put the phone on the bed beside her. As usual, there was plenty of room. Hers was a lonely life, not compatible with having a partner or family. Seeing her parents and their comfortable, loving, familiar relationship had reminded her again how alone she was – her job had seen to that. Some might say her commitment to her work was the problem rather than the job itself, as Nicky had told her more than once, but undercover work was all or nothing. It had to be.

Now, though, as she had reminded herself, she no longer worked directly for the Met. Her time could be her own, if she wanted it to be. She would still need to work, but allowing herself more time to relax, to enjoy herself, to see her family was now possible.

Closing her eyes, she rolled onto her side. Less than two hours to sleep.

23

The people he passed shone and shifted, their voices loud and musical. Ryan paused outside a takeaway, the scent of meat and onions so intense he felt he could taste them, though he had no need of food. He grinned at his reflection in the window, knowing he was untouchable.

A young woman glanced at him, stared. He winked at her, certain she liked what she saw. He was well dressed, clean, his hair trimmed, his shoes new. All thanks to the stupid bastard who'd had five hundred quid in his wallet to impress the bloke he'd hired to be his toy for the night. The young woman turned away, said something to her friend, and they laughed together. Ryan's smiled widened. He would have liked to stay and talk to them, but there wasn't the time. He had to keep moving, earn more cash. Five hundred didn't go far these days.

Further down the road he saw an elderly man waiting at a bus stop, standing apart from the rest of the queue. He wore a brown raincoat, had a bald head and crumpled skin. Ryan started at him, seeing his grandfather. The man took out a wallet, began fumbling through it. Ryan smirked. Big mistake. The wallet already had his name on it. There was an Underground station down the road, and if he could make it before someone grabbed him, he would be away. And he knew he would make it. They wouldn't catch him, couldn't stop him.

He increased his pace, seeing a bus lumbering down the road and the people in the queue start shuffling in anticipation. Jostling, pushing, like sheep in a pen. Ryan hated them. Not the man with the wallet, though – he was a friend, and a generous one.

The bus slowed, almost at the stop. The man took a hesitant step towards the kerb, and as he did so, Ryan reached him, grabbed the wallet and ran. There were shouts behind him, but he didn't care. They couldn't catch him, wouldn't even try when they saw it was pointless. He was away on his toes and cruising, in control, the station and his escape route just ahead.

He dodged a group of laughing teenagers, weaved around a wheelchair and a man carrying a little girl on his shoulders. So slow, they were all so fucking slow. There was no one behind him, though. No reaching hands, no shouts of abuse.

The station was across the road now, and he felt a laugh escape him as he jogged towards it. It had been so easy. By the time anyone had realised what was happening, especially the doddering old sod he'd robbed, he'd vanished. Too clever, too quick.

Too late.

He never saw the car, but he felt the impact.

24

The first knock was more of a tap, but as Caelan struggled to force her eyes open, it quickly became more insistent. She rubbed at her face with both hands, feeling worse than when she had got into bed. Checking her phone, she realised Achebe and Somerville had allowed her an extra half an hour's rest.

'Five minutes,' she called as she rolled out of bed and reached for her clothes. She hadn't bothered with her usual jogging bottoms and T-shirt. Sleeping naked had felt almost as though she was doing something wrong, that she wasn't taking the job seriously, turning her back on protocol. In the hotel, behind a locked door and with the security of knowing she was no longer entirely under the Met's thumb, she found she didn't care.

She showered quickly, brushed her teeth, washed her face again with cold water before dressing. As she pushed her feet into her trainers, there was another knock. There was a security chain on the door, and Caelan slipped it on, more out of habit than anything else before stepping to one side and turning the handle. Somerville, Achebe and Ewan were waiting in the corridor.

'Hello, sleepyhead,' Jen Somerville said. Wordlessly Caelan stared back at them. All three gave her wary smiles, as though expecting a mouthful of abuse.

'Can we come in?' Achebe asked. He had two paper cups in his hands, and he held one out to Caelan. 'We have coffee.'

She opened the door wide. 'The coffee's welcome. I'm not sure about you three.' Taking the cup, she grinned as she opened the lid and sniffed. 'Thank you.'

Achebe smiled. 'Jen's idea.'

Somerville held up her own cup. 'Cheers. Thought you might need it.'

Caelan sat on the bed, her back against the headboard, as the others found places to park themselves. Somerville took the chair at the tiny desk, Achebe the sofa and Ewan the small armchair by the window. Caelan smiled at him.

'Did you sleep?' she asked.

Ewan pulled a face. 'For about forty minutes.' He held up his own coffee. 'Could do with a few litres of this stuff.' He glanced at Achebe, who was clearly ready to start. 'Sorry.'

'No worries. I know the two of you haven't had much chance to rest.' Achebe sat back, crossing his legs. 'Okay. Can we talk about Nathan Nash first?'

'Have they done the post-mortem?' Caelan asked. Achebe nodded. 'And what can you tell us?

'As expected, cause of death was a massive bleed on the brain. But,' Achebe exchanged a glance with Jen Somerville, 'it's what's happened to him before that's thrown us.'

'Before? What do you mean?' Caelan remembered what Brady had said about the possibility of Nash having a broken jaw. She hadn't noticed when they'd found his body, but then she hadn't examined him closely.

Somerville got to her feet, pulling her phone from her bag. She took a few seconds to scroll to whatever it was they wanted Caelan to see and held the handset out to her without a word, then leant against the wall beside the bed and folded her arms. The atmosphere in the room had changed. When Achebe and Somerville had arrived, they'd been smiling, handing over coffee, seeming relaxed. Now, ready to get down to business, their faces were grim.

Caelan looked at the image displayed on the phone's screen. Immediately she saw what Achebe was talking about. The photograph had been taken during – most likely at the beginning of – the post-mortem. The body lay face down on a steel table. Caelan stared, then forced herself to study the screen, but it was an effort. Nathan Nash's back looked like raw meat. The area between his shoulder blades and his buttocks was a mess of deep cuts, torn flesh and bruising.

Horrified, she looked up at Somerville, then at Achebe. 'What the hell happened to him? He was… whipped? Flogged?'

'We think so,' Achebe said. 'The pathologist found healing wounds on his wrists and ankles too. It's looking like he was bound to something with cable ties, maybe a table or post, and then…' He waved a hand, looking as sick as Caelan felt. Sometimes, however long you'd been in the job, however much you'd seen, something would happen that stopped you in your tracks.

Caelan stared at Nash's tortured body for another second, then turned to Ewan and held up the phone.

'You need to see this too.'

He crossed the room, had a look. Caelan saw him swallow, perhaps reminded of things he had seen during his time in the army that he wanted to forget.

'Poor bastard,' was all he said. Somerville reached out and took back her phone.

'Pretty much covers it,' she said as she sat back down.

Achebe leant forward on the sofa. 'You don't need me to tell you that this changes things. We don't know who did this to Nash, or why. It could have been to extract information from him, or as some kind of punishment.'

'Or a warning to his brother,' Ewan said.

Achebe nodded. 'Or to Nathan himself.'

Caelan took a breath and let it out slowly, trying to erase the image of Nash's ruined flesh from her mind. The photograph had affected her more than finding the body had. 'Did the pathologist have any idea what might have been used to… do this to him?'

'Probably some kind of plastic-coated cable, but it's difficult to be sure. There were no traces of rope in the wounds, for example.' Achebe spoke without emotion, but Caelan knew that didn't mean he wasn't feeling it. The beating Nash had suffered had been calculated, inflicted by a person apparently undisturbed by the cruelty and brutality of what they were doing. This assault had been deliberate and prolonged, meted out by someone who had the stomach to watch the injuries they were causing deepen and worsen as they brought the cable down on Nash's back over and over again. Someone able to ignore his cries of agony.

Someone like…

'James Mulligan has been accused of torturing people for information before,' said Somerville, as though reading Caelan's mind.

'You think Mulligan ordered this?' Caelan considered it. 'Why would he? Who would he have asked to do it? The two men he employed are in jail, and we don't know of anyone else he trusted.'

'Doesn't mean they aren't out there, though,' Somerville said.

Caelan glanced at the other woman, saw no animosity on her face. 'True.'

'There's something else,' said Achebe. 'Nathan Nash's jaw was definitely broken, but not by a fist.'

'Considering the bruising, the pathologist guessed at a blunt instrument, possibly a baseball bat,' Somerville added.

'And Mulligan was hit with a baseball bat too. The same one?' Caelan asked.

Achebe's shoulders twitched. 'We don't know, maybe never will. We didn't find anything at either scene or on the victims we could compare. No splinters, no shards of wood.'

'Bit of a coincidence if it wasn't the same bat, though,' said Somerville.

There was a silence.

'To me, this adds weight to the idea that Mulligan didn't order the beating Nathan was given. I think someone else is behind the attacks on them both.' Caelan screwed up her face, thinking about it.

'My money would be on Stefan Harris,' Achebe put in. 'Nathan made him look a twat and Mulligan owed him money.'

'Makes sense,' Somerville said with a nod.

'What about Nathan's back, though? Harris has the muscle men to inflict the damage, but why? Nathan didn't hesitate when he had a go at Harris in the club. He wouldn't have taken a thrashing like that without fighting back, even days later.'

'Maybe that's why he ended up with a knife at Harris's throat,' Ewan said.

'But wouldn't he have said so? "This is for what you did to me", or whatever?' Achebe rubbed his eyes. 'I don't know. This whole thing is tying me in knots.'

'I'm surprised Nathan was able to walk around, much less throw himself at Harris like he did, considering the pain he must have been in.' Caelan hadn't thought about it before, but the wounds must have been causing agony, yet Nathan Nash had shown no sign of being in pain when she'd seen him.

'The results haven't come back from the lab yet, but the pathologist is guessing some heavy-duty painkillers and stim-ulants, both legal and otherwise, will show up in his system,' Achebe said. 'You told the chief super that Nathan seemed drunk, or high? Maybe that's why. He'd swallowed a shit ton of stuff to take the edge off.'

Caelan nodded. 'It doesn't help us explain anything, though. I need to ask Reuben Nash about his brother's injuries.'

Somerville inclined her head. 'You mean *we* do. You wouldn't know about them if we hadn't told you, and Victoria Smith would have no idea.'

'Unless I prod Reuben in the right direction and he tells me himself.'

'If he knows about it at all.' Somerville folded her arms. 'Nathan rented a flat in Ealing Broadway, not far from his brother's club. We've gone over it – there was blood on the bed sheets, bandages, cotton wool and antiseptic in a bag on the kitchen table, plus some that had been opened and used in the bathroom. Now we know about the mess his back was in, what we found makes sense.'

'You think he went back there after... well, whatever happened to him, and lay low?' Ewan asked.

Somerville turned to him. 'Again, we need to find out. We're talking to his neighbours, local taxi firms, anyone we think might be able to help us, but without a more definite time frame, it's even harder than usual. It seems as though he tried to clean and dress his wounds – or someone else did.'

Ewan nodded. 'It would have to be someone else, wouldn't it? He wouldn't be able to do it himself, not his back.'

'Jolene Townsend's fingerprints were found in Nathan's flat, but so were Reuben Nash's, as you'd expect. There were loads more we couldn't identify,' Achebe said.

'What about any prints on the medical stuff?' Ewan wanted to know. Caelan was pleased to see him asking questions, making suggestions. She knew he lacked confidence and was also aware he needed to adjust to his new role in his own time.

'They couldn't get anything useful, not even from the bottle of antiseptic. Too many people have handled it,' Somerville said. She uncrossed her arms, tucked her hair behind her ears. Caelan knew the other woman usually wore a wedding ring, but she saw it was missing and wondered if Achebe had realised. Somerville didn't seem the type to confide in anyone, but she doubted Achebe missed much. She looked away, not wanting Somerville to notice her interest. It was none of her business.

'Maybe Jolene helped Nathan after he was hurt then?' she said.

'It's possible. We found a receipt in the bag with the bandages and stuff showing they'd been purchased in one of the local branches of Tesco three days ago,' said Achebe.

'We're pretty sure it was Nathan himself who bought the items, looking at the CCTV from the store, but it's not definite,'

Somerville added. 'It was a cash sale, one of the self-service checkouts. The person buying them is the right height and build, but it's the usual story – baseball cap, head down… almost as though they knew we'd come looking for them.'

'Maybe the person who did it, or ordered it to happen, sent Nathan on his way with a bag of supplies to tidy himself up afterwards?' Ewan looked disgusted and Caelan couldn't blame him.

'There must have been more than one person involved,' Somerville pointed out. 'Maybe even three or four. Nathan had been tied to something, which means he must have been overpowered. Even if he was drugged, it would take more than one person to lift him, get him upright or onto a table.'

'Harris and his men,' Achebe said, though he didn't sound convinced.

'Maybe Nathan never saw who gave him the beating. A bag over his head, face down on the table or against a post…' Caelan said.

'Depends what the point of it was, I suppose,' said Somerville. 'If they wanted information, someone would have needed to speak to him. If it was meant as a warning, maybe not.'

'When did the pathologist say the wounds were inflicted?' Caelan asked.

'He said a couple of days before death, which ties in with the CCTV from the supermarket.' Achebe finished his coffee and crossed the room to drop the cup into the bin. 'There are people we need to talk to – Johnny Bates and Chris Walsh to begin with.'

'Johnny… You're talking about the two men who babysit Harris?' Caelan said.

Achebe looked at her. 'Do you know their backgrounds?'

'No. I'm assuming they both have records?'

'And both have served time. Couple of months here, a year or two there. The usual list – assault, ABH, unlawful wounding.

No weapons used by either of them, but they're not shy about using their fists,' Achebe said. 'Obviously we have a record of their fingerprints but none were found in Nathan's flat.'

'There were no traces of the flogging having taken place in Nathan's home, though?' Caelan asked, though she was sure it would have been mentioned already.

'None, and there would have been,' said Somerville.

'And the neighbours would have heard. I doubt anyone could have taken a thrashing like that without making a sound, and there are flats above, below and to either side. We've spoken to most of the neighbours, and so far no one can help us.'

'We have to talk to the brother again.' Somerville's tone was that of someone closing an argument.

'When?' Caelan looked from Somerville to Achebe. Achebe smiled.

'I suppose you want to see him first?'

She thought about it. 'No. I think I might get more from him later if you interview him now. He'll probably be angry, upset – he might want someone to complain to.' She met Achebe's eyes. 'What do you think?'

'Sounds like a plan. We'll be making it official this time, bringing him to the station, cautioning him. Reckon it might ruffle his feathers if he realises he's a suspect.'

There was a silence. Caelan finished her coffee and set the empty cup on the tiny shelf beside the bed.

'What about the attack on Mulligan?' she asked.

'It's early days, but so far it's the same story,' Somerville said. 'No one saw anything, not even some bloke with a baseball bat marching into his house, which you think would have raised eyebrows. Some of the neighbours are still at work, so we haven't spoken to them yet, but we're not hopeful. What could they have seen if they weren't at home when it happened?'

'Truth told, we have nothing,' said Achebe.

'Except the link with the baseball bat,' Ewan pointed out.

'And that's probably at the bottom of the Thames by now.' Achebe massaged his temples, wincing as he did so.

'Headache?' Caelan asked. Her own had subsided, but she still felt as though she could sleep for a week.

'Hoping it doesn't turn into a migraine. If it does, I'll be useless for the rest of the day, and the boss won't be happy.' Achebe took a box of headache tablets from his jacket pocket and popped two into his palm. 'Okay if I use the bathroom?'

'Of course.' Caelan wouldn't want to have to tell Adele Brady she was going home with a headache either.

'Cheers.'

Achebe didn't bother to close the door, and they heard the tap running, then him spluttering.

'Is there any update on Lucy Mulligan?' Caelan asked as he came back into the room.

'Nothing. No activity on her debit or credit card or bank account. Housemates haven't seen or heard from her, she hasn't been in touch with the unit her mother's in, and she usually calls at least once a week to check on her. There's been no contact with anyone at the university either, which in my view is the most concerning thing.' Achebe sat back down on the sofa. 'She's the perfect student, totally dedicated.'

Caelan nodded. 'She told Penrith she couldn't go into a safe house because it would disrupt her studies.'

'There you go then. Wherever she is, I doubt she went there voluntarily.'

'What about her computer? Have we been able to examine it? Penrith said it had been smashed up.'

'It had, and whoever was responsible did a thorough job. Our geeks have managed to have a poke around, but there's nothing that can help us.' Achebe's frustration showed on his face. 'As I understand it, she'd pretty much wiped it clean.'

'Really? As though she knew someone might come for her?' Caelan made it a question, though it seemed the obvious conclusion.

'Maybe,' Somerville said. 'Though it must be backed up in the Cloud somewhere, or whatever the terminology is these days. Again, the geeks are seeing what they can do.'

'Apart from the injuries to Nathan's back, that's all we have. Three cases, and the progress we've made on any of them sits somewhere between nothing and zero.'

'We're no closer to being able to identify the murdered woman in the photo sent to Lucy Mulligan, or the other two victims?' Caelan saw the three faces in her mind. Three anonymous, voiceless people, forgotten and abandoned. Unmissed. She remembered what Mulligan had said: *A quiet funeral, no big do with full honours for you, because let's face it, no one knows who you are. You're faceless.* She pushed the memory away, focusing on Achebe.

'Still nothing,' he said. 'No matches in any missing person report we've been able to access. No matches when we checked their fingerprints or DNA either. We'll keep trying, but...' He spread his hands, frustrated. 'I hate not being able to at least give them a name.'

'We will,' Somerville told him.

Achebe didn't look convinced as he checked his watch. 'Jen, we should be going. Can you call and ask for Reuben Nash to be brought in, please?'

Somerville rose and left the room without a word. Achebe watched her go and then stood.

'Is she okay?' Caelan asked.

'Jen? I think so. Some stuff going on at home.' Achebe headed for the door, then checked himself and turned back. 'There is something else. Ryan Glennister.'

'You've found him? I assumed someone would be on it. Penrith said he'd speak to Brady.'

Achebe laughed. 'He did, but we haven't been looking. Even Ian Penrith can't expect us to run four investigations simultaneously. No, you could say Ryan made it easy for us. I had a call about it on the way over here – he was involved in a hit and run earlier. Smacked off his tits and stumbled in front of a car, ended up in A and E. He's a bit banged up, but he'll be okay. Might be time for him to check back into rehab.'

'The driver didn't stop?' Caelan was already thinking about what this might mean. She'd wondered from the start if Glennister could tell them anything about Mulligan and his dodgy dealings, but Penrith hadn't seen it as worth pursuing. Maybe it was coincidence, but maybe someone else saw Glennister as a possible source of information too. She had told Mulligan about Glennister being at Lucy's house, and though Mulligan couldn't have been driving the car that hit Glennister, he could have paid someone else to do it. She rubbed her aching eyes, despairing of the whole situation.

'More questions, no answers.' Achebe's smile was knowing.

'Has anyone spoken to him?'

'Local officers took a statement, but it doesn't make much sense. The hospital did find another man's wallet in Glennister's pocket, though. He wouldn't explain how he'd got it, but I doubt he tripped over it in the street. They're going to have another chat when he comes down from whatever he's on plus whatever the hospital gave him.'

'Where did it happen?' Caelan asked.

'I wasn't told. I think he was taken to the Royal Free. Listen, I need to go. No doubt we'll talk again soon.'

With a wave, Achebe was gone. Caelan turned to Ewan.

'What do you think?' she said.

'About Glennister?'

'I knew I should have been looking for him.'

'But Penrith said—'

'I know what he said.' Caelan raised a hand. 'Sorry. It's just…'

'Frustrating.' Ewan gave her a sidelong glance.

'What?' Caelan spoke quietly, realising there was more he wanted to say.

'Well, Nathan Nash is dead, Mulligan's in intensive care, his sister's still missing and now Ryan Glennister's been hurt too. It's worrying. I thought we were just here to gather information, but since we started poking around…'

'Everything's gone to shit.'

He smiled. 'Exactly.'

'Mulligan keeping quiet about the money he owes Harris didn't help. We could have handled it differently if we'd known. Now I'm trapped between Harris and Reuben Nash.'

Ewan shuffled his feet. 'After what he did to you today... I know you can handle it, handle him, but he could have had a knife, a gun, anything. You're putting yourself in danger based on the word of Mulligan, who will do anything to keep himself out of prison. You told Penrith this was a waste of time, and I think you were right. You don't work for the Met any more – you can walk away at any time.'

Caelan paused. 'Maybe, but...'

'Lucy Mulligan's still missing. I know.'

'And while she is, I can't tell Penrith to stick the whole job up his arse.'

'Can't you?'

She looked at him. 'You know I can't.'

'Fair enough. What's next?'

'We do as we're told.'

25

Caelan and Ewan went back to the newsagent's where Jolene Townsend worked.

'Let's hope she's still here,' Caelan said as they neared the shop. 'She'll probably lock the door when she sees us – me, anyway.'

They slowed their pace as a man approached the shop and went inside.

'One of her customers?' Ewan said softly.

Caelan picked up the pace again. 'Let's see if we can find out.'

She pushed the door open. Jolene was behind the counter, the man they'd just seen handing over some banknotes. Jolene looked up and scowled.

'Fuck's sake, what do you want now? Why don't you just bring sleeping bags and move in?'

Caelan approached the counter. 'I want to talk to you.'

Jolene's customer looked nervously over his shoulder. 'Look, I was here first.'

'Yeah, well take the shit she's peddling you and get out,' Caelan told him.

'Cheeky bitch.' Jolene held her fist over the man's open palm and his fingers closed around whatever he was buying. Caelan guessed it was spice or weed. The man turned and fled. Jolene folded her arms.

'I'm trying to make a living here,' she said. 'Tell me what you want and then piss off.'

'I want some answers.'

'Yeah? I hear Google's good for that.'

'You said you didn't know who my cousin's housemates are?'

Jolene assumed a blank expression. 'What?'

'You heard. Which one of them do you sell to?'

A quick glance towards the back of the shop. 'I don't have to tell you anything.'

Caelan took another couple of steps forward and stood at the side of the counter, her own arms folded and her face set. Taking in her expression, Jolene gave her a nervous glance. 'I only need to scream and my uncle will be in here with his shotgun.'

Caelan made a show of hesitating, though she didn't believe it. 'His what?'

Jolene smirked. 'Come on, who has a shotgun? Made you think, though, didn't it?' She uncrossed her arms, set her phone on the counter. 'You going to tell me what's going on? How's Mulligan?'

She almost sounded friendly, and Caelan wondered at her quick change of attitude. 'Still alive, but who knows how long he'll stay that way,' she said. 'Help me out, Jolene. I need to find Lucy, make sure she's okay. People are getting hurt around here.'

'Hurt?' Jolene scoffed. 'Killed, you mean.'

'Then tell me what you know.'

'Nothing to tell. I know someone who lives in the house next door to Lucy's. I'm not giving you a name, because I sell to him, but he's on the same course as one of Lucy's housemates. He told me this bloke's obsessed with Lucy – follows her around, watches her, probably sniffs her dirty washing too.'

Tom Haslam, Caelan thought. 'And?'

'And what?'

Frowning, Jolene paused. 'You realise I'm taking a risk here? What if you go to the police?'

'The police?' Caelan gave the loudest snort she could muster. 'You think I want them anywhere near me or my family?'

'You told me they're investigating what happened to Mulligan.'

'Of course they are. Even the police can't fail to take notice when a man's lying by his front door with his head smashed in. Doesn't mean they'll get anywhere. Doesn't mean they want to.' Now Caelan leant in. 'Tell me. I'll keep your name out of it, your customer's too. Help me, and I'll leave you alone to get on with your business.' She decided to take a chance and lowered her voice. 'I'm going to need people to help me now I'm around. Let's face it, Mulligan's struggling – I mean with business, though since the attack he's fucked every which way as far as I can see. You want to make money, and so do I. Maybe we can help each other out.'

She waited, wondering if she'd gone too far. Jolene was close to Reuben Nash, Mulligan and Stefan Harris too. Who knew which way she would turn or where her loyalties lay.

Jolene bit her bottom lip as she thought about it. 'I do need money. I'm… I owe someone.'

'Is it Harris?' Caelan asked without thinking.

Jolene scowled. 'None of your fucking business.'

'All right, I'm sorry. All I'm saying is, we don't have to be enemies. There's room for us all to get rich.'

Would Jolene bite? If she did owe Harris money, she might be tempted. Who knew what he had her doing in order to pay him back?

After a few seconds, she exhaled heavily. 'Yeah, all right, I'll tell you. Only because this girl's missing, not because I want to. You really going to cut me in?'

'I said so, didn't I? Listen, I want James to recover, of course I do. But chances are he's going to need time to get back to normal, if he ever does. This is an opportunity, and I reckon the blokes around here have run things long enough.'

Jolene laughed. 'Girl power now, is it?' She stopped and stared. 'What happened to your neck?'

Caelan ignored that. 'Listen, I have contacts – I used to import my own gear when I was in Scotland. I can pick that up again, no worries, and you can stop peddling from this shithole and start earning some real money.'

'Shithole?' Jolene glared. 'Cheeky cow.'

'You know what I mean.'

'Anyway, what I do here is a sideline.' Jolene smoothed her hair. 'I have other stuff going on too.'

'Yeah? And it's making you rich, is it, conning people?'

'How the—' Jolene stopped, nodded to herself. 'Mulligan.'

'He made a comment, but I worked it out myself.'

'Well done.'

Caelan held up her hands. 'Come on, I'm impressed. It takes balls to run a scheme like that.'

'Yeah, I do okay, but it's not regular income, if you know what I mean. Depends who I meet, how stupid they are.'

'Well, I'm offering you a partnership. The money we make would be split fifty-fifty. I'd have a contract drawn up.'

'A contract? You're kidding.'

'Straight up,' Caelan lied. 'I know a legal bloke, takes on this kind of job on the side. It wouldn't be specific about what we're selling, but it'd do the job. Protect us both, wouldn't it?'

'If you say so.' Jolene nodded at Ewan. 'What about him?'

Caelan smiled. 'He'd protect us both too. He'll make himself useful, don't worry, but he's not a businessman.'

'Just happy to spend the profits,' Ewan said with a smirk.

Curling her lip at him, Jolene turned back to Caelan. 'That's the deal?'

'Best I can do. Can't say any fairer than fifty-fifty. Like I said, a partnership.'

'And you're offering me this because you want to find a cousin you hardly know?' Jolene looked sceptical, and Caelan couldn't blame her. 'You must be crazy.'

Caelan knew she had to keep talking. 'It's not only that. You know the place, the people. You already have customers. I'm not new to the game but I'm new to the area.'

Jolene's eyes strayed towards her mobile, which was still on the counter between them.

'How do I know I can trust you?' she said.

Now Caelan smiled. 'You don't, any more than I know I can trust you.' She grabbed Jolene's phone before the other woman could stop her and held it up. 'You're recording this, aren't you?'

Jolene stuck out her chin. 'No. Why should I be?'

'Because you want proof that I came in here offering you a deal? Because you want to go running to one of your boyfriends to tell tales? I don't know, Jolene. You tell me.'

Lunging across the counter, Jolene made a grab for the phone, but Caelan stepped back and held it out of reach.

'Give me the code to unlock it.'

She spoke quietly but with authority. Jolene's face contorted. 'Fuck off,' she snarled.

Caelan smiled. 'I'm going to stop this recording one way or another, so either you tell me the code, or I drop the phone on the floor and keep stamping until there's nothing left but a five-hundred-piece jigsaw.'

'Bitch.'

'Yeah, yeah, you've already told me.' Caelan lowered the phone to hip height, her eyes not leaving Jolene's. 'Five seconds. One, two—'

Jolene smacked her palm against the counter. 'All right. Fucking crazy bitch. It's one nine zero seven seven three.'

Caelan tapped in the numbers and scrolled until she found what she was looking for. 'Thank you.' She held out the phone. 'What's the number mean? Is it someone's birthday?'

Jolene snatched the phone, shoved it into her pocket. 'Yeah, my mum's. She's dead, in case you're interested.'

'I'm sorry. I didn't know.' Caelan felt a tug of guilt.

'Why should you? You just want to push me around, make me do what you want me to.' Jolene ran an angry hand over her eyes. 'Like everyone else does. Like they always have.'

'Jolene, I—'

'No, you're going to listen to me for a change.' Jolene's eyes were fixed on Caelan's, her gaze steady, her voice cold. 'My mum died when I was fourteen. She argued with her boyfriend in the pub one night and he marched her home, gave her a kicking and threw her down the stairs.' She took a breath. 'Then he came into my bedroom and...' Her voice faltered and she glanced at Ewan. He didn't move, gave no sign he had heard her.

'We get it,' Caelan said softly.

Jolene looked at her feet. 'Yeah, well. Everyone's got a story, haven't they?'

'Some are worse than others.'

'Maybe.' Jolene raised her head. 'Anyway, he ran from the house, left my mum lying there. I managed to get downstairs to her, but I was...' She faltered, cleared her throat. 'I was hurt myself. Anyway, I was too late. By the time the ambulance arrived, she was gone. I went to hospital, then into foster care. My mum was cremated by the council and her bastard boyfriend went down for life once they found him.' She bared her teeth in a vicious smile. 'And eventually he found out what a life sentence can really mean.'

'What do you mean?'

'Someone shanked him last year.' Jolene drew a finger across her throat. 'Bled out in a couple of minutes. Heartbreaking.'

Caelan was silent, thinking about another man she'd known who had died in prison in exactly the same way. Suspicion flared in her mind. 'Do they know who did it?'

Jolene gave a dismissive flick of her hand. 'Does it matter?'

'Probably not.' Caelan maintained eye contact. 'Was it someone James knew?' Or someone he had threatened?

'Might have been. All I'm saying, is, don't think you can push me around. Whatever you think you're threatening me with, I've been through ten times worse. You don't scare me and you won't own me.'

'I'm not trying to. I said partners – equal partners.'

'And I won't drop Mulligan in the shit, not ever. He's been good to me. If he gets better, all of this is off.'

Caelan still wasn't sure about Jolene's motives, especially since she apparently owed money. Her expression when Caelan had asked about Stefan Harris had been telling. 'Then you agree?'

Jolene held out a hand. 'Fuck it, yeah, though I don't know what we're going to sell. Mulligan said he needed a deal. Does that mean you do too?'

Caelan gave a reluctant nod as she shook Jolene's hand, hoping she was going to be able to keep up the pretence. Her role was becoming more complicated by the day. 'Like I said, I have contacts.'

'Me too. I know a bird can get you anything you want, though she's pricey. Has to be, her stuff's the best. We'll need money up front, though.'

'Which is the main problem.' Caelan chewed the inside of her cheek, pretending to think about it. 'Let me talk to my contact. He might let us have some credit.'

'No chance. These guys never do. I've known this woman I buy from for years and she still wouldn't lend me a fiver.'

'Maybe. Let me see if I can persuade him. I've done favours for him in the past.' Caelan flicked a glance at Ewan, and Jolene leered.

'Yeah, got you. Well, let me know.'

Caelan hoped Ewan would keep his mouth closed, and he did, though he didn't look happy. Caelan wondered whether it was genuine. She was used to lying with every second breath, but he wasn't and she wondered if he might be struggling.

'Your turn.' She pointed a finger at Jolene. 'Tell me what your customer said. I need to find my cousin.'

'All right. Damon – shit, I mean my customer – was sitting behind someone in a lecture one day. They all have laptops or tablets out, supposed to be making notes, but this one guy, the one in front of Damon, was watching a video.' Jolene paused, ran a hand across her mouth. 'Oh, I don't know about this. I feel like a grass.'

Caelan wanted to scream at her. 'Come on, Jolene. We've agreed a deal.'

In truth, what Jolene had already let slip might be enough to help them. They could go back to Tom Haslam, throw their knowledge about his obsession with Lucy in his face and see how he reacted, but if there was more, Caelan wanted the whole story.

'Yeah, you could be ripping me off. I could spill my guts and never see you again.'

'Not going to happen,' Caelan told her.

'Prove it.'

Fuck, Caelan thought. 'How am I supposed to do that?'

Jolene's smile was cunning. 'You know the debt you owe Stefan?'

'You mean the fifteen thousand James owes him? Yeah, rings a bell. Why?'

'How'd you like to make it twenty?'

'Twenty? What do you mean?' But Caelan already knew.

'That's my price.'

'Five grand? Five grand to give me information that could save someone's life?'

Jolene scoffed at her. 'Dramatic, aren't you? I still reckon she's gone off with her boyfriend.'

'No one knows, that's the point.'

Another smile. 'Can't take the risk then, can you? Agree to pay the five K for me and I'll tell you everything I know.'

'And if I don't pay?'

'Then I'll go to Stefan and tell him you're planning on muscling in on his patch.'

'What if I go to your mate Damon myself? Shouldn't be too hard to track him down.'

'Same applies. I go to Stefan.'

Caelan narrowed her eyes. 'Who's the bitch now?'

Jolene laughed. 'You said it yourself – we can help each other out here.'

'No choice then, have I?' Caelan shook her head as though resigned to being outmanoeuvred. 'All right. Looks like I'm paying your bill too.'

'What the fuck?' Ewan exploded. 'You don't have the money to pay Harris a couple of grand, never mind twenty. Why don't you walk away, let your cousins sort out their own shit? You owe them nothing. You don't even know if she,' he glared at Jolene, 'has anything worth saying.'

'Owen—' Caelan started to say, wondering what the hell Ewan was thinking.

'Come on.' Jolene held up her hands. 'I'm giving you information, my time, my contacts and my loyalty.'

He snorted. 'Loyalty? Do you even know what the word means? Back-stabbing bastards, the lot of you.'

Caelan turned on him. 'Can you let me handle this?'

'Yeah, do as you're told,' Jolene told him. 'You're only here to look pretty, remember?'

Ewan turned on his heel and walked out of the shop. Caelan looked at Jolene.

'Finished?'

'Not my fault he's a touchy bastard. Where were we?'

Caelan exhaled through her nose, told herself to stay calm. Whether Ewan's anger had been fake or genuine, she wasn't going to run after him.

'You were going to tell me what you know,' she said.

'Well, Damon was in the lecture, yeah, and this guy in front of him is watching some video on his phone, kind of hiding it behind his laptop screen.'

'But not hiding it from Damon?' Caelan was instantly suspicious. Was this a set-up?

'Damon was a couple of rows behind. He came in late, sat down quickly and quietly. He didn't think the other guy knew he was there.'

'Convenient. You think he'd have been more careful.'

Jolene scowled. 'Do you want to hear this or not?'

'You know I do.'

'All right. So Damon's half listening to the lecture, and watching this video at the same time, only he realises it's not a video at all. It's live footage.' Jolene raised her eyebrows. 'You see what I'm saying?'

Caelan was beginning to. Her heart began to thump. 'You mean—'

'I *mean*, this pervert had hidden a camera in this girl's room and was watching her every chance he got, even when he should have been listening to his teacher. It was her bedroom, and Damon said you could see she had no idea she was being watched. She was getting changed, doing her hair... He must have seen her naked hundreds of times. Maybe he's even broadcasting it, making other people pay to watch.'

'You're saying he was spying on my cousin,' Caelan said flatly. She felt sick, but this might be a break. If there was a camera in Lucy's room when she disappeared, wouldn't it have picked up what had happened?

'Woman in her twenties, long red hair? That's exactly what I'm saying.' Jolene sounded disgusted too.

'Did your friend Damon give you a name? If they were on the same course, I assume he recognised him?'

'Of course he did. He said his name's Tom. Tom Haslam.'

Caelan nodded, angry but not wanting Jolene to pick up on it. 'We've met him. I spoke to him when we went to Lucy's house earlier.' And he lied to us.

'Yeah?' Jolene curled her lip. 'Lucky you. He must have one of those cameras you set up to watch your front door or your dog. You know the ones? You log in through an app on your phone to see what's happening?'

'I've seen them.'

'He could have got into her room and hidden it somewhere.'

But how? Caelan wondered. When? Lucy Mulligan was a computer expert, surely well versed in the latest technology.

Wouldn't she have noticed a camera suddenly appearing, even if it was well hidden? She didn't want the other woman to think she wasn't taking her story seriously, but she knew she had to be cautious. Jolene had just palmed off her own debt and thought she had Caelan trapped. She was a con artist, and spinning a line or two would be what she did best. But this time, she wasn't aware Caelan knew more than she did.

'You'd think she'd have realised,' was all Caelan said.

'Why would she? You don't expect people to be watching you, do you?' Jolene shook her head. 'No. Poor cow hadn't a clue.'

'But how would he have set it up? He told us Lucy's room was always locked when she wasn't in there.'

'Don't know, do I? He probably sneaked in when she was in the shower or something. I doubt she locked the door every time she went to the toilet or kitchen. Wouldn't bother, would you?'

'Seems she should have done.'

'Telling me.'

Caelan considered what Jolene had said. However outraged she was about the invasion of Lucy Mulligan's privacy, however abhorrent she found Haslam's actions, she knew the images he had seen might help them. If Lucy had been abducted somehow, or at least forced to leave the house under duress, Haslam might have seen what had happened, even from afar. He wouldn't have been able to tell the police, or Caelan and Ewan when they had seen him, without landing himself in a lot of trouble.

'Dirty little fucker,' she muttered. 'Didn't this mate of yours think to confront him? Not even when Lucy went missing?' Normally she would have asked why he hadn't gone to the police, but she knew the woman she was supposed to be would want to deal with the situation herself, not run to the law. Anyone involved in buying or dealing drugs might think twice too, whatever the situation.

Jolene looked shifty. 'Well, he thought… I mean, he didn't see any harm in it at first.'

Caelan stared. 'What?'

'I know, I know… blokes for you. Some blokes, anyway. He thought it was funny, that's why he told me about it. Thought I was going to laugh along with him.' Jolene pressed her lips together. 'Wanker. I soon put him straight. Anyway, when I spoke to him after I heard Mulligan's sister had disappeared, he pretended he didn't remember telling me about it, said he'd been off his face and I should have ignored him. Told me to forget about it.'

'Shit.' Again Caelan wondered how much she could trust what Jolene was saying.

'Yeah. Tell you the truth, I wouldn't be surprised if he was planning to blackmail this perv with the camera.' Jolene tucked her hair behind her ears. 'And if he tried it, maybe this Tom Haslam has already taken the camera away. If he has, even if you got back into the house, you'd never prove what Damon told me is true.'

Caelan hid a smile. And you're banking on me not being able to, she thought. 'He must have taken it away,' she said. 'The police went into Lucy's room, Haslam told me that himself. They'd have found it.'

'Maybe they did. Maybe they're planning to arrest him,' Jolene said.

Caelan knew she'd have to check, though if the camera had been found and identified as Haslam's, she knew her colleagues would have brought him in for questioning at least. They would have had to consider the possibility that he had been involved in Lucy's disappearance. No. He must have removed it before the police arrived, but how would he have known they were coming if he wasn't aware Lucy had disappeared? His obsession now seemed even more sinister.

Appearing to read her mind, Jolene said, 'So what are you going to do?'

'I don't know yet.' Caelan wasn't lying. She should go to Penrith, to Brady, Achebe and Somerville, but it would be obvious where the information had come from if the police went knocking on Haslam's door again. Jolene and Damon would run for the hills, but not before Jolene had told Stefan Harris what Caelan was planning, and the whole operation would be blown. It was another problem to add to a case already thick with them. 'Maybe I should go back and see Haslam again.'

'Well, when you decide, remember to keep me out of it. Damon told me it was our little secret, and I don't want him thinking I can't be trusted. He's a good customer, and word would get around.'

'But you'll sell him out for five grand?'

Jolene grinned. 'Business, isn't it? Now, this partnership of ours. When do we start?'

'When we've got something to sell.'

'But you've no money, and we need to invest equally, don't we? To get started?'

Caelan had to admit Jolene had a point. 'Yeah. It's only fair.'

'Screwed then, aren't you?' Jolene flicked her hair over her shoulder. 'Because before we can start our business, you need to pay Stefan his twenty grand.' She laughed. 'Now, it's time for my break. I'll see you around.'

26

Ewan was leaning against the wall outside, staring at his phone. When he saw Caelan, he shoved it into his pocket. She ignored him, walked past him, forcing him to scurry to catch her up.

'I'm sorry,' he said as he reached her.

'For what?'

'Behaving like a twat.'

She smiled. 'Was it real, or were you pretending? Because if you were acting, it was bloody convincing.'

Ewan blew out his cheeks. 'Both, I suppose. It's just, you're—'

'Doing my job?'

'Getting more and more involved with these people. Jolene, she was stringing you along in there. She's using you.'

Caelan stopped and stared at him. They shouldn't be having this conversation on the street, but there was no one around, and even if anyone saw them, from a distance they would just look like a couple having a row.

'Don't you think I know that? I'm using her too,' Caelan told him. 'That's how this works. We have to get closer, more involved, as you called it. It doesn't matter if I owe Stefan Harris fifteen, twenty or five hundred grand, because I'm never going to pay him. He's going inside and I'll be on to the next job.'

'He'll only go inside if he's guilty of something. So far, we've no proof he's involved in anything but assaulting women.' He lifted his hand as though he was going to lay it on Caelan's arm, then ran it through his hair instead. His voice softened. 'What if he doesn't go to prison? What if he comes after you? He would, especially if he knew—'

'We can't think like that. Not on this operation, not ever. If we did, we couldn't do the job. When you were in the army, in Afghanistan, did you worry you were going to be killed every second of the day?'

Now he smiled. 'Honestly? Yeah, pretty much.'

She didn't smile back. 'Well I can't. Harris strikes me as a coward. He's loud, arrogant. He likes to make threats but he has other people to do the dirty work.'

'Meaning he wouldn't kill you himself, he'd get someone else to do it. It's hardly a comfort.'

Caelan started walking again. 'You know, he's like Mulligan. They both need to have people around them doing their bidding to make them feel safe, powerful. Whereas Reuben Nash seems to work alone.'

'He had his brother,' Ewan pointed out.

'But did he? From what I saw, he treated Nathan like a child. He told me he allowed Nathan to invest in his business as a way to keep him busy, not because he wanted him as a partner.'

'Who else, then?'

'Jolene said Reuben had bouncers who would kick the shit out of you. We saw them dealing with Harris without any problems. It's possible they do more than just provide Reuben with security at the club. Maybe we need to have another look at them.'

'We?'

'You know what I mean.' Caelan took out her phone to check the time. 'Too early to go to Reuben's.' She told Ewan what Jolene had revealed about Tom Haslam. 'Whether she's telling the truth or not, I think we should pay him another visit.'

'You think Haslam hurt Lucy?'

'I think we need to consider it. Like I said, let's go and talk to him.'

'What about the boss?'

'Penrith?' Caelan pulled a face. Ewan was right – they should report back first, but she was tired of having to cross London every time they had a new piece of information. 'I think he should come to us for a change.' She took out her phone. When Penrith answered, she didn't give him a chance to speak. He wouldn't be happy about having to leave his lair again, but Caelan knew that if she told him they had a new lead, he would do so.

'We need to talk to you,' she said. 'Where can you meet us?'

–

'How do you want to play this?' Ewan said as they sat in another Underground carriage, this one almost empty. 'Haslam's got to be a person of interest now in Lucy's disappearance, hasn't he?'

'Ideally, we'd send forensics in. As it is, if Ian agrees, we'll be on our own. I think we have to be clever. We want Haslam to know we suspect he's hiding something, but at the same time we don't want to spook him.'

'Maybe we should suggest following him,' Ewan said. 'What if Lucy's alive but he's stashed her somewhere? Maybe that's why he moved the camera, so he could keep an eye on her wherever he's holding her.'

Caelan looked at him. 'There's a horrible thought.'

'Wouldn't be the first, though, would he?'

'Or the last.' Caelan clicked her tongue a few times, thinking about it. 'Could he have abducted Lucy, alone, from a house they shared with several other people, though? From the photograph I've seen of Lucy, she's slim, and if she's anything like her brother she'll be fairly short, but then Haslam's not exactly Mr Muscle. I don't know.'

Ewan lifted his shoulders. 'He might have drugged and restrained her during the day when the house was empty, hidden her in his room, then taken her elsewhere during the night.'

Caelan didn't like the idea but she had to admit it was possible. 'But if she was drugged, she'd have been a dead weight. I don't see Haslam being able to move her on his own.'

Ewan blinked, and Caelan wondered if he was remembering his time in Afghanistan. He and another soldier had been hiding out, surrounded by Taliban fighters, the dead bodies of four men in the building with them rapidly beginning to decompose in the heat. Had he and his colleague been forced to move the bodies as far as possible from the room they were hiding in? She didn't know, and she wasn't going to ask. She waited, knowing he would come back to her. Another blink, and he said, 'He could have had a helper.'

Caelan's stomach lurched. 'Or he *was* the helper.'

'How do you mean?'

'We've been told Tom Haslam was obsessed with Lucy. We also know someone threatened her as a way of forcing Mulligan to keep his mouth shut. If this person approached Haslam, told him some bullshit story about wanting to take Lucy away to protect her but she wouldn't play ball, they might have got him to help them.'

'I don't know,' Ewan said. 'Would you do that to someone you cared about, even if you thought you were protecting them?'

'Haslam hates James Mulligan,' Caelan said. 'Remember his tone when he talked about him? He said it was too late for Mulligan to start worrying about Lucy now, something like that. If he told the person who wanted Lucy the same thing, they could have used it to manipulate him.'

Ewan looked doubtful. 'It's a lot of ifs and buts,' he said.

Caelan sat back with a sigh. 'I know. All we have is ideas.'

As the train drew to a halt, they got to their feet.

Outside, drizzle was falling. Caelan scowled up at the sky. 'Where the hell is he?'

As she spoke, a black cab drew up at the kerb. She waited to see if anyone got out; when they didn't, she took out her phone. As expected, it rang immediately.

'Ready to go to the ball, Cinderella?'

She didn't reply, ended the call. 'That's him,' she told Ewan.

There were five seats in the back of the cab, three across the rear window and two opposite, with their backs to the driver. Penrith sat in the middle of the three, his arms folded. He nodded at the two seats opposite as Caelan climbed inside.

'Could you sit over there? Travelling backwards makes me feel sick.'

'You sure that's not all the coffee and pastries?' Caelan glanced at the driver but didn't recognise him. She knew he would be a police officer – this wasn't an ordinary London cab but one used exclusively by the Met.

Penrith ignored her, and when Ewan had settled next to Caelan, the driver pulled out into the traffic.

'What's so urgent?' he demanded.

Caelan told him about her conversation with Jolene, and the ideas she and Ewan had had about what Haslam's involvement might mean. Unusually, Penrith listened without interrupting, only speaking when Caelan fell silent.

'They didn't find a camera in Lucy's room,' he said. 'As you've pointed out, though, that doesn't mean one wasn't there at some point.' He rubbed his chin, tapping his foot. 'I think we need to take a closer look at Haslam – subtly.' He gave her a meaningful stare, which Caelan ignored.

'I'm guessing nothing was found in the search of the room to suggest she'd been hurt in there?' she said.

'Don't you think I'd have mentioned it?'

'Just checking. We need to have a look at Haslam's phone.'

'Not going to happen, at least not yet. We'd never get permission.'

'There are other ways...' Caelan said, but Penrith raised a hand.

'No. None of your cowboy stuff. We need to do this properly.'

'Come on, Ian. You've said it yourself, we've nothing on Haslam. Jolene will never repeat what she told me today in any way we can officially use.'

'We don't know if this camera ever existed.' Penrith sounded sceptical. 'You've met Haslam. Do you think it's likely?'

Caelan thought about Haslam's bitterness when she had asked him about Lucy's boyfriend, his anger at knowing nothing about this rival.

'It's clear his interest in her is bordering on obsession – his behaviour, and what Liss Tucker, one of the other housemates, told us proves that.'

'Liss Tucker also said Haslam would sometimes find out where Lucy was going to be and turn up there himself – it's not a huge jump from that to hiding a camera in her room, is it?' Ewan said.

'Hardly a jump at all,' Penrith agreed.

'What about fingerprints?' Caelan asked. 'Were any of Haslam's found in Lucy's room?'

'Some on the inside and outside of the door and on the door handle, I believe, and some on the top of the back of the chair.'

'The prints on the chair – do they indicate he might have picked the chair up, or just that he leant on it?'

Penrith frowned. 'I'd have to check.'

'And what about the top of the wardrobe, or on any shelves? Any fingerprints, or signs of dust being disturbed?'

'I don't have the entire report in my head, Caelan. You're asking if there could be evidence of where Haslam set up a camera, if he used the chair to climb up to wherever he put it?'

'Yes, exactly. I'm also wondering if he created the mess in Lucy's room himself – trashed it, to use his own words – to disguise the fact that he'd abducted her, or at least had been in there to remove the camera.'

'His prints weren't found on any of Lucy's belongings, as far as I recall, but he might have worn gloves. He's a student, after all, he must have a brain in there somewhere,' said Penrith.

'He told us he didn't know Lucy was missing until the police turned up at the door,' said Ewan. 'If he had been in there that day to remove the camera, it seems a huge coincidence that he did it without knowing she was missing. Looks to me like he might have already known.'

'Also, he seemed familiar with Lucy's room,' said Caelan, 'which makes sense now we've been told he was watching her – he knew which things should have been on the desk, that there were usually cushions on the bed...'

'He might have been poking around in her room every time she was out for all we know,' Penrith said.

'I doubt she invited him in there,' Caelan said. 'Not often, at least. Liss Tucker said Lucy found Haslam creepy.'

'Really? A man who kept turning up wherever she was, uninvited? I can't think why.'

'We should speak to the housemates again, see if they noticed Haslam hanging around Lucy's room.'

'And ask if they ever saw him leaving the house carrying her over his shoulder?' Penrith said. 'It would help to know if he has a car, because I don't see how he could have got her out of there otherwise, especially without someone seeing him. As a student in London, though, I doubt it.'

Caelan groaned. 'Maybe we're making too much of this. As you said, we've only Jolene's word for it the camera ever existed, and we can't ask anyone else without potentially jeopardising everything we're investigating. She's the person who links everyone – she's friends with Mulligan, she owes Stefan Harris money, she's in a casual relationship with Reuben Nash, and she sells drugs to a man who lives next door to Lucy Mulligan, as well as working in a shop in her street.'

'She's also a con artist,' Penrith reminded her quietly. 'We need to remember that when dealing with her.'

'I do, though I can see she's good at what she does.'

'Maybe I should try to recruit her.'

'She'd make more money ripping people off.' Caelan smiled at Penrith. 'Do you know if Somerville and Achebe have asked

Reuben Nash yet whether he was aware of the injuries on his brother's back?'

'If they have, they haven't updated me,' Penrith said. He looked at Caelan, clearly expecting her to have more to say, but she remained silent. She still believed they should focus on Tom Haslam.

Eventually Ewan cleared his throat. 'What about Ryan Glennister?' he said.

Penrith and Caelan both looked at him.

'Glennister? What about him?' Penrith looked confused.

'He was at Lucy's house, wasn't he? We've been considering whether Haslam had a helper, or if he was possibly helping someone else, whether accidentally or not. We know Glennister was at the house looking for Lucy, though we don't know why.'

Caelan frowned, thinking about it. 'Glennister has reason to dislike Mulligan too, and we know he's always desperate for money, especially if he's using again. Liss Tucker said she told him Lucy wasn't home, but what if Haslam overheard the conversation? He'd be desperate to know what Glennister wanted, what his connection was to Lucy. He wouldn't have been able to help himself.'

'Back to needing to find Glennister then,' Penrith said. 'He left the hospital.'

Caelan stared at him. 'Are you joking?'

'Yes, I thought it was the perfect time to try to be funny.'

'Why didn't you tell us about his accident?'

Penrith sniffed. 'Because I knew Tim Achebe would.'

'I thought Glennister was injured?'

'Not enough to stop him legging it, obviously.'

Caelan paused. This was Penrith at his most annoying, twisting and turning, skittering away from her questions.

'Wasn't anyone watching him?'

'No.' Penrith didn't elaborate and Caelan knew there was no point asking him to.

'And we've really no idea where he went?' she said.

'I've had someone on it – the same person who failed to find him before he walked in front of a vehicle.'

'Let me guess. Richard Adamson.'

Penrith leant back in his seat. 'Well, since you and Ewan are both here and I have no one else in the team, it's a fair assumption.'

'He's found nothing?'

'There are quite a few places Glennister might be in London. You may not have noticed, but it's a big place.'

'Then we need to focus on Haslam,' Caelan said. 'His phone records, emails, finances. Where he's been and who he knows.'

Penrith regarded her steadily. 'I've already said, we have no grounds for going in hard on him.'

Caelan knew he was right. 'Then we'll speak to him again ourselves, say we've been told he was obsessed with Lucy. Without mentioning names, we could tell him she confided in a friend that she was worried she was being watched.'

'No. Too obvious.'

'It would give us a chance to see from his reaction whether he had a camera in there or not.' Caelan hoped she sounded more confident than she felt. She thought it was their only option, but even she had to admit it was a long shot.

'You honestly believe that if Haslam saw someone kidnapping his beloved Lucy, he'd have kept quiet about it?' Penrith demanded.

'If it meant having to reveal what he'd been up to, yes. Wouldn't you?'

'Does it matter?'

'Then what's your plan? What's our next move?'

He drummed his fingers on the table. 'You go back to focusing on your original brief – the people trafficking and our three unidentified victims. You seem to have lost sight of that.'

'No, we haven't, but you have to admit, things have moved quickly.'

'I'll say. This morning you owed Stefan Harris fifteen thousand pounds. Now it's twenty.'

Caelan shrugged. 'But we have the information about Haslam.'

'Which may or not be genuine. You have to admit, if Jolene Townsend was lying, it's an expensive mistake on your part.'

'Thanks for backing me up.' Caelan glanced out of the window, the London streets slipping by. 'Can you let us out?'

'Not yet.' Penrith waited until she met his eyes. 'You've managed to wheedle your way between Harris and Reuben Nash. Use that.'

'I intend to. I still think it's worth us talking to Haslam. He's afraid of Ewan—'

Penrith snorted. 'And no doubt terrified of you.'

'I kept it polite.'

'And you think he'll respond if you're a little more persuasive?'

'Well I don't see him putting up much of a fight.'

Tipping his head back, Penrith stared at the roof of the cab. 'All right, but just ruffle his feathers.' He leant forward, tapped on the glass between them and the driver. 'Mind if we chuck you out here?'

Caelan had another look out of the window. 'Where are we?'

Penrith grinned as the cab drew up to the kerb. 'Haven't a clue, but we haven't gone far. I'm sure you'll work it out.'

27

Caelan hammered on the door with her fist, counted to three and hammered again. Eventually it opened a few inches and a man's face appeared in the gap. He stared at them, frowning.

'Any reason you're trying to batter the front door down?'

'We're here to see Tom Haslam,' Caelan told him. 'Is he in?'

'Tom?' He glanced behind him. 'No idea. We don't keep tabs on each other.'

'Yeah?' Caelan sneered at him. 'Well maybe you should.'

The man shook his head and started to close the door. Ewan stepped forward, stuck his foot in the gap.

'Listen, mate, we want to talk to Tom. We met him earlier.'

'You can't just walk in here.' The man was glaring now, but Caelan could see he was rattled. He wasn't much taller than she was, five eight or so. He looked up at Ewan and she knew he was going to give in. 'You just want to talk to him?'

Ewan held up his hands. 'Scout's honour.'

Caelan decided to take a chance. 'It's about Lucy Mulligan. She's my cousin.'

The man's face cleared. 'You're the people looking for Lucy? Tom was babbling about it, but I didn't take much notice. He's' – he looked over his shoulder again – 'kind of...' His voice trailed off.

'Obsessed with Lucy?' Caelan finished for him. He nodded, clearly relieved.

'You already know. Yeah, it was obvious when she first moved in that he liked her, but he's got weirder and weirder about it.' He opened the door fully and held out his hand. 'Joel Kingsley.'

Caelan shook it briefly. 'Is Tom upstairs?'

'He was ten minutes ago. I went up to the bathroom and he came out of his room, going on about Lucy's cousin turning up.'

'And he hasn't left?'

Kingsley shook his head. 'But then I've been cooking, listening to a podcast. I might not have heard him.'

Caelan and Ewan exchanged a glance. 'Which room?'

'You know which is Lucy's? Tom's across the landing.'

They approached quietly. Lucy's door was closed, the tape the police had left behind still sealing it, but Haslam's was ajar. Again Caelan met Ewan's eyes. There was no reason for them to believe Haslam to be in danger and no sign so far that he was, but she held up a hand and they approached cautiously all the same. Caelan stood to the side of the door and tapped softly.

'Tom?'

No reply. She tried again.

'Tom, it's Victoria Smith. We met earlier?'

Still nothing. No sound, no movement. Caelan swallowed.

'Why isn't he answering? He should be in there,' Joel Kingsley said from behind them, concern clear in his voice.

Caelan wrapped her sleeve around her fingers and pushed the door open, then eased herself around it so she could see into the room.

A double bed with navy-blue sheets, the duvet neatly arranged, the pillows plumped. A desk, its surface empty except for a laptop computer, a chair tucked neatly beneath it. A bookcase, the books arranged by size. A chest of drawers with a TV and DVD player on top. Caelan moved further inside. The place was as bare and impersonal as a hotel room. No photographs, no clothes thrown on the chair, no shoes kicked off in the corner.

'He's not here.' She beckoned Ewan inside. 'What do you think?'

He looked around, raising his eyebrows. 'Looks like some-where a serial killer would sleep.'

Kingsley was in the doorway, and Caelan turned to him.

'Have you been in here before?'

He shook his head, his eyes wide.

'You can't tell us if there's anything missing?'

'Except for Tom? Not a clue.'

'He's probably just gone to the corner shop.'

Kingsley nodded, backing out of the room. Caelan went over to the desk and opened the laptop, her movements made awkward by the sleeves still over her hands. She pressed the button to power the computer up, but it didn't respond. She closed the lid, turned away.

'No doubt password-protected anyway,' she said as she reached for the desk drawer. There was no way of locking it, and it slid open easily.

'Shit.'

She stared down at a wallet, an Oyster card and a mobile phone.

28

'Let's not panic,' Caelan said quietly to Ewan, though in truth she was worried. Like Lucy, would Haslam have left his posses- sions behind? If he wasn't using his Oyster card, did he not want his movements to be traced? He would still be able to buy a Travelcard for the Underground with cash if he wanted to get around London, but wouldn't he have taken his wallet? His phone? She closed the drawer. 'We need to get out of here,' she said. Ewan nodded, understanding immediately. This was not the place to discuss what they'd found.

Downstairs, Kingsley was waiting by the front door.

'Do I need to call the police?' he asked.

'I'd leave it for now,' Caelan said. 'Maybe you missed Tom leaving, if you had your music on.'

'Maybe,' Kingsley said, though he didn't sound convinced. 'No one came into the house, though, I know that for sure. I would have heard anyone knocking at the front door.'

Not if they walked in without asking, Caelan thought. She didn't believe it was likely that Haslam had been taken against his will, but they had to consider all possibilities.

'What about the back door?' she asked.

'No one uses it,' Kingsley said. 'We have keys, but it's kept bolted. I've never seen it open.'

'But you could let someone in through it?'

He shrugged. 'Yeah, if you wanted to, but why would you?'

'Who knows.' She smiled at him. 'Thanks for your help.'

She turned, reaching out to open the front door.

'What shall I do?' Kingsley demanded. 'What if Tom's in trouble?'

'He'll be fine. If he's not home tomorrow and you're worried, go to the police.' She knew he would be wasting his time since Haslam was already involved in a police investigation and no one would tell him anything, but she needed to reassure him.

As they left the house, Kingsley stood on the doorstep watching them go down the street.

'This gets weirder,' Ewan said softly.

'Does it mean Haslam was working with whoever has Lucy, or that they see him as a threat because he knows more than he told us?' Caelan slid her phone out of her pocket, checked the time. 'Assuming Lucy hasn't just taken herself off on holiday.' She felt like screaming. Picking up the pace, she strode towards the station. 'Does it mean Jolene was in touch with Haslam, that she told him we know what he's been up to? She could be selling to him too. No one else knew we'd been to see him.'

'Except Penrith and Liss Tucker,' Ewan pointed out.

'I don't see Tucker being involved, but who knows. Anyway, she has no idea about the camera.'

'Unless Lucy really did suspect she was being watched and told her.'

'Tucker said they aren't close, but it's possible. Then again, Haslam might have panicked when we showed up, especially if he has been watching Lucy. He could have done a runner, left his stuff behind so we'd think it was linked to Lucy's disappearance.'

'Are we going to Reuben's?

'I am. You should see Penrith, or at least speak to him. He can get Achebe and Somerville onto trying to trace Haslam.'

Ewan nodded. 'Maybe we should have told Kingsley to call the police straight away. Then he'd be expecting them to arrive and start poking around.'

Caelan smiled. 'Fair point, but it's early days and Haslam won't be considered vulnerable. It's unlikely the police would take Kingsley seriously.'

'Even though Lucy disappeared from the same house in the same way?'

'They're not kids. Anyway, I don't know if the information on Lucy's appearance will be available to everyone in the force. I'd guess it's been restricted because of...' She waved a hand, gesturing to herself and Ewan.

They parted at the station, Caelan dropping a kiss onto Ewan's cheek for appearance's sake. She didn't believe they were being followed, but someone knew they had spoken to Tom Haslam and had acted, or Haslam had decided it was time to disappear. Either way, she guessed it was a hint that they were on the right track, and it was best to keep up the pretence. She watched Ewan turn away and wondered what he was thinking. His confidence was growing; he was making suggestions, giving opinions, but she knew he wasn't always comfortable with the way she had to work. Any police officer took risks on every shift. Their role could be more dangerous than most, but it wasn't a job you could do unless you were entirely committed. Caelan had seen marriages and relationships disintegrate, colleagues develop addictions, people burned out and defeated by the constant pressure of living as someone else. She didn't know what it said about her that she kept going, but she doubted it was because she was any different to the others she had known. She probably just had less to lose.

–

The queue outside Reuben's was shorter tonight, though Caelan had arrived earlier than she had when Mulligan had brought them here. The same two bouncers were on the door, and both smiled when they saw her.

'Victoria Smith?' the male bouncer asked. 'Mr Nash is waiting for you in his office.'

He spoke politely, without a hint of a leer and Caelan smiled back, though her heartbeat quickened. 'Thank you.'

The female bouncer met her eyes as she passed them, her expression difficult to read. Caelan thought she read sympathy there, and the realisation did nothing to calm the anxiety she was already feeling. After her encounter with Harris, she had been expecting the meeting with Nash to be easier, safer, but she had to remember her first impression of him. Nash and Harris might hate each other, but Caelan knew they were two of a kind. Harris might never get his hands dirty and Nash might fancy himself a businessman, but in the end they both peddled misery. The question was, which of them was also selling people? Maybe it was neither, but Mulligan had made a point of introducing Caelan to them both. Now she had to work out why.

Inside, the same bartenders were already hard at work. One of them, the man with the beard, waved Caelan over when he saw her and handed her a glass.

'Champagne,' he said with a smile. 'Compliments of the boss.'

Caelan thanked him, held it up to her lips as she walked away but didn't drink, then headed for the darkest corner she could see. With a quick, surreptitious movement she tipped the liquid onto the carpet and left the empty glass on the nearest table. She knew of many things that could be slipped into a drink and didn't feel like sampling any of them. Even if the glass had only contained champagne, she wanted to keep a clear head.

She crossed the dance floor, her eyes fixed on the stairs that led up to Nash's office, as though she was keen to see him. In truth, now that she was here, she realised, she would rather have dealt with Harris again. Harris was predictable, Nash was anything but. His anguish when he'd sobbed over the body of his brother had appeared genuine, but Caelan had seen parents cry over children they'd killed, husbands and wives weeping while still clutching a bloodstained knife or a length of rope.

There was a man at the bottom of the stairs, one of the bouncers who had dragged Stefan Harris away from her when he'd grabbed her arm, who had held onto Harris when Nathan Nash punched him. He caught her eye, looked her up and down and winked at her.

'Evening. The boss is ready for you.'

Caelan forced a smile. 'Is he now?'

He laughed. 'As he'll ever be, I reckon.'

She kept walking, aware of his eyes on her body. She'd been back to the hotel to shower and change, knowing she had to pay enough attention to her outfit, hair and make-up to make it look as though she wanted to impress when all she'd really wanted to do was crawl into bed. From the bouncer's reaction, she had achieved her aim, though the realisation made her skin crawl.

At the top of the stairs she paused and glanced around. There were a few people there, but none she recognised. Standing by the door to Nash's office was another bouncer, this one stern-faced, stocky, his arms folded. Caelan couldn't see if he wore an earpiece, but he had clearly been warned of her arrival, as his eyes immediately fixed on her. She approached him and he nodded, as though giving her permission to knock.

Caelan's anxiety had increased, her senses heightened. She already knew where the exits were from her previous visit, but she found herself running over them again in her mind. Why had the bouncers been told to watch for her? The fact that she had arrived must have been passed up the chain, from the bouncers at the club's entrance to the one at the bottom of the stairs and now this man. No doubt Reuben Nash himself had also been following her progress. She didn't like it. It was different, unexpected, and in her business that could mean trouble.

She remembered the expression on the female bouncer's face and wondered again what it meant. It could be as simple as the woman having had the same sort of casual relationship with Nash as Jolene Townsend, and her sympathising with Nash's potential next plaything. Another possibility was one Caelan had been trying to ignore since she'd approached the building – that she was walking into a trap. She couldn't rule out the possibility that Nash was suspicious of her motivations for talking to Jolene, to Tom Haslam. She had no doubt Jolene was feeding information back to him, probably to Harris too.

'Are you going in, or not?' the bouncer said.

Caelan lifted her chin, looked him in the eye. 'That's the idea.'

He stepped back, arms still crossed, looking down his nose at her, and Caelan suspected he also guessed she would be Nash's latest conquest.

Maybe that was what the sofas in Nash's office were for.

She knocked, and the door opened. Nash stood there smiling at her. He wore a charcoal suit with a white shirt and smelled as though he had bathed in aftershave. Caelan forced herself to stay relaxed as he bent to kiss her cheek, though her instinct was to recoil.

'Victoria. I've been waiting for you.' There was no admonishment in his voice, though his hand snaked around her wrist and held it. He looked over her head towards the man outside. 'Make sure we're not disturbed.' He flashed Caelan another grin and playfully pulled her inside. She allowed it to happen, knowing he assumed she was here for more than a business meeting and accepting she needed to play along for now.

For now.

Nash released her and closed the door. Caelan held her breath, but he didn't lock it.

'Did they give you the champagne?' he asked.

'They did. Thank you.'

He nodded towards the sofas at the other end of the room. On the coffee table, a bottle of champagne stood in a silver bucket, two glasses beside it. Caelan saw that the cork was still in the bottle and was reassured: she could risk drinking a glass if she had to.

'Fancy another?' Nash asked.

'Why not?'

He poured the drinks, moved towards the nearest sofa, beckoning for her to join him. It was a three-seater, though there wasn't much room. Predictably Nash settled in the middle, forcing Caelan to sit far too close for comfort. He handed her a glass and leant back, crossing his legs. Caelan knew she should relax her own posture, but lounging against the cushions would leave her in a more vulnerable position than she was comfortable with, and she stayed on the edge of the seat.

Nash laughed. 'What's wrong?'

Caelan took a deep breath as though to steady herself. It wasn't entirely an act. 'I need to talk to you about Stefan Harris,' she said.

The reaction was instantaneous. Nash's eyes narrowed, his nostrils flaring. 'That murdering fucker. What's he done now?'

Wordlessly Caelan pointed at the bruising on her throat. 'He wasn't happy when I told him I didn't have his money.'

Nash peered at her injuries. 'The bastard. Who did it, Johnny or Chris?'

'Neither of them,' she said. 'I had the pleasure of a private meeting with Harris himself.'

'Aren't you the lucky one? And now you're having one with me.' Nash got up, wandered over to his desk. He drank half of his champagne, watching her. 'What does he want from you? I doubt he'd have suggested a payment plan.'

Caelan took a sip of her own drink. 'Well, in a way. He offered me the chance to work off the debt. Apparently he owns me now.'

Nash looked incredulous. 'Owns you? He said that?'

'Yeah, he made it pretty clear. He also asked questions about my relationship with you, what we'd talked about.'

'And?'

'I told him the truth, that we'd discussed business but that the conversation came to an end after his name was mentioned.'

She swallowed, again not having to pretend to be bothered by the memory. 'It's not easy to think of a convincing lie with someone's hands around your throat.'

Nash finished his champagne. 'I can imagine.' He went back to the bottle, held it up to Caelan, who shook her head. With a shrug, he poured himself another glass. 'You can tell Stefan anything you like. I'm not worried about him. Anyway,' he grinned, 'it's not as though you know much about me – yet.'

She ignored that. 'He also gave me instructions.'

'Which were?'

'He wants me to find out what I can about your business and report back to him. He wants to get his hands on this place.'

'The club?' His laugh was scornful. 'Not a chance.'

'He told me he tried to buy it before but the previous owner wouldn't sell to him.'

Nash nodded. 'For once he was telling the truth. The bloke I bought it from wouldn't give Harris the time of day. I offered less, but he took me up on it. I think he'd have given the place away rather than let Harris buy it.'

'Why?'

'He hated Harris almost as much as I do, but with him, it was personal.'

'What do you mean?'

Nash moved back to sit on the sofa again, his thigh pressed against Caelan's. 'You already know how Harris treats women – you've experienced it for yourself. Shaun had a sister – Hayley. She was quiet, sensible, focused on her studies – none of the usual teenager shit. Then she met Harris. A week later she was smoking anything she could get her hands on, and within a month she was injecting heroin.' He paused for a drink. 'Six weeks after she met Harris, she was dead.'

'How?'

'Overdose. They could never prove it was Harris who gave her the stuff, but it's not like he would have allowed her to buy it from anyone else.'

'She was a teenager?'

Nash waved a hand. 'Eighteen when she died, I think. Anyway, my mate hates him.'

'That's understandable.'

'And I benefited, got this place at a knockdown price.' He grinned, nodded at her glass. 'Aren't you drinking that?'

Sickened, Caelan sipped the champagne. She knew she had to keep Nash talking, see what else he would tell her. 'What do I say to Harris?'

'Let me think about it. If he thinks he's got you trapped, we might be able to use it to our advantage.'

Now she met his eyes. 'Our?'

He nodded, not smiling now, his face expressionless. 'I've been asking around about you,' he said.

'I'm flattered.' Caelan kept her breathing steady, a slight smile on her face, though her heart was hammering. She hoped Penrith had done his bit and given her a plausible background.

'You should be. It means I'm interested in you… in working with you, I mean.' He chuckled, the sound knowing and unpleasant. 'Where's your boyfriend tonight?'

'I left him with a crate of beers and the TV remote. He's probably asleep by now.'

'More fool him.' Nash shifted so he was sitting even closer to her. 'I have contacts in Glasgow, in Edinburgh,' he went on. 'No one in Glasgow had heard of you, but in Edinburgh you were on the radar.' He nudged her. 'Small-time, I was told. Keeping your head down, making your money.'

'Depends what you call small-time.'

Nash raised his hands. 'I'm not criticising. It makes sense. You know the main man up there? The one with most of Edinburgh in his pocket?'

Was this a test? Caelan dredged her memory and took a chance. 'Alastair Gordon? Only by reputation.'

Nash leant even closer, his breath tickling her ear as Harris's had done. Again Caelan didn't react, though she knew she might need to. She had to remain in control, of both herself and the situation. 'You're out of touch,' he said softly, his voice cold. 'Ali Gordon died a month ago.'

Caelan froze. She knew she had to respond, and quickly. It was a stupid mistake, one that shouldn't have happened. She should have known more about the Scottish drug trade, especially when Mulligan had mentioned Edinburgh specifically. Her first thought was that Penrith shouldn't have sent her in unprepared, but she knew she couldn't blame him. It was her responsibility too. Now she had to reassure Nash, make him believe she knew what she was talking about. If she couldn't, she was in trouble.

'News to me,' she said. 'I haven't been back to Edinburgh, and there was no one I wanted to keep in touch with.'

Abruptly Nash got to his feet. He took a few steps away before turning back to face her. 'It means there's a gap in the city. Ali's son Robbie is making moves to fill it, but my mate thinks he's too weak.'

Relieved, Caelan tipped her head to the side, pretending to think it over. 'Maybe I should head back up there.' Her mouth was dry and she took another sip of champagne. As she lifted the glass again, her mouth hidden behind her hand, she took a deep breath and let it out slowly, trying to bring her racing thoughts and thumping heart under control. She couldn't let Nash see she was rattled.

'Don't you want to know what happened to Ali Gordon?' Nash asked.

'Does it matter?'

'The police seem to think so. They say he was murdered.'

Caelan raised an eyebrow. 'Yeah?'

'Yeah. With a baseball bat. Head like a smashed pumpkin, I'm told.' He pushed his hands into his trouser pockets. 'Interesting, wouldn't you say?'

'It's the risk you take. You'll always have rivals in this game, people who want you out of the way.'

'I mean it's interesting you left Edinburgh recently and came down here. Even more interesting that people immediately started being attacked with baseball bats.'

She managed a laugh. 'Are you serious? You think I've got something to do with Gordon's death?'

'No, but I'm wondering if it gave you some ideas.'

'Even though I didn't know about it until you mentioned it?'

'So you say.' His glass was empty again and he moved over to the bottle. This time, he didn't offer her any. 'The way I see it, you've recognised an opportunity down here. I understand that, I respect it. Your cousin Mulligan's out of your way now.'

'Come on, you think I was behind the attack on him? That's ridiculous.'

'Is it?' His eyes were locked with hers. 'It's a handy weapon – anyone can use it, you don't need much strength, and it's easy to dispose of.'

'Perfect for me, then.' Caelan risked a smile. 'Come on, Reuben. Are you serious?'

He kept staring at her, his eyes blank as stones. Caelan was reminded of the faces of those young victims again, three pairs of sightless eyes. She blinked, her throat tight, stomach knotted, running through the escape routes again in her head. Then Nash smiled.

'Serious? Not really. I think Harris was behind it, just like I think he ordered the murder of my brother.' Caelan heard him swallow. 'We just need to prove it.' He turned away, raising his arm once he'd turned his back. Caelan guessed he was wiping his eyes, composing himself, or pretending to. After a few seconds, he turned back. 'The police came for me earlier,' he said, his eyes on hers again.

Caelan raised her eyebrows. 'The police? What do you mean?'

'They said they wanted a chat, but I wasn't given a choice about whether I wanted to go with them or not.'

'I assume it was about Nathan?' Was Nash surprised? His brother had been killed, whether by accident or design, and he wasn't expecting the police to want to speak to him?

'They... told me something. Something about Nathan.'

Caelan kept her eyes on his face, watching for signs he had known about Nathan's injuries before today. She could see none but knew she couldn't rely on her impressions.

'What do you mean?'

Nash rubbed his face with both hands as he moved back to sit beside her. 'Some fucker had beaten him, ruined his back.'

Caelan pulled her best bemused face. 'How do you ruin someone's back?'

'Ripped it to fucking shreds.' Nash exhaled sharply through his nose. 'And when I find them...'

'What do you mean? With a knife, or...?'

'They said he'd been whipped, fucking whipped. I don't get it. Why would he just take it? Who would even dare try? Nathan was my brother, but he was a fucking psycho. Even I was scared of him.'

She doubted it. 'Whipped... You mean like an S and M thing?' As she spoke, Caelan realised it was a possibility they hadn't considered, though the injuries seemed far too extreme to be consensual.

'If you like being half killed during sex, maybe.' Nash gave a harsh laugh. 'No, this was a punishment beating, or a warning to keep his mouth shut.'

'About what?' He was furious, and Caelan knew she would have to be careful how far she pushed him. He was too wound up to realise she was firing question after question at him, wanting to rant at someone, let out his anger and frustration. She didn't want him to turn it on her.

'I don't know. He's made enemies over the years, we both have. But this... You've got to be a cold-hearted bastard to do that to someone.' He ran his hand over his mouth. 'They showed me a photograph. His back was just... raw flesh. Meat.'

'Didn't Nathan tell you about it?'

He glared at her. 'Don't you think I'd have gone after the bastards if he had?'

Caelan waited a beat. 'You think more than one person was involved?' Careful, she told herself.

'It'd have to be. How else could they have done it? It wasn't like he was only hit once; it would have taken time to do that kind of damage.' Nash stopped, frowning. 'It's got to be Harris again.'

'Why?'

He spoke through clenched teeth, as though angry she wasn't understanding. 'Because Nathan knocked him on his arse. Harris would want to teach him a lesson, humiliate him.'

'But the argument between Harris and Nathan happened just before Nathan was killed. He must have already had the injuries,' Caelan pointed out.

Nash stared at her. 'Yeah, I… You're right, it couldn't have happened like that. I'm not thinking straight.'

'You said you've made enemies. What if Harris wasn't involved at all?'

Again Nash pushed himself out of his seat. This time he stood over her, arms crossed. 'He was. Maybe you can find me some proof.'

Caelan looked up at him. 'You want me to spy on Harris while I'm spying on you for him?'

He laughed. 'Got it in one. I'll even make it worth your while.'

She wanted to get to her feet, but he was deliberately preventing her from doing so, using his body to try to intimidate her, his crotch almost level with her face. He was leaving himself vulnerable, but Caelan doubted he would realise until she landed a punch. She looked up, her eyes fixed on his, showing him she wasn't going to be cowed.

'How?' she asked.

'The fifteen grand you owe Harris?' He rocked back on his heels, well pleased with himself. 'How about I lend you some money, get him off your back?'

'If I pay him, there's no reason for him to keep me hanging around.'

He smirked. 'Oh, I think there is. Anyway, I'm not talking about the full fifteen. Just enough to keep him sweet.'

Caelan hesitated. This was unexpected, and unwelcome. How was she going to wriggle out of it? 'Why would you do that?'

'Because I like you. Because I want you to stay close to Harris, and because I can.' He smiled, took a step backwards. 'And... well, it'd mean I'd own part of you too.'

She said nothing, hating him and his attitude. She studied her champagne glass, determined not to be the one to break the silence. Nash took another step back, still smirking at her. 'Best offer you've had all day, isn't it?'

'If not all week.' Caelan stood, moved away to study the print of New York City on the wall. She tensed as Nash came to stand close behind her, trapping her.

'Have you ever been?' he asked softly.

'To New York? No.' It was true.

'You should. Maybe I could show you the sights?'

His hand was on her wrist. Gently he pulled her arm so she had to turn to face him. Looking down at her, he smiled. 'What would your boyfriend do if you didn't come home?'

'Come looking for me? He knows where I am.'

'And he still let you come here alone.'

She pretended to be indignant. 'He didn't *let* me do anything. He doesn't own me.'

Nash found that amusing, as Caelan had guessed he would. 'No, Stefan Harris does. Until...' He waved a hand towards the room's other door, the one Caelan had wondered about on her first visit.

She glanced at it. 'What's in there, the Royal Mint?'

Nash laughed. 'Almost.'

He pulled a bunch of keys from his trouser pocket. Caelan saw they were attached to a chain, which she guessed was secured to his belt. He worked through them but kept the bunch in his hand, not allowing her to see which ones he'd selected. 'Follow me.' He approached the door and knocked on it approvingly. 'As secure as it gets.'

'Steel-reinforced?' Caelan had guessed it would be when she'd seen it before.

'And then some. Twelve-point locking system, upgraded reinforcement.' He knocked again. 'Bullet-resistant.'

She ran a hand down the frame. 'Get shot at often, do you?'

'Only once.' He stepped between Caelan and the door and worked at the locks. Glancing over his shoulder, he winked. 'They missed.'

The door swung open and Nash flicked on an overhead light, the bulb unshaded. The room was small, around ten feet by six. There were no windows, and no other door. The walls had been painted white but the floor was bare boards. There was a black safe, over a metre tall, against the back wall, but otherwise the space was empty.

Caelan made a point of not gazing around, but she was intrigued. The room was smaller than she'd expected, based on the size of Nash's office. If the door was steel-reinforced, bullet-resistant, wouldn't he have decided that the walls, even the floor and ceiling, should be too? Some strongrooms might be too heavy for an upstairs location, but she knew more lightweight options were available.

Nash moved to the safe and crouched in front of it. 'You won't take offence if I ask you to look away while I open it? We have to have some secrets, don't we?'

Caelan turned her back. 'I'm sure we both have plenty.'

She heard keys, clicking and the creak of the metal door opening.

'Who needs the Royal Mint?' Nash stood back, grinning as Caelan turned.

Inside the safe were closely packed bundles of used banknotes, four shelves stacked high.

She whistled. 'Wow.'

Nash laughed. 'I thought you'd be impressed.'

'Makes my earnings look pathetic.'

'Rubbish. From what I've heard, you were doing okay.'

She smiled. 'If only I hadn't spent it all.'

He raised a finger. 'First rule of business: don't blow all your profits.'

'I'll try to remember that,' was her only comment, whatever else she felt like saying. There was a locked box at the bottom of the safe, and she wondered what was inside. She doubted Brady's search team would have been authorised to access the strongroom. 'Is this your income from the club?'

'Officially, yeah. As you can see, I do pretty well.' Nash seemed to be waiting for applause.

He'd said 'I', Caelan noted, not 'we'. Often the newly bereaved spoke about the person they had lost as though they were still alive, until acceptance of their situation began to creep in. Either Nash had reached this state of mind quicker than most, or his brother's presence had never registered much in the first place.

'And if the taxman followed me in here, you'd be able to account for all this?' She put a hand on her hip, tipping her head to the side as she studied him; not flirtatious, but definitely teasing. He moved towards her, sliding his arm around her shoulders.

'Why don't you let me worry about that?'

'Happy to.' She ducked away from him, went over to admire the safe. She wasn't an expert, but she knew an expensive bit of kit when she saw it. 'This must have cost a fortune,' she said.

'Almost ten grand. Worth it when you're storing an actual fortune inside – amongst other things.' Nash squatted by the safe and reached inside, pulling out a bundle of banknotes at random and holding it towards her. 'How many do you want?'

Caelan didn't move to take it. 'Depends on the interest rate. Harris's is extortionate.'

'Interest? Nothing – for now. I want you close to Harris, feeding back whatever information you can. He has people on the streets selling for him, and I want to put him out of business.'

'Expand your empire?'

Nash smiled. 'Empire. I like that.'

'Do you mean…' Caelan hesitated. 'You want Harris put out of business permanently?'

He stood up, laughing, the money still in his hand. 'You mean am I planning to have him killed? Come on, what do you think I am? I'm a businessman, not a mobster.'

It can be a fine line, Caelan thought. Again there was no hint of grief for his brother. He'd also let information slip, telling her he had people he could call on to do his bidding. She knew she had to be cautious. Maybe he was behind Nathan's death, even if he hadn't swung the bat himself. He was showing a great deal of trust in her by inviting her into this room, showing her the safe and the cash inside. If he only wanted to use her to get at Harris, it seemed like overkill, so what else did he want?

'But you've got a decent set-up here,' she said. 'Why get your hands dirty?'

'I wouldn't have to.' Nash was watching her. 'Harris has other ways of making money than running knackered taxis and forcing smackheads to sell for him.'

'He said the same about you.'

'Yeah, well he's wrong, and that's why I want a piece of whatever he's up to. More than a piece.'

'You don't know what he's involved in?'

'I have my suspicions, but I want you to find out for sure.' He threw the bundle of money to her, forcing her to catch it or let it fall to the floor. 'I know I can trust you to help me out.'

'Do you?'

'Why do you think I brought you in here?' Then he was beside her, his hand on her shoulder. 'I told you – you help me, and I'll help you. But if you let me down, if Harris gets to hear about what I've got tucked away in here, I'll know you were the one who told him.' His fingers dug into her shoulder for a second, but it was long enough and painful enough to make his point. 'This is our secret, you understand? Not a word to your boyfriend either. In fact, why don't you send him back to Scotland?' This time he pulled her close and kissed her cheek. 'I think we'd work well together.'

She wanted to scrub at her face with her sleeve, but she forced a tiny smile. 'Maybe. I'll see what I can do.'

Abruptly he released her, making her stumble. 'Good. Don't keep me waiting.' He pulled out his phone, checked the screen. 'I need to be downstairs soon, making sure everything's running smoothly. Do you have a bag?'

Shaken now, Caelan feigned confusion. 'No. Why do I need one?'

Nash nodded at the safe. 'Don't think seven grand will fit in your purse, do you?'

He was actually going to give her the money, and Caelan knew she'd have to take it. This pretence was becoming more complicated by the second, and she had no idea how she was going to wriggle out from her current position, trapped between Harris and Nash with both of them expecting information, loyalty, money and sex.

Maybe she and Ewan should both disappear and pretend none of this had ever happened. If it wasn't for Lucy Mulligan, she would seriously consider it. As it was, for now, Victoria Smith would have to do as she was told.

'I can't walk around carrying seven thousand pounds in a carrier bag,' she said.

Nash moved to the door. 'You need a handbag or something. You don't want to raise suspicion. I'll go and see what I can find.'

Uneasy, Caelan said, 'You're not leaving me here with the safe open?'

He smiled. 'I am, but I'm locking you in.' He disappeared through the door, and Caelan heard keys turning before she could react.

She didn't move, guessing there would be cameras watching her, though she couldn't see any. What was Nash's game? Did he want her to go to the safe and rummage through the contents? Help herself to more of his money? Like Harris, he wanted power over her, using the money he was forcing her to borrow to ensure her subservience. Having been manipulated and threatened by him, she could easily imagine him trafficking people. Had that been what he'd meant when he'd mentioned Harris making money from more than his legitimate businesses and drug dealing? Harris also wanted to know how Nash made his money, and Caelan had no way of telling who was selling what unless she stuck close to them both.

With her head bowed, her eyes scanned the room. If Reuben Nash had slipped out of his office to attack his brother, she couldn't see an alternative way out here. It was built for security, and an escape route would compromise that. She studied the safe again, though it seemed unlikely there was a door or hatch concealed behind it. In any case, she doubted Nash would be able to move it on his own. She needed to know whether this room had been searched, and she was also intrigued by the box in the bottom of the safe. She judged it big enough to hold a pistol of some kind, but why would Nash keep such a thing in a property that had already been searched by the police? He could have brought it here once the search had been completed, but he would still be taking a huge risk.

She looked down at the money in her hand. If Nash did insist on her accepting the rest he had promised, she decided she would take it straight to Stefan Harris. She didn't want to see him, not so soon after he had attacked her, but she knew she had no choice. She didn't want the cash in her possession for any longer than was necessary.

What was taking Nash so long? A thought crossed her mind, an unpleasant and unwelcome one. What if he wasn't coming back? What if he'd intended to trap her in here all along? She didn't know why he would, but she closed her eyes, cursing her stupidity. The most basic of basic errors. Taking out her phone, she glanced at the screen, already knowing what she would see. No signal.

Refusing to panic, she shuffled her feet, stretched her back as though tiring of waiting. The room would do just as well as a prison cell, as effective at keeping people in as it would be at keeping them out. The thought gave her pause. They had no proof that Nash was involved in the disappearance of Lucy Mulligan, but here was a room ready-made for holding a captive. There were no signs anyone had ever spent more than a few minutes in here, but Nash would have cleaned up carefully. Then again, Caelan was probably reaching, finding answers where none existed.

She heard keys jangle on the other side of the door and tensed. On the balls of her feet, she waited as the door opened and Reuben Nash appeared.

'Miss me?'

'I was starting to think you'd forgotten about me,' she said.

'You? Never.' He held out a rucksack. 'Here you go. I see you didn't help yourself.'

Caelan took the bag from him. 'I didn't think you'd appreciate it.'

He nodded. 'Didn't even move from where you were standing.'

'Were you watching me?' Caelan allowed some indignation into her voice. Again he was telling her he was in charge, he had power over her.

That he owned her.

'Watching you? Not personally, but...' He grinned. 'Can't be too careful.'

'I'm surprised you let me in here at all.'

He spread his hands. 'I wanted you to see I'm not some small-timer like your cousin Mulligan. I have the money and the contacts to take over this part of the city.'

Good, Caelan thought. Now tell me about them. 'Who runs it at the moment?'

He went to the safe and grabbed some more bundles of notes. 'Depends who you ask. I know of at least three people who think they do. They all need to learn they're wrong.' Holding out the money, he beckoned to her. Caelan took the bundles and pushed them into the rucksack. Seven thousand pounds carried in something that looked like a kid's school bag. Nash smiled at her like a proud parent.

'I'm glad you're letting me help you.'

She wouldn't call it that. 'I'd rather work with you than Harris.'

He moved close, stroked her cheek. Caelan looked into his eyes, knowing she would have to let him kiss her. It went against every instinct, but this was her job.

In the end, it was over quickly; a lingering peck and Nash stepped away. 'Take the money to Harris and call me when you've done it. I want to know what he says.'

Caelan hoisted the bag onto her shoulder, bridling at his tone. 'Talk to you soon.'

He watched her leave, his smirk following her out of the door.

29

The bouncer was still in position at the top of the stairs, and as Caelan passed him he called, 'Nice bag.'

She turned back, scowling. He raised his hands as she approached him.

'If Mr Nash has given you an errand to run, it's none of my business,' he said.

'An errand.' Caelan nodded as though he'd said something fascinating. 'Do you run many errands for him yourself?'

Now his hands went to his hips and he leant towards her. 'My job is keeping this place safe, making sure people can enjoy themselves without any problems.'

'Except Stefan Harris.'

'Harris? That bloke deserves everything he gets. He was lucky we let him walk out of here.'

'After Nathan Nash had a knife to his throat?' Caelan adjusted the bag, the notes heavy on her shoulder.

'Harris needed teaching a lesson. He's no respect.'

'And then Nathan died.'

The bouncer frowned. 'If Harris was involved, he'll pay. The boss hates him already, and if he even suspects Nathan was killed on Harris's orders, he's dead.'

Caelan smiled at him. 'You don't think Harris would have attacked Nathan himself?'

A mocking laugh. 'No chance. Cowardly bastard.'

'What about Johnny and Chris?'

'Who?'

'The two geezers who follow Harris around everywhere.'

'Those two? Arses with both hands comes to mind.'

'You don't rate them?'

'I don't rate many people.' He folded his arms. 'Jury's out on you, though.'

'I'll remember that.'

'The boss likes loyalty and people who do as they're told. Remember that and you'll be fine. And, you know...'

'What?'

'Let him bend you over his desk every now and again.' He winked. 'Easier for you women to make an impression, isn't it?'

Caelan took a step towards him. 'You always do as you're told, then?'

'Whatever the boss tells me, yeah.' He watched her as she moved closer. 'Like I said, he appreciates loyalty and I wouldn't let him down.'

Caelan was almost nose to nose with him now. 'He's never asked you to do anything you didn't want to do?'

His eyes skipped away. 'As long as he pays me, I keep my mouth shut.'

'Good to know.' She leant closer still. 'What about Nathan?'

'What about him?'

'Someone killed him, whether they meant to or not.'

'Don't look at me.'

'I'm not. But your boss might be. I'd think carefully about that if I were you.'

–

Downstairs, Caelan pushed through the crowd, always conscious of the bag of money. She considered pulling it from her shoulder and holding it against her chest, but that would make it obvious there was something of value inside. She kept moving.

She saw Nash's tame drug dealers approaching people, the quick handover of cash then merchandise, and quickened her pace. She ignored the bar staff, marched past the bouncers. The place felt toxic, and she couldn't wait to leave it behind.

Outside, the air was cold, freezing drizzle stinging her cheeks. She paused at the spot where they had found Nathan Nash's body, knowing she was no closer to discovering who had killed him than she had been then.

Looking up at the building she had just left, she tried to work out where Nash's safe room would be located. Since it didn't have a window, it was difficult to guess, but she thought it would be on the other side of the building, where it was attached to the shop next door. She made her way down the alley, onto the street. The kebab shop was doing a decent trade, three men standing outside eating from polystyrene trays, the shapes of people waiting in a queue inside visible through the steamed-up windows. Caelan kept walking, not wanting to attract attention. One of the men looked up from his food, and she waited for a comment or laughter, but it didn't come. She told herself to relax, to trust herself and her training. She crossed the road, took shelter under a bus stop and tried to get her bearings. The back of the club was attached to the kebab shop, the entrance down the alleyway between them. Could Nash's strongroom be over the alleyway? And if so…

She waited for the people inside the shop to receive their food and crowd onto the pavement. The three men had already disappeared into a taxi, and the group began to make their way down the street, laughing as they tried to eat and walk.

Inside, the shop was warm, the smells of meat, pizza and chips reminding Caelan she needed to eat. There were two men behind the counter, one cooking, one serving. They both looked up as she approached, and she guessed they were brothers.

'What can I get you?' the man standing by the till said with a smile. His name tag read *Arif*.

Smiling back, she looked up at the menu board behind him.

'Chicken burger and fries, please.' She thought it would take the longest to cook. Handing over a twenty-pound note, she waited for him to count out her change before she said, 'Busy tonight?'

Arif nodded. 'Yeah, fairly.'

The other man was scooping salad into a burger bun, keeping an eye on the fryer.

'You must get a lot more customers when the club closes,' Caelan said.

'Sometimes. Rain doesn't help. Lot of people just want to get home when they've had a skinful.'

'Hear a bloke died there recently.'

'Outside the club, yeah.' He grinned. 'Nothing to do with our food, though.'

She laughed, though the other man raised his eyes to the ceiling. He'd probably heard the joke several times already.

'Did you know him?' Caelan knew she was firing questions, moving too quickly, but she needed to get to Harris. From there, she didn't have a clue, but if she was ever going to leave this assignment behind, she had to find some answers. It didn't seem as though Achebe, Brady and Somerville were close to providing any.

'Nathan? Yeah, he came in here quite often. Working late, couldn't be arsed to cook. You know how it is.'

'I only met him once, but I know his brother.' Caelan checked on the progress of her order. The fries weren't ready, so she doubted the burger was. Keep talking.

'Reuben? Yeah, I know Reuben.' Arif's tone made his opinion clear.

'You don't like him?'

He screwed up his face. 'It's his attitude. He owns a crappy little club in Ealing Broadway, walks around like he's king of the world, but when he comes in here, he expects freebies 'cos we're neighbours.'

'Maybe if he let you into the club for free...?'

He snorted. 'Not exactly a favour. Have you been in there?'

'Yeah, just now.'

He saw the bag on her shoulder and frowned. 'Like that, is it?'

'What?'

'I know what goes on in there, know what he has people doing. I don't want that shit in my shop.'

'Food's ready,' the other man said.

'Good.' Arif turned from the counter, grabbed the white polystyrene carton and set it on the counter. 'Take it, and your bag of crap, and close the door behind you. No offence, but if that's how you make your living, we don't want your custom again.'

Even though she knew he was wrong about her, Caelan was stung. 'Listen, you know nothing about me. I'm not into that stuff.'

'But you know Reuben Nash, you go to the club.' He pushed the food towards her. 'Take it,' he said again.

Caelan stood her ground. 'What's your problem with Reuben?'

He stared at her. 'You really don't know?'

'I've only just met him.' That at least was true.

'Watch your mouth, Arif,' the other man warned as he lifted more fries from the oil and shook them. 'We don't know who she is.'

Arif grunted. 'As if it matters. We're out of here in five days.'

'You're closing?' Caelan sensed they had more to tell her, though whether it would help her or not, she had no idea.

Head tipped to the side, Arif studied her. 'Want my advice? Go back into the club, give back whatever you have in that bag and run. Nash is bad news.'

Despite herself, Caelan felt a pulse of fear. 'Why?'

'I told you. Drugs.' He pointed with his thumb. 'This is my brother. Our cousin? He's banged up for five years because he went to work for Nash. We never found out what he was doing, but I don't think it was serving drinks.'

'Nash owns this building, and a couple more in this street.' The other man came to stand beside his brother, arms folded. His own tag read *Kadim*. 'He bought the place last year, and he wants us out of here next week. Our mum and dad started this shop twenty years ago, when they first came to London. Now we're being kicked out because some greedy bastard wants to charge more rent than we could ever afford.'

'What will you do?' Caelan asked.

'What can we do? Pack our bags. One of our mates has the newsagent's down the street. Nash raised his rent but our friend couldn't pay. Overnight, the shop windows were smashed, the door forced, the place ransacked.' Kadim gave a humourless smile. 'Nash charged him for the clean-up, and the new glass as well.'

'Is he still there?'

'Until he finds a job, yeah. He lives above the place with his family, so they need a house too. Young kids, his mother-in-law lives with them and she's disabled. Nash doesn't give a shit if they end up on the streets.'

'What about you? Do you live here?'

Arif nodded. 'I do. There's a flat upstairs.'

'More like a wardrobe,' Kadim said.

'Anyway, I'll have to move back in with my parents.' Arif blinked. 'It's the way he's gone about it, you know? Just throwing us out.'

'Did he tell you this himself?'

Laughter.

Arif shook his head. 'As if. He sent a couple of blokes round.'

'Blokes?'

'Heavies, you know what I mean. One speaks, the other stands there glaring like he wants to rip your head off. We got the message.'

She wanted to ask for a description, but thought she would be going too far. She got the idea. The brothers' story had put a new slant on the conversation she'd had with Nash earlier:

Expand your empire? she had said, and Nash had smiled. *Empire. I like that.*

Arif nodded at the box of food. 'Aren't you eating?'

Caelan hesitated. How should she play this? 'All right, cards on the table,' she said. 'I work for someone who'd like to see Nash put out of business.' Again, she was telling the truth. Ian Penrith and Stefan Harris would both agree with her. 'I'm no more a drug dealer than you are – I'm trying to get close to Nash to see what I can find out. Can I trust you?'

They looked at each other.

'We don't want any trouble,' Kadim said. 'I've a family to think of.'

Arif glanced at him. 'Why don't you go and get some cigarettes?'

Kadim frowned. 'Cigarettes?'

'Just get out of here for a few minutes.'

Kadim frowned, then nodded. 'Be careful, Arif.'

He opened the hatch in the counter and walked out of the shop without looking back. Arif waited until he was out of sight before speaking.

'My brother's cautious, but he has three kids, and with losing the shop... It's a worrying time.'

'I understand. What else can you tell me about Nash?'

'I've mentioned the way he's forced people out of business. We've heard rumours about beatings, people who've refused to do what he wants getting hurt.'

Caelan thought of Nathan Nash's injuries. 'Hurt? In what way?'

'I don't know the details, but I doubt Nash was ever involved himself. He has people who work for him.' He stopped, rubbed his face with both hands. 'This is hearsay, you understand? I couldn't swear to any of it, probably wouldn't if I was asked to. It's just what I've heard.'

'None of it will get back to Nash, I promise you.'

He glanced around. 'It's like he owns us as well as the building, you know? We're not people, we're just here to make money for him, and if we don't play along, we're out.'

'Is there any way of getting from the club into this building without going outside? Any connecting doors, any way through the roof space?'

His face was blank. 'I don't think so. My flat's on the first floor, and there's no hatch leading to the loft or anything like that.'

And if Nash had somehow come through from the nightclub to the upstairs of this building, run downstairs through the shop to kill his brother then done the journey in reverse, Arif and Kadim would have seen him.

Maybe they had, and he'd paid them to keep their mouths shut? Caelan studied Arif's face and knew that hadn't happened.

'Does anyone else work here, or is it just you and your brother?'

'Just the two of us. Family business.' He gave a sad smile. 'Or it was.'

30

Caelan left the shop after thanking Arif, the food forgotten. She passed Kadim as she hurried up the street, his head down against the rain, or more likely to avoid meeting her eyes. He didn't acknowledge her and she ignored him too to protect him.

She needed to speak to Penrith, but with seven grand of drug money on her back, she also needed to keep moving. Deciding to take a chance she ducked into a doorway, trying to shelter from the drizzle, and took out her phone. He answered immediately.

'What now?'

She told him what she'd heard. 'Nash is now busy raising rents so high the current tenants can't afford to pay them, and doling out beatings if anyone stands up to him.'

'Nash is investing in property? Interesting.'

'And he's also just handed over seven grand in used notes.'

'To you?' Penrith chuckled. 'You must have your persuasive head on.'

'It's a loan, for me to give to Harris. Seems I have two masters now. Well, three.'

Penrith's tone sharpened. 'You're going to play them off against each other? Be careful.'

She ignored him. 'I don't see how the club brings in enough money for Nash to be buying up property, not in London, not even with the dealing that goes on in there.'

Penrith was silent. Caelan pictured him frowning, pinching his lower lip. 'You mean you think he's our people trafficker?' he asked.

'Harris says he doesn't know how Nash makes his money, and even if he's increasing the rent on the places he already owns, the sums don't add up.'

'And you believe Harris? I thought he was your prime suspect?'

'He's an arsehole who treats women like shit, but he doesn't appear to have the money Nash does.'

'Even though he allowed Mulligan to have a load of coke on a try now, pay later basis?'

'Jolene Townsend owes Harris too, but Nash let me borrow seven thousand pounds without thinking twice. He allowed me a good long look inside his safe. I'd guess there was about a quarter of million in there.'

'Really.' Penrith sounded unimpressed.

'And a box that might have contained a gun.'

'*Might* have?'

'I couldn't really go and examine it. I guessed Nash would be watching me.'

'Maybe he wanted you to look inside.'

'You told me our three unidentified victims were shot in the back of the head,' she said.

'Correct.'

'Which sounds like an execution.'

'Right again. You think Nash pulled the trigger?'

'I don't know. It's just—'

'Guesswork. We can't rely on guesswork. You said Leyton Grey has money, Jolene Townsend's a con artist. Either of them could be organising the trafficking, or it's possible none of the people Mulligan has pointed you towards are involved. We don't know. We need something concrete.'

There was another pause.

'Have you found Tom Haslam?' Caelan asked as she tried to press further into the doorway. The temperature was falling along with the drizzle, the moon a blur above her.

'No,' Penrith said. 'And before you ask, we still don't know where Ryan Glennister ran to, or where Lucy Mulligan is either.' He sounded weary, defeated. It was unlike him. 'There are no updates on Nathan Nash's death, or the attack on Mulligan. You need to keep pushing for answers.'

'I don't even know what the questions are.'

'Now who's talking as though they're in a soap opera?' Penrith bit back. 'What are your plans?'

She rubbed her eyes, exhaustion clawing at them again. 'I need to give this money to Harris. After that, I'll be speaking to Nash, on the phone, and then… I've no idea. I need some rest. I'm hoping either Achebe and Somerville come up with something, or you decide to bring me in.'

He sniffed. 'Cancel the operation? Why would I?'

Caelan didn't answer, watching the drizzle glimmer and dissolve under the street lights. She needed to get out of the rain. She doubted the rucksack was waterproof, and turning up to see Harris with a bag of soggy banknotes wouldn't be ideal.

'Where will you take the money?' Penrith asked.

'I'll need to ask Harris, but I'm not going to his house.' She baulked at the thought. 'If he wants the cash, he'll have to meet me somewhere else.'

'Keep me informed.' Penrith rang off, leaving Caelan staring at her phone. Should she call Ewan? She didn't know where he was, though if he had any sense, he would be back at the hotel, catching up on sleep. She would have liked some backup, but dragging him out into a cold, wet night seemed pointless when she had no intention of spending a second longer than she had to with Harris.

She found Harris's phone number, her stomach clenching. He didn't answer immediately, but when he did, she could hear talking, laughter.

'What do you want?'

'I have some money for you.'

Harris laughed. 'Yeah? Won on a scratch card, have you?'

'Where do want me to bring it?'

'How much have you got?'

'Seven.'

More laughter. 'Seven? Why are you bothering?' There was some muffled rustling and Caelan heard him talking to whoever he was with. 'My mum will still be at my office. Take the money there. I'm busy tonight.'

He ended the call and Caelan put her phone in her pocket, relieved to have sidestepped seeing him again.

–

'Stop here, please.' Caelan said to the cab driver. He turned in his seat to stare at her, bemused.

'You called a taxi to bring you to… more taxis?'

She handed him a twenty-pound note. 'That's right. Keep the change.' She scrambled out and he drove away, still shaking his head.

There was only one Kwik Kabs vehicle parked at the kerb. Caelan hugged the rucksack to her chest. She was soaked, exhausted and pissed off. More than ever, she was sure Mulligan had been spinning them a line, trying to keep himself out of prison.

Harris's mum looked like she hadn't moved since Caelan and Ewan had walked out of the building hours before. She had a headset on and was scribbling on a notepad, a cup of coffee by her elbow. She hadn't heard Caelan come in, and almost leapt off her chair when she tapped her on the shoulder.

Spinning around, she pulled off her headset and threw it onto her desk. 'Shit. You trying to kill me?'

There was a hint of accent in her voice that Caelan couldn't place. She held out the bag.

'Stefan told me to leave this with you.'

The woman took it from her. 'I know. He called me.' She peered inside. 'What's this? Saved your pocket money?'

Caelan hesitated. She needed a lift back to the hotel, but she wasn't going to let anyone from Kwik Kabs drive her there. 'Just give it to Stefan,' she said.

Mrs Harris dropped the bag at her feet, waving an impatient hand as though shooing Caelan away. She put her headset back on and picked up her pen. As Caelan turned away, she heard the door open.

The woman who marched inside was young, auburn-haired and clearly raging. She marched up to Caelan and stuck a finger in her face.

'I need to talk to you,' Lucy Mulligan said.

31

'You've been going around London pretending to be a relative of mine, and I want to know why,' Lucy continued. Caelan held up her hands, confused, disbelieving, and very aware of Stefan Harris's mother sitting behind them. Where the hell had Lucy sprung from? How had she known where Caelan was?

She stepped forward, knowing she needed to take control of the situation. Manhandling Lucy out of the office would raise Mrs Harris's suspicions, but she couldn't allow the young woman to keep talking. Mrs Harris was still wearing her headset, but she was watching them.

'Can we...' Caelan started to say. She reached out a hand, intending to grab Lucy's arm, knowing she could easily over-power her and force her out of the building, but if she showed how desperate she was to silence her, Mrs Harris would know for certain something was wrong.

'No, we can't.' Lucy glared at her, hands on hips. 'Even if your name is Victoria Smith, you're not related to me. I've never met you, never heard of you. I spoke to my mum earlier today and she hasn't either.'

'You might not remember me, but I know your brother.' Caelan glanced at Mrs Harris, who had removed her headset again.

Furious, Lucy shook her head. 'You're lying. You don't know either of us, so what's your game? Who are you?'

Caelan didn't know what to say; only knew she had to shut Lucy up and get them both out of here any way she could.

'Can we go somewhere and talk?' she said.

Lucy was having none of it. 'My brother's in intensive care, my mum, who's ill anyway, is now terrified and confused because I rang her asking about someone who didn't exist.' She took her phone out of her bag and held it up. 'Tell me who you are, or I'm calling the police.'

Mrs Harris got to her feet. 'No. I'll phone my son.'

Caelan's mouth was dry, her brain refusing to work. What could she say? What lies could she concoct? In all her roles, all the hours and weeks she'd spent pretending to be someone she wasn't, she had never been confronted, exposed as a fraud. She had been withdrawn from operations because suspicions had been raised, told to come in because another officer had dropped her in it, but never had she had her own fake persona thrown back in her face.

'Well?' Lucy's fists clenched, and for a second Caelan thought she was going to hit her. Mrs Harris looked on, a strange expression on her face.

Caelan hesitated, infuriating Lucy further.

'Fine,' she spat. 'Have it your way, but you'll have to speak to the police.' She focused on the screen of her phone, but Mrs Harris laid a hand on her arm.

'My son will come, I'll call him now. He knows this woman. He'll make her talk.'

Lucy stopped. 'Make her talk? What does that mean?' She moved her arm from the other woman's touch, staring at her. Her eyes flicked between Caelan and Mrs Harris, as though unsure who she should trust, then she looked around her, as if realising for the first time that she was alone.

'Persuade her, I meant,' Mrs Harris said. 'This is his business. He won't want the police here.'

'Why not?' Lucy demanded. 'It doesn't matter. Whoever she is, she's lied to everyone. I'm sure your son will want to know what's going on, if he knows her. Thinks he knows her.'

Mrs Harris gave a sly smile. 'I'm sure he will.'

Caelan knew she had two choices. She could run, or she could stand her ground. Running wasn't a real option, because she had to protect Lucy. Leaving her here at Harris's mercy was unthinkable. The questions about where she had been and what she'd been doing could come later. She looked well, unharmed, no different to the photograph Caelan had seen before.

The problem was Mrs Harris.

Her fingers were moving across the screen of her phone, and Caelan knew she had to act. She stepped backwards, away from Lucy, then sprang at the older woman, seizing her forearm with one hand and the phone with the other. Mrs Harris squealed, Lucy gasped, but neither of them tried to prevent what was happening. Using a move similar to the one that had put Mulligan on the floor in the cell at Acton, though with more consideration, Caelan pivoted the woman over her thigh and lowered her gently to the ground. She knelt over her, keeping hold of her wrist so she couldn't struggle. Mrs Harris wriggled, cursing and flailing, but she couldn't break free. With her other hand, Caelan removed the phone from her grasp and tucked it into her coat pocket.

Lucy stared down at her. 'Who the hell are you?' Her voice was soft now, fearful. 'Some kind of spy?'

'No. I told you, I know your brother. You're not safe here. Please, go and wait by the door.'

Lucy nodded, compliant now, her movements quick and panicked.

Mrs Harris cried, 'My son will be here soon.'

Lucy froze as Caelan took out the phone again. The screen hadn't locked yet, and she was able to check the recent calls and texts. 'No, he won't. He didn't answer.'

'He'll know something's wrong. He'll be here.'

Caelan didn't believe her, but she knew staying here would be a bad idea. She needed to get Lucy to Penrith, and that meant taking Mrs Harris along for the ride. She looked at Lucy's fearful face and tightened her grip on Mrs Harris's arm.

'There's a cab outside. Where are the keys?'

Mrs Harris pouted. 'I'm not telling you anything.'

Caelan knew she could break the woman's wrist with one twist, but she would never do it. She only hurt people who were intent on hurting her. 'If you don't tell me, I'll walk out of here now and take that bag of money with me. You'll have to explain to your son that you lost it, and I'm guessing he won't be happy. I only want to borrow the car. I'll bring it back, good as new.'

She knew the operation was blown, but with Lucy here, safe and well, it was time to admit defeat. Achebe, Somerville and Brady could pick up the pieces. She was going to walk away once she had delivered Lucy to her boss.

She stared down at Mrs Harris, curled on the floor, her face showing her terror, and hardened her heart. 'Well?' she said. 'Shall I phone Stefan, or do you want to tell him yourself?'

Mrs Harris tried to twist away, but Caelan held on.

'Bitch,' Mrs Harris snarled. 'Stefan will kill you for this. In the desk drawer. Don't take anything else. He'll know.'

Caelan looked at Lucy. 'Would you mind getting them? I'll explain everything in the car, I promise.'

Mechanically, Lucy nodded, but she didn't speak. She moved to the desk. Caelan saw her stop for a second as she reached into the drawer, but then she held up the keys. Caelan leant over Mrs Harris.

'Now, I'm going to let you go. I want you to go back to your desk and start answering calls again as though nothing has happened. Whatever you do, don't contact Stefan.'

'Why? What can you do to stop me?'

Caelan smiled. 'Like I said, I'll take his money with me. You might sniff at seven grand, but I don't think your son would. Not when it's money he's owed.'

The other woman swallowed, and Caelan felt another sting of guilt. Mrs Harris was afraid of Harris, that much was clear, and Caelan was using that fear to intimidate her. It didn't sit well.

'He isn't my son,' Mrs Harris mumbled.

Caelan hesitated. 'What did you say?'

'He isn't my son.'

Relaxing her grip, Caelan allowed her to move into a sitting position. Lucy stood with the car keys in her hand, staring down at them.

'What do you mean?' Caelan asked, gentle now.

'I'm not Mrs Harris. I never have been. Stefan's mother disappeared years ago.'

'Then who—'

The woman's laugh was bitter. 'His father's whore. He brought me here from Poland twenty-five years ago, along with my sisters and my brother. I was seventeen. We were promised the usual things – work, a house, money.' The same short laugh. 'Once we arrived, I never saw my sisters again, though Victor, Stefan's father, was only too pleased to tell me they had been put to work on their backs. My brother went to a farm of some kind.'

'You mean you were trafficked?' Lucy said.

The woman turned on her. 'You think it wasn't happening then? Humans have always bought and sold other humans. People are the worst creatures on earth.'

Caelan knew she was telling the truth; there was no question of her making this up. She knew she should run, get herself and Lucy out of there, but there was something in the woman's voice that made her hesitate. The agony in her eyes, the trembling of her body. This was a story she had longed to tell for years. Caelan hesitated. Harris hadn't been summoned, she'd checked, and she had a duty to protect this woman too.

'What's your real name?' she asked softly. Another person whose identity had been stripped from them.

The woman released a shuddering breath. 'Justyna. Victor always called me Tina – more English, you know.' She gave a shaky smile. 'That mattered to him.'

'Why does Stefan call you his mother?' Caelan was still gently grasping Justyna's wrist, but now she adjusted her grip so she was holding her hand in support rather than controlling her. Justyna shook her head.

'It amuses him. He knew I was his father's prisoner, his slave.'

Lucy stood with her hands by her sides, clearly shaken. 'His slave?'

'He was in control of everything, from what I ate to what I wore. Who I spoke to.' Justyna blinked, her mouth working. 'Who I had sex with. If I argued, he beat me. He said if I tried to get away he would find me and kill me.'

'He prostituted you?' Lucy looked appalled.

Justyna managed a smile. 'To his friends, only they didn't have to pay. Then... then to his son.'

Caelan's grip tightened. 'Stefan?'

'On Stefan's fourteenth birthday, Victor decided it was time he lost his virginity. He gave me to Stefan as a present. Lent me, I should say. Stefan wasn't allowed to keep me.' She blinked again. 'Not until his father died, anyway.'

'What happened to him?' Caelan asked.

Justyna turned to look directly into her eyes. 'Stefan's father? He fell down the stairs. It was an accident.'

Caelan understood it had been no such thing. 'I see.'

'He was drunk. He hit his head, I think broke his neck.' She gave a careless shrug. 'Either way, he was gone.'

'It happens.'

'And Stefan is easier to control.' Justyna smiled.

'You said Victor brought you into the country, you and your sisters and brother. Do you know if... Does Stefan...?'

Justyna nodded. 'His father taught him the family business and now Stefan is in charge.'

Caelan had heard enough. 'You're coming with us.' She looked at Lucy. 'Let's go.'

Lucy held out the keys. 'I still don't know who you are. Why should we trust you?'

'Because you have to. I'll explain on the way. Come on, please. Time to go.'

She pulled Justyna to her feet, was ready to grab Lucy's hand too and drag her along with them if she had to. She needed to get them both to Penrith, and quickly.

'Hang on a minute.'

Caelan froze. The voice came from behind them. It was smug, male, and she recognised it immediately.

Johnny.

Stefan Harris's right-hand man had been in the building all the time. Why hadn't Justyna said so? But as she glanced at the other woman's face, she knew the answer. Justyna was stunned, terrified. She hadn't known.

Caelan turned. Immediately she knew they were in trouble. By his side, Johnny held a gun. Now he raised it, gestured at Caelan and nodded towards the door.

'All of you, throw your mobile phones on the floor. Now.' They did as they were told. Johnny kicked the phones under the desk, out of sight. He looked at Caelan. 'You've got the keys. Let's go.'

Slowly Caelan moved her feet and raised her arms slightly, making herself bigger, putting her body between Johnny and Justyna. Lucy was still standing behind the desk, shifting restlessly, and Caelan turned so Johnny wouldn't have a clear shot at her either. She felt no fear, just anger at herself for not checking the building, and for not leaving sooner. They could have heard Justyna's story in the car. She met Johnny's eyes.

'Where?'

'To see the boss. He's busy tonight, but I'm sure he'd be delighted to see you all, especially,' he gave Justyna a cold smile, 'his dear mother.'

Caelan shook her head. 'Let them go, and I'll do whatever you say.'

He gave her a bored stare. 'Start walking, or the ginger one gets a bullet in the knee, then I'll work my way up.'

Caelan squeezed Justyna's hand and then released it. Lucy was staring at Johnny, panic clear on her face.

'Follow me,' Caelan told her. 'Trust me. It'll be okay.'

Behind them, Johnny chuckled. 'That's what I like to see, blind optimism. Come on, move.'

He pushed past them, grabbing Justyna as he went and standing by the door with the gun at her temple. He nodded at Caelan. 'You can drive, Ginger sits in the passenger seat. I'm in the back with Mrs Harris here, and you go where I tell you. The second you take a wrong turn, try and draw attention to us or do anything other than exactly what I tell you, I'll shoot her. You understand me?'

'Yes.' Caelan knew that for the moment she had to do as she was told. She should never have allowed this situation to happen, but now she had to think, react, plan. Beside her, Lucy looked shell-shocked, her face white, her breathing too fast. Caelan squeezed her arm.

'You're okay,' she said.

Johnny laughed. 'Yeah, everything's great, sweetheart. Now get outside.'

He held Justyna close as they went through the door. 'You two, don't move. You,' he dug the gun into Justyna's ribs, 'should have the key. Lock the door and then give the key to me.'

She nodded, fumbling in her jeans pocket.

'Hurry up,' Johnny hissed. Caelan watched, hoping for an opportunity to attack him, but he kept Justyna too close and she dared not take the risk.

Justyna locked the door and held out the key in a trembling hand. Johnny smiled, his cheek pressed against hers as he held her in front of him. To an onlooker it would look as though he was hugging her, not holding her prisoner.

'Put it in my jacket pocket,' he said. She did as she was told and he forced her to turn towards the taxi. 'Get in, all of you, and remember: do as you're told.'

Caelan opened the passenger door for Lucy and ushered her inside. Lucy didn't resist, pulling the seat belt over her chest, stunned and wide-eyed, her movements mechanical. Caelan scrambled around to the driver's side, hoping to see a police car, Ewan, Penrith, anyone who could help them. No such luck. There was no one in sight, not a pedestrian, not a vehicle.

She got in and started the engine. Johnny pushed Justyna into the back seat and climbed in beside her.

'Now drive,' he said.

32

It was an industrial estate, somewhere past Heathrow Airport. The unit Johnny directed Caelan to was tucked out of the way, a household recycling centre on one side, a scrapyard on the other. Both closed, both in darkness.

'Drive around the back,' Johnny said. 'There's a car park.'

Caelan did as she was told, following the narrow tarmac road along the side of the building. There were no signs, nothing to indicate what sort of business went on here. She was sure they were about to find out.

She turned the corner into the car park, surprised to see so many cars there. It was close to midnight, wintry rain and freezing gusts tugging at their clothes and numbing their faces as they got out of the car. Lucy stumbled as she put her feet on the ground. Caelan went to help her, and immediately Johnny turned the gun on them, keeping hold of Justyna with his other hand.

'What are you doing? I told you, behave yourselves.'

'She tripped,' Caelan said. 'It happens.'

He grinned, waving them forward with the gun. 'When you're shit scared, yeah.'

Caelan didn't reply, keeping an arm around Lucy's trembling shoulders. She wanted to ask her where she'd been, what had happened. Now, though, they needed to concentrate on staying alive. The estate was silent, deserted. No witnesses.

Johnny led them over to a black double door and rapped on it with the gun. Immediately it opened, and he hauled Justyna inside. 'Come on,' he barked over his shoulder.

Caelan kept hold of Lucy, and they stepped through the door into a corridor. She looked around, wanting to commit every detail to memory. If she got out of here, she would need to be able to describe it. The floor was concrete, the walls white. She could hear a man's voice. He was talking quickly, his voice amplified somehow, but she couldn't make out what he was saying. To their left was a metal staircase with a chain across it to discourage anyone from going up or coming down, though it wasn't much of an obstacle. In front of them, about five metres away, was another black door. A man stood beside it, his face obscured by a dark scarf and a knitted hat pulled low over his brow. He wore black trousers and boots, a black jacket, no labels or designs, nothing to help anyone if they were asked to describe him. He stood with his back straight, chin up. Caelan guessed it was Chris, Harris's other hired muscle, but she couldn't be sure. Johnny nodded to him, but neither man spoke as he marched them all through the door.

Beyond was a huge room with a stage at one end. Here, the voice they had heard was loud and clear, and Caelan realised immediately what was happening. She felt light-headed, nauseous, the floor seeming to rise and fall beneath her feet. She felt Lucy go rigid beside her as Johnny stopped, allowing them to see what was happening. He was grinning, highly amused by their reactions. Justyna's knees sagged and he hauled her upright, holding her tightly so she was forced to watch.

It was an auction.

In front of them were rows of chairs, most of them occupied. On the stage, a middle-aged man, sweating and smiling, stood at a podium. He was plump, wearing tiny glasses, and kept stroking his straggly moustache. To his right, a young woman stood blinking at the crowd. She was naked except for a pair of red high-heeled shoes and an elaborate pink feather headdress bearing the number 12. Her arms were by her sides, her eyes fixed on a point at the back of the room.

Caelan felt as though she'd been kicked in the stomach. Pink feathers. Penrith had told her the three young people they had found dead had had pink feathers or fluff in their hair. They had been here, on this stage, or at least in the building, before they were executed. What had they done? Protested? Tried to escape? She stared around her, numb and disbelieving. This was what Stefan Harris was doing. This was why he wanted to buy Reuben Nash's club. He'd told her he had plans for it, and this was what he had meant – this human cattle sale.

'…Ladies and gentlemen, beautiful Lot Twelve. To recap, she's twenty-one, and free from all STDs. As you can see, she has blonde hair, blue eyes, a full set of perfect white teeth.' He paused, smiling. 'Willing to work hard and play hard, if you know what I mean.' He stopped again as though waiting for laughter, though none came. The atmosphere was charged, a room full of people smacking their lips, waiting to feast. Caelan drew in a deep breath and let it out slowly. She hadn't been able to keep her arm around Lucy, but now she reached again for her hand. Lucy's grip was tight, almost painful. Beside them, Justyna looked ready to collapse.

'We'll start the bidding at five thousand pounds,' the auctioneer said. Immediately, hands went up and the bids rose swiftly. 'Ten thousand, eleven, twelve, thirteen, thank you, sir.' He paused and wiped his brow. On the floor at the front of the stage someone waved to the young woman who was being sold up there. Blankly she looked down, and Caelan saw who was speaking to her.

Jolene Townsend.

Caelan's guts lurched and rolled as Lot 12 lifted her head and managed a smile. Jolene must have told her to look as though she was enjoying herself. The rage Caelan had felt inside since Justyna had shared her story began to build. She would close this place down, and every one of these filthy bastards with their hands in the air would go down too. How, she didn't know, but she would do it.

'Do I hear fifteen thousand?' the auctioneer was saying. Johnny jerked his head.

'Follow me.'

Caelan kept hold of Lucy's hand, her eyes searching for an opportunity, anything she could grab to use as a weapon. She would be gambling with Justyna's life, probably with her own and Lucy's too. Would that save these people who were being sold like antique furniture or paintings? No. She had to be patient.

Johnny led them down the side of the room, to a door next to the stage. Lucy gripped Caelan's hand even tighter as they saw the naked young woman glance at them. Her chin trembled, and she blinked rapidly. Caelan wanted to hurl herself onto the stage, to grab her, cover her and get her out of here. She looked at the faces of the people in the crowd – mostly men, but there were women present too – and hated every one of them. She didn't have time to dwell on how she felt about their actions – this reducing of fellow humans to pieces of meat, play things, property. That would come, if she escaped this place.

Through the door, and this room was even worse than the last. There were people inside, but there was also complete silence. Johnny stood back, pushing Justyna, Caelan and Lucy forward. At first, all Caelan could see was eyes. Twenty people sat on the floor, each wearing a white robe and with a pile of clothes beside them. Caelan knew there were twenty, because their headdresses ranged from number 13 to number 32. Number 15 wept silently, her mascara running, shadowing her blue eyes. Number 22 drummed her fingers on her thighs, over and over. Number 29 was male. He sat with his head bowed, hairy legs straight out in front of him. Beside him, number 30 closed her eyes and pressed her hands together. Caelan guessed she was praying and hoped she would find some comfort in it.

There was sudden pressure at her back, and she knew without looking that Johnny held the gun there.

'Something to show you,' he whispered. Caelan didn't answer, and he grabbed her arm, twisting it painfully. As their hands were wrenched apart, Lucy moaned, and Justyna was immediately by her side.

Johnny led her back to the stairs. The chain had been removed and he marched her up them. There was a small landing, and two doors. He pointed.

'Behind that one... Go on, open it.'

Caelan didn't know if they were alone up here, but he still had the gun and she had seen nothing she could use as a weapon. No handy length of pipe or wood, not even a pen. He waved the gun at her.

'I said open it.'

If he was expecting her to be cowed, he was going to be disappointed. She stared at him for a long moment, then strode towards the door. Her hand trembled, but he wouldn't be able to see it. Her throat was choked, the anger, disgust and despair at what people were capable of doing to each other seeming to rise from her stomach to suffocate her. Whatever was on the other side of this door couldn't be any worse than what she had seen downstairs.

Except it was.

Sitting back to back, their hands behind them, handcuffed together, were Ryan Glennister and Tom Haslam. They too were naked, their heads lolling but the numbers on their head-dresses still visible – 33 and 34.

'We gave them the choice – they could be killed or sold,' Johnny said conversationally. 'They chose to be sold, though I've no idea why. Who's going to want a scrawny druggie and a mentally ill stalker?' He shoved Glennister's leg with the toe of his boot. 'I doubt they'll get any bids, and then what are we going to do with them?'

Caelan didn't answer, wanting to drive her fist into his face. He stepped closer, pinning her against the wall, the gun under her chin. Lazily he drew it across her throat, pressed it against her temple. 'What would you choose?' he whispered. Behind them, Caelan heard laughter. She stared into his eyes.

'Death.'

Johnny laughed. 'I thought you might. And we'd make it quick.'

'A bullet in the back of the head, and it's goodnight,' a different voice said.

Recognising it instantly, Caelan stiffened.

Reuben Nash. He stood, arms folded, a mocking grin on his face. What was he doing here? Where was Harris?

Beside him was another man. He was as tall as Nash, wearing a dark suit and a bored expression. Small dark eyes skimmed Caelan's body, assessing her like a farmer at a livestock market. There was nothing sexual about the way he studied her – he might have been looking at a painting, or a car. He said nothing.

Nash sauntered towards her, hands in pockets, looking pleased with himself. 'So here you are. Now you know most of my secrets, but I'm told I don't know any of yours.' He held out his hand. 'Come on, darling.'

Caelan sneered at him. 'Make me.'

The other man said, 'Shut your mouth.' He spoke quietly, turning away as though there could be no doubt she would do as he said. His accent was strong, though Caelan couldn't place it. She wondered whether he could be Albanian, like the men Mulligan had employed, or Polish, like Justyna. Nash shot him an anxious glance. This man was clearly involved in the horrible scheme; maybe he was even the one in charge of bringing people into the UK from the countries they had called home.

'Surely you're not going to be awkward when there's a man with a gun standing beside you?' Nash said.

Johnny stepped forward. 'Do as you're told.'

Caelan allowed Nash to take her hand. He lifted it to his lips and kissed it, then wrenched it behind her back. Caelan gasped but knew better than to struggle. In this position she could break Nash's hold, but he could also snap her arm. Then there was the other man, plus Johnny and his gun.

'You lied to me,' Nash hissed in her ear. 'Who are you?'

'You already know. Victoria Smith. Check my passport, my driving licence.' She was breathing hard, harder than she needed to. She wanted him to think he was hurting her, that she was weakening.

Nash twisted her arm further, setting her off balance, making her vision blur for a second. She had to make him let go before he caused her real damage.

'Stop, please,' she squealed, laying it on thick.

Nash laughed, delighted. 'Come on,' he said to Johnny 'Bring her to the storeroom. I'm sure when she sees the blood on the walls, she'll tell us.' He made a gun from his fingers and pointed it at her. 'And if she doesn't... Well, she's already told us what her choice will be.'

He turned and walked away. Johnny gave her a shove and Caelan started walking, her mind spinning as she took in what Nash was saying. People were given a choice – be sold or be killed? She couldn't believe he was serious, but the bullets in the back of the heads of the three unidentified victims told their own story. Still, it didn't make sense. Nash was in this for the profit – why would he give his merchandise a way out when he could sell them?

The gun jabbed her spine again and she kept moving. Nash waited at the top of the stairs, beaming. He crooked a finger at Caelan, and she followed him down. In the corridor, the drone of the auctioneer's voice continued, every thump of his gavel another life sold. Nash stopped to check his phone as Johnny marched Caelan past him.

Lucy and Justyna huddled together at the bottom of the stairs, both pale-faced, terrified. Again Johnny pushed the gun into Caelan's back, and she moved to stand beside them. Lucy reached for her as Johnny turned away, looking to Nash for his next command. Caelan froze for a second as Lucy's hand found hers.

Nash put his phone away. 'We're going this way.'

Caelan moved against the wall, changing the position of her body as Johnny turned back. He glared at her.

'You heard. Keep moving,' he said, pointing with his gun.

Caelan did as she was told, making her way down the corridor, moving as slowly as she dared. She didn't want to leave Lucy and Justyna, but with Johnny and Nash beside her she had no choice.

Halfway down, Jolene Townsend stood with her arms folded, what looked like a toolbox at her feet. Her face was blank, her eyes fixed on the opposite wall. Beyond her was a man who had his back to them, shoulders hunched. Caelan guessed his identity before he turned.

Leyton Grey.

He too had a case, clutched to his chest. His expression was desolate, his eyes on the ground. When he lifted them and met Caelan's gaze, he didn't flinch, and she knew what he was trying to tell her: *I had no choice.*

She stared back at him as she passed, because there was always a choice. Whether you decided to take the right path or went for self-preservation was up to you.

Nash nudged her as they walked along. 'As you can see, the gang's all here.' He stopped, checked his watch, then hurried back towards the stairs, pulling Caelan along with him. Johnny followed, while the other man disappeared through the door at the far end of the corridor.

'Stefan?' Nash bellowed, his fingers digging into Caelan's arm. 'Stef?'

Stef. Caelan blinked. They were in it together. Nash and Harris, pretending to hate each other, all the while running this despicable scheme.

This was what Mulligan had been trying to tell her all along – they were all involved. Reuben Nash, Stefan Harris, Jolene Townsend and Leyton Grey. She guessed Mulligan had struggled to point the finger at Jolene and Leyton, but he had done so in the end. Whether his conscience hadn't allowed him to protect them or it had been his own line in self-preservation, keeping him out of prison, Caelan didn't know.

Harris descended the stairs, looking as nonchalant as Nash.

'Evening, all,' he said. He spotted Justyna, who turned her face away from him. He went to her, grabbed her by the throat. 'Hello, Mother,' he said, and threw her against the wall.

Nash raised a hand. 'Easy, Stefan. We don't want her hurt.'

Harris was still snarling, but he allowed Nash to lead him away and stalked back up the stairs muttering to himself.

Nash smiled as there was a knock on the outside door. He opened it with a flourish.

Caelan saw Ewan first, stumbling inside, his eyes swollen, his mouth bleeding. Mulligan was next, pale and sweating. She stared at him and he managed a grin.

'Evening, Cousin Victoria. Don't suppose you've any aspirin? I've a shocking headache.'

Lucy said, 'James,' and tried to reach for her brother. Johnny shoved her back, and Caelan saw Mulligan's eyes blaze. She met Ewan's gaze and gave a tiny shake of her head: *Let me handle this.* He frowned, but she knew he would do as she asked.

'Let's keep it friendly, shall we?' Nash said.

Caelan looked at the cases Townsend and Grey carried and the nausea rose again as she remembered the torture inflicted on Nathan Nash. Had Jolene been involved? Leyton? She couldn't see it, but she had been wrong about so much already. She was trapped, more so than she had ever been in her career. She was exposed, vulnerable, and she had too many people around her to risk any heroics. Then again, you could only bide your time for so long. If she wanted to get out of here alive, she might have to act regardless.

Nash was a talker, a show-off. She already knew that and wondered if she could use it. She had questions, after all.

'Who killed Nathan?' She spoke loudly, and Nash narrowed his eyes.

'Haven't you worked it out yet, Miss Marple? People will do anything for money, or better still, for drugs. Fortunately for me, and for Stefan, poor Leyton over there has problems with both. He's good with a pair of scissors, less so with a baseball bat. He killed the man he was supposed to threaten and tickled the man he was supposed to kill.' He spoke about the death of his brother as though it was no more than a minor inconvenience. Grey looked ill. He had set his case on the floor, wrapped his arms around his body.

'Tickled?' Despite it all, Mulligan sounded indignant. 'I've been in the bloody hospital; this isn't a migraine we're talking about. I'd be there now if you hadn't—'

Casually Nash stepped forward and punched him in the stomach. Mulligan dropped to his knees, gasping and choking. His sister made to rush forward, then thought better of it.

Caelan raised her voice. 'And Jolene? What's her role here?'

'Making our friends look presentable,' Nash said. 'Make-up, hairstyling. Leyton does a few trims. Jolene also stays with our friends in the green room – the one they're waiting in now – before they go onstage.'

Caelan listened in horrified fascination. Their friends? The green room?

'She chats to them while they wait, offers them a little something to calm their nerves if they need it. Nathan used to do that too, but then he… well, he let us down.'

'How?' Caelan thought she'd guessed, but she wanted to hear Nash say it.

'He had a crisis of conscience, much like your friend Mulligan. He wanted out, didn't like the thought of what we do here. Jolene and Leyton, well, they might not enjoy it either, but they keep their heads down and do the job, because when you owe as much money as they do, what choice do you have?'

Grey gave a strangled sob, and Nash laughed. 'It was Leyton who flogged my brother until he screamed for mercy. You'd never think it looking at him now, snivelling like a baby, but when we told him to get on with it or we'd practise on him first, he soon picked up the whip. Kept his eyes closed most of the time, but he got the job done. People can do anything if it saves their own skin.' He stepped closer to Caelan. Still she didn't flinch, not when his hand stroked her cheek or when he ran his fingers through her hair. He leant into her, trapping her against the wall. She hoped Ewan wouldn't react as Nash ran his lips down her throat and kissed her ear. She held herself rigid.

He gave up, pushing her away from him. 'Now that I've answered your questions, how about you tell me who you really are?'

'I'm Victoria Smith.'

He rubbed his chin, pretending to be deep in thought. 'Except a woman you claim is your cousin has never heard of you, certainly doesn't recognise you.'

'I... must have got confused,' Lucy stammered. 'I don't know all of the family; there are so many on the Smith side...'

Nash ignored her. He looked at Mulligan, who was now back on his feet, though his face was purple, his eyes streaming.

'Looks like it's up to you, James,' he said. He beckoned to Johnny, who stepped forward. 'The gun,' Nash snapped. Scowling, Johnny handed it over. Nash smiled, testing the weight of the weapon in his hand. 'Feels good,' he said. 'Lighter than I expected. You ever fired a gun, James?'

Mulligan licked his lips. 'Once or twice.'

Nash nodded, then with a sudden movement jammed the barrel against Mulligan's temple. Grey moaned; tears were running down Lucy's cheeks. Caelan twitched. The situation was more desperate than ever. What could she do? How could she stop this? She could attack, but it was still too risky. Play along, and be ready to take your chance, she told herself.

'Now, James, man to man,' Nash said. 'All right, you're the one with the gun to your head, but let's play fair. I won't blow your brains out if you tell me who this bitch really is.'

Mulligan gulped. Over Nash's shoulder he met Caelan's eyes, and she knew what he was going to say. She knew then that she would die in this place, for this job. Mulligan didn't look away, kept his eyes fixed on Caelan as he spoke.

'She's my cousin. Lucy doesn't know her, of course she doesn't. We only met Victoria once as kids, and Lucy wasn't much more than a baby. We didn't speak again till recently, when Vic heard I was in the same business as her. I mean, it's not something you shout about, is it? Don't bring it up at weddings and funerals. Check her background, ask around in Edinburgh.'

'I have,' Nash said.

'And?'

'People said she was legit.' Wavering, Nash ran his free hand through his hair.

'There you go,' Mulligan said. Caelan was amazed at his calmness. He hadn't betrayed her, at least not yet. She had no idea what he was doing, but it was buying them time. 'You know what she was up to,' he went on. 'She saw I was useless, wanted to work with a proper businessman. Whether that was you or Stefan, she didn't care. Either way, one of you would be forced out of the area.'

'You think?' Stefan bellowed from upstairs. 'Cheeky bastard.'

'Wait,' Nash said. He turned to Lucy. 'You. Follow me.' He looked at Caelan. 'You too.'

Caelan met Lucy's eyes and nodded. What else could they do? Nash still held the gun.

'Where are you taking them?' Mulligan demanded.

Nash smiled. 'Why don't you come with us and you'll find out?'

Johnny grabbed Mulligan by the front of his jacket. 'Start walking,' he said.

Lucy glared at the bodyguard. 'Leave him alone.'

He laughed. 'Found some guts, have you? About time.'

'Fuck off,' Lucy spat.

Nash waved the gun. 'Through the door, all of you.'

Nash hustled them past the stage, into the room where the people in white robes sat, waiting their turn. He ignored them, didn't even look, but Mulligan's eyes widened.

'What the fuck?'

Johnny laughed. 'What? Where did you think your shipments ended up? Not coming over here for a holiday, were they?'

Mulligan's face worked. 'This is fucking barbaric.'

'Didn't bother you when you were spending the money, did it?'

'James?' Lucy's voice was little more than a whisper. 'You're not involved in this? You wouldn't—'

'Of course he would,' Johnny said cheerfully. 'Hope the two of you don't have a granny, because he'd sell her as well.'

Mulligan reached out a hand to his sister, but she shoved him away.

Nash kept them moving, through another door. This room was about twenty feet square, and empty. The skin on the back of Caelan's neck prickled. This place... People had died in here, she would swear to it.

'Over there, by the wall,' he ordered.

Johnny closed the door and stood beside it, arms folded, a smile on his face like he was having the time of his life. Mulligan stumbled towards the far side of the room, Lucy close behind him. Brother and sister stood side by side, Lucy's face wet with tears, Mulligan's red and furious. Caelan followed, terrified, adrenalin making her frantic, her mind racing through possibilities. Nash had the gun, Johnny was guarding the only door, and there were no windows. Stefan Harris was out there, as was the second bodyguard, Chris.

'On your knees,' Nash ordered.

Caelan heard Mulligan whimper. Slowly, Lucy crouched. Mulligan dropped to the ground beside her. Nash waved the gun at Caelan.

'On your knees,' he repeated.

She stared back at him, knowing he'd never held a gun before in his life. He'd just told them as much, but at this range, inexperience wouldn't matter.

He wouldn't need to be an expert to kill her.

Still she defied him. Nash's hand trembled as he raised the gun again, pointing it at Caelan's face.

Johnny shifted. 'Boss, why don't you let me—'

'Shut up,' Nash screamed.

The door opened and the man in the dark suit walked in. He took in the scene immediately. Walking up to Nash, he held out his hand. 'Give it to me.'

'I know what I'm doing,' Nash protested.

'No. Give it to me.'

Scowling, humiliated, Nash handed the weapon over. The man weighed it in his hand and smiled. Caelan revised her plan. This was a man familiar with firearms, comfortable with them. He looked at her.

'Come here,' was all he said. She looked at him and he nodded, pointed at the floor with the gun. 'Now.'

She moved quickly, stood beside him.

'Good. Stay.' He walked across to where Lucy and Mulligan cowered. 'Now,' he said to Caelan. 'My colleague asked you a question. You need to answer.'

'Who are you?' Nash said softly.

Caelan knew she had no choice. Lucy watched her, dry-eyed now. Still Caelan didn't speak; she couldn't. Her mouth was parched, her throat closed.

'Well?' The man with the gun clicked his tongue. He pointed the gun at the back of Mulligan's head – Mulligan, torturer, liar, drug dealer, people trafficker, and all Caelan could think about was how she was going to save his life. The odds were so heavily stacked against her it was laughable, but she knew she had to try.

'You don't think I'll shoot?' the man in the suit asked quietly.

Johnny laughed. 'I don't think she believes—'

His words disappeared as the back of his head exploded, blood and gore splattering the wall behind him. Lucy shrieked, Mulligan let out a scream. Nash whimpered, flung his arms around himself.

'Yes, I will shoot,' the man said. Caelan gave a casual nod while her mind screamed against the murder she had just witnessed. She forced her eyes away from Johnny's body, from the oozing matter on the wall.

'So.' The gun was at Mulligan's head again. 'Your friend. Tell me her name.'

Mulligan gulped, looking up at Caelan. *Tell him*, she mouthed. Mulligan swallowed, lips pressed together. 'You won't say?' A chuckle. 'Maybe the young lady will.'

As he took a step to the side, Caelan dropped to one knee, pulling the gun Lucy had passed to her at the bottom of the stairs from the waistband of her jeans. She fired once, the bullet finding its mark, the shoulder of the fancy suit instantly covered in blood. The man fell backwards, his own weapon skittering across the floor as he lay bellowing in pain.

Mulligan came to life, scrabbling for the gun, but Nash was there first. He grabbed it as Caelan straightened, pointing it at her again. She saw the panic and fear in his eyes and knew he was more dangerous now than he had been before, probably more so than the man in the suit had been. He had murdered Johnny, but Reuben, with his wild eyes and trembling body, could end up killing them all.

'You bitch,' he said. His voice was shaking almost as much as his hand was. 'Who the fuck do you think you are?'

Caelan held up her hands, still holding her gun. She didn't take her eyes off his as she kept moving, hands in the air, slowly rotating, Nash following her movements unconsciously, until her body was between Nash and Lucy and Mulligan.

'Give me the gun, Reuben,' she said softly. 'It'll be better for you.'

He snorted. 'What are you talking about? I'm walking out of here.'

'And where will you go?'

'I don't know. Anywhere.' He looked at the man on the floor, blood still leaking from his shoulder. 'He's dying.'

Perfectly calm, Caelan shook her head. 'Unlike you lot, I don't shoot to kill.'

Nash looked at the gun in his own hand as though he was surprised to see it there. 'Tell me who you are.'

Caelan waited, hoping she had read him right, hoping this wasn't where the whole thing went to shit.

'Tell me,' Nash yelled, lunging for her. Caelan stepped back, spun on the ball of her left foot and whipped out her right leg, the crack as her foot connected with Nash's outstretched arm sounding almost as loud as the shots had. He screamed, fell, and she bent to pick up the gun. As he writhed on the ground, she stood over him, both weapons safely pointed at the ground. He was crying, moaning, and she knew he wouldn't hear her.

'I'm a police officer,' she said.

33

10 December

'They intended to sell you too, you know.' Ian Penrith opened a bottle of whisky and began to pour generous measures into glasses. He looked at Ewan, Mulligan, Lucy and Caelan in turn. 'All of you.'

'Are you serious?' Caelan shook her head. She felt as though she was still trembling as shock, horror and disbelief set in.

'Why not? It would have got rid of the lot of you in one stroke.' Penrith pressed a button on the phone on his desk. No one spoke, Caelan and the others absorbing what he had said, Penrith himself continuing to pour whisky. The door opened and DS Jen Somerville appeared. She handed several evidence bags to Penrith and left the room. Penrith put down the whisky bottle.

'And here are some they prepared earlier.' He held up a bag containing one of the numbered pink feather head-dresses. 'Thirty-five.' He nodded at Caelan and then held up the others. 'Thirty-six, thirty-seven, thirty-eight, thirty-nine. Lucy, Justyna, Mulligan, Ewan.' He stood, held out the tray of glasses. 'Anyway, cheers.'

–

When they were alone, Caelan said, 'How much did you know?'

Penrith sipped his whisky, affecting an air of innocence. 'I don't know what you mean.'

'Yes you do. You got someone to throw the brick through Lucy's window, made sure Mulligan heard about it while he was still inside.'

'No comment.'

'You hid Lucy away and came to me with your sob story. Mulligan was released. Did he know your plan?'

Penrith smiled. 'He was… cooperative. I think we might have a role for him here.'

'He's a murderer, a torturer.'

'And he saved your life.' Penrith drained his drink and reached for the bottle.

'And that makes up for everything else?' Caelan felt like throwing her own glass at the wall.

Penrith watched her steadily.

'What?' she demanded.

'Do you know where Lucy was?' he asked.

She made a noise of frustration. 'Obviously not.'

'In the hotel where you're staying. Same floor, five doors down. You wouldn't have seen her; she was instructed not to leave the room.'

Caelan stared at him. 'Are you joking?'

'Do I ever? Mulligan told her to go there, before we were even involved, and he paid for it too. Consider that when you're wondering if I orchestrated the whole thing. He lied about that, not me. I had no idea.'

Did she believe him? Caelan wasn't sure. Did it matter any more? 'What about Mulligan? He was in intensive care.'

Penrith smiled. 'No, he wasn't. I told you he was, and you took me at my word. He was also staying in the hotel – we put him in the room next to Ewan's.'

'You—' Caelan took a breath, controlled her anger. 'You were protecting him.'

'I had to. He knew you were beginning to make progress, even if you hadn't realised it yet.'

'Even though he's—'

He looked at her, serious now. 'You did well. They're still processing all those…' He swallowed a word, searched for another, 'All the punters who were there to bid, as well as Nash, Harris and their friends.'

'What about the man I shot?'

Penrith grinned. 'There'll be a queue of people wanting to shake your hand. He's wanted for all kinds of crimes throughout Europe. Albanian, very nasty man.'

'And he knows who I am.'

'Well, if you will go around shooting people… Where did you get the gun?'

'It was in a drawer in Harris's office. Lucy saw it when she got the car keys and slipped it into her pocket. No one searched her, and eventually she managed to pass it to me.'

Penrith nodded. 'Impressive.'

It was. 'It was… a surprise. I knew it was loaded from the weight, but there was no guarantee I'd have a chance to use it. We were lucky.'

'Why would Harris have a gun in his desk drawer?'

'To impress people, maybe, or intimidate them. To remind Justyna who was boss? You'll have to ask him.'

'I'm sure someone will.'

Caelan rubbed her eyes. 'You lied to me. I trusted you, *again*, and you lied.'

'No. I wound you up and let you go. I knew you could do this, would do it.' He flicked through a pile of papers on his desk, found the one he wanted and held it out. 'We have names for our three victims; we can return their bodies to their families. When you're thinking about who's done what and what could have happened, remember that. You couldn't save them, but you saved the people who were wearing these,' he waved the headdresses, 'and all the others who would have followed them.'

Suddenly Caelan was exhausted. 'You lied.' She knew she sounded like a child, couldn't help it.

Penrith held up a hand. 'I'm not going to discuss this with you now. You're tired, you've had… a difficult day. Go back to the hotel and we'll meet tomorrow. You can scream at me as much as you like then.' He grinned. 'And bring me that invoice.'

–

When Caelan reached the street outside, she crossed the road and stood looking out over the Thames, watching the London Eye slowly turn, her arms wrapped around her body as she tried not to shiver. Shock, or just the cold? She didn't know, couldn't think, couldn't begin to understand what had happened over the last few days.

After a couple of minutes, she became aware of someone standing beside her. She turned.

'Thank you,' Lucy Mulligan said. She too looked exhausted, shattered and hollowed out by what she'd seen and endured.

To Caelan's horror, tears welled in her eyes. She swallowed them down. 'Quite a few hours,' she said.

Lucy gave a shaky smile, though it was clearly an effort. 'I've had better days.'

Images flashed through Caelan's mind – the shots, the blood, the tumbling bodies. 'Me too.'

'Sorry if I hurt your hand. I remember grabbing it a few times.'

'Giving me the gun… You took a hell of a chance.'

Lucy shrugged. 'What choice did I have? I didn't know how to use it.'

Caelan glanced at her, angry though she knew Lucy wasn't to blame. 'I thought you were missing. How did you end up in the hotel?'

She stared at the ground. 'James contacted me, told me he was in trouble, that I had to stay in a hotel he'd booked for me. He'd send some mates round to pick me up, make it look as though I was being abducted. Said it would confuse the people who were after him, and that I should stay hidden until he contacted me again. Well, he didn't.' She snorted. 'I didn't know at the time that he was in a room down the corridor. I had my laptop, a few books and plenty of work to do. James had got them to leave me loads to eat, so I was fine. Lonely, bored, but fine.'

'Then what happened?'

'Like I said, I didn't hear from James, and I began to panic. Then I got a message from Tom – Tom Haslam – saying you'd been asking questions, saying you were my cousin.'

Caelan frowned. 'You had your phone?' Penrith had said she had left it behind.

Lucy shook her head. 'Not mine. James told me to leave my personal stuff in my room, make it more convincing. He'd arranged for another one to be left at the hotel. Tom emailed, said he hoped I'd be able to read it as he knew I didn't have my phone. I was confused, angry – I didn't know what to do, what to think. James wasn't answering his phone, and I thought I'd go and find out what was going on. Tom told me he could help; he told me where you'd be.'

'But Nash and Harris already had Tom.'

'They sent the email as if it was from him. I should have realised – it was a different email address, and it sounded strange, but then Tom can be... Well, anyway, I decided to go to Kwik Kabs. I didn't question how Tom knew you'd be there, and I should have done.'

'Because Stefan Harris knew I would be.' Caelan ran both hands over her face.

'You must be exhausted,' Lucy said.

'Exhausted, hungry, confused, angry. Those people...'

Lucy closed her eyes. 'I know. I've never... I can't imagine...'

'They'll be helped,' Caelan said, to reassure herself as much as Lucy.

'Do you know what James told me? The woman who was there doing the make-up – the auctioneer was her uncle. He used to do it for a living, apparently.'

Caelan's mouth twisted. 'Keeping it in the family. Lovely.'

They were quiet, listening to the sounds of the city, watching the river. After Big Ben chimed eleven o'clock, Lucy turned back to Caelan and smiled.

'Fancy getting some breakfast?'

Caelan hesitated. She wanted to shower and sleep, but she heard the plea in Lucy's voice. She didn't want to be alone, and if Caelan was honest, it wouldn't be a chore to keep her company.

As they crossed Westminster Bridge, Caelan's phone rang. With an apology to Lucy, she answered.

'Caelan?' Nicky Sturgess said. 'I'm sorry. Can we meet?'

Acknowledgements

It's that time again…

Thank you to the lovely people at Canelo, and special thanks to Michael Bhaskar (as always) for his patience, understanding and advice.

Thank you to Jane Selley for her ace editing skills, and to Tom Sanderson for the amazing cover.

To anyone who has read my books, written a review or blog post, taken the time to contact me about my work – thank you.

Thank you to my wonderful family and friends, and my furry writing companions.

And finally, Tracy: thank you for your support, belief, and encouragement. I couldn't have done it without you, and I wouldn't want to even try.

Detective Caelan Small Series

Ask No Questions
Tell No Lies
Time To Go